AT HIS SERVICE:
MILLIONAIRE'S MISTRESS

ANNE OLIVER

KELLY HUNTER

CATHY WILLIAMS

Mills & Boon, an imprint of Harlequin (UK) Limited, Eton House, 18-24 Paradise Road, Richmond, Surrey TW9 1SR

AT HIS SERVICE: MILLIONAIRE'S MISTRESS

ISBN: 978 0 263 90225 9

026-1112

Harlequin (UK) policy is to use papers that are natural, renewable and recyclable products and made from wood grown in sustainable forests. The logging and manufacturing processes conform to the legal environmental regulations of the country of origin.

Printed and bound in Spain
by Blackprint CPI, Barcelona

Memoirs of a Millionaire's Mistress

ANNE
OLIVER

When not teaching or writing, **Anne Oliver** loves nothing more than escaping into a book. She keeps a box of tissues handy—her favourite stories are intense, passionate, against-all-odds romances. Eight years ago she began creating her own characters in paranormal and time travel adventures, before turning to contemporary romance. Other interests include quilting, astronomy, all things Scottish, and eating anything she doesn't have to cook. Sharing her characters' journeys with readers all over the world is a privilege...and a dream come true. The winner of Australia's Romantic Book of the Year Award for short category in both 2007 and 2008, Anne lives in Adelaide, South Australia, and has two adult children.

Visit her website at www.anne-oliver.com. She loves to hear from readers. E-mail her at anne@anne-oliver.com

With thanks to my editor, Meg Lewis.
For my colleagues and friends who supported me through tough times during the writing of this book, especially Gay—thanks for the roses!

CHAPTER ONE

'DON'T date this man.'

Didi O'Flanagan paid scant attention to her workmate's warning, barely glancing up as she scoured her bag for lip gloss. 'Whatever he did, Roz, he probably doesn't deserve to have his photo plastered to the mirror in a public restroom…' Her words segued to a hum of approval, lip gloss momentarily forgotten.

Maybe he did deserve it. His eyes—deep dark blue—were the kind of eyes that could persuade you to do things you'd never do in your right mind…

'Only the woman who put it here knows that.' Roz leaned in for a closer look. 'You must've really ticked her off, Cameron Black. Still, you are a bit of a hunk.'

'Yeah…' Didi had to agree. Dark hair, squared jaw. Perfect kissing lips. What did the rest of him look like? she wondered. She imagined a man with looks like that would keep his body toned to match. In fact she could imagine quite a lot about that body. 'We could try Googling those "don't date him" websites…'

'Hmm, revenge. Undoubtedly a dish best served online…' Roz agreed. 'But right now, if we want to keep our jobs, we'd better get out there and start serving those impatient big-shots,' Roz reminded her, heading for the door.

Didi blinked, feeling as if she'd somehow stepped out of a time warp. 'Right behind you.'

Cameron Black. Why did that name sound familiar? Didi wondered. Shaking the thought away for now, she unscrewed her tube of colour, slicked coral gloss over her lips.

She twitched at a few blonde spikes, straightened her uniform's little bow tie and fiddled with her name-tag, which always seemed to tilt at an angle no matter how many times she adjusted it.

She couldn't resist; her gaze slid back to the printout on the mirror. Below the picture were the words, 'He's not the man you think he is.' On impulse, she reached out. She didn't care what he'd done, it wasn't right. That was what she told herself as she peeled it off. There were two sides to every story. Not that she knew much about relationships. In her twenty-three years there'd been only one serious relationship, and that mistake had coloured her perception in a very *un*colourful way.

But she couldn't bring herself to crumple the paper and toss it in the waste basket on her way out as she'd intended. It seemed a sacrilege to spoil that perfect face. She folded it into quarters, then again, carefully creasing the lines before sliding it into the pocket of her black trousers.

A few moments later Didi circulated the crowded room with her tray of finger food. Predominantly male executives in business attire made for a sea of sombre suits interspersed with splashes of colour and the occasional whiff of feminine perfume.

Didi aimed a winning smile at the group of men she'd targeted as being the head honchos. 'Would you like to try a crab cake with lemongrass sauce? Or perhaps one of these baked cheese olive balls?'

As expected, her smile was ignored as they continued their discussion around the model of a proposed development for one of Melbourne's inner city precincts on a table in front of them, but a few greedy fingers plucked her dainty morsels off the tray.

Rude, rude, rude. Her smile remained, but inside she gritted her teeth as she skirted the group to reappear around the other side. She hated this subservient, thankless job. But right now she had no alternative if she didn't want to slink home to Sydney and admit she'd made a mistake—

'Thank you, Didi.'

The unexpected rich baritone voice had her looking up—way up—at the man who'd taken the last crab cake *and* had the courtesy to use her name. 'You're welcome. I hope you enjoy…it…' Her voice faded away as her gaze met a pair of twinkling blue eyes…

This couldn't be the man whose photo was warming her right hip even as he smiled. Could it?

Yes. It could—and it most definitely was. So the woman who'd left the picture in the Ladies had known he'd be here—maybe she still was, and wanted to witness his humiliation.

The cheap printout didn't do him justice—he was *gorgeous*. His eyes were navy, almost black. And focused wholly on her. He'd shaved tonight; no sign of that stubble. Just smooth tanned skin… Her palms itched to find out just how smooth. The maroon and black tie's sheen accentuated his snowy white shirt, drawing her attention to a prominent Adam's apple and solid neck. His hair was shorter than it was in the picture and the room's light caught threads of auburn amongst the brown.

He wore a pinstriped charcoal suit and she knew from her experience with fabrics that it was Italian and expensive. Touchable. Warm from his body heat. Her insides did a slow roll and her fingers tightened on the tray.

As she watched he lifted the crab cake to his lips before popping it into his mouth, still smiling at her, and for an instant she bathed in the warmth before he turned away.

No. She wanted to bask in that heat a moment longer. 'You forgot to dip,' she found herself saying. Loudly. Too loudly. His gaze swung back. 'And that was the last one…' She trailed off, lost for a moment in his eyes.

His lips stretched into a smile as he continued chewing.

She had a completely inappropriate image of dipping her fingers in the sauce then sliding them between his lips, and her pulse quickened.

'That's too bad,' he said, his voice a tone or two lower, his eyes a tad darker. As if he was sharing the same fantasy. 'It was delicious nevertheless.'

'Try a cheese and olive ball.' She offered her tray up like some kind of entreaty. 'It's a different texture but if you like olives—' Cheeks heating, she caught her runaway tongue between her lips to stem the verbal tide. *What the heck was she doing?*

'I love olives.' He selected one, his gaze once again focused on her, warming her from the inside out.

'When you've quite finished.' A man with thick white hair aimed his glare at her over the rim of a pair of butt-ugly spectacles. 'As I was saying, Cam…'

Cam held Didi's eyes for a second longer, then gave a conspiratorial wink before getting back to business.

Cam… *Cameron Black.* Didi mentally repeated his name as she watched one long tapered finger touch the model of his proposed development as he spoke. What would it feel like to have that finger touch her? Anywhere. For any reason…

Get real, she admonished herself. *Step away before you make a complete and utter fool of yourself.*

This man was into property deals and big-business networking. He didn't have time for the simpler things like social conversation. No doubt he spent his entire life dealing with men like Mr White Hair. He was one of those men for whom making money was more important than relationships—hence the poster, no doubt.

As she stepped back she couldn't help noticing the arched façade of the model he was touching. She frowned, squinting without her glasses. It looked like her apartment building.

It *was* her apartment building. They'd been served with eviction notices months ago, but Didi hadn't got around to finding herself a new place yet. At least not one she could afford.

Resentment simmered beneath her carefully cultivated waitress persona. *That* was where she'd seen his name. Cameron Black Property Developers were kicking her out along with several other families in three weeks; she'd seen the signage on the vacant lot next door where a pawn shop and a sleazy tattoo parlour had recently been demolished. All destined to be part of a new complex that would take months to complete.

A different kind of heat fired through her veins. The burn of disappointment, anger. Outrage. Greed was Cameron's motivation. Certainly not concern for the residents who couldn't afford to move to the more upmarket parts of town.

She should bite her tongue, turn around and head to the kitchen to refill her depleted tray. But she'd never been one who could keep her mouth shut. 'Excuse me.'

Six heads turned, six pairs of eyes drilled into hers, but it was Cameron Black she focused on. 'Have you given any thought to the tenants you're turfing out at number two hundred and three?'

His jaw firmed, the warmth in his eyes vanished. 'I beg your pardon?'

She waved a hand over the model. 'I don't know how people like you sleep at night.' She scoffed out a humourless laugh. 'Mrs Jacobs has been there for fifteen years—she's had to go to Geelong to live with her daughter's family. And Clem Mason's—'

'Watch yourself, girlie,' Mr White Hair warned.

Fired up now, Didi didn't spare him a glance. 'Do you know how hard it is to find suitable accommodation at affordable rates, Mr Black? Do you care at all about the ordinary people trying to get by on the basics who live—make that *lived*—in that building?'

'I'm not aware of any problems.' His voice was cool professionalism.

'Of course you're not.' And he'd probably trotted out that

same line to the pinner-upper of the photo in her pocket. She could only shake her head on behalf of women everywhere. 'Maybe that's why you're the current Pin-Up Boy in the ladies' loo.' Her voice carried way further than she'd meant it to and a hush descended around them like a suffocating shroud.

Twin spots of colour slashed Cameron Black's cheeks and his mouth opened as if to speak, but she turned away, her runaway tongue cleaving to the roof of her mouth. Before she made matters worse, she set her tray on a nearby table and quickly made her way towards the restroom.

She pushed through the door, found it empty and leaned back against its solid barrier with a heartfelt sigh. Tonight her mouth might just have cost her this job.

She stepped to the vanity counter and turned on the tap, dabbing her neck with cold water. Thankless or not, she needed this work. Why couldn't she control her tongue? And why did the man-to-die-for have to be her evil landlord?

The door swung open with a whoosh, pushed wide by a very tanned, very firm, very *masculine* hand. Didi's breath snagged in her chest. Then she steeled herself to meet Cameron Black's grim reflection in the mirror.

Instead of feeling threatened; she felt…anticipation. It buzzed through her body, turning her legs to liquid and drawing her nipples into tight points of sensation. *Damn him,* she didn't want to feel as if she were poised and breathless on the edge of a lava pit. She wanted to get herself together, and how could she do that when he'd invaded the only place she'd thought safe?

She turned so that she could meet him face to face on equal terms, gripping her fingers on the counter top at her sides for support. Except he had a good fourteen inches on her. Struggling to keep the nerves from her voice, she lifted her chin and met his gaze. 'I think you made a wrong turn somewhere.'

'Not me. You.' His gaze darkened, indigo satin over hot coals, and his voice was silky smooth when he advised, 'You really shouldn't bad-mouth the people who help contribute to your pay at the end of the evening.'

How was it that even though his eyes remained fused with hers he managed to conjure a shimmer of heat up the entire length of her body as if he'd swept a hand from ankle to clavicle and every place in between?

She shook her head. 'I tell the truth, Mr Black. Unfortunately the truth often gets me in trouble…'

When his gaze finally released her he scanned the room. 'And how do you know my name?'

She arched a brow. 'I'd suggest most of the women at this function know your name by now.'

His eyes narrowed. The door swung closed behind him, swirling the air and leaving the two of them alone. The scent of his cologne reached her nostrils in the draught he'd created. Without thought she breathed deep, inhaling its fragrance: snowflakes on cedar-wood. As if by some force she didn't know she had, it seemed to draw him closer. It seemed to draw the walls in, suck the air away, until he was standing so close she could feel his body heat through the fine-textured weave of his shirt.

He placed his hands firmly on the counter top, a fingerprint away from hers, boxing her in. 'What game are you playing at—' and even though she was certain he remembered her name, his gaze slid over the swell of her left breast where her name-tag hung at its permanent forty-five-degree angle '—Didi?'

She slid an unsteady hand into her trouser pocket, the backs of her fingers bumping against his and sending fireworks shooting up her arm in the process, and pulled out the folded sheet of paper, thrust it at his chest. 'It's not my game.'

Straightening, he unfolded it and scanned the contents. She watched his jaw bunch, his knuckles whiten on the paper. In the silence that followed she could hear the quickened rasp of his breathing, could almost feel his anger as a third entity in the room with them.

'I found it on the mirror.'

She flinched again when he closed a substantial fist around it, crumpled it beyond redemption with an impatient crackle, then shoved it in his pocket. She had to bite her lip to stop herself from asking for it back. Of course she wanted it back…so she could grind her heel into his face when she left her flat in three weeks' time with nowhere to live.

'Thank you,' he said quietly. 'I've been having some trouble with an ex girlfriend.'

'No kidding. Did you kick her out too?'

'As a matter of fact it was she who did the kicking.'

She was tempted to dole out more sarcasm but the complete lack of emotion in his expression stopped her—too complete. Too controlled. He'd blocked the pain, she thought, and stuffed her hands into her trouser pockets to curb her natural instinct to reach out to him. He was hurting, and she understood too well how it felt to be tossed aside. 'Yeah, well, you're better off without someone like that.'

And I'm better off not knowing. She needed to remember who he was: *Evil Landlord.* He might be hot sex in a pinstripe suit but his motive in life was greed. Keeping her backside against the counter top, she sidled closer to the door—she had to get out before she changed her mind and offered something stupid, like sympathy. Or sex on the vanity unit.

Cam sensed her imminent departure but he wasn't done with her. He slammed his hands back on the tiles on either side of hers. Wide and wary silver eyes snapped to his. She was petite. Dainty. But he knew the aura of fragility was purely that—an aura. He liked that about her—a woman with guts in a compact little package.

She'd furrowed hands through her gelled hair and it stood up now in spiky disarray. With her name-tag askew and resting on one small pert breast, she reminded him of a rather untidy pixie. The jolt of attraction was swift and unexpected. And hot.

He gritted his teeth and forced himself to focus. 'Do you want to come with me now and voice your concerns about the new development to the rest of the investors?'

'With that irritable and arrogant old man? No point. More important, I've still got half an hour of paid employment to go and, unlike *some,* I need the money.' She made a noise of disgust and her breasts rose as she drew in a short sharp breath. 'It's people like you who barge in and buy up big, ripping up homes and businesses and lives and call it "development" when in reality it's just a money-grabbing venture.'

'It's not—'

'People like *you,*' she interrupted, 'wouldn't understand the first thing about people from the other side of the tracks.'

He had a fleeting but graphic image of a past he'd spent half his life trying to forget and his gut clenched. He pushed back from the counter, his fingers tightening into fists at his sides as he remembered how long and hard he'd fought to earn the wealth and respect he now enjoyed. 'You know nothing about me.'

She waved an accusatory hand at the peach-coloured sofa. 'You followed me in *here,* didn't you? That tells me something, and, let me tell *you,* it's not flattering.'

Her eyes flashed at him, a silver blowtorch, all heat and sparks and energy, setting spot fires snapping to life through his veins. In his thirty-two years no woman had ever ignited such a reaction in him.

If he could direct that passion elsewhere… His groin tightened at the thought of where he could direct that delicate-looking hand with its clear varnished nails… 'Tell me something else, Didi. Why did you fold my picture with such obvious care and put it in your pocket? Why not throw it in the waste bin?'

Her cheeks turned a delicious shade of pink and her gaze dropped to her shoes. 'I…wasn't thinking.' Then she pushed, her palm hitting him firmly mid-chest. 'Now move.'

Her touch was like a brand, searing his flesh. Heat radiated throughout his body and his first instinct was to cover that small hand with his and keep her there just a few more seconds and argue that she *was,* in fact, thinking. About him.

But he stepped aside, the imprint of her hand still burning, and watched her march the two steps to the door, yank it open. If he wasn't wrong, those rosy cheeks gave her away. *Attraction.* And right now she was about to walk. He should be relieved—he didn't need the distraction; he certainly didn't intend dating her. So why he found himself asking for her phone number was beyond his comprehension.

She paused mid-stride, her fingers curved around the door frame, her eyes barely meeting his. 'Why?'

'I may decide to press charges against my ex.'

She scoffed and resumed walking. 'You can do that without my help.'

He stood a moment, breathing in the sweet nutty fragrance she'd left behind, feeling oddly put out. 'Damn right, Didi. I don't need your help.' *I certainly don't need you.*

He'd barely moved when her elfin face reappeared around the door. 'What makes you think I'd want to help you?' she continued as if she'd never left. 'Maybe she did us girls a favour. Apparently you're not the man she thought you were.'

She looked him up and down thoroughly from his now sweat-damp brow to his black Italian leather shoes and he had the disturbing sensation she wasn't looking at his clothes. 'Makes one wonder what she meant considering you're on the wrong side of the door here. Perhaps she knows something the rest of us girls don't.'

He didn't bother with a reply. *Didi* whoever-she-was could imply whatever the hell she liked; Cam knew exactly what Katrina had meant.

When Didi arrived home she knew she'd made the right choice in not giving Cameron Black her phone number. He was the single most dangerous man she'd ever met. He owned her apartment. He was going to tear it down.

And she had the worst case of lust for him that she'd ever experienced. How dumb was that?

Still in her coat, she was stepping out of her shoes when her mobile rang. She froze momentarily, then coughed out a laugh. Of course it couldn't be him… Pulling her phone out of her bag, she checked caller ID, breathed a sigh of relief, but only for an instant because her friend Donna was on her own with a toddler and it was well past midnight.

'Donna, what's up?'

'I've broken my leg…' Distress tightened her voice. 'Trent's not home for another two weeks and I've got no one to help look after Fraser. Can you come?'

Didi rubbed her tired eyes. Donna lived in the Yarra Valley, a couple of hours' drive from Melbourne—too far for Didi to commute on a daily basis with her unreliable car.

They'd met as volunteers at a kids' breakfast club in Sydney, then Donna had married and moved to Victoria with her husband, but he worked on an offshore oil rig half the time. Didi would have to stay with her, which meant she'd be unavailable for work—if she still had a job, that was.

She glanced at her chaotic apartment and empty cartons. If you couldn't help a friend in need… 'I'll be there as soon as I can.'

Didi threw a handful of clothes and essentials into a couple of canvas supermarket bags. At least she'd managed to pack away her precious art supplies. She still had three weeks before she had to vacate—cutting it fine, but it couldn't be helped. She wasn't about to let Donna down—Cameron Black and his big bad bulldozer would just have to wait.

Cameron wasn't sure which got to him more. The fact that Katrina had stalked him to a business function and left her poison, or that someone—a very appealing someone called Didi—had announced the fact to him at a crucial moment in negotiations.

Negotiating with Bill Smith needed subtlety and diplomacy. And as much as the man pained him, Cam needed Bill's support to help smooth things over with the council. He might have had that support sooner if Didi O'Flanagan hadn't announced Cam's poster-boy status along with her condemnation of Cameron Black Property Developers. He'd had to schedule another meeting he didn't have time for, but he'd won the older man over at least.

He stared out of his office window with its view of Telstra Stadium and the Yarra River. Didi O'Flanagan. It had been a simple matter to access her phone number through the rental agency that serviced the building and cross-reference it with the catering firm he always used. Apparently it hadn't taken Bill long either because when he'd rung they assured Cam she was no longer working with their company and did Cam wish to file a complaint as well?

Of course the name rang a bell—she lived in the building she'd been fighting for. It was due for major renovation in two weeks. They'd been served eviction notices as soon as the project had been finalised months ago. And they'd all vacated the premises except for Miss O'Flanagan in apartment six.

He expelled a long breath. She didn't deserve to lose her job for having the guts to stand up for her beliefs, however misguided they were in this particular circumstance. And she'd done him a favour by removing his photo. She obviously cared about others and respected their rights—even his, he thought, with a wry twist of his lips.

He wanted a chance to explain his vision for the development and the reasons behind it. If she'd stop for one second and listen, that was. As for living arrangements…maybe he could speed things up if she was having trouble finding a place. Find her an apartment in one of his complexes somewhere.

On the other side of the city.

The warning rang in his head. Yeah. The further away, the better.

Because he had a feeling this little pixie could run amok over his well-ordered life—the life he'd built from scratch—with just one look from her silver eyes or one word from that tempt-me mouth.

CHAPTER TWO

Two weeks later

IT WAS a night for disasters.

Rain pelted the pavement, but that was Melbourne.

Didi's apartment building was all locked up—*one week early*—and that was entirely Cameron Black's work and the reason she now huddled on the front steps thinking of ways she might enjoy killing him. Slowly. *After* she got her stuff out.

She'd had to abandon her excuse for a car on the other side of the city with some sort of mechanical failure that no one was willing to look at until tomorrow. Not that she had any hope of paying for repairs since she'd learned she was now unemployed when she'd rung to explain why she wouldn't be able to work for the next couple of weeks.

So she considered the fact that she'd managed the rest of the way by public transport with a bag of clothing and a box of abandoned and distressed young cat she'd found beside a public toilet block a minor miracle.

Only to find herself locked out of her own apartment.

And she couldn't ring anyone from here because in her rush to help Donna she'd left her mobile behind in her apartment somewhere. She'd had to make do with Donna's landline for the past two weeks.

The busy inner suburban street was awash with wet colour, the untidy web of overhead cables dripped moisture. Trams jostled amongst the steady stream of vehicles on their way home, pedestrians huddled under umbrellas, and the aroma of Asian takeaway steamed the air. She'd kill for a fried rice about now.

At least it was relatively dry here on the top step—an awning shielded her from the worst of the weather. She pulled out the tuna sandwiches she'd bought earlier, feeding the cat tiny portions through a peephole she'd created in the side of the box. Sometime soon she was going to have to find somewhere for the little guy to pee.

'It'll be okay, Charlie,' she said, popping a bite into her own mouth, feeling more and more incensed with every passing minute. 'It's just you and me against the world and we're not going down without a fight.'

Finally. Cam came to an abrupt stop on the pavement and watched Didi from beneath his large black umbrella. She gazed up at the time- and weather-worn semi-circle of red bricks that created the arch above her, drawing his attention to the creamy curve of her neck. His own neck prickled beneath his cashmere scarf as a surge of heat engulfed him and he wondered how it would feel to trace a finger down that smooth column to the soft spot at the base of her throat—

'This the place?'

The removalist's gruff voice caught Cam's attention. He nodded at the two men who'd appeared beside him, digging out the building's keys as he climbed the steps. 'Apartment six.'

At his approach, Didi's gaze darted to his. Wariness changed to recognition, then her brow puckered and her pretty lips twisted into something resembling a sneer. 'Well, if it isn't the man himself.' She pushed up, scattering crumbs. 'What the hell is going on?'

He stopped a few steps away. 'My sentiments exactly,

Miss O'Flanagan. I've been trying to contact you for the past two weeks.'

'Why?' Her eyes narrowed. 'I had a personal emergency to take care of.'

'And now you have another. I've been forced to call in the removalists.' He kept his tone civil, firm. 'If you can't give me an alternative address you leave me no choice but to have your belongings placed in storage.'

She blinked. '*Storage?* I've got another week.'

'No, Miss O'Flanagan, you do not. Which you'd know if you'd bothered to answer your phone.'

Her chin came up. 'The phone I *didn't* give you the number for.'

'There's always a way.'

She stiffened. 'Yes, I'm sure there is for someone like you. As it happens I don't have my phone at the moment.' The derision in her gaze fled as it shifted to the two men beside him, then to the truck parked at the kerb. 'I need more time. I have no job, thanks to that night—how am I going to rent an apartment?'

He shook his head. 'Reconstruction starts tomorrow morning.'

'*Tomorrow morning?* Well, that's just peachy.' Her mouth pouted in a way that made him want to lick the fruity word right off her lips.

He quashed the urge and resultant heat immediately. Damn. Rather than her own lack of action, she made it sound as if *he* were the party responsible for her situation. Guilt niggled at him. She *had* shielded him from personal embarrassment, at least initially, by removing that poster. And he was her landlord after all.

'You can't put my things in storage,' she stated, a hint of nerves behind the grit. 'I *need* them.'

'So, you'll give me an address.'

'I told you, I don't have one.'

'You don't have a friend you can stay with?'

'I've only been in Melbourne a couple of months, so no.'

'You've obviously been staying with *someone* the past couple of weeks.' He didn't care for the image that unfurled in his mind—her compact body entwined with—

'Not in Melbourne—not that it's any of your business. *And as I've already told you, I had another week!*' Her blade-sharp voice sliced the exhaust-heavy air.

'No. You didn't.'

'I rang the agent last month about a week's extension and was told it was okay. As the landlord you're accountable for this mess.'

'Obviously there's been some sort of miscommunication.' He frowned as he stepped past her, unlocked the door and motioned to the waiting removalists. 'No extension would have been granted.'

'But it was.'

Grabbing her bag and box, she squeezed ahead of him into the narrow passage. He allowed her the dignity of opening her own front door with her key and followed her inside. She'd made some attempt at packing, he noted, glancing at the boxes stacked in the centre of the tiny living space. The odour of sour milk wafted from a carton on the kitchen sink. Perhaps she really had had an emergency.

She set the stuff she carried on the floor and marched to the fridge. 'There.' She gestured to the calendar, silver eyes sharp as knives, aimed at him. She'd written *Eviction Day* in bold red letters that dripped blood beneath it. On the wrong date.

Did she get things wrong on a regular basis? he wondered. She certainly had a knack for getting herself into trouble of one kind or another. But she was right about one thing; no matter whom she'd spoken to at the rental agency, as her landlord, Cam was ultimately accountable.

'Look, why don't we have a coffee and let the guys do their

job?' he suggested, hoping to smooth things along. 'Perhaps we can work something out.'

'I'm not letting them out of my sight.' She glared at the removalists loitering uncertainly in the doorway.

'Start with the furniture,' Cam suggested to the men. 'We'll sort out the rest in a while.' Then to Didi, 'Pack what you need for now. Why don't you try your workmates? Perhaps they can put you up for a couple of days while we look for something suitable.'

She flashed him a look that damn near froze him to the spot, then grabbed her bag and box, disappeared into the bedroom and shut the door. He watched the men take the dilapidated furniture—what little there was of it—while he made a call delaying his planned dinner meeting.

Five minutes later she reappeared. 'I've tried my workmates. One's quit and gone interstate, one's living with an aunt in a one-bedroom apartment, the other lives in a hostel. I've got stuff here I can't—won't—put in storage. It's simply too precious.' She bit her lip, looking perilously close to tears.

'Okay. Put it aside. I'll have it delivered to my apartment, it'll be safe there.'

She stared grimly at him. 'Not a chance.'

'For God's sake, be reasonable.' He could tell she was fiercely independent. Judging by the fact that she'd torn down the poster and spoken out for her fellow evictees he also knew she was a woman with scruples. 'We'll find you a place for the night. Leave it to me.'

She blew out a breath. 'Okay. But I'll be looking for you if any of my stuff goes missing.'

It took forty minutes longer to clear out the apartment but finally the van was gone, the items to be delivered to Cam's apartment clearly labelled. He waited until she'd exited, then locked up the building.

He turned at the bottom of the steps when he realised she wasn't following. She stood beneath the awning with her cardboard box and carry bag beside her. Her shoulders drooped and her body seemed to shrink inside the worn coat she wore, which may have been a fashion statement in the eighties but now looked sadly outdated.

He fought the ridiculous urge to bound up the steps and gather her into his arms. The same urge he used to get when his little sister came home at dawn high on whatever her drug of choice was that particular night.

'Let's go. What are you waiting for?' When she didn't move he stifled an impatient breath—Amy hadn't wanted his support either. 'You can't stay here.'

Her eyes flashed with defiance. 'You have a better suggestion?'

You could sleep in my bed. The associating image smoked through his brain. Her spiky hair tickling his nose as she stretched out on top of him, eyes closed in pleasure. Fingers intertwined and above his head, breasts to chest, thigh to thigh…

He wasn't sure how, but he had the feeling she knew exactly where his wayward thoughts were going. He spoke stiffly through a clenched jaw. 'I'll book you a room for the evening until we work something out tomorrow.'

Her response was an instant, 'No.'

'Didi, it's too late to do anything else tonight—'

'I mean…I can't go to a hotel.'

'Why ever not?'

Her gaze dropped to a cardboard carton on the step beside her. He'd not noticed earlier, but now it drew his attention because some sort of scratching noise emanated from within.

'I rescued a cat on the way here. I'd never get it past the desk, and I need a litter tray and some food.' Her eyes met his. 'And don't suggest I take him to a shelter because I won't do it.'

'You'd sit on this step all night because of a cat?'

'Yes.' Her mouth set in a determined line as she bent down, scooted the box closer. 'You may not have a heart, Cameron

Black, but I'll safeguard this animal from harm if it's the last thing I do.'

'Which it could very well be.' He shook his head. 'Amazing.' *She* was amazing—amazingly naïve or amazingly foolhardy. Or both. He checked his watch. It left him with no option but to move matters along immediately if he wanted to keep his already delayed dinner appointment on the other side of the city. Without looking at her he backtracked, picked up her overstuffed canvas shopping bag.

Didi watched him close one large fist over the straps then scrambled up. 'Hang about—where are you going with that?'

'My apartment.'

'No.' She made a grab for the bag but he'd already started down the steps.

She did *not* want to accompany Don't-Date-This-Man to his bachelor apartment. Wherever that might be. Where he ate breakfast or lounged semi-naked in front of sports TV. She did not want to know—her pulse skipped a beat in panic—whether he slept alone. She wanted nothing to do with his living arrangements or his lifestyle…or his crazy women. 'Stop!'

His stride barely faltered. 'You're coming home with me and I don't have time to argue about it.'

Home with him? She knew next to nothing about him—except how he made her insides roll about as if they'd become detached. 'I can't…' She caught up with him on the bottom step and tugged. Hard. One of the straps ripped away with a loud shirring sound, tipping the bag and spilling a few articles of intimate clothing onto the wet pavement. Water immediately soaked into the garments. 'Now look what you made me do.'

She regretted her slip the moment it left her mouth. His gaze landed on a lolly-pink thong centimetres from his shiny black shoes. Her *old* thong with the fraying elastic and the words 'Tempt me' faded by washing but still way too visible.

Oh, no. She dropped to her haunches, her fingers scrabbling on the wet pavement.

Too late.

Heat prickled her neck as she rose. The minuscule garment swung from one long finger. If she'd met his eyes she might have seen humour there but, frankly, right now he didn't seem the type and she wasn't risking it. She muttered a word she almost never used beneath her breath, careful to avoid skin contact as she snatched it from him.

She scooped the rest up, stuffing them back where they came from while rain splattered the pavement and her hair. Until Cameron shifted the umbrella so that it shielded her while leaving him exposed to the weather. 'It's all your fault,' she bit out.

'Am I to be held responsible for all your misfortunes, Didi?'

She straightened quickly, her eyes skidding straight into his with the inevitability of a train wreck. 'My life's been a disaster since the night I met you.' And even though she knew it was ridiculous, 'So, yes, I'm holding you responsible.'

His midnight-blue gaze didn't alter but a muscle twitched beneath his right eye. 'Makes one wonder what'll happen next. Maybe you should give up now—your misfortunes have a recurring habit of rubbing off on me.'

'I'm not rubbing anything off on you, Mr Black, you're managing your own rubbing very well.' Unfortunate choice of words. She forced herself to hold his gaze, which seemed to darken as they glared at each other.

Moisture sheened his face and raindrops lay like diamonds on the shoulders and collar of his very expensive wool coat. She knew it was wool because she could smell its distinctive scent chafing comfortably with his very expensive cologne. No, a man like him wouldn't tolerate something as inconvenient as another's misfortune.

'Maybe we could trade places some time,' she shot at him. But as she tripped up the steps again she had to admit he was offering her a generous and possibly very *in*convenient solution—for both of them. Or had she misunderstood? She picked up the cat's box, hefted its wobbling weight under one arm. 'Okay, so what exactly are you suggesting here, so I don't misunderstand?'

'You don't have a place to stay—and I'll take responsibility for that—so my apartment's a logical choice.'

'With my friend here? I'm not going anywhere without him.'

He glanced at the cat box, frowned. 'I guess it's settled, then. Tomorrow you can look for somewhere more suitable.'

She blew out a sigh, her breath fogging the air in front of her. Realistically, what alternative did she have? His offer was only for one night. A bed, somewhere safe…

She made the mistake of looking up at him again. At the dark eyes and sensual mouth—right now it was firm and inflexible. And absolutely captivating. How would it feel to be captivated by such a mouth? She drew a deep breath of chill night air. *Safe?*

'Tonight, then. Thank you.' She tried to keep her voice a notch above a croak. 'I'll need to stop at a pet shop for supplies on the way.'

He nodded, retrieving her one-handled bag, tucking it beneath one arm. She followed, dodging traffic and a tram as he headed towards a shiny late-model vehicle on the other side of the street while he fired rapid instructions into his mobile regarding the delivery of her stuff to the security guy at his apartment building.

The next experience was sitting beside him in his big classy car that suddenly didn't feel so big. Soft leather seats, the lingering fragrance of aftershave and mints. Body heat.

She shrank against the door as far away as she could get and concentrated on the box on her knee, soothing the more and more agitated animal within with quiet murmurs. In the absence of radio or CD noise he sounded more like his larger jungle cousins. At least it gave her something else to focus on.

Until that familiar hand with its sprinkling of dark hair appeared in front of her as he leaned sideways to adjust an air vent on the dash sending a spurt of warm air her way. She held her breath. As if she needed any more warmth.

'So…this friend you've been with…' Checking the rear mirror, he replaced his hand on the steering wheel. 'That's not an option for a few days, I take it?'

'Accommodation-wise?' she said, keeping her tone enigmatic. 'Marysville's a long drive away. My working life's here, in Melbourne.' When she found another job, that was.

She had something to prove. To her family, to herself. It didn't help that she'd told them she'd found work in a gallery and had a stunning apartment overlooking the Yarra. When she'd returned from a couple of years overseas after leaving school, they'd told her if she didn't intend going to university or making some sort of commitment and/or compromise she was on her own. She'd taken them literally and moved out.

They saw her passion for textile design as a waste of time—an argument she was never going to win. Creativity didn't pay; artists didn't make money. And until she did, until she showed them what she was capable of, she was stuck with waitressing—or not, since she was now unemployed.

They stopped at a small supermarket for pet supplies, and fifteen minutes later she followed his broad-shouldered shape through the revolving glass door of a luxury building.

Then he was whisking her skywards to his apartment. His penthouse apartment. But as she stepped into the living room surprise knocked her back a step. She hadn't expected to find his taste so…formal, so cool. So impersonal.

Maybe she should have.

Still holding the cat's box, she took in her surroundings. Almost everything was white. Stark white sofas bordered a black rug over white marbled floor tiles that seemed to go on for ever, giving an impression of endless space. A couple of glass-topped occasional tables with black-shaded lamps that threw out a harsh bleached light. Oyster-coloured curtains framed night-darkened floor-to-ceiling windows, which offered a stunning view of Melbourne's high rises.

Not a speck of dust, she noted as her eyes scanned the room. Nothing out of place. Not a coffee cup, TV guide, or book in sight. Nothing to make it homey or liveable. How did anyone live in such sparse surroundings? Because he probably spent little time here, she decided. Probably busy sleeping elsewhere.

She wandered to the window. 'Great view from up here. I imagine you see some beautiful sunsets—if you take the time to look.'

'Sunrise actually.' He set her bag on the floor. 'The view faces east. And yes, I make the time.'

'I didn't take you for the contemplative sort.'

'You wouldn't, would you? You're the sort who makes snap decisions about people before you have the facts. You're also impulsive and driven by emotions. You only see what you want to see.'

His blunt appraisal stung. Some sort of comeback was due and she lifted her chin. 'Whereas you're driven by cool, calculating intellect.' More like sunrise was a pretty backdrop while he planned how to make his next million. 'Sunrise should be about a new day—hope—something that comes from the heart… Oh, my…'

She trailed off as her gaze snagged on a major piece of textile art that hadn't been visible from the entrance. Without taking her eyes from it, she fished in her bag for her rose-tinted reading glasses and moved in for a closer inspection.

The asymmetric mural took up almost the entire wall, a forest bound with thread and paint beneath swirling drifts of snowflakes constructed with silver thread and beads in a disordered hexagonal fashion. She couldn't resist reaching out to touch the tactile feast, the subtly different shades of texture. 'A Sheila Dodd original. It must be worth a fortune.'

'Yes, and yes. You're familiar with her work?' His tone turned considering, as if he didn't believe someone like Didi would know anything about artists like Sheila Dodd. Or Monet for that matter.

She met his speculative gaze full-on. 'She's my inspiration.'

'Inspiration… For what exactly?'

'What I do.' Didi turned back to admire the work but didn't elaborate on the fact that she produced pieces along similar lines to the prominent Aussie artist and hoped to one day bathe in the same limelight. 'I enjoy creating things, whether it's food or fashion or fabric.' She flicked him a glance. 'That surprises you.'

'I'm fast learning not to be surprised by anything about you.'

He was watching her with an expression she either couldn't or didn't want to read. All she knew was it made her…prickly, itchy. Bitchy. 'It's a pity it's all so—' she waved her free hand at the room '—monochrome.'

One eyebrow rose. 'My designer thought otherwise.' Then he seemed to reflect on that a moment and said, 'What would you change?' as if he'd never given his choice of interior decoration a thought.

'Personal opinion of course, but you don't think it's lacking a little warmth and intimacy?' When he didn't reply she looked around at the bare surfaces. 'Where's the ambience? A few homey pieces like photos, a rock collection, a pottery figurine. A mix of plump red or apricot cushions, warm yellow light and a bluesy CD.'

Typical Didi-speak, but now the warmth and intimacy thing seemed to take hold as he continued to watch her. To distract herself she set her box on the floor, withdrew Charlie, buried her face in his soft fur and changed the topic. 'Hey, you're safe now, little guy.' *But was she?*

'It suits me the way it is.' He turned his attention to Charlie. 'That cat looks remarkably healthy for a stray. Are you sure it was abandoned?'

She rubbed the round tight tummy. 'True, but if you found a cat stuffed in a box tied up with string and left by a toilet block what would you assume?'

He nodded, straightened, all formal again. 'The bedroom's this way.' His tone matched his choice of furnishings—minimalist. 'It has an enclosed balcony. Please keep the cat confined to that area.'

She followed him down a wide corridor. As she passed she glimpsed what must be his bedroom, then another filled with gym equipment…and her stuff.

'Davis, the security guy downstairs, had your gear put in here.' He gestured towards it, then stopped at the third door, swung it open. The mountain of cream and gold quilt looked inviting on the big double bed. 'The guest bathroom's at the end of the corridor.'

'Great,' she said into the tense silence. Her initial snap judgement might have been premature. How many people would have put themselves out this way for a virtual stranger? She murmured, 'Thank you.'

He nodded, checked his watch. 'I'm unlikely to be back before midnight so make yourself at home. If you're hungry, feel free to fix something to eat.'

'Thanks.' Her gaze turned back to the bedroom. To the bed covered in *his* sheets. A shaft of heat slid through her belly. 'Um…thanks again, I'll be fine. Goodnight,' she managed, and stepped inside. Closed the door.

She waited till she heard his footsteps fade. 'Well, Charlie…' She smoothed his fur and set him down. 'So I guess it's tuna fish dinner for you and a hot bath for me.' But even though she forced herself to keep thoughts and self-talk upbeat she wondered with an ever-increasing knot in her stomach what she'd got herself into.

CHAPTER THREE

CAM glanced at the time on his computer screen as he checked his last unread email. Half past midnight. Surely his house-guest would be asleep by now? Because he didn't want to have to deal with her again tonight he'd stopped by his office on his way home from dinner.

Nor did he want to dwell on the fact that for some perverse reason she'd been slipping into his dreams over the past couple of weeks and doing wicked things to his libido. Of course she'd been on his mind, he told himself—she'd caused him unnecessary inconvenience and concern.

He switched off his computer, swiped his hands over the back of his neck. Okay, dreams—he could deal with those—but in-the-flesh reality was a different matter. So he'd give her another half-hour to be on the safe side.

But that didn't stop him from imagining her in his apartment. Relaxing in the bathroom's spa and steaming it up with her intriguing blend of feminine fragrance. Drinking from his cups. Curled between his sheets with only one room separating them.

He made a coffee in the kitchenette, then sat at his secretary's desk and flicked through *The Age* to kill time and divert his thoughts from what was going on in his apartment.

But his mind refused to glance further than the latest headlines. Would Didi remember his instructions to keep the no doubt flea-infested cat in her room, preferably on the balcony? Had she even heard them? he wondered, then shook his head. He had a feeling she wasn't good at following instructions.

She'd not yet shared with him the information that she'd lost her job. Perhaps she had something else lined up already, but he seriously doubted it. Because Didi O'Flanagan seemed to be a woman who danced to her own tune, when and wherever it suited her.

Irresponsible? He blew on his coffee. He'd reserve judgement on that. But he *was* surprised she recognised his Sheila Dodd.

Was that a tad pretentious of him?

He flicked through the pages with disinterest until his gaze snagged on a photo of his ex and thoughts of Didi fled as his fingers tightened on the paper. Katrina. On the arm of Melbourne's latest most eligible bachelor—soon to be ex-bachelor judging by the size of that rock on Kat's finger. The coffee turned bitter on his tongue. Unlike Cam, Jacob Beaumont Junior was from old money. His father owned half a shipping fleet and an airline—the perfect pedigree required for a suitable match for the daughter of an influential MP on his way to Australia's top job.

His harsh jeer echoed around the empty room. He'd thought Katrina the perfect woman. Tall, dark-haired, educated, meticulously groomed. Unashamedly uninhibited in the bedroom, the perfect conversationalist whatever company they surrounded themselves with, as driven to succeed as he was.

Until he'd revealed his background.

Her demolition of their relationship had been swift and vehement. In her eyes his family's history defined who *he* was—and consigned him to the lowest form of life. It didn't matter that he'd clawed his way out of the gutter, and had constructed a life he could take pride in. That he was stronger for past experiences, wiser, more perceptive of others' needs and motivation.

The page came away from the rest of the paper as he crumpled it in his fist, then tossed it in the bin. Her betrayal had severed an artery. Aristocrats were never going to let him into their world, no matter how successful he was now.

He liked women. He enjoyed their company. He liked the way they smelled, the feel of feminine softness against his body. But laying his heart on the line again was not going to happen. From now on he'd trust no one with his past. He didn't intend to remain celibate for the rest of his life, but from this day forward there'd be no emotional entanglements.

Cam let himself in with careful stealth so as not to awaken his sleeping guest. He didn't notice her at first. He just assumed she'd left every light in the apartment on because she had no idea about energy conservation. Annoyance prickled at him as he strode to the kitchen and flicked off the switch.

He was about to turn off the living-room lamp when he saw her. Rather, he saw her pyjama-clad backside—poking out from behind his white leather sofa. Red and green tartan flannelette.

He remained perfectly still while every male cell in his body jerked to attention. From where he stood he could see the soles of her feet and a band of creamy skin above the pyjama's waistband. What the hell was she up to?

Then he heard her croon softly, her voice muffled by the sofa, and watched, immobile, blood pooling in his groin as the compact little bottom wiggled and began backing out, her movements inevitably tugging the elastic lower…

'Problem?'

The wiggling stopped, then resumed at a frantic pace accompanied by a hiss, then the disconcerting sound of fabric tearing. 'Ouch!'

Didi appeared clutching an angry armful of spiked fur, damp blonde hair in similar disarray, her eyes huge, too huge for her elfin face, reminding him again of that pixie.

'I didn't hear you,' she said with a breathy catch to her voice that made him think of hot nights, hotter bodies.

'Obviously.'

'Charlie escaped. Um…there's a tiny claw hole—a couple actually…in the back of your sofa.' She closed her teeth over her bottom lip, then smiled up at him. 'Lucky for us they're not where you can see them, isn't it?'

The way she did that…artfully innocent or cunningly cute? He shook his head. 'Lucky for Charlie.'

Her smile dimmed. Snuggling the creature against her, she rose. 'If you have a pair of nail trimmers handy, I'll fix these claws right now.'

The shapeless flannelette swamped her. It should have been a blessing but it had the opposite effect. A sliver of protectiveness—or lust—snaked through his veins and coiled low in his body.

It had to be lust.

He crossed to the window, stood with his back to her to hide his body's response. 'Just take yourself and that damn cat back to bed and shut the door behind you.' *And stay there.*

'You don't like animals. How sad.'

The quiet censure in her tone put him on the defensive. 'I don't like animals *in my apartment.*'

'That's why I'd never live in an apartment. No garden, no fresh air and sky, no pets.'

He tried to confine his gaze to his own reflection in the night-darkened glass, but like lightning to metal his eyes were drawn to the image of the woman behind him. To the way her delicate fingers massaged the cat's fur. To the way her pyjama top dipped on one side exposing a sharply delineated collarbone—

'So you'll be wanting to find yourself somewhere more to your liking as soon as possible.'

The air stirred with a tense silence that echoed around his heart. Pulled at him as he heard her say, 'Naturally,' and watched her reflection turn and walk away, shoulders slumped. His fingers curled and tightened at his sides. Damn it.

Why had he taken his hostility towards Kat out on his house-guest? Even if she did rub him the wrong way. In so many ways… Shaking unwanted feelings off, he followed her ribbon of freshly showered almonds-and-honey scent along the hall. 'Didi…'

She halted at her door, hugging her cat to her like a child with a teddy bear. But she gave him no time to form the words he might have said. 'Thank you for your generosity this evening, Cameron Black. Goodnight.'

The door closed with a tight click, leaving only her fragrance to mingle with his self-recrimination.

He stared at the barrier a moment, listening to the sound of her moving around on the other side and wondering what she was doing. When the sound stopped abruptly, he couldn't help but picture her climbing into bed in those oversized pyjamas.

A big picture, a bad picture. A very bad picture because he didn't want to think about what those pyjamas hid. Nor did he want to imagine how he might go about finding out once and for all what that mobile mouth of hers tasted like, even if it was just to shut her up for a moment or two.

He gulped in a deep breath, heard it whistle out through his teeth. Finally he peeled his gaze away from the paintwork. Right now was a good time to hit the treadmill running.

The sound of his mobile woke Cameron from a sleep crowded with unwanted dreams of passionate pixies. Eyes still closed, he reached for the phone. 'Cameron Black.'

'Good morning, Mr Black. Sasha Needham calling for Sheila Dodd. I apologise for ringing you this early but I've just had a call from Sheila in the UK.'

'Yes?' Cam dragged his eyes open, checked the digital clock on his night stand. Five forty-five a.m.

'Sheila sends her sincere apologies but she's unable to finish the piece you commissioned within the agreed time frame. She's had a family crisis and will be staying on in the UK for the next few weeks.'

He pushed upright, wide awake now and already one step ahead. 'The gallery opens in less than three weeks.'

'I'm so sorry, Mr Black. Sheila realises it's short notice. She's given me the names of some possible alternatives…'

He closed his eyes again, scrubbed a hand over his morning stubble. 'Email them to me along with their credentials et cetera and I'll get back to you.'

Tossing off the quilt, he rose quickly, his bare feet barely registering the change from plush carpet to cool tiles as he moved to the bathroom and splashed cold water over his face.

Over the past two years he'd worked like a demon to turn a graffiti-covered warehouse in Melbourne's inner suburbs into something unique. An art gallery, not only for prominent artists but also for undiscovered talent from the lower socio-economic areas. An opportunity for those willing to put in the effort to start something worthwhile. A second chance.

The way he'd been given a second chance.

He stared into his own eyes. Heaven knew where he'd be now without it. He'd been one of those kids, and this gallery was a memorial to the one person who'd made it possible to start over.

Cam had poured a large sum of money into publicity; the minister for the arts was attending the official opening along with the press. If he couldn't have Sheila's work on display in time for the opening, he'd damn well have to find someone else pronto.

Twenty minutes later, showered and dressed, Cam slid open the French doors and welcomed the sounds of distant early morning traffic and brisk winter wind blowing through the potted palms on his sky garden patio. The fading glow of sunrise tinged the clouds a dirty pink, crisp air tingled his cheeks. He shrugged inside his suit jacket. Who said apartment living and nature were mutually exclusive?

Didi O'Flanagan.

Her image exploded into his mind and he pinched the bridge of his nose. As if he hadn't seen enough of her in his dreams last night; reclining on his desk, wearing nothing but those damn pink glasses and munching on red apples, for heaven's sake. He shook it away. He should have arranged a time to meet this morning to discuss further arrangements. If he wasn't careful she could end up here for God knew how long.

Right now he had a more urgent problem. Slurping strong black coffee, he checked his mobile for the names Sheila's assistant had promised to send. Nothing yet.

'Wow!'

He turned at the sound of Didi's voice, mighty relieved when she appeared wearing a cover-all pink dressing gown. 'Good morning.' His relief was short-lived—she smiled at him as she bit into a shiny red apple.

'Good morning.' Silver eyes sparkling, she waved the thing in the air like a damn trophy, indicating their surroundings. 'This garden's amazing! Is that a kumquat tree?' she said, barely drawing breath and moving to his tubbed specimen laden with tiny orange fruit. 'I just love kumquat marmalade.'

'Ah, we need to discuss—'

His mobile cut the rest of his sentence off. Didi studied him as he took the call. Impeccably dressed in dark suit, wrinkle-free white shirt and a tie the colour of blueberries. His cedarwood fragrance wafting on the air, the broad shape of his shoulders, the sexy strip of neck between his jacket and newly cut hair as he turned and began walking inside. Heat shivered through her and lodged low in her belly. Tall, dark, gorgeous.

Forget gorgeous.

Yep, she seriously needed to forget gorgeous. Cameron Black was the reason she no longer had an apartment. And because of her outburst at that function a fortnight ago, *thanks to him,* she needed to look for another job, which left her no time to work on the important things like establishing her career as an artist.

If she could just win that chance…

To give him privacy while he took his call, she chomped on the apple she'd helped herself to in the kitchen and admired the view a few moments, then rescued his coffee and carried it inside.

She found him studying his laptop at the dining-room table, brow furrowed, mouth pursed in a seriously sexy way, and for an insane moment she wondered how he'd react if she walked over there and pressed her lips against his.

Bad thought. This man was so not her type. This man was the type of successful entrepreneur her parents would approve of, which made him *all wrong*.

So she had to ask, 'What, no destitute families to evict today?' as she set his coffee cup on the table beside him.

He didn't look up; his only reply was, 'Humph.'

Had he even heard her? Then she made the mistake of looking at his eyes. Framed by ridiculously long lashes, they were the colour of his tie—dark blueberry—and the clouds in them had her softening despite herself. 'Anything I can do?'

Fingers tense on the table, he leaned back against the chair, his suit jacket falling open and giving her a view of broad chest, his dark nipples barely visible beneath the white shirt. 'Not unless you know someone with Sheila Dodd's expertise who can whip up something remarkable at short notice.'

Processing his words, she dragged her gaze away from his superhero body. 'Why?' she queried carefully.

'I'm opening a gallery in less than three weeks. The press will be there, along with a host of art critics, and I need something spectacular for the main wall. I commissioned Sheila but she's overseas dealing with some sort of family crisis.' His breath steamed out through his nostrils and he smacked the table with a hefty palm. 'Damn it!'

'So you want someone similarly experienced with textiles.' Dared she mention Didi O'Flanagan's considerably *less* experienced expertise?

He scrubbed his hands over his cheeks, a wholly masculine sound—the only sound in the quiet room apart from the thump of Didi's heart galloping in nervous anticipation.

'Right now I'd settle for anything, bar tomboy stitch or macramé.'

'Hmm.' She drew in a tentative breath. 'Leave it with me. I'll have something for you to look at by tonight.'

His hands paused on his jaw and Didi found those unnerving blueberry eyes focused on her. 'You know someone?' Spoken with barely concealed incredulity.

'Yes.' *Surprising as that might seem to you. And just wait till you find out who.*

'Who?' he demanded.

She shook her head. 'No questions.' Her mouth turned dry. Could she impress this guy enough to display her work? 'You're going to the office, right?' A horrible thought occurred to her. 'You *do* have an office somewhere, don't you?' Preferably a long way away.

'I do.' But as he lowered his hands to the table top she couldn't help but note the inflexible set of his jaw and his eyes didn't precisely brim with confidence.

'Look, I know we didn't exactly hit it off, and last night… well, all is forgiven if—'

'*You're* forgiving *me?*' His brows rose. 'By the way, how's that cat this morning? More to the point, *where is* that cat this morning?'

Didi huffed out a breath, knowing she'd made a wrong turn somewhere. 'Charlie's fine, sleeping on my pyjamas last time I looked.' She waved a hand as if it could erase last night's little foray behind the sofa. 'Forget about that for now.' *Please.* 'Do you trust me in your apartment?'

His shoulders lifted inside his jacket, then he seemed to

relax momentarily and a corner of his mouth kicked up. 'What's the worst that can happen?'

Several scenarios presented themselves, none of which Didi wanted to contemplate. She forced a smile back at him. 'You give macramé a go?'

Didi waited fifteen minutes just in case Cameron changed his mind and came back. The phone rang and she had a moment when she thought he might have changed his mind, but it must have been a wrong number because whoever it was hung up. Thoughtful, she stared at the handset as she replaced it on its base. Was it him checking in with last-minute instructions? Or was he checking that she hadn't run off with his valuables? Or perhaps it was a lady friend who'd hung up at the sound of a female voice?

She shrugged away the odd little niggle that thought provoked, then hurried to where her boxes of supplies had been stashed, dragged them out and got busy. She unearthed her portfolio with photographs of smaller pieces she'd either sold or still had in her boxes. She had no idea what he wanted for the gallery, but first she had to impress him with her work.

She had several pieces in various stages of completion, but her pride and joy was a quilt-sized work stretched on a frame, covered in black plastic and taped for safety. And how serendipitous that it blended so well with his living room, she thought, unwrapping it. Similar to Sheila's work with black, white and silver and various shades between, but Didi had used fire-engine red as a focal colour.

She set the piece against a bare wall, stood back and cast a critical eye over it.

Twigs she'd painstakingly collected and bound in black, white and silver thread made up the tree, the leaves silver filigree she'd constructed by hand at a jewellery class. An embroidered black serpent wound its way through the branches along a piece of old barbed wire. Just visible behind the action were the subtly spray-painted but unmistakeably erotic shapes of male and female. The apples of red silk layered with organza, thread and delicately spray-painted for a three-dimensional effect completed the picture.

She'd never shown her family. It would hurt too much to hear their dismissal of something she'd put her heart and soul into for months, using any spare cash she earned to purchase the supplies she needed.

The big question was would it be good enough to convince Cameron Black to take a chance on her?

He arrived home late. Didi had spent the day working on new material and suddenly there he was, watching her from across the living room with a doubtful expression in his eyes. Of course, he would, wouldn't he? With every square centimetre of his ever-so-clean table covered in her stuff.

'Hi.' She threaded her needle through a piece of fabric, took off her glasses, blinking up at him as her eyes adjusted. 'I'm sorry about the mess—I'll clean it up right this—'

'Forget the mess. I don't have time to waste. I've got less than three weeks.' Crossing the room, he shrugged off his jacket, slung it on the back of a dining-room chair at the far end of the table. Didi couldn't help but notice Mr Immaculate's shirt looked as pristine as it had when he'd left this morning.

His eyes took in her scraps of fabric and silks then flicked to the sheet-draped work against the wall, back to her. Comprehension dawned. 'So, you're the artist.' He sounded disappointed.

Her pulse took a leap. Squashing down her insecurities, she replied, 'I hope so.'

'That's why you recognised Sheila's work.'

She nodded. 'I've always loved textiles. I took one of her workshops in Sydney a few years ago.'

He crossed his arms over his chest. 'So…what do you have to show me?'

A hiatus while she stopped breathing. Oh, cripes, she wished he hadn't said it in quite that way with quite that expression in his eyes. Scepticism. Her art was the one thing that truly mattered to her.

Somehow she managed to make it across the room. Her arm trembled as she withdrew the sheet. And waited for a response. Any response.

The right response.

She thought she heard him mutter, 'Apples again,' and saw his jaw tighten.

He had something against apples? 'It's called Before the Temptation.'

'What else could you call it?' His wry response still gave her no clue to his thoughts.

Almost unbearable. How long he studied it, immobile, feet spread and arms crossed, she couldn't be sure. Seconds? Minutes? She counted the beats of her heart. Lost count.

Finally, he nodded. 'Okay, Didi, you've got yourself a commission. Two and a half weeks to come up with something of the same standard.'

Relief and excitement sent her soaring on helium balloons, making her voice breathless when she said, 'I'll need to know what you have in mind.'

'Something half as big again. The rest's up to you. I want your best.'

'You'll have it.'

'Don't let me down,' he continued. 'The press will be there, the minister for arts. I can't afford—'

'I won't let you down.'

He nodded. 'I'm not an artist, but I'm guessing it'll take all your time with only two and a half weeks to completion. All day, possibly some evening work too. Have you considered that?'

She nodded. 'Not a problem. I no longer work for the catering company, so I'm all yours.'

Hands dipping into trouser pockets, his gaze swung to her at last, and she was blasted by the full force of those eyes—not sceptical now, but…unreadable in the room's cool electric lights. They darkened considerably as his gaze flicked down over her tight black T-shirt and apricot chiffon scarf around her waist, to the black leggings and bare feet.

Oh… Her toes curled against the smooth tiles, her fingers slid down the front of her thighs as her heart did a strange tumble. Why the heck did her body react to him the way it did? As if he could draw her into those bottomless pools and— No. She'd let herself be drawn into a man's eyes once, and that had been one time too many. Jay had captivated her from the start, the way he had so many women. It was because of him she'd never trust a man's looks again, nor the way he might make her feel.

Because whatever her feelings might be towards a man, she couldn't trust him to reciprocate. Even when his eyes told her otherwise. She could only nod before clearing her throat. 'I—'

'You'll need space to work.'

'Yes.' No. Her balloons deflated. She didn't *have* space.

'So you'll remain here until the work's completed.' Blunt, a rusty knife on sandstone.

No time to reply.

He swivelled away, back bristling with tension, and headed towards the kitchen. 'Less than three weeks, Didi. You've got yourself a chance—use it.'

CHAPTER FOUR

DIDI heard the sound of the fridge door open, something hit the kitchen bench with a thwack, and realised she'd eaten nothing since that apple at breakfast. Nor could she now with her stomach twisted into hard, indigestible knots.

Work *here?* In this man's apartment? The man who ostensibly didn't give a fig for the less fortunate yet took in a stranger with a cat, no questions asked...well, almost none.

He wasn't the man she'd first assumed, she had to admit. And he was giving her the chance of a lifetime.

To anchor herself she clutched the front of her T-shirt while she replayed the last few moments. She'd wanted, more than she'd ever wanted anything, him to give her the commission, she just hadn't thought beyond that happy moment to the day-to-day/day-to-*night* practicalities.

Several long days. And nights.

Cam hadn't even bothered to comment on her work. The first person she'd exposed her best piece to, laying her vulnerability on the line, and not a single comment apart from a rude 'apples again'—what was that all about? Typical of the wealthy, she thought with an inward sneer. It reminded her of her family's dismissive attitude towards her art.

And yet...he had an original Sheila Dodd on his wall and he was opening a gallery, which had to mean he valued art. She thought of his eyes, the pulse-accelerating way he'd looked at her… Perhaps there was another reason he'd stalked off as if the demons from hell snapped at his heels…

She shook off the thought and all its complications—forget all that. This was her big chance, maybe her only chance to show what she was capable of.

Cam put two frozen gourmet meals in the microwave, set the timer, then leaned against the bench, uncomfortably aware that if Didi chose that moment to follow, she'd be in no doubt as to why he'd walked away before they'd formalised any kind of agreement.

For a moment he'd considered remaining in front of the open refrigerator door for a few moments. Cool the fires within. The woman was a sorceress in pixie clothing. How else could she have bewitched him so utterly? One glance and he knew for certain that underneath the figure-hugging black she was moulded just the way he'd dreamed. All she needed was the wings.

Hell.

And he'd just made an arrangement that required her here, in his apartment, for the next two and a half weeks. He shook his head at the irony.

No. This was strictly business. If she was going to be working in the dining/living room in the evenings—which was the ideal room with its floor-to-ceiling windows and huge table—wearing those figure-hugging outfits… He'd stay longer at the office and sleep on the futon. Maybe he should check into a hotel.

Then how would he keep an eye on her progress?

He needed to set some parameters, but some sort of celebratory offering was probably required first. A drink? He moved to the refrigerator once more, whipped out a bottle of Moët et Chandon Vintage Rosé, grabbed two glasses and headed to the living area.

Struck again by the sight of her sensational art against the wall, he slowed to study it once more. Who'd have thought the somewhat crazy little waitress was so talented? It would look right at home in the best galleries in the country. It looked right at home in his living room.

So did Didi.

She stood facing the windows, her hands laced together behind her head. The down-lights spangled her contrived riot of hair and he could smell her sweet almond fragrance from the other side of the room. He did his best to ignore her relaxed pose against Melbourne's diamond-studded deep velvet panorama as she stretched her body from side to side, no doubt flexing her spine after hours of close work.

But there was something spellbinding about the way she moved, as if she listened to some inner rhythm, that had his feet stapled to the floor. His blood pounded thickly as his gaze devoured the slim waist and compact little ass like some ravenous beast. And those legs… How would they feel clamped around his waist?

Dangerous curves.

Dangerous thoughts.

'We haven't ironed out the details of this arrangement,' she said.

Her voice startled him out of his semi-dazed state. Using his trick and watching him in the glass. Their eyes met for a brief moment, then again when she turned to face him. It was in her gaze too—a mutual awareness, quickly banked. If he'd blinked he'd have missed it.

'No, we haven't.' He moved to the table, set down the bottle and glasses, dismissing the urge to suggest an alternative and completely inappropriate way to celebrate: *Sealed with a kiss.* Like a spark to oxygen, the thought of locking lips with Didi exploded into stunning, breathtaking life. He grappled with the bottle's foil and cork. With those full rosy lips she'd suck away any bargaining power he possessed, of that he had no doubt. And on that not-so-sobering note, he said, 'We'll drink to it first.'

Didi shook her head. As much as she loved champers—and this looked like a bottle of the very expensive variety—this was way too important. 'Details first. How much am I worth?'

He named a figure that swept the air out of her lungs with a whoosh.

'That's if you're finished within the time frame,' he reminded her.

She was suddenly elated and terrified all at once. That amount was seriously serious. It would set her up for a long time. Show her family artists *did* make money and finally, maybe, they'd accept her choice. Accept her. How long had she craved their acceptance, their pride? Doubts crept in. Was she up for it? 'I'll need an advance to purchase supplies.'

'No problem. I can order you a credit card or give you cash, whichever you prefer. The apartment's at your disposal day and night.'

She nodded, trying to absorb the details. At least he'd be out during the day, but evenings… 'I'm not used to people watching me work—or looking at the unfinished product.'

'I'm paying you enough—that gives me the right to view it any time.'

He poured the bubbly into the glasses, looking satisfied with the deal. And why not? He dealt with mega bucks on a daily basis; this was probably no more than a drop in the Pacific Ocean to him. And he was correct—that amount of money on an unknown artist gave him every right to track her progress.

'I'll need time to design and collect materials.'

'Not too long. I want to see something tangible within a few days.'

Panic stations. 'Artists don't work like that.'

'Ah, but this one will. It's too important, for both of us.'

He held up a full glass, sparkling with pink liquid, his eyes focused on hers and she felt…respect? No one had ever afforded her work that compliment so she wasn't sure of her perceptions. She stood by the window too strung out with emotion to move. Or speak.

'Lost for words, Didi?' His voice held a hint of humour, deep and warm, and he walked towards her with both glasses. 'I have every confidence in you. Don't doubt yourself or your abilities.'

She drew herself up as he approached. 'I don't.'

'Good.'

'Even though *you* haven't said a word about my work,' she pointed out.

'Doesn't the fact that I'm commissioning you say it all?' His knuckles inevitably skimmed hers as he handed her the pink bubbly, sending a fizz of sensation through her fingers and up her arm. That first brief skin-to-skin contact left her wanting…more.

'We're in this together,' he said. 'A team. You create and I'll provide you with meals, coffee, chocolate, headache pills if necessary…whatever you need.'

She clinked her glass to his. 'Okay. To teamwork.' The fruity bubbles sparkled through her system as she took the first sip, their happy hiss and pop tickling her nose and prompting her to smile and say, 'I'll tell you now, I only eat dark chocolate. Soft centres.'

'Ah, a woman after my own taste.'

He grinned, an easy grin that reminded her of the first uncomplicated moment when she'd met him when he was just an attractive man with a flirtatious wit. Like Jay. Despite the warning bells that told her to avoid such men at all costs, she grinned right back. And why not? It wasn't as if they were going to fall into bed—she wouldn't let that happen. 'And olives,' she continued. 'You like olives, if my memory serves correctly.'

'Cheese and olive balls…' His smile faded and just like that the atmosphere changed from light and casual to something darker, deeper. Different.

His gaze dropped to her mouth, which suddenly felt dry and chapped and tingly and she had to force herself not to run her tongue over her lips.

Her relationship with Jay had tarnished the way she viewed men. But none had made her feel so aware of herself as a woman. And if she was right in her assumption of his reaction, a desirable woman. He could even—perhaps—polish that tarnish away.

If she moved closer would he kiss her?

She couldn't help it, she looked right back. She could imagine being kissed by those lips. Her own were practically puckering up in anticipation.

And where would that leave her?

In that big bad bed of his having the best sex of her life?

And more breathless and brainless than she already was, no doubt.

Big mistake. She knew next to nothing about him except that he was rich, gorgeous…and attracted to her. And his poster-boy status suggested a playboy and put her defences on alert. Yep, way too much like Jay.

So she chose the only alternative and stepped back. Away. Paying careful attention to keep her glass—and her voice—steady as she said, 'Tell me about this gallery of yours.'

He regarded her a moment through thoughtful eyes as if he, too, was mulling over the sexual tension between them. 'It's my latest building development.'

'Another bunch of displaced people, then?' And instantly felt less-than-stellar for the jibe. Did she want to blow this whole deal before she got started? Especially when his eyes glinted with some emotion she didn't recognise… Regret? For past business actions maybe? Or for something that struck much deeper and closer to the heart.

She was still frowning when he said, 'I'm not the bastard you seem to think I am.' And took a breath—

She perked up, ready to listen. Personal information, great, he hadn't volunteered a word about his personal life. But either the sound of scratching and an annoyed yowl from her bedroom distracted him or he deliberately chose not to elaborate.

'Charlie,' she murmured. 'He's lonely. And hungry, no doubt.'

'No doubt.' The dismissive tone didn't bode well for poor Charlie. 'It was a disused warehouse,' he continued, ignoring the feline sounds. 'Boarded up and covered in graffiti. High ceilings, plenty of space. It has a whole new look.'

'What type of art are you showcasing?'

'Paintings, textiles, jewellery, you name it. The idea is to foster new talent.'

'So why a Sheila Dodd commission? She's hardly new.'

'I've admired her work for several years and a big name brings in more customers and encourages new sales.'

'Why me? With your contacts you must know others who fit the bill.'

'This opening's being publicised as a big event in the art community. I don't have the time to look for someone at such short notice.' He glanced at the piece, looked back to her. 'Your work's unique—I'm prepared to take a chance. I want you.'

His voice was neutral, all business, but his eyes…his eyes imbued a different meaning to those last three words. Her pulse seemed to throb in her throat, making it difficult to swallow. She gulped down more wine and held his gaze.

But he didn't want her so much as *need* her and that gave her a sense of power that she'd never had. Which emboldened her to say, 'I have another request… Perhaps favour is a better word? It's about Charlie.'

'Ah. Yes. Charlie.' His tone predictably cooled.

'Could we perhaps compromise?' Her parents had often mentioned the word and Didi in the same breath. 'If I'm here for nearly three weeks, it's hardly fair to keep him shut away by himself all day while I work. Would you agree to him being in here with me?' Cameron didn't look impressed with her idea—his brows lowered, his lips thinned, then pursed as if about to speak. 'And I know he'd love the sky garden,' she hurried on. 'He couldn't do much damage there and if I could leave the door open a fraction…'

He blew out a sigh. 'I guess we can try it before he strips the paintwork on the bedroom door to kingdom come.'

She paused, knowing, hating that she had to say, 'I love him to bits, but I know I'm going to have trouble finding a place that will take me *and* a pet…if you know anyone who wants a cat…' She blinked away a sudden moisture.

'I'll ask around at the office,' he said. 'Meanwhile he's okay here.'

'Thank you.' She polished off her wine and felt the grin pull at her cheeks as the bubbly danced through her system. 'And it's a wonderful compromise. I'll go tell him the good news now.'

'You do that. Then we'll eat; I assume you're hungry?'

'Famished,' she called as she all but skipped on those pretty bare feet across the room and disappeared from view down the passage. 'All I've had today is an apple.'

Yeah. The apple. Cameron stared at the place where she'd been seconds ago. It was as if she'd left something of herself there. Hell, his whole apartment suddenly seemed crammed with her presence. His gaze lobbed on the usually pristine dining-room table, now a jumble stall jammed with her stuff. Littering his floor was a haphazard scatter of cardboard boxes brimming with colour. A fresh spicy fragrance permeated the air.

It was as if a cellar had been opened to let in the sunshine.

He slammed the door on his overactive imagination. Shaking his head at the absurdity, he strode to the kitchen. What the hell was wrong with him? He despised clutter. Didn't tolerate disorganised people. The squalid mess of his childhood would live with him for the rest of his life.

Three weeks. For art's sake he could manage three weeks. And what was that about compromise? She obviously had no idea of the meaning of the word… What *was* that odour?

He glared at the two containers as he yanked them out of the microwave. One hot gourmet dinner and one ruined tray of greying prime fillet steak, steamed beyond redemption. Blast it.

'What's that smell?' Didi appeared at the door with the cat in her arms and wrinkling her nose.

'Charlie's dinner. What say we eat out? My treat.' He whisked the remaining gourmet plate to the back of the bench then, grabbing a knife, he sliced the plastic off the other tray, cut the meat into chunks, put it on a saucer.

'Sounds good.' Then her perky voice altered. 'Ooh,' she almost crooned, the sound washing through him like liquid sex, causing his hand to slip on the knife. 'You didn't have to go to so much trouble for Charlie. I've got plenty of cat food.'

He set the saucer on the floor, noticing a pair of bare feet approach as he did so. 'I won't be making a habit of it,' he muttered. She had gold nail polish on her toes, he noticed, with little black snowflakes in the middle of each. Slim ankles, shapely calves—

Four white furry paws bounded into view and the feet moved away as he straightened up to clear the empty meat tray, but Didi got there first.

'Cameron. That steak wasn't for Charlie, was it?' She was smoothing out the plastic wrap and checking the price sticker. 'Come on, fess up. Even with your wealth you wouldn't pay mega bucks for a cat's dinner. You wouldn't pay for a cat's dinner at all if you had your way.'

To his chagrin he watched her lean over the counter top and check out the second container: the gourmet meal. 'Hey, I'm guessing you took out the wrong container. So you made a mistake—no big deal.' She grinned at him through silky gold lashes, her eyes slightly unfocused. 'Why do you feel you need to play Mr Perfecto in your own home? There's only you and me here.'

He was all too aware of that fact, which for some reason had every hair on his body rising, not to mention his blood pressure, and other bodily parts.

He snatched the empty container and plastic out from beneath her hands, catching a whiff of alcohol on her breath as he dumped them in the kitchen bin. Was the woman tipsy on one glass?

'Maintain the Image, perhaps?' she went on when he didn't reply, waving one end of her chiffon scarf. 'I bet you maintain that Mr Perfecto image in your sleep. All buttoned up and stiff…'

Registering the tiny hitch in her breath, he swivelled his head to see her soft cheeks suffused with instant colour. *Right on the mark.*

He turned away, moved to the sink to rinse the mugs left over from breakfast and said the first thing that sprang to his lips. 'What do you feel like eating?'

'Whatever you're having.' Her voice had dropped a notch, turned husky.

His fingers slipped on the mug he was drying as her words slid over him, through him. Ropes of fire snaked along his veins, tugging at his libido, stampeding his imagination into savage, steamy life. Didi riding him, her hair wild, long legs spurring him on, unbuttoning his image with quick deft hands…

He closed his eyes. Very carefully set the mug down. Unclenched his teeth. Wiped his hands on the towel and sent up a silent prayer for sanity.

No doubt about it, she was tipsy. What had he been thinking, giving her champagne on an empty stomach? *That's it, focus on practicalities.* 'You didn't eat lunch,' he barked. 'I told you to help yourself.'

'I forgot.'

Next he knew she'd planted her butt on the bench beside him. He didn't know how she'd got there—one moment she was standing behind him safely out of his line of vision, the next moment she was on the counter top. Perhaps she flew.

He made the mistake of looking at her. Astute silver eyes stared back at him. She wasn't worried about losing her commission or her accommodation, he realised—as he'd already said, he needed her. And they both knew it.

Leaning one elbow alongside her on the counter top, he forced himself to hold her gaze. *Ignore the normal red-blooded male's reaction.* The one still racking his system.

But he *was* a normal red-blooded male. And the warmth of her skin, fair and fresh and fragrant, teased him, tempting him to reach out and touch. He curled his fingers, confining the urge, shooting temptation straight to his already tormented lower body.

Plump rosy lips curved ever so slightly, hinted at a sense of fun. He hadn't experienced anything remotely funny in a long time. When was the last time he'd laughed? Did he even have a sense of humour any more? he wondered. He had the feeling Didi would be the type to breathe life back into it.

Breathe. He could hear the soft sound of her steady exhalations. Breasts rising, falling… He wanted to look down and see for himself. His fingers itched again to test the weight of her womanly flesh and feel her nipples rise in anticipation against his palms.

A good reason to focus on her face. The eyes brimming with hidden thoughts, the high cheekbones, the neat flat ear lobes— 'You're wearing two different earrings.'

She tipped her head to one side, setting the left one tinkling. 'It's The Look.'

'The look?'

'Asymmetric. Like your Sheila Dodd. Like your tie.' Her eyes dipped and she studied his throat through long silky lashes.

He swallowed over the lump that had suddenly mushroomed from nowhere. 'My tie's asymmetric?'

Wiggling her bottom along the bench until she was within reach, she slotted her fingers behind it, loosening the knot and yanking the silk sideways in one swift movement. 'It is now.' Grinning, she smoothed it all the way down his chest, her eyes following the path of her fingers, every part of his body responding to the touch. 'That's better. It looked like it was strangling you.'

Perceptive girl. Or maybe it was blazingly obvious, he thought, reaching up now to undo the top button of his shirt. He'd never thought this apartment overly warm. Until this woman had turned the heat up.

'Okay. I made a mistake. I intended to impress you with my gourmet dinners specially imported from the Six Spice Deli around the corner.'

Now it was he who manoeuvred along the counter top so Didi was directly in front of him, her knees bumping his waist. So he could rest his hands on her hips. So he could look directly into her eyes and say, 'And I'm probably about to make another one,' as he laid his lips on hers.

CHAPTER FIVE

THE first touch of Didi's mouth against his detonated an explosion that knocked Cameron sideways and shattered the illusion that control was his rock-solid foundation, that he could pull away any time.

Sparks. They sizzled along his nerves with the spectacular ferocity of frayed power cables, snapping and crackling through his blood, sending his hormones spearing into the sky like some crazed Eureka Tower.

He felt her instant response—the heave of her breasts as she struggled to drag in air and push him away, then her mouth softening, opening, hands rising to clutch at his shirt. The moan deep in her throat as he changed the angle for better access.

Her taste was a sweet temptation, luring him deeper to sample the dark lusciousness of her tongue, to drink in its hot honey flavour as it writhed with his.

This was no ordinary kiss. This was the force of a wrecking ball at its most dramatic, splintering thought and crumbling to dust barriers he'd thought impenetrable.

Had he thought himself immune to emotion? He tried telling himself this was a severe case of lust but somehow the condition sounded grossly inadequate. Because something else was happening here. Something he didn't want to think about because if he did he'd know he'd made a bigger mistake than he'd ever dreamed of.

Instead he pulled her closer, shifted nearer, between thighs that seemed to melt apart at his wordless command so he could feel her sultry heat seep through his shirt and into his skin.

Her softness yielded to his burgeoning hardness, hot blood beating through his body as his hands slid from her hips to the curve of her bottom and found the hem of her T-shirt. Fingers barely steady crept beneath to find smooth alabaster skin, the delicate arch of her spine as she leaned into him.

Her grip on his shirt tightened. Jersey-clad legs clamped around his waist, locking their lower bodies in an iron embrace. He rocked against her. Sweat broke out on his brow, his lungs seized. The urge to rip away the thin barrier and drive into her—right here, right now, without thought for the consequences—

He wrenched his mouth away from her satiny warmth. Backed up a step. It was torture to slide his hands beneath her thighs, over firm shapely calves and untangle her legs from around him. Madness to look into her wide silver eyes and see his own ardour reflected back. Had he forgotten so soon? Lust was one thing, this emotional whatever it was…was something else.

He didn't do emotion. Not since Katrina.

Chewing on passion-plumped lips, she drew in a breath, her breasts rising with the effort, drawing his attention to her nipples outlined clearly against her T-shirt.

'A-a-ah.' Her breathy voice drew the sound out like spun toffee.

'I—' A stab of pain in his lower leg cut through his senses and he stumbled back a step. 'What the…?'

Charlie. He glared down at the cat, who'd apparently polished off his silver-service main course and decided trouser-clad legs were a convenient dessert.

'What?' Didi still had a death-grip on his shirt and now one of the animal's damn claws seemed to be lodged tight in the leg of his Armani trousers. He teetered dangerously for a couple of seconds before rocking forward on the balls of his feet only to feel one shoe land on something squishy.

'Bloody cat.' He shook his leg free and the animal bounded away with a hiss of annoyance, no doubt in search of its next victim of choice—the French silk drapes, perhaps.

His body still pulsed, his leg throbbed, his pride was dust beneath his feet. There was a rip in the fabric and—he checked—a disgusting disc of squashed fillet steak on the bottom of his shoe.

He looked back at Didi, who'd relinquished her hold on his shirt to cup her hands over her mouth and nose. 'It's okay,' he reassured her. 'Hardly a scratch.'

Didi stared at Cameron while she tried to regain control of her runaway emotions. Her lips felt as if they'd been buzzed by a supersonic jet; her pulse was galloping for a win in the Melbourne Cup.

Alcohol on an empty stomach had snatched away reason and common sense. Planting her butt on the counter top had been her first mistake.

He looked…worried? No, he looked confused. Blame the champers for the fit of giggles that bubbled up her throat. She must be borderline loony because why would she feel like laughing when she'd just been kissed senseless and he was probably going to kill her cat and fire her and life was never going to be the same again?

She couldn't help it; the half-laugh, half-cough tumbled out, convulsive and slightly hysterical.

His gaze narrowed slightly, his bemused expression didn't alter. 'Are you laughing?'

'I'm sorry, it's just…' She dabbed at her eyes with the corner of her scarf. Her sudden amusement faded as he bent and she saw him twitch at the hem of his trouser leg to inspect the damage to his flesh—twin stripes of red. 'Are you okay?'

He grabbed a tissue, moistened it under the tap and dabbed

at the wound. 'I'm probably going to die of blood poisoning or tetanus but don't let that spoil your evening.'

'Let's have a look.' She slid off the bench but he was scraping meat from the bottom of his shoe and she couldn't see. 'Where's your first-aid box?'

'I don't need first aid. Or maybe I do, but not for my leg.' He straightened and met her eyes. 'What just happened here—'

'Was a kiss, Cameron.'

At least that was what she'd thought it was. But she'd never thought a simple kiss by the kind of man you'd sworn to avoid could suck the air from your lungs and leave you in need of an oxygen mask. Burn you from the inside out until you were cinders. Send your heart spinning in a thousand different directions until you didn't know which way was up. The answer: it wasn't a simple kiss. Which only led to another question: what *was* it?

But she was hardly going to tell him all that, was she? The best option was to feign nonchalance. As if she exchanged saliva with almost-strangers every day of the week. So she shrugged. 'It was fun, Cameron.'

'Fun.' His tone mocked and his eyes, darkly assessing, pinned her own, holding her immobile, stripping away clothes, flesh and façade until she understood the meaning of naked to the core.

It took all her strength to drag her eyes away. 'My guess would be you thought so too,' she managed, whirling away to drag open cupboards. 'About that first-aid box…'

But she could feel his gaze tracking her movements, like a hot glue gun oozing heat down her spine, her bottom, her legging-clad thighs.

Suddenly he was behind her. She felt his shirt brush her sleeve, his breath against her bare arm as she reached for the next cupboard. Her heart rate, barely back to something approaching normal, picked up pace once more.

Then he leaned closer, the hard planes of his chest abrading her spine, her nape, the back of her head as he reached to the top shelf. She could smell the residue of cologne he'd used this morning, and, beneath that, the scent of soap and man. This man. She'd smell it in her sleep tonight, and a few nights more. Many nights more.

'Here,' he snapped. Rather than the super-dooper kit she expected, he pulled out an old ice-cream tub with a loose assortment of Band-Aids, painkillers, tubes and bottles. He stepped back and Didi swayed at the sudden loss of contact. Her head was spinning, her legs felt numb.

He lifted out a tube of antiseptic cream, barely glanced at her as he said, 'Looks like you should sit down. Or perhaps you should eat.' He flicked his head at the counter top. 'There's a dinner there. It should still be hot.'

Probably a sensible idea, even if her stomach churned at the thought of food. 'I think I will.' She peeled off the lid, grabbed a spoon, filled a tumbler of water and perched on a kitchen bar stool at the end of the counter top. But even the fragrance of sweet-spiced Moroccan lamb didn't tempt her appetite out of hiding.

She dug out a token chickpea or two, rolled them around her mouth, barely swallowed. Gulped water. Then the sight of Cameron placing one foot on a chair, rolling up his trouser leg and exposing one firm calf with thick masculine hair dried her mouth all over again.

The two distinct raised welts were dealt with swiftly and she stared as he rubbed in antiseptic cream with long blunt fingers.

Dark olive skin overlaid the hard muscle. Her own fingers tingled and her creativity took flight. Oh, how would it feel to run her hands up his leg? What was it about this guy? She'd never even looked at Jay this way. This wicked, wanton way.

She'd take off his shoe, his sock. Start at the toes and work her way up. From the smooth skin of his instep to the rougher skin above the sock line. She'd watch his eyes darken to that gorgeous blueberry as she crept her fingers higher, beneath the trousers to fondle his kneecap. Higher, where the tops of his thighs would be hard, like wood, then to the inner thigh where it would be softer, hotter…

'How is it?'

His voice penetrated the sexual shroud she found herself immersed in. As she blinked it away she became aware of her own heart beating a thick, heavy rhythm against her ribs. Aware of his eyes studying her with a searing intensity that made her wonder if he could read her thoughts.

She managed a smile, hoped it looked casual and tried for light. 'Mmm, good. Want a taste?'

His gaze dropped to her mouth, the sexual glitter in his eyes making her lips feel swollen and sensual, as if she'd invited him to taste something far more intimate. A taste he'd already acquainted himself with, and her pulse spiked at the memory.

Which was probably why he said, 'Thanks, but I'll eat later. When I've finished at the office.' He rolled down his trouser leg, capped the tube. He didn't want an encore. In fact she got the distinct feeling he did, in fact, consider it a mistake, as he'd said before he kissed her.

She told herself she was *not* disappointed. She did *not* need another reminder of her own mistakes. Rather, she felt a growing unease that he was leaving his own apartment on her account. Guilt because he shouldn't have to do that. She set the spoon on the counter top with a chink of silver on granite. 'I thought you'd finished for the day?'

'I've got some last-minute details to finalise before I leave for Sydney.'

'You're going to Sydney?'

'First thing in the morning. I'm viewing some glass figurines and wooden carvings I intend purchasing for the gallery. I'll be gone a couple of days. You'll be okay here alone, won't you?'

He didn't pause for an answer, just dragged a wallet from the back pocket of his trousers, pulled out a couple of business cards and a wad of fifty-dollar bills. 'I haven't had time to organise a credit card but this should cover your expenses while I'm away. I use a limo service; I'll let them know the car's at your disposal.' He counted the cash, laid it on the table.

She stared. She'd never seen anyone lay down such a large amount of cash at one time and not blink an eye. Perhaps it simply wasn't enough for him to bother about. 'You're not afraid I'll do a runner with your money?'

He shook his head once. 'You'll hang out for the prize. You stand to earn ten times that amount—and earn a name for yourself at the same time.' Spoken with an almost indiscernible disdain for those beneath his privileged position of wealth and power. She recognised it and anger flared, hot and harsh. 'How dare you presume to pigeonhole me—or anyone else for that matter—because I don't live at a fancy address?'

He flashed her a look, a cold blue flame that froze and burned, holding her in its grip for a few tense heartbeats, and for a gut-curdling moment a stranger seemed to stare back at her. *He's not the man you think he is.* The poster pinned to the ladies' room mirror streaked through her mind.

She slid off the stool and took a step back, rubbing arms that suddenly felt chilled. Who was this man she'd committed herself to work for? Whose apartment she'd be living in for the next couple of weeks?

The man who'd kissed her with toe-curling expertise.

The man she'd kissed back.

His gaze relented a little but his face remained stony and unforgiving, the lines around his mouth suddenly looked deeper. 'You're mistaken,' he said quietly. 'I judge people by the way they live their life, not their address.'

'I'm—'

'Any problems, speak to Davis downstairs or call my mobile.' He turned and headed to the dining room, collected his jacket.

Trailing in his wake, Didi nodded, hugging her own threatened security within her crossed arms.

As he shrugged into his jacket he said, 'If you're cold, turn up the thermostat; it's on the wall by the front door.'

'I'm not cold.' Just uncertain.

'I'll be late back tonight and gone early. Have some work in progress for me to look at when I get back.'

'I will.' Spoken with a certain amount of trepidation.

He paused, looking grimly awkward. 'We should clear the air about that moment…'

She was almost tempted to let him bumble through an explanation, but, really, she didn't want to discuss it either. 'I told you, it was a bit of fun. Let's leave it at that.'

He nodded and she sensed his relief. His remote expression relaxed into some semblance of the guy who'd toasted their partnership with her less than an hour ago. 'See you on Friday.'

Then he was gone. Didi sank into the nearest available sofa. She hoped her creativity wasn't shot to pieces. Charlie wandered in, jumped up onto her lap and began purring, bumping his head against her hand. 'There you are. You just wanted in on the action, didn't you? Or were you jealous, hey? Well, you don't have to worry, there won't be any more.' Cameron's kiss might be the hottest thing since supernovae were discovered but they'd never be compatible.

Except in bed.

She had no doubt he'd be an absolute god in bed. But he'd never be suitable in the ways that counted. Yet she hardly knew him, how could she make any kind of judgement?

Well, she knew some things. He'd never understand what it was like to wonder where your next dollar was coming from or where you were going to sleep tonight. Mind you, neither had she until she'd made the decision to go it alone.

'Don't bother coming back until you're prepared to take your place as a part of our family and communicate rationally,' her mother had said when Didi had flounced into the lounge room and announced she was leaving. Fitting in with her family's lifestyle had never suited her. A lifestyle Cameron Black would be totally at home with.

But who was he really? With his lifestyle, looks, his way with women, he reminded her too much of the man who, to her humiliation, had left her to cancel their wedding plans alone. But she'd seen glimpses—shadows—of someone else behind that polished façade. Drained of energy, she closed her eyes. Cameron Black Property Developers might have a reputable name but Cameron Black, the man, was someone else entirely.

The wide steel doors slid open on a cushion of air and Cam stepped into his night-darkened office on the fifteenth floor with its twinkling vista of lights below, but he barely gave them a glance as he strode past the empty reception area. He'd kissed her. Didi. The woman he'd commissioned to work for him.

Why, for God's sake? Because he'd been unable to help himself. He'd been bewitched. No, he told himself, it was simpler than that—he was horny. Scowling, he rifled through his files until he found the Sydney contacts. She didn't call the shots where his sex life was concerned. So why had it felt as if he'd been sledgehammered? As if he'd been the one out of control?

He tossed the necessary paperwork into his briefcase then moved to his computer, booted it up. He'd not go to Sydney next weekend as he'd originally planned, but tomorrow.

Just a kiss. That was all it was, right?

Who knew what might have happened if the damn cat hadn't decided to take a piece out of him?

Sex might have happened.

Fast furious sex on his kitchen counter. The image of him whipping her leggings down and plunging himself into that warm wet heat had his pulse stepping up, his blood rushing to his groin. He swore. He didn't do emotional, he didn't do trust, not where women were concerned. Not any more.

He tapped keys, booked a seat on the six a.m. flight and printed out his boarding pass. He wanted the best Didi could do with her *needlework.* He needed her creativity on the wall, not in his bed.

Didi spent the following morning designing something on paper, deciding on materials, sorting through what she already had and what she needed to purchase.

This was what she needed to concentrate her thoughts on, she told herself as she pulled out skeins of tangerine and vermilion silk and matched them to the aubergine. Not the sexy man who was paying her, offering her the chance she'd been waiting for.

Next she took Cameron's offer of the limo service and shopped like a queen—for supplies. But it was liberating selecting materials without having to think of the cost. Paying for them with the cash he'd left, then riding back to his apartment without having to depend on an unreliable car, the hassles of parking or public transport. The carefree way she'd done as a child.

She and her sister had been raised as the privileged daughters of a society couple. Their parents graced the social pages regularly and she'd attended numerous functions over the years. As a teenager, she'd accompanied her mother to her charitable events, had witnessed firsthand what it was like to live in the gutter with no support, no hope. She'd seen the despair in those eyes and what that desperation led to—drugs, crime, death. It had changed the way Didi viewed her place in the world.

Over the years she'd devoted regular early mornings to helping out with the kids' breakfast club on the seamier side of the city, lent her expertise to an arts programme for women and children in shelters, volunteered late shifts at a halfway house for those undergoing drug rehabilitation.

People were all equals as far as Didi was concerned.

Mum didn't see it that way. *They're not like us, dear.* Her mother would tell Didi, 'It's our duty as Christians to help those less fortunate than ourselves.' But she didn't want to soil her silk ensembles doing it.

Nor could Didi imagine Cameron Black getting his designer suits dirty in a soup kitchen or handing out blankets to the homeless on a frosty night.

Bulging shopping bags hanging from both arms, she stepped onto the footpath in front of his apartment building, glancing at a young woman at the entrance as she passed. Even in skinny jeans and a casual black velvet jacket, she was stunning. At around six foot, she was a statuesque brunette with clear blue eyes. Yes, she'd fit right in amongst the tenants who resided here, Didi thought.

Whereas she'd never fitted in. Her older sister, Veronica, took after their parents—tall, dark. Immaculate. At eighteen she'd married a wealthy middle-aged owner of several luxury yachts that ferried rich tourists around the Harbour and now lived a life of luxury in one of Sydney's most affluent suburbs.

She nodded to Davis at the security desk and crossed the ornate foyer, stepped into the elevator. If her sister could see Didi now…

Should she answer that? Didi frowned at her mobile over her glasses while the familiar tune rang out over the soft CD she'd been working to. She didn't need any distractions, but what if it was Cameron checking up on her with some request or other? She could tell him she'd started, even if she didn't need to hear his deep velvet voice on the other end of the line.

She set down the frame she was in the process of constructing and answered with a crisp, 'Hello?'

'Surprise!'

'Veronica?' Thinking of the devil in Prada had somehow conjured her up. Didi leaned back in her chair, removed her glasses, stunned to hear her sister's voice. Veronica hadn't spoken to her since she'd left Sydney. She rarely spoke to Didi in any case, unless it was to denigrate her. So why was she ringing now? Didi rubbed the frown pleating her brow. 'How are you?'

'I'm well. Are you busy?' When Didi didn't answer, Veronica said, 'I didn't know if you'd be able to take personal calls while you're working. Some work-places have a strict policy on mobile phones. I was going to leave a message.'

'Ah-h-h… No, it's cool.' The little lie tripped off her tongue—as far as her family knew, she worked in a gallery and she wanted to keep it that way. 'We're fairly casual here.'

'Great. Listen, I'm in Melbourne for a couple of days—Daniel's at a residential conference in Brisbane and I told him I needed a break to explore Melbourne's shopping arcades. And to see you of course,' she added. It sounded like an afterthought. Definitely an afterthought.

More like you're checking up on me. Didi's stomach dived to her feet as her hand tightened on the phone. 'You're in Melbourne? *Now?*' Oh, she was so dead.

'I'm at the airport. I should be in the city in, say, thirty minutes. What's the gallery's address? I'll come straight there.'

'No!' *Think.*

'What's wrong?' A definite edge of suspicion. 'I'll only stay a few moments. We can catch up after—'

'I'm not actually working at the gallery today…' She paused, looked around at *her apartment.* Cameron wasn't due home till tomorrow night. He'd never know Veronica had set foot in the place. 'I'm working from home,' she continued. 'I've been commissioned to do a piece for the opening of a new gallery.' That part was true, at least.

'Oh…that's…great.'

She heard her sister's tentative approval and breathed a sigh of almost-relief. Her sister could go home and report everything was fine with Didi and maybe, just maybe, her family would accept her choice and let her back into their lives again without disgrace. She gave her Cameron's address. 'Speak to Security, they'll buzz you through.'

'I can't wait to see this new apartment and it'll give us time to catch up. I'll stay overnight if that's okay.'

'Oh…' A jolt of alarm shot through her, and she sprang out of her chair. 'Fine,' she finished faintly. What else could she say? 'See you soon.'

Two bedrooms. Veronica could sleep in the room she'd been using.

Which left Didi with Cameron's room…

CHAPTER SIX

SHE stabbed the disconnect button and flew towards the hall. Did she dare…? *No choice.*

Swiftly she gathered up her meagre supply of clothes and toiletries and lugged them down to Cameron's room. But she paused at the closed door. She'd never been in here. She'd barely seen past the crack in the door on her way past.

She had thirty minutes tops.

As she flung the door open the cedar-wood scent of his cologne wafted past her. She stood a moment breathing it in while she cast her eyes over the room. A stunning view of nearby high-rise buildings cast a reflected afternoon glow on the cream carpet and deep blue quilt atop the king-sized bed. Matching drapes graced floor-to-ceiling windows, which opened onto a balcony filled with soft ferns.

A partially open door revealed an en-suite bathroom in cream and gold. Shuffling to the far side with her arms full, she pulled open a cupboard door and discovered it led to a walk-in wardrobe filled with racks of top designer suits and enough pressed shirts to last a year.

In what seemed another life she'd had a cupboard like this. She'd given her designer labels to charity, walked away from her family's disapproval to become an artist. It was vital Veronica thought Didi successful.

She stuffed her clothes next to a rack of shiny leather

shoes, then moved to the bathroom, swept Cameron's toiletries out of sight beneath the vanity and arranged her own. Just in case…

And tomorrow morning her sister would be gone—Didi would see to it personally, even if it meant accompanying Veronica on her shopping spree and waving her off to the airport in a taxi.

At the cost of having something for Cameron to look at?

She shook the disturbing thought away. She'd roughed out a plan, hadn't she? She'd bought supplies, put together a frame to work on. The sound of the elevator doors alerted her and she hurried from Cameron's room, closing the door.

'Hi.' Didi gave Veronica a quick hug and took charge of her suitcase.

'Hmm.' Veronica's eyes swept the apartment. 'I never imagined this. It must cost you a fortune.' She cast Didi an assessing glance. 'How do you afford it?'

Aware of her tatty jeans and dishevelled hair, Didi noted the classic lines of her sister's designer outfit, the pink suede boots, the perfect make-up and long dark hair salon-streaked with auburn highlights. Was it any wonder Veronica would ask that question? And why hadn't she anticipated an answer?

'Ah, the gallery owner was leasing it out at low cost since he's interstate at present.' Didi, who never lied, who hated deception, was getting in deeper with every passing moment. Spinning on her heel, she set the rolling case in motion. 'Your room's this way. I hope you don't mind sharing it with a cat,' she said over her shoulder.

'Not at all. You know I love cats, but Daniel's allergic, you know.'

She knew. Daniel Davenport was allergic to most things, including anyone remotely connected with poverty. Didi showed Veronica to her room, indicated the bathroom at her disposal, then left her to freshen up.

A few moments later, Veronica appeared, requesting a tour

of the apartment. Didi whisked her through the rooms, then suggested they go out for lunch before hitting the shops.

Veronica spent a fortune; Didi helped her. Later they swapped childhood stories over a leisurely dinner. Even though she wasn't a nightclub fan, Didi suggested they cruise to a couple of nightspots so that by the time they returned home it was well after one a.m.

Didi sighed a breath of relief when Veronica said she was exhausted and intended showering then going to bed. Didi happily agreed to do the same.

As she tiptoed into Cameron's room her skin prickled with the feeling that he was somehow there with her, breathing down her neck. She closed the door behind her and, leaving the light off, wandered to the sliding door that looked out onto the balcony. Ferns shifted in the breeze. Turning, she took in the immaculate room. Shadows and light played over the walls. The sibilance of the air-conditioning overlaid the muted traffic noise.

Even though none of his personal items were visible, his presence lingered. The room smelled of him. How could she possibly get any sleep in here? she wondered, gazing back at the twinkling streetscape below.

A hot shower might help. She stripped off her clothes, tossed them on the bottom of the bed and padded across the carpet in the semi-darkness.

Light flooded the bathroom as she flicked on the switch. She startled at her own reflection, then chastised herself for being foolish. 'Your secret's safe,' she whispered. Why was she whispering, for goodness' sake? 'He's hundreds of kilometres away,' she said out loud to convince herself. 'Only a few more hours and he'll never know.'

She turned on the spray, smothered her face in cleanser, massaging it in until the room began to steam, then stepped under the water's glorious heat.

She'd left her personal soap in the other bathroom. Which

meant she had to use Cameron's soap. The one she'd smelled on him last night. As she lathered up and rubbed the slippery suds over her arms and breasts her nipples turned to tight little peaks, blood rising to the surface and turning her skin a blushing pink, reminding her of how he'd made her feel last night.

Hot. Turned on. Every body part excruciatingly sensitive.

She reached for her exfoliating mitt, scrubbed her skin with unnecessary vigour, hoping the harsh abrasive action would relieve the discomfort. No. It merely deepened the blush in places, which gave the appearance of sunburned patchwork.

She yanked off the mitt. This was bad. Worse, this inappropriate preoccupation with Cameron Black had to stop. Right now. Closing her eyes, she leaned back against the cool tiles, lifted her head to the spray and let the water pound her. One more minute…

Cameron frequently employed the element of surprise. He keyed in his entry code and watched the floor numbers illuminate as he rode the elevator towards his apartment. Expect the unexpected—it kept employees on their toes.

The same went for sexy little waitresses who moonlighted as live-in commissioned artists. Still, a buoyant feeling of anticipation lifted him, stirring memories of the last time he'd seen her—deliciously mussed, her lips red-cherry plump. The fact that it had been him plucking the fruit only added to the intensity.

That aside, he knew little about her. He *did* know she kept him second-guessing, stimulated him with her bubbly personality and quick tongue. And, to his never-ending surprise and discomfort, aroused his libido far too frequently.

She had the looks of a pixie but she kissed like an angel.

The reason he'd taken off for Sydney earlier than planned. The fact that she'd called that moment in the kitchen 'fun' merely demonstrated the type of woman she was—carelessly casual. That *was* the type of woman he preferred now, wasn't it? So the fact that it had rocked him more than it had her was disturbing in the extreme and best forgotten.

He needed to keep his distance, put some perspective on the situation, he assured his muted reflection in the impersonal elevator's mirrored walls. No way was he going to jeopardise this commission; it was too important. He was taking a risk on an unknown, probably paying her far more than he should. He didn't even know if she was up for the task at such short notice.

He'd been naïve to trust a woman he barely knew in his apartment with a load of cash. Which was why he'd decided to return a day earlier.

Not for any burning desire to see her again.

The elevator doors swished open, heightening that sense of anticipation. He forced himself to concentrate on important matters. If she was asleep, he could view her work at leisure without her looking over his shoulder and distracting him.

Light from the hallway beckoned. She wasn't in bed yet, then. His blood pumped that little bit faster. He turned into the hall—and saw a tall, dark-haired woman in a slim-fitting blue nightgown strolling out of the guest bathroom as if she had every right to be there.

He stilled, every hair on his body rising as a fierce disappointment stabbed through him. He'd been right to come home early. The moment his back was turned Didi was entertaining guests. He supposed he should be relieved it wasn't a male. But she'd abused his trust, something he couldn't, *wouldn't* tolerate.

The woman came to an abrupt halt, clutching a bag of toiletries to her breasts, dark eyes wary. 'Who are you and what are you doing here?'

'I live here,' he said grimly. 'Who the hell are you?'

'Dymphna's sister.'

'Dim...*who?*'

'Didi,' she clarified. Her disparaging gaze swept over him despite the fact he wore well-pressed trousers and a sky-blue business shirt. 'She didn't say anything about a boarder.'

'Boarder.' The word exploded from his mouth. 'She said that?'

She shook her head. 'I already told you, she didn't mention anyone else living here, so, no, she didn't say that.'

'No, I don't suppose she did.' A red haze shimmered before his eyes. She wouldn't. Not if she wanted to play lady of the manor, or whatever her game was, in his apartment.

The woman moved swiftly towards Didi's room, keeping close to the wall. 'I'm calling Security if you don't identify yourself.'

'Go ahead. In fact, I'll call them for you.' Keeping his eye on her, he backed up to the security panel in the wall, hit the button. 'Davis, Cam Black here. There's a woman in my apartment calling herself—what's your name?'

'Veronica Davenport.'

Cam listened while Davis explained that Miss O'Flanagan had a guest staying overnight and enquired was everything all right.

'Fine,' Cam clipped, and disconnected.

'Not Veronica O'Flanagan, then.' He studied her from the top of her shiny dark hair to the tips of her manicured toenails, saw her register the fact that he knew Didi's surname.

The woman reeked of wealth. The kind of inherited wealth Cam despised. It didn't fit. Didi was nothing like this model of sophistication in any way, shape or form.

'Davenport's my married name.' She tilted her head so that she looked down her nose at him, but he didn't miss the appreciative way she cast her eyes over his body. 'You haven't explained yet who *you* are.'

No, I haven't, have I? 'Where's Didi now?' he demanded. He strolled to the entrance to Didi's room, blocking the other woman's path and casting a quick glance inside. The bed was empty and he could see an open Louis Vuitton suitcase on the floor by the window.

'She's gone to bed.' She indicated behind him with a stiff tilt of her head.

His room.

His whole body stiffened. Didi was sleeping in his room? In his bed, between his sheets. Heat and anger warred within him but desire snaked through the mix like a restless serpent in a stormy sea. He moved away from the door, gestured her inside. 'Then I suggest you do the same, since you're obviously spending the night.'

'Not until you identify yourself to my satisfaction. How do I know you're not here to do my sister harm?'

He pulled out his driver's licence, flashed it at her. 'I told you—I live here. You want to speak to Security yourself, be my guest. Otherwise do as I ask. Leave Didi to me. I assure you, she's perfectly safe.' If he didn't throttle her first.

But the woman must have read something in his expression because a small smile twitched at the edge of her mouth, as if she'd just discovered a delicious secret. 'Didi didn't tell me she had a man in her life.'

His jaw clenched at that but he aimed an imperious finger at the door and spoke through stiff lips. 'Goodnight, Veronica.'

Still clutching her toiletry bag and her innate poise—and the smile—she slipped inside with a murmured, 'Goodnight,' and closed the door.

Cameron let out the breath he hadn't realised had backed up in his lungs. Steeling himself for the sight of Didi's tartan pyjama-clad body in his bed, he strode to his room, his traitorous palms tingling in anticipation of waking her.

He didn't knock, shoving at the door with an open-handed *thwack.* The scent of his soap and Melbourne's glimmering skyline through the windows greeted him. He was halfway across the room, arm outstretched to wake her, before he realised that she wasn't in bed. That the sound he could hear wasn't his blood pounding through his ears, it was running water, and that the fragrance billowed from steam clouds through the door of the en-suite.

The partially open door.

Too late to deny what he'd seen. Somehow he dragged his gaze away from the outline of her body in his shower stall, but it was indelibly printed behind his retinas. Her creamy flesh in a pose that rivalled anything in a men's magazine. The swell of her buttocks, the way she'd tipped back her head against the tiles so that her throat arched wantonly. As if waiting for a lover to take a bite. His mouth turned dry, his body hardened.

The water stopped and he heard her open the shower door. He stood rooted to the floor as possible scenarios flashed through his mind in that split second. Stranger. Stalker. She'd scream. Veronica and the cops would join the party.

He took the best option he could think of, given the circumstances. Diving into the bathroom, he grabbed a towel from the rail and held it in front of her with one hand. He did *not* see the tight rosy nipples, the cute little belly button, the erotic patch at the juncture of her thighs.

Her eyes widened and predictably she opened her mouth but his free hand got there first, clamping on damp, petal-soft skin. 'Didi. It's Cameron. Don't scream.'

Her shoulders relaxed a little but he watched as her predicament dawned on her and they tensed right back up again. She struggled to cover herself with the towel, her breath hot on his palm as she made a noise of distress.

He felt her delicate jawbone tense beneath his fingers but his hold didn't slacken. 'Don't,' he warned. 'Veronica'll have my balls for breakfast.'

Her lashes flickered at that and she nodded, continuing to watch him steadily. Satisfied she wasn't going to cause a ruckus, he relaxed his hand a little but he didn't want to let her go quite yet. He was enjoying her rare quietness and it gave him a moment to think how he was going to handle this.

Drops of water lay on her flushed skin, her hair, her eyelashes. The knowledge that she'd used his personal soap on her body spun through his head like an aphrodisiac. She was clutching the towel to her breasts, pushing them higher. He watched as a single droplet fell from her hair and trickled into that forbidden valley.

It occurred to him that she could have pulled away without too much effort. No doubt she was using the time for reflection and planning her excuses as well. He clenched his jaw and reminded himself that she'd helped herself to his apartment behind his back.

Mind spinning, Didi stared up at the man gripping her jaw and mouth, watching her with a speculative glint in his midnight eyes…and something more…something predatory? And no wonder; dear heaven, he'd seen her naked. How long had he been standing there while she lingered provocatively against the tiles like some hooker?

She shivered as her mind veered in another direction while he continued devouring her with that rapacious expression. He was *here.* In *his* bathroom. *Not* in Sydney.

Oh. My. God. What had she done? And how was she going to *un*do it?

His hand moved away from her mouth but one finger continued to slide sensuously over her lower lip, a dangerous touch, a hypnotic caress that slowed time and wiped everything from her mind but the pleasure it provoked. Beneath their calloused texture she could feel the tension ready to clamp her mouth shut again if she didn't co-operate.

His voice held the same deceptively languid quality when he said, 'So, Didi…or should I call you Dymphna?'

Her whole body rebelled and she speared him with her eyes. 'Don't call me that—never call me that.'

His mouth curved slightly. 'I agree it's a crime to punish

an innocent child with such a name. Then again…' he whisked his thumb back and forth over her jaw, firmed his other hand against the back of her head, imprisoning her '…maybe it isn't such a crime… Maybe you're not so innocent.'

In the room's dimness the lights from a nearby skyscraper stroked the unyielding angle of his jaw, his eyes mesmerised her, his grasp on her head paralysed her. His finger continued to fondle the edge of her lip, sending shivery tingles to every extremity and sparking erotic images of letting him use that same lazy thoroughness to explore other body parts. She fought an insane urge to suck its pleasure-giving warmth into her mouth.

'Well, are you going to try and defend yourself?' His tone sharper, eyes piercing. 'Or maybe I'll tell you what I think and you can try to deny it.'

She shook her head but it didn't move beneath his grip. 'I didn't expect you back until tomorrow night.' Her voice came out hoarse and pitifully desperate.

'That was the original plan.'

'I'm sorry. My sister flew into Melbourne unexpectedly. I told her I live here, that I work in a gallery, which is all a lie, I know. You weren't here, I didn't think it would matter—just for one night, Cameron.' The familiar sting of rejection, the secret heartache of not belonging, washed through her. 'But it matters to me.' Unshed tears pricked at her eyes. 'That she thinks I'm a success, that my family thinks I'm a success.'

There was a softening in his eyes, as if he…understood her. His hold loosened a little, though his hand continued to massage the back of her head, and a rare, wry humour lifted the corner of his mouth. 'She *thinks* I'm your lover.'

The image ran through her like quicksilver. Too easy with her head cradled in his expert hand to let herself remember what had happened in the kitchen… 'She…does?' Well, naturally she would since there was only one other bedroom…

She sensed his mood lighten and her own initial fears thawed a little. He'd invested a heap of money in her already. He wouldn't turf her out until the job was finished. Would he? No, she assured herself, he didn't have time to find a replacement. Question was, could she negotiate with only a towel held to her breasts?

She stepped back. He let her, and she used the opportunity to wrap and secure the towel around her. 'Can we play along with this here? It's only one night—she'll be gone tomorrow.'

'Play.' The way he said it made kindergarten sound like an orgy. Then a dark brow lifted. 'You mean lie.'

She bit her lip. 'Just a little bit. Just for tonight. You don't know how important this is.'

'Why don't you tell me?'

'Later.' After they'd sorted out the logistics of how they were both going to share the room for the night. 'Right now I need you. And you need me.'

'Didi?' Veronica's voice in the hallway. In the doorway. Even in the semi-darkness, the light from the bathroom illuminated concern—or was it suspicion?—on the familiar face.

Didi's hands tightened on the edge of the towel. Her gaze flicked up to Cameron's, silently pleading with him, to her sister. Back to Cameron.

'Are you all right, Didi? Is this man—?'

'She's fine.' Cameron's hands closed over Didi's upper arms, rubbing seductive circles over her shoulders with hard flat palms, a conspiratorial gleam in his eyes. 'Aren't you, Fairybread?'

Fairy bread? 'Fine,' she managed, holding his gaze, ignoring her sister. She stretched her stiff lips into a smile. 'Now that you're home.' She didn't even have to try to make her voice husky—that gleam in Cameron's eyes, the feel of his hands on her flesh did that.

'That's my girl.' He smiled back, his thumbs massaging the sensitive place where shoulder met torso as he pulled her flush against his hard, lean body. 'Goodnight again, Veronica.'

And leaning down he pressed a firm, open-mouthed kiss on Didi's surprised mouth. His tongue slid across the seam, coaxing her to open, dipping inside when her jaw dropped. Just a tantalising taste, an appetiser, and oh…it felt…good. But she couldn't allow herself to enjoy it—this was an act, a show. A skilfully executed piece of theatre for her sister's benefit.

She could feel Veronica's stunned gaze. Didi was no less than one hundred and ten per cent stunned herself. Her nipples rasped against the towel, making them throb as he shifted his body for a better fit. *Don't be fooled—this isn't real.*

'If you're sure…' Veronica's voice seemed to float at the edge of Didi's consciousness.

'She's very sure,' Cameron muttered against her mouth.

A moment later Didi heard the swish of her sister's gown and her bedroom door clicked shut. Releasing her arms as suddenly as he'd taken her, he stepped back, withdrawing the warmth of his body with him. But while he'd put physical distance between them, the intensity of his gaze completely possessed her.

A shaft of heat knifed through her. Could he be…turned on by a ten-second performance?

His eyes didn't leave hers as he strode to the door, kicked it shut. Her damp skin prickled in the draught he'd created. As he approached her he shrugged out of his suit jacket, let it fall where it would. Yanked off his tie, tossed it behind him. Undid the buttons of his cuffs.

What did he intend? *Isn't it obvious?* a tiny voice whispered. A shiver of doubt snuck through the heat. Her fingers crept over the top of her towel, needing to keep herself secure, protected. 'Um…thanks…' She flicked a finger, couldn't manage the hand. 'For…that.'

He didn't reply. He just kept coming, like an approaching storm, big and dark and all-powerful, making her feel insignificant, a fugitive with no place to hide.

His hands curled over hers on the towel, knuckles rough

against the swell of her still-throbbing breasts and his eyes turned molten, lightning on cobalt.

'What was that about needing me, Didi?'

CHAPTER SEVEN

DIDI'S breath snagged mid-chest. She gulped in air. 'I said... we...both needed *one another...*' Oh, cripes...with Cameron's hands covering hers covering her breasts and his gaze hotter than hell's kitchen that did *not* come out sounding the way she'd intended. 'I mean I think we need to discuss...I nee—have to explain...'

Her words—indeed her entire brain function—seized up as he lowered his head again. 'Tell you what, why don't you shut up for a bit?'

His breath feathered across her brow, her cheeks. She could smell fresh winter rain on his clothes, the foresty scent of his aftershave. As if her head were being manipulated by some invisible puppeteer, it tilted up, her lips opening of their own volition. Waiting, trembling...

She had a glimpse of eyes, dark and bright with purpose, a frown of concentration—or was it something else?—between heavily lowered brows before his mouth met hers once more and her eyes slid shut.

This time his tongue didn't linger around the edges of her mouth, it delved inside, seeking, exploring, finding hers. His flavour filled her mouth. She already knew how he tasted but this was more. Now she experienced, not only the flavours of peppermint and coffee, but the exhilarating essence of desire that slid like sun-warmed silk over her tongue, her teeth, inside her lower lip.

His hands left hers to better hold her head, to whisk his fingers over cheeks and jaw, leaving her own hands free to touch his shirt, absorb its crisp feel against her fingertips. To feel the steel muscles of his stomach tighten as she flattened then curled her hands against him.

To feel the quickened tempo of his breathing, his chest expanding as his hands left her head to slide over her shoulders, the shh as they shimmied over the towel, warmth from his palms stroking her, lower, lower. Her limbs turned to jelly, her brain liquefied and she felt herself dissolving against him. Total meltdown…

He lifted his head the tiniest bit. 'Do you need me, Didi?' he murmured, seduction oozing from the words.

She heard herself murmur something unintelligible back. Was that her voice all deep and drowsy and detached, as if it came from somewhere outside her?

'Do you need me to touch you…' she jolted, her hands whipping back to hug the security of her towel when she felt his fingers curl under the hem to touch the bare flesh of her thigh '…here?'

Her eyes snapped open to find his eyes focused on hers. She didn't answer. Couldn't. Holding her breath as his hand glided towards her inner thigh, calluses at the base of his fingers creating a delicious friction and sending shivers spiralling from his touch. Moisture swamped her most feminine place.

His hand changed direction, sliding slowly, inexorably towards the source of that moisture, every second an exercise in torture, every inch a scandalous pleasure. She sucked in a breath but there wasn't any oxygen, only hot airless space filled with his scent. Then her breathing stalled completely as his thumb found the source of her heat, the pinnacle of her pleasure.

'Or maybe you need me here…' He prodded the swollen knot of need with gentle pressure.

'Ah-h-h…' Oh, yes, right…*there.* She shuddered on the edge of the world, unable to look away from his eyes glittering in the muted light from the bathroom. His facial muscles bunched, his lips firmed, then curved ever so slightly in the knowledge that he'd taken her to the brink of no return with a single flick of his wrist.

It was humiliating to realise that at this moment the man had total and absolute control over her mind and body. But somewhere in her semi-coherent brain a fragment of sanity still clung. 'No,' she whispered, knowing her eyes made a liar of her. Knowing the engorged knot throbbing wantonly against him made a mockery of her.

He wiggled his thumb. 'Your body's sending me an entirely different message.'

'My body doesn't want to listen to reason,' she said over a parched throat. 'I don't even like you.'

A brief hesitation, then his lips stretched into a smile, and she realised he didn't care one way or the other. 'Since when did that stop two people from enjoying such a mutually satisfying experience?' he said reasonably, continuing to stroke her moisture as she rocked helplessly against him.

She swallowed. *Yeah, since when?* Over his shoulder she saw a gibbous moon sail silently from behind a high-rise, bathing the room in silver light.

'Didi.' He removed his clever hand to tilt her face to his, thumbs rasping over her cheeks, eyes dark with intensity. 'I played along with you, didn't I? Don't you want to convince Veronica I'm the real deal?'

'I think we managed that a few moments ago.'

'Ah, but tomorrow morning she'll be expecting to see the afterglow in your smile.'

'Afterglow…?' Her breath caught as every internal organ leaped up and changed places.

'I promise,' he said. Low and smooth and sexy. Confident. Arrogant, even.

And she had no doubt he could deliver. She shuddered even as she willed those talented fingers to find their way beneath her towel again.

The hot tub of desire in his eyes swirled and swallowed her up. 'Why don't we find out what this thing between us is all about?'

'This *thing?*' This angsty, itchy thing that hadn't given her a decent night's sleep since she'd met him? 'The thing about "things" is they get complicated and someone ends up getting hurt.'

'It doesn't have to be complicated.' He paused. 'Unless there's someone else?'

She glared at him, her back stiffening, shoulders tensing as Jay's image flitted through her mind. 'Would I be standing here naked with you if there was?' *Sweet heaven, naked with Cameron Black.*

He must have read her wistful expression because he looked into her eyes and said, 'Who was he, Didi?'

'Just a guy I…thought I loved.'

'He hurt you. He's scum.'

She bit her lip. 'I'm over him. And I don't want to talk about him.'

She tried to pull away but he held her fast. 'Neither do I.' He tightened his fingers on her cheeks. 'As I said, we can keep this simple. This time we know up front how it's going to be—no one gets hurt.'

She shook her head. 'We have a working relationship—'

His finger on her lips stopped her. 'Work's for tomorrow. So stop analysing, stop talking and for Pete's sakes relax…'

The knot in the towel came undone at his touch. Cool air breathed over her body, a stunning contrast to the heat emanating from his gaze as the towel slid to the floor. He took in every curve, from the hollow at the base of her neck where her pulse beat like horses' hooves, the fullness of her breasts swelling beneath his scrutiny, her waist, the flare of her hips.

'You're a work of art yourself, Ms O'Flanagan.' His voice was smooth and sensual and Didi could imagine he used that self-assured tone with women all the time. But there was something in his eyes reflected in the moon's silver light that hinted at that innate vulnerability she'd seen that night in the ladies' loo before he blinked it away.

He reached out. One fingertip brushed against her neck, over her left breast to draw a circle around the stiff nipple. Another.

Oh-h-h. Her already aroused body hummed with unbearable tension. Seeing him clothed while she stood as naked as a Greek statue was unspeakably erotic. A few more seconds of this protracted torment and she was likely to snap.

'Relax?' She managed, barely, to get the word out. 'Right now this *work of art* is fraying at the edges.'

His hitherto solemn expression transformed to a grin. 'That so?'

'Damn right.' *Don't think about whether this is a wise decision.* Because even if she did, she didn't think she could pull back. Long-suppressed need asserted itself. She took a step closer so that their bodies were a shiver away and poked his chest. 'In fact it's in danger of disintegrating…' Her fingertip discovered a shirt button, found the edge of his shirt, wiggled through to find hard, hairy skin. 'It needs serious attention. Now.'

She emphasised her demand by closing the gap and bumping her body against his. To explore the sensation of cotton against her breasts, the ridge of belt buckle, the coarser weave of fine skin-warmed wool along her thighs.

To spread her prickling palm against the front of his trousers and soothe the itch along every inch of his hard, hot length.

It didn't soothe—neither her nor him. The itch was a virus spreading through her body, as powerful as it was contagious. His sexy grin vanished, he jerked beneath her hand and a sound, something between a growl and a groan, erupted from his chest.

Then she was being swept up in the hard strength of his powerful arms and deposited in the middle of his bed. She lay, breathless and waiting as she watched him yank the shirt over his head, buttons popping.

He toed off his shoes. Undid his belt. His zipper being lowered was the only sound in the room, then his trousers pooled at his feet and he stepped out of them. Naked with that magnificent erection jutting at her, he transformed from urban sophisticate to primeval man.

She was in awe. Aroused, yes. Apprehensive, definitely. But, watching his long thighs with their dusting of dark masculine hair flex as he climbed onto the bed with her, she was mostly in awe.

He straddled her, gripped her wrists, holding them above her head, and looked into her eyes. 'Leave your arms there,' he instructed. The only body parts touching were their hands and his knees against her hips. Then he slid to the bottom of the bed and pushed her thighs apart.

And the world ceased to exist.

Only the feel of his tongue, moist and warm, leaving a damp trail that cooled in the air as he worked his way from instep to ankle, to the inside of her knee. Higher…

She might have come right there, right then, but he only skimmed the place yearning for him most and moved on to suckle each of her nipples gently with teeth and lips and tongue, teasing them into stiff, aching peaks. And all the while his hands were moving, touching, exploring, fingers gliding up the inside of her arms to twine once more with hers.

That simple connection, the joining of hands as he looked into her eyes… She closed her eyes to block him out. No one had ever made love to her like this before. No one had ever made her feel this way before. But uncomplicated sex was all she was looking for, she told herself, and so was he—they'd both just admitted as much.

So she concentrated on his warm masculine scent, the

friction of hot skin on hot skin. Every movement, every murmur, every breath, invoked a different sensation, a new experience in delight. She wanted to touch him the way he'd touched her, but the grip of his fingers held her fast.

Cameron didn't want to loosen his grip, even when he felt her resistance. 'Not yet,' he whispered against her ear.

He had her right where he wanted her, with her hard little nipples prodding his chest, her heart beating out the wild rhythm echoing his own. Somewhere in the back of his mind it mystified him that someone as individual as Didi, as opposed to him as north and south, should match him in any way.

She was all compact curves and sinuous limbs. Fire roared through his veins, hammered in his groin. The urge to plunge into her wet heat without further preliminaries and satisfy himself slammed into him like a fully loaded cement truck on steroids. But he'd barely started. He wanted to see the passion build in those silver eyes, to watch her come undone beneath him—and he had to unlock their hands to do that.

He banked the fire, let it smoulder through his system. Slow. Freeing her to do her own exploring while taking her with him on his leisurely tour of discovery. As he brushed his lips over skin as smooth as satin—a cheek, a shoulder, the softer flesh of her neck, each with their own unique fragrance and texture.

She might be somewhat naïve but she wasn't shy—a surprise given her innocent pixie-like charms. He hadn't counted on the ability of those small deft fingers to fan the embers into a red-hot need with such swiftness.

Another surprise. He didn't *need* women, he enjoyed them. And when the enjoyment faded, so did the relationship. Only Kat had managed to inveigle her way beneath his defences. His hand tightened a little over Didi's breast. Never again.

What had happened with her ex-lover? he wondered, watching her eyes turn to pewter as her fingernails scraped over his nipples, a tease of pleasure, a hint of pain. He slammed the thought to the back of his mind. But he couldn't shake the uneasy, unfamiliar feeling it evoked. Jealousy? Hardly.

His fingers tightened again on her flesh and an overwhelming need to possess her *now* seized him, tossed him high where there was only heat and need and greed. Forget slow—skimming the dip of her belly, he plunged three fingers into her tight wet centre.

She arched into his hand, writhed against him, eyes glassy and unfocused. 'Yes!'

At her urgent demand, he levered himself up, swung a thigh over her hips, and, taking his weight on his hands, he looked down at the woman beneath him. My God, she looked beautiful in passion. 'Protection.'

Her mouth rounded into a soft 'Oh…' and she stared at him, her gaze sharpening. 'Yes-s-s…' She trailed off and their fast unsteady breaths mingling in the tight space between them were the only sounds in the room's silence. Her eyes widened. 'Don't tell me you haven't…'

'Of course I have.' He shifted slightly, pulled open a drawer in his night-stand and withdrew a foil packet.

'Of course you have.' A crisp edge to her tone—and her eyes—as she watched him rip the foil, roll on the condom. As if she thought he got laid by a different woman every night of the week.

'Didi.' Taking his weight on his hands again he positioned himself above her. 'It's you and me. *Only* you and me.' Terms and conditions yet to be negotiated.

He waited a beat, every muscle in his arms quivering, every pulse-point hammering. Saw her understanding and acknowledgement, then, with a groan that seemed to come from some uncharted place inside him, he entered her in one long deep thrust.

She was different, was all he could think as he began to move inside her. Hotter, faster, it swept him up until everything faded except her body clinging to his, the fragrance of her fresh-soaped skin, her wet tightness surrounding him, accepting him. Claiming him.

He felt her teeter on the brink then shudder, her inner muscles drawing him deeper, further, harder until he dived over the edge with her.

Hours later, as dawn painted the clouds purple and gold behind the skyscrapers, Cam watched Didi's gold lashes rest on her cheeks. Not only was she beautiful in passion, he thought, but also in repose. If he could take the image from his brain, scan it into his computer and have a master painter recreate it, it could hang in the most prestigious art galleries of the world.

He watched her sigh, then snuggle into the quilt, and a small smile touched her lips, as if she was dreaming happy dreams. At some point they'd climbed beneath the covers. The room was warm, he couldn't resist—he lowered the quilt so that they were both naked from the waist up and he could get a look at her breasts dusted in the new day's light. He couldn't resist some more and blew on them gently, making them pebble as he watched.

His sex stirred. He wanted her again, with dawn's light smattering pink into her silver eyes. She was the most responsive woman he'd ever had. Sure he'd had women who knew a few good tricks in the bedroom, but they'd performed them with the polished ease of practice. What Didi lacked in polish she more than made up for in a delightfully naïve spontaneity.

A glance at his bedside clock warned him it wasn't going to happen now. He was due at the office for an early meeting and before he left he wanted answers. She'd promised them this morning. Then they were going to have a discussion about what they expected from this new direction their relationship had taken. And it all had to happen before they could leave this room because her sister would be waiting.

He leaned over, brushing his lips over hers. 'Wake up, Didi.'

Didi drifted on a tide of contentment. As she surfaced contentment turned to wariness as a deep voice and memories of last night dragged her awake. She opened her eyes.

Cameron Black.

She'd spent the night in his bed.

And didn't her body know it? she thought as vaguely pleasant aches and twinges in various places made themselves known.

'Good morning,' he murmured.

Had she ever woken to a more mouth-watering sight than that of Cameron sporting nothing but morning stubble and a smile? 'Good morning.'

Morning. The feeling of well-being faded and tension grabbed at her belly. Their little whatever-it-was was over and now she'd have to live under his roof—and his gaze—and endure the consequences of what they'd done. And there was still the problem of Veronica.

Suddenly all too aware of her nakedness, she dragged the quilt up to her chin, then, shoving a hand through what must look like porcupine hair, she sat up. 'What time is it?'

'Six-thirty.' He played with the ends of her bed hair and there was a twinkle in his eye when he said, 'We have a few things to discuss, Fairybread.'

'I was going to get to that. *Fairy bread?*'

'You know, buttered and covered in sprinkles and cut into tri—'

'I know what it is—what I don't know is why you called me that.'

'Because it's pretty—' he kissed her nose '—it tastes sweet—' he moved lower to nuzzle her neck '—and it was the best I could think of at short notice. We need to get our story straight before we face the dragon lady.'

She saw his amusement sober as he shifted away creating a space between them, but her mouth was dry and she needed a moment to gather her thoughts. 'Any chance of a coffee?'

'No. For all we know, your sister could be prowling the apartment looking for evidence to put me away.'

'More like she wants to catch *me* out,' Didi said. 'She knows this isn't real.'

His brows rose and something intimate crossed his expression. 'After that performance last night?'

Her cheeks heated. That was just it—it was only a performance. As for the rest…how he'd taken her to heights she'd never been…she couldn't think about that now.

'Why would she want to catch you out, Didi?' he asked quietly.

'My family…' She steepled her hands at her lips. She wished she could put on a robe, anything to cover her vulnerability, but she couldn't bring herself to climb out of bed naked. 'My parents are…well off, my older sister's married to a…' *pompous ass* '…wealthy owner of a string of luxury yachts.

'I never fitted in. You've seen my sister—tall, elegant, poised, sophisticated. Like my parents. They despaired of me right from the start. They wanted me to take piano lessons and study multiple languages. I wanted to use Mum's silk brocade curtains to make clothes, learn origami and study art.

'When I finished school I spent a couple of years overseas. But when I came back my parents said if I didn't go to uni I was on my own. So I found a boarding house on the cheap side of the city and got a job in a café. I took casual employment for the next couple of years, including stocking supermarket shelves and kitchen hand.'

'And somewhere along the way you met this guy who messed you up.'

She sighed, staring at the ceiling. 'I thought he was serious. Turned out there was someone else—*that there'd always been* that someone else. Which is why I don't want a serious relationship ever again.'

There had been too many painful memories of her broken heart and humiliation in Sydney. 'I decided to come to

Melbourne to make a fresh start, so I told my parents I'd got a job in an exclusive gallery with a luxury apartment to boot.'

His chest hair rasped against her shoulder as he slid an arm around her in wordless support.

'She's just come to gloat. I couldn't let her. I just couldn't. Not when I saw an opportunity. I'm sorry I went behind your back.'

He dropped a kiss on her head. 'I've got a strong back. How do you want to play it today?'

'Keep up the charade that we're...involved—'

'Lovers,' he reminded her. 'And it's not a charade. Not any more.'

'Until she leaves this afternoon,' she finished, her cheeks heating as her body reminded her in all kinds of ways of the fact that, no, it hadn't been a charade.

She felt him shift again, then he tilted her face to his. In his eyes something flickered and sent her pulse scrambling. 'Didi, how do you feel about extending this arrangement a little longer? Say, two and a half weeks?'

'What do you mean?' She tried to keep her voice even, her expression neutral.

But she knew what he meant and blood pounded through her veins. A ball of fire lodged behind her breastbone, shooting flares up and down the length of her body.

He wanted her, here. In this bed. And she didn't need rocket science to work it out.

If she wanted, for two and a half weeks she could be Cameron Black's live-in mistress.

CHAPTER EIGHT

DIDI backed up on the mattress towards the edge of the bed, holding the sheet in front of her breasts, her gaze scouring the room. Better, she thought, to look for something to cover herself than to look him in the eye because one glance at her response and he'd know the effect he'd had on her. And that would be a distinct disadvantage.

So he'd used the word 'lover' in this morning's conversation—now he was suggesting an 'arrangement'. And suggesting amazingly coolly for something as hot as an affair with Cameron Black would be. Too coolly. As if he were negotiating one of his property deals.

'You know exactly what I mean,' he murmured. 'What do you say?' His tone told her he expected an affirmative answer.

And how easy would it be—mistress to a millionaire, a heap of money in commissions? She'd walk away richer at the end. Ah, but would she still be happy when she walked away? Better, safer, to stick to their original agreement.

'I…don't think so,' she said. Pleased with how calm she sounded even if she was coming apart inside, still avoiding eye contact. Still feeling vulnerable. 'Um…do you have a bathrobe I can put on?'

With that same cool confidence he padded naked to the bathroom, plucked a terry robe from behind the door. Ah, and she couldn't help but look, could she? But it didn't seem to faze him—nor the fact that he was in a state of semi-arousal. No, well, it was that male pride thing, obviously.

He tossed her the robe on his way back and retrieved last night's discarded trousers from the floor. He didn't bother with underwear. He came around to her side of the bed. Her body hummed as remnants of last night's electricity arced between them. Then he ran a thumb over her lower lip. 'So…you don't think so, huh?'

She jerked as if that electricity had zapped her. 'I told you last night, I don't like your type.' To put on the robe she had to let go of the sheet… She closed her eyes so she couldn't see him watching her and slipped her arms inside. Rising, she moved to the window and watched the morning traffic build.

'No,' he said behind her. 'Last night you said you didn't like *me*. There's a difference. Tell me more about my *type*.'

'I've told you before…' She trailed off as she tightened the sash, aware of the robe's familiar soap scent enveloping her. Cameron's scent.

Her opinion of the type of man he was *had* changed since that first night. She'd seen a different side of him: a caring, thoughtful man who'd trusted her with a large sum of cash and allowed her to stay in his apartment—and look what she'd done to repay him. She'd brought in an uninvited guest last night and she'd barely scratched the canvas she'd promised she'd start.

Still, she didn't have to like him on principle, she decided, hugging her arms around her. With his million-dollar lifestyle and Italian-made suits. She might have had a similar upbringing but she'd always been aware of the poverty never far from her door.

It was a long way from his.

She'd decided it was easier and less complicated to *not* like him…except now it was too late for easy and it had just got a whole lot more complicated.

She'd had sex with him.

'Didi,' he said behind her. 'Regardless of my *type,* why stop at one night when there's clearly a chemistry between us we could explore further?'

She could feel that simmering chemistry from half a dozen steps away. How could he feel so hot yet sound so cool? Nor did she need any further investigation. She already knew his was the kind of love-making that burned all the way through and left a brand on your heart and a glow on your skin.

Only if you let it.

'As I said last night we have a working relationship,' she said. 'And in three weeks we won't even have that.'

'So we lay some ground rules.' He planted an open-mouthed kiss on the back of her neck. Another on the soft flesh between neck and shoulder. Then steadied her with his hands as he turned her to face him.

'Ground rules…?' Her heart was pumping so hard she wondered it didn't explode out of her chest.

'You work here during the day and I work at the office.'

'And nights…?'

'We explore what we have in common.' The glitter in his eyes didn't need clarification. It was all about the sex and they both knew it.

'And when the time's up I walk away, no complications on either side.'

'Exactly.'

Like a business transaction. 'That's plain enough.' She stepped away from him again and began picking up her clothes from where she'd dropped them at the bottom of the bed last night.

What did she expect? She'd flirted with him, pushed his buttons, got him to play along with this crazy idea of convincing her sister he was her lover.

'You don't seem too thrilled about it.'

She flashed him a glare over her shoulder as she picked her T-shirt up off the floor. 'Should I be?'

'You liked it well enough last night. Didi.' His voice softened. 'What happened with your last guy won't happen with us because we both know up front what we're getting into. So long as we have mutual respect and understanding.'

She straightened and forced herself to look at him.

'And I'll include other benefits, of course.'

'Other benefits?'

'I attend a lot of charity events; some are quite formal affairs where a partner is expected. If we go out in the evening, I'll pay any expenses, clothes, salon procedures et cetera.'

'You mean you want me to accompany you? To functions where you're exhibiting your next property development?' She scoffed. 'Like, I'm on the other side of the fence—how could I do *that* with a clear conscience?'

A look she couldn't interpret crossed his face. 'You're not as far away from my side as you think, Didi.' He scratched his chin. 'The alternative would be for me to chaperone some other woman and I don't think that arrangement would work.'

The thought of him with *some other woman* while she sat in his apartment working her fingers to the bone poured acid on her empty stomach, but she remembered, 'Did you forget I may need to work through evenings?'

He shook his head. 'Not every evening, Didi. You'll need some down-time. I'm the last person who'd want to compromise your creativity. And I'll ensure it's not something you wouldn't feel comfortable attending before I accept.'

She couldn't look at him while she made her decision so she studied the pile of clothes in her hand. She'd have to be very, very careful not to let herself fall for him. Because she would *not* go through that kind of pain again.

She had to remember to keep her heart out of the mix. Keep it temporary. Casual sex. Except she'd never done casual sex.

But she knew this inexplicable attraction was mutual and she wanted to explore that attraction while she was here. And, damn it, why shouldn't she? They were both single, unattached and available and this was twenty-first-century Australia.

Finally, she met his gaze. 'I'll be wearing my own clothes if we go out, thanks. And believe it when I tell you no one can manage my hair but me.'

Cam let out a deep slow breath as he watched Didi run her hands through the unruly tufts. He hadn't realised he'd been holding his breath and mentally shook his head at the sheer madness of whatever-the-hell-it-was that had gripped him until he saw the agreement in her eyes.

Sex was the motivation, right? Yet this crazy feeling was like nothing he'd ever felt before. Before he could stop himself he crossed the room to take that beautiful bewitching face between his hands and watch last night's afterglow in her eyes sparkle.

She smelled of sleep and sex and his mouth fell onto hers as if he'd relinquished control of his movements to some unseen force. Unthinkable to resist. Impossible to pretend he wasn't instantly aroused by her warm womanly shape beneath the terry-towelling robe, by the feel of her hands sliding around his naked back as she fashioned herself against him.

Exclusively his for the next two and a half weeks.

The sound of someone passing by the door pulled him out of the moment. Reluctant, he drew back, soothing her lips with his before he said, 'I'd better make myself presentable while you go see if our guest wants some breakfast.' *And I need to put some priorities in order, starting now.*

'Hmm.' Her fingers found their way beneath his waistband and she looked up at him. 'I kind of like you unpresentable.'

Drawing her hands away, he clasped them together. 'Go. Now. Before I forget I'm supposed to be the host.' *And that today's another business day with a couple of site inspections and three meetings scheduled.*

Twenty minutes later he helped himself to a mug of coffee. Veronica was sipping from her own mug on the sofa by the living-room window while Didi took eggs from the refrigerator. The apartment's open-plan living arrangement allowed him to view both women simultaneously.

Two sisters couldn't be more different. It wasn't lost on him that at a purely superficial level Veronica was more like the usual type of woman who shared the occasional breakfast here before they went their separate ways to work.

Charlie greeted Cam as he carried his steaming mug towards the sofa. Why was it that cats invariably chose to smooch people who ignored them? But he bent down to fondle the silky ears as he nodded at their guest. 'Veronica. I apologise for not being up earlier. I trust you slept well?'

'I did. Thank you.' Sipping delicately, she eyed him with a hint of the distrust she'd shown last night. 'You have a lovely apartment.'

'We like it.' He smiled at Didi, who was whipping up eggs with one eye and watching them with another.

Veronica arched a brow. 'How long have you been here, Didi?'

The whisk faltered but only for a second. 'Um…not long…'

'Didi's a relative newcomer but I've been here a few years.' Cam covered the hitch smoothly.

'Ah…' Veronica eyed him with an I-know-your-game glint and when she spoke her voice was silk. 'You're the gallery owner who leases it to my sister for a low rent. How…convenient. But you're not interstate—Didi told me you were.'

He glanced at Didi, back to Veronica. 'And so I was…yesterday.'

Glancing at the Sheila Dodd and Didi's work against the wall, she observed, 'You're also an art collector.'

'Actually, the Before the Temptation one is mine,' Didi said, setting two frying pans on the stove with satisfied clangs. 'Scrambled eggs okay?'

'Yes. Fine.' Veronica paused, sculptured brows rising. 'Yours?'

'Yep. As in I made it.'

'Beautifully crafted, isn't it?' Cam said, smiling, watching Veronica's bemused expression. 'It should fetch a tidy price at the gallery.'

'It's not for sale,' Didi said over the counter top.

'Ah…yes. Very nice.' Veronica set her mug down with a delicate clink. No well-deserved praise, Cam noted.

'Mum and Dad send their love.' Casually spoken but Cam felt the immediate undercurrent between the two sisters.

Wouldn't they have had this conversation yesterday? This was purely for his benefit.

Didi only glanced up as she stirred eggs into one pan, set bacon sizzling in the other. 'I've been very busy.'

'Too busy to call?'

Silence except for the crackle of bacon. 'I'll do things my way, Veronica,' Didi said finally. 'When I'm ready.' She sliced avocado onto plates.

Cam watched the interaction. Clearly Didi had further issues with her parents that she'd yet to share with him.

'So where did you two meet?'

Didi caught Cam's eye, then said, 'At a cocktail party.'

He grinned back at Didi over his coffee. 'I turned around and there she was. It was literally sparks at three paces.'

'Really? So, Cameron, this gallery you own…' Her pursed lips were quite deliberate. 'That makes you Didi's boss?'

'Not exactly. Didi's working on a commission at present,' Cam said carefully. 'Her work's going to be demanding a small fortune soon.' No lies there. 'You'll have to put in an order before word gets out.'

'It's not really my thing,' Veronica said with a lazy disinterest that annoyed Cam. 'Fabric and threads collect dust. Daniel's allergies wouldn't allow it.'

How could she be so dismissive of her sister's talent? 'Unfortunate,' was all Cam allowed himself to say but he felt his hackles rise on Didi's account. He suppressed the urge to slice into Veronica. 'Smells like breakfast's ready. Shall we adjourn to the breakfast bar?'

Veronica left a short time later with Cameron's limo made available until her flight departed. As Didi cleared the dishes into the dishwasher she turned to see that her lover had disappeared behind a neatly pressed businessman with money-making on his agenda. He was studying her work-in-progress—or lack of—with a calculating eye.

Tension gripped the base of her skull but she refused to let his authoritarian stance intimidate her, or the fact that they'd spent the night naked together prevent her from saying, 'I spent yesterday sketching designs and collecting supplies.'

'What have you decided on?' he asked, flipping through her boxes of threads and silks.

'This one.' She handed him the outline she'd decided on. 'I thought fire. It's fluid and alive; a rising-from-the-ashes kind of thing. Contrasts—obscurity and brilliance.'

'The eternal flame,' Cameron mused. 'A memorial. Appropriate.' He paced to the window, hands in his pockets, stared out for a long moment before turning to her. 'You have everything you need?'

'For now, yes. A memorial to whom?'

An expression of barely veiled regret crossed his face before he blinked it away and a wistfulness crept into his eyes, a small smile tipped his mouth. 'Someone I knew. Someone I owe.'

Who had he known? Who did he owe? Why didn't he tell her?

Because this arrangement was only temporary, she reminded herself. She didn't need to know his life history. And this was the right choice of theme, she thought, watching him. This was the emotion she wanted to capture—darkness into light—and it obviously resonated with him.

He seemed to shake away whatever it was that put the shadows in his eyes. 'I'll see you this evening, then.' He spoke briskly as he crossed the room to pick up his briefcase from beside the sofa.

Not a hint of the man who'd practically worshipped her body last night with hands and mouth and…more. He could have been talking to anyone. The only concession he made was a chaste almost impersonal kiss on her cheek. 'Have a productive day.'

She was tempted to throw her arms around his neck and demand something of last night's passion but she kept her hands at her sides, remembered their deal and said, 'You too.'

He didn't even give her time to see if a remnant of the night's heat lingered in his eyes because he was already walking away, leaving a souvenir of his scent on the air.

She stood watching the elevator doors long after they'd closed. Long after she'd heard its muted hum as it took him away to his world of wheeling and dealing and knocking down buildings.

Didi forced the hot memories to the back of her mind the way he obviously had. *Think business arrangement.* For Cameron there was no blurring of lines. She needed to do the same. Keep it in perspective. In three weeks their *business* would be concluded.

Didi did her best work to music so she chose one of her own CDs and slid it into Cameron's sound system, cranked up the volume. Ravel's 'Bolero' throbbed out of the speakers, eerie, edgy.

She closed her eyes a few moments, absorbed its building passion, the throbbing swirl of emotion. Not until she'd visualised the finished work did she slip on her glasses and begin.

Hours passed. Hunger was forgotten, cramped muscles ignored, aching fingers disregarded. She worked until the surrounding buildings' lengthening shadows slid through the windows and the sky grew scarlet behind the silhouette of the Rialto Towers, turning the Yarra River to blood.

It took a few moments to emerge from her labours. Placing her glasses on the table, she stood back to study the day's work with a critical eye. Nothing much to see yet, but she'd made a start on the foundation.

Stretching, rolling tense shoulders, she moved to the window and watched the city's lights appear in a rainbow of colours. That tension at the base of her skull was back, a dull echo to her heartbeat, and her eyes felt gritty. It occurred to her that she had no idea what time Cameron would be home.

The thought of seeing him again sent a wave of excitement through her, and a rising panic. Did he expect her to dress up for him? Or dress 'down'—as in gauzy negligee with a welcome-home glass of champagne in her hand? Did the 'evening' part of their arrangement begin at sunset? Or did it only exist between the sheets?

When did his employee transform into his magical mistress?

She scoffed at her new persona, but her laugh caught in her throat when she stepped into the bedroom. The unmade bed, with its sheets wrinkled and quilt dragging on the thick carpet, was a testament to their torrid night. Was making beds a part of her job description now? Which had her wondering, did Cameron carry out those domestic tasks himself or did he have a regular cleaning service?

The phone on the night-stand shrilled. 'Hello?' As had happened yesterday, whoever it was disconnected without speaking. She stared at the receiver while a sick feeling of betrayal rose up inside her, throbbing in time with the pulse in her head. A woman, she was sure of it.

His ex that maybe wasn't an ex any more?

She shook her head. Just because Jay had gone back to his ex-lover didn't mean Cameron would. It was paranoia making her think that way. But it *was* a timely reminder of the temporary nature of their relationship.

She picked up her towelling robe from the bed, determined

to put the incident out of her mind. She needed to stretch out the kinks with a long, fragrant soak in that guest bathroom's spa before she felt even human again, let alone magical.

And as for dressing up—or down—it wasn't an option. Either he accepted her somewhat offbeat and eclectic style or he didn't. She no longer had the luxury of money to waste on frivolous dresses or seduce-me nightgowns, nor did she feel a need to conform to the gurus of fashion.

And if she didn't do something about this developing migraine, she thought as she rummaged in her bag for medication, she'd be no use to anyone, including herself.

She stripped off, shrugged into the robe's comforting warmth, sat on the edge of the bed. Tempting to lay her head on the pillow—the one that smelled of him—just for a moment. Then she'd have that soak and then…

CHAPTER NINE

CAM closed his folder and glanced at his watch as the last of the attendees exited the room. The meeting had run late. He'd been running late since he arrived this morning.

It didn't usually bother him—he practically lived at the office, often making up for lost time well after midnight when necessary. Tonight wasn't one of those nights. Tonight anticipation snapped at his heels and he couldn't wait to be out the door.

That brought him up short. *Slow down, Cam.* It wasn't as if he needed to see *her,* he assured himself. He didn't *need* anyone. Need threatened control, something he'd fought for most of his life, and won.

So he sent his driver home and set out to walk the forty minutes to his apartment. He deliberately took his time, strolling along tree-lined Collins Street where spring was showing itself with tiny green buds gleaming in the street lights. Ducking rattling trams and harried pedestrians at one of the busy intersections. Workers were cramming cafés for an early dinner, hitting the city gyms or shopping. The smell of fast food mingled with car exhaust fumes.

He found his pace picking up and slowed once more. Didi was in his head again, and too much for his peace of mind. He wanted to see how the work was coming along, the artist herself was a…fringe benefit. A diversion.

Yet even as he told himself that was all it was he knew he

was fooling himself. Didi O'Flanagan was one hell of a diversion…and a whole lot more. The fact that they clashed on so many points only added to the appeal.

And the sex was… More. It was the only description he could come up with.

He found himself outside his apartment building and rode the elevator up. He'd been surprised to learn she came from wealth; she clearly championed for the disadvantaged. Why would her parents have nothing to do with her? There was obviously more to it than she was willing to let him see. A woman with secrets—a good reason not to trust her too easily.

The apartment was silent when he stepped inside. Charlie trotted towards him, twining himself around his legs, a furry ribbon with an appetite. Priorities, he reminded himself. He went to the living room to view the work-in-progress. Not much to see yet, but she'd been busy. Her glasses lay amongst the scatter. He fed the cat. So, now…where was Didi—and what was she doing?

His pulse rate accelerated as he headed for his bedroom and his steps quickened. As he stepped inside the spill of low light from the bedside lamp highlighted her face, glinted on her hair. Fast asleep, her complexion pale, smudges beneath her eyes.

Then his gaze fell on a bottle of pills on the night-stand. Gut-curdling dread clawed its way up his throat, choking off his air. Visions from the past flashed before his eyes. Amy had done this to herself on a regular basis. His mother had died of an overdose of prescription drugs.

He grabbed the bottle as he shook her shoulder with rough impatience. 'Didi.' *For God's sake.* 'Wake up!' Belatedly a glance at the bottle informed him they were prescription pills for migraine.

She stirred. 'Huh? What?' He saw her wince as she opened her eyes, squinting in the glare. 'What is it?'

He blew out a slow breath. 'I'm sorry. I shouldn't have

woken you. I just…' He noted his hand wasn't steady as he brushed hair from her brow. 'Go back to sleep.'

She blinked up at him as her eyes adjusted to the light. 'I was going to take a dip in that swimming-pool spa of yours. I guess I zonked out.'

'Do you still have your headache?' He cleared the residual panic from his throat and let his hand rest on her shoulder. She felt warm, soft. Alive.

'No.' She sounded surprised and rubbed her brow, checking. 'No.'

'Lie there for a bit. I have to go out for a while. Do you think you'll feel like eating later? I can bring something back if you want.'

She rolled onto her side, the robe dipping and slipping, tempting his own appetite with generous slices of cleavage and thigh. She moistened her lips, drawing his gaze. 'Why do you have to go out? Friday night's for relaxing. Stay.'

He doubted she knew how husky she sounded, how provocative she looked, drowsy from sleep and sexy as sin. The whole effect shook him to his foundations and, coupled with the near heart attack she'd just given him, he was in no mood to analyse his angry response, nor why he felt the need to distance himself.

He rose. 'I have a standing appointment on Friday evenings and I don't intend to break it. Not even for you.' In three weeks she'd be gone, a pleasant memory.

Her expression cooled. 'This *arrangement* we have—I thought it was exclusive.'

'It is.' He turned away, strode to his wardrobe.

Didi flopped onto her back and stared at the ceiling, unaccountably hurt, unreasonably disappointed. Why was she feeling this way? Because the memory of that earlier mystery phone call hammered at her and it was all too easy to draw her own conclusions. 'I'm not going to sit here and wait for you every night,' she said, listening to the rustle of clothes on the other side of the partially open door.

She could almost hear his eyes rolling back in his head as he said, 'It's not every night, Didi, it's Friday nights.'

He strode back into the room and every accusation—every thought—dried on her tongue.

He was wearing jeans. Blue jeans. Faded, scruffy, worn jeans with a T-shirt that had been black once, and two sizes too small because it stretched over his chest like elastic over the Harbour Bridge.

And she'd thought he looked sexy in a business suit... She'd thought he couldn't look more sexy, but he did, in a dangerous, bad-boy way that called to the wanton woman inside her.

And he was going out. Without her.

She so didn't care. She wished she had a nail file and polish handy, or a magazine so she could flick through the pages ever so carelessly and show him just how much she so didn't care. Instead she shrugged. 'Slumming it tonight, huh?'

He stilled, every hard ripple in that impressive chest tense, every muscle in his jaw bunched. His lips compressed into a tight angry line. Something dangerous flashed in his eyes—not in that bad-boy way, but in a way that made her want to shrink back and wish the sarcastic words unsaid. Definitely the lowest form of wit.

'Get dressed,' he said calmly. Too calmly. 'You want to see slumming? Come with me. Be ready in five minutes. I can't be late. I *won't* be late. Wear comfortable shoes and bring a jacket.'

There was no thought of refusal. Her fingers trembled as she dragged on jeans and a jumper she found amongst her stuff. This showed a side of Cameron she'd never seen, never known existed. A quick glance in the mirror reflected a face devoid of make-up, hollows beneath her eyes. She spiked her hair with her fingers—that would have to do. She dragged out her worn coat, slipped it on.

They rode the elevator down to the underground car park in silence, climbed into the car and merged into the evening traffic the same way. Considering the dress code it was almost absurd to be driving in such luxury with something classically high-brow playing through the speakers.

Whatever it was, this was very important to Cameron, and it would give her some insight into the man who didn't talk about himself.

Fitzroy's busy inner suburban street was crammed with traffic, tram lines and overhanging cables, some of the beautiful architecture of a bygone era mottled with peeling paint, boarded up or covered in graffiti. Light years away from Cameron's exclusive Collins Street address. He parked in a side street.

'You're leaving this expensive piece of automotive engineering here?' she said, incredulous.

'It's only a car, Didi.'

She bit back a retort that only an hour ago she wouldn't have hesitated to use and climbed out.

It became obvious he was heading for what had once been an old department store. The tired red bricks on the second and third storey remained but the street-level façade had been given fresh paint and the windows at the front were large and brightly lit. Inviting. The sign read, 'Come In Centre'.

She saw a medical clinic, still open. Lights spilled from the room Cameron explained was a youth counselling service. The atmosphere was vibrant and alive, busy. She followed him through a large recreational room where people, mostly teenagers, watched TV, played table tennis, or sat at tables talking.

She could smell unwashed bodies, poverty, fear, but she also sensed optimism and hope and determination.

'This building's for abused teenagers and runaways,' he said as they made their way through the high-ceilinged room towards a canteen. 'Here they can get a meal, see a doctor, talk with professionals who care, and generally hang out.'

'You did this.' Didi looked up at him with new-found respect, but his eyes were an unforgiving navy steel. 'You renovated this building. You financed it yourself.'

His shoulders tensed, he put his hands in the back pockets of his jeans and kept walking. 'It doesn't happen on its own.'

'Stop.' She caught his arm, felt the resistance beneath her fingers. He didn't want to be touched, but she needed the contact. Needed to say, 'Hang on a minute. I'm sorry I said what I said back at the apartment. I'm sorry for a lot of things I've said to you,' she finished quietly.

The steel in his eyes didn't soften. If it was possible, they hardened. 'You couldn't begin to understand the meaning of destitute. You *chose* the way you currently live your life. You *chose* to leave your family. These kids don't have that luxury.'

She knew. It made her feel ashamed. But Cameron… 'Why did you do it? Why are you involved?'

Shadows flitted over his gaze but he shook his head and kept walking.

They reached the restaurant-sized kitchen where a round woman with flyaway brown hair and two double chins was dishing greens and mash and some sort of spicy-smelling stew onto plates for the kids lined up at the counter.

'Ah, Cameron, right on time.' The woman smiled at them over her ladle. 'And you've brought us a new assistant. Good, because we're really busy tonight. Sandra couldn't make it.'

'Hello, Joan. This is Didi,' he said, walking behind the counter. He tossed Didi an apron. 'Let's get started, then. Joan'll fill you in on what needs to be done. I'll be back in a few moments.'

'Welcome, Didi.' She smiled with genuine warmth, brown eyes twinkling. 'I hope you're wearing comfortable shoes.' Joan glanced at Didi's sneakers, filled another plate. 'Cameron's never brought a girlfriend here before.'

Didi felt her cheeks warm. 'I'm not his girlfriend.' *Just his temporary mistress.* 'I'm working on an arts project for him.'

'And supporting him in your free time, good for you. There's not many willing to put in the effort on a Friday night.' She pulled loaves of bread from the shelf behind them, set them in front of Didi. 'You can start on the sandwiches. You'll find everything you need in the fridge. You'll need a knife.' She handed her a key, gestured to a drawer. 'We keep them locked away—one never knows…'

They worked side by side, ladling stew and cutting sandwiches.

'*You're* working here on a Friday night,' Didi prompted after a few moments. 'Do you help out often?'

'Every week. Cameron looked out for my son when he turned up here lost and alone. Thanks to him, my abusive ex is locked up and I have my son back.' She flicked hair off her face with the back of her hand. 'I don't know where these kids would be without him.'

Every so often Didi saw Cameron walk through the canteen, talking to kids. Holding a hand, squeezing a shoulder. Listening. Caring.

Who was this man? She'd mentally accused him of not wanting to soil his suit yet here he was, hands-on and involved. Again, why? In the short time they'd known each other he'd not spoken of family and she hadn't asked. What was the point? It wasn't as if he were going to introduce her, nor did she want to meet them. Their relationship wasn't the kind that involved family.

Shaking off the hollow feeling, she plastered ham and tomato onto buttered bread. She didn't want to dissect her emotions because right now they were too close to the surface and too vulnerable. If she let him, he could steal her heart and leave her dead inside.

No. Once was more than enough. But now, as he leaned over a table to speak with a couple of boys in their late teens she couldn't seem to take her eyes off him.

She tried observing him from a purely feminine viewpoint without the tug of emotion. Below the T-shirt's short sleeves, the hard definition of his arms, olive-skinned and dusted with dark hair. The innate strength in that upper body. The way his jeans hugged his tight backside, the faded denim down the front of his thighs and where the zipper chafed…

I know what's inside those jeans.

The recent memory of his body over hers—inside hers—speared through her and the knife she held slipped on the tomato she was holding. Which was okay, she told herself. It was a purely sexual zing—no emotions hence no vulnerability.

Until he glanced over as if he'd known she was watching and their gazes locked. Intense cobalt eyes studied her. Even from across the room she felt the heat all the way down to her toes. *Sexual attraction,* she assured herself. Tonight they'd act on that attraction. Again. Another zing hummed through her like an electrical jolt. Anticipation.

But the sound of voices, the smell of food and kids, faded. The whole scene blurred around the edges. Only Cameron remained in focus, as if she were looking through a tunnel. She saw his fingers tighten on the edge of the table. His jaw tightened infinitesimally. He didn't straighten but she knew the muscles in his back had turned rigid.

She knew because it was happening to her.

His eyes relayed a message she didn't want to read—emotion. She felt her own emotions flow to him on a tide of something perilously close to trust.

Vulnerability.

No. Dragging her eyes away, she concentrated on loosening her grip on the knife, rolled tension from her shoulders. *That* wasn't supposed to happen. Wasn't going to happen. Not even when she noticed he was making his way towards her, still watching her with those bluer-than-blue eyes.

'Not your boyfriend, eh?' Joan chuckled. 'He's been distracted all evening. And you too, I think.'

Didi glared at the sandwich as she sliced it into ruthless triangles, *not* being distracted by the man and her unwise reaction to him. 'I don't need a man in my life.'

'Ah, but maybe he needs you,' Joan murmured.

Didi's laugh came too fast, sounded too brittle. She reached for more bread, more ham. Cameron's 'need' for Didi wasn't the kind Joan was referring to. It would never be anything else. *Cameron* had made it quite clear their three-week arrangement was all there was.

And she'd agreed.

So…maybe that made it okay to watch him as a purely sexual being… She lifted her eyes… He was talking to a boy with a baseball cap on backwards and dirt-stained hands.

A shout nearby had Didi turning sharply. A teenager had collapsed and was lying on the floor. Cameron was beside the girl in seconds. 'Call an ambulance!' he yelled as pandemonium broke out amongst the crowd gathering around the unconscious girl. 'Everyone move back. Joey, go wait out the front for the ambos.'

Joan flew into action, phoning the emergency services while Didi rushed around the counter and elbowed her way to Cameron's side. 'Anything I can do?' Didi's heart was thumping. The girl was sheet white, her lips blue, skin cold to the touch when Didi took her hand.

'Stay out of the way.' His attention didn't waver as Didi chafed the girl's hand and kids jostled for a better look.

'And get those kids back,' he barked. 'She's unresponsive, barely breathing.' He shoved up her sleeve, revealing the telltale bruising. 'Overdose.' He expelled a four-letter word, then muttered, 'Lizzie, when are you going to learn?'

He knew her name, Didi thought. He knew the kids' names. Didi absorbed that information for a split second, then, snapping into action, she shooed the audience back, giving Cameron air and space to work.

He checked the patient again. 'Mask.' His voice snapped with authority—no nerves, just an iron control—obviously he'd done this before, and more than once.

Joan appeared, dropping to her knees beside him, handing

him the requested mask. He placed it over the girl's mouth and nose and immediately began resuscitation.

Seconds dragged by without end. Cameron worked steadily, breathing for the girl while Joan checked her pulse and Didi kept a clear space between them and the onlookers.

Finally, finally, the wail of a siren. Chaos, noise as paramedics rushed in with equipment. Pressing her lips together to bring the circulation back, Didi turned away. She couldn't look at Cameron right now. Black spots danced in front of her own eyes. Blame her earlier migraine and medication and lack of food, but, damn, she would *not* pass out in front of him.

She knew now why he'd been so panicked when he woke her earlier. She'd left her pills on the night-stand, he'd jumped to conclusions. And little wonder. She sank onto the nearest chair.

A few moments later she heard the wail of the sirens fade as the ambulance sped away, the background noise of voices and chairs scraping and the drum of her own heartbeat.

She didn't know how long she sat there. She knew Cameron and Joan were busy, calming kids, talking to those who'd been with Lizzie. Making phone calls.

'You okay?' Cameron sat down at the table opposite her, his warm steady hand enveloped her own and dark eyes met hers. Sweat dotted his brow. The lines around his mouth looked deeper. He'd probably been on the go all day and then this…and now her. 'Yes. Is…she going to be all right?'

The worry lines etched deeper into his brow. 'We've done what we can, now we wait. I'll phone the hospital later.'

'You were brilliant back there.'

He shook his head. 'You look beat. Let's get you out of here.'

She squared her shoulders and sat straighter. 'I might look a little under the weather tonight, but I'm not the fragile woman you think I am. I've worked in drop-in centres like this in Sydney. I've seen it before.'

She saw a new respect in his eyes but he only said, 'You were ill this afternoon.'

'I'm fine now. I can wait if you're not done.'

'I was on my way over to tell you we were leaving.'

'I need to help Joan clean—'

'She's got it covered. We're closing up now.'

Didi noticed the kids dispersing. A security guard manned the door. 'Where will they go now?'

'Wherever they came from.' He blew out a breath. 'At least they know they'll be safe here, if only for a little while. Come on.'

'They trust you,' Didi murmured. And trust, not the sexual buzz she got from his touch, had her putting her hand in his when he offered it over the table top.

CHAPTER TEN

CAM parked the car in the basement. He must be mad—a willing woman waiting to warm his bed and blot out the memories that stalked him tonight more than most, and he was hesitating.

The tension in the car had been building all the way home. He'd blanked out the past hour's events and concentrated on nothing except how quickly he could get Didi naked. A survival mechanism, he supposed.

Now he burned, his groin hardening to her proximity, her subtle soap scent teasing his nostrils. He could be inside her slick wet heat in under five minutes, filling his hands with silky flesh and familiarising himself with her taste in all those musky feminine places he'd not explored to his satisfaction yet.

Blocking out the bad.

So why was he gripping the steering wheel and saying, 'How about a stroll?'

She turned to him, her eyes unreadable. 'If you want.'

But he couldn't interpret that tone of voice as he watched her push open the door. He'd made a mistake taking her there tonight, he thought now, grabbing a jacket from the back seat. Allowing her to see more of him than he'd intended.

He pressed his keypad, the click of the locks echoed in the car park's stillness, then he turned to Didi. Her skin appeared almost translucent under the harsh fluorescent light and he hesitated. 'You sure you're up to it?'

She wrapped her coat tighter about her. 'Of course I am.'

They walked a few moments, not touching. They crossed Flinders Street and took the pedestrian bridge over the River Yarra to Southbank. The night breeze carried the smell of the river. An enticing aroma of Japanese cooking. He could hear the ebb and flow of voices and a band playing a nightspot nearby. If he looked up, the Eureka Tower blotted out the stars. If only he could blot out the past as easily.

His mouth was dry; he longed for a double whisky on ice. Something to dull the edge. 'I could do with a drink. There's a bar I think you'll like.' He took her hand in his.

Polished auburn marble spread warmth throughout the lobby, shards of light refracted rainbows from the huge chandeliers.

'We're not dressed for this place,' Didi said as they passed function attendees in glittering gowns and crisp dinner suits making their way down the wide curving staircase. 'It's five star, for goodness' sake.'

'You should feel right at home, then.' Realising sarcasm was inappropriate, he squeezed her fingers. 'No one's looking at us.'

It occurred to him that Kat wouldn't be seen dead in worn jeans in a place like this. Kat wouldn't be seen in worn jeans, period, nor had she ever accompanied him to the drop-in centre. Whereas Didi had apparently been involved in a similar voluntary capacity.

He found a spot in the lounge bar, relatively private, overlooking the lobby where water rippled over marble and ornate gilt mirrors reflected elaborate floral arrangements on glass-topped tables.

'What would you like?'

She shook her head as she removed her coat. 'Nothing alcoholic; I took that medication earlier. A pot of green tea if they serve it.'

'Tea, it is.'

She folded her arms, rested them on the table, her shadowed cleavage above a faded pink T-shirt a temptation to forget about Lizzie and Amy and the whole damn world and concentrate on the sweet diversion she could offer.

When the world went crazy… 'Aside from the tea what would you really like?'

Her eyes sparkled in the lights. 'To be able to snuggle back into my dressing gown on a couch deep enough to get lost in and…' She trailed off, her voice husky with memories of last night as her eyes met his. And the sparkle turned hot.

He allowed the unspoken to smoulder a moment. 'Forget the dressing gown and tell me the rest.'

Her cheeks turned pink. 'You've got other things on your mind. I—'

'Damn right, I've got things on my mind. Starting with you, Didi…'

Their order arrived and the words hung between them with all their erotic possibilities. Ice clinked, china rattled as the waiter set the tea and a tumbler of whisky over ice on the table. Cam paid the waiter, then sat back and watched Didi's colour heighten further.

'Shall I tell you what I'm thinking about?' he went on when the waiter had moved away. He leaned closer so he could see flecks of gold amongst the silver in her eyes. 'I'm thinking about peeling those clothes off you. Slowly. Then sampling every inch of your skin. With my hands. With my tongue. Every inch.' He let his gaze travel over the swell of her breasts. 'Or maybe I'll savour the anticipation and let you strip while I watch before I—'

'I'm thinking *you* should get naked first.' The colour had bled into her neck. Her eyes flicked to his lap. 'I want to watch you get turned on.'

Just the thought of those eyes stroking him with liquid heat shot bullets of fire to his groin. 'Too late,' he murmured, watching her eyes widen, her pupils dilate. 'I already am.'

'Well, then.' She picked up her cup, sipped, her expression touched by the humour of it. 'It's too bad we have a twenty-five-minute walk ahead of us. In the cold.'

Suddenly he didn't want to make that long chilly walk. A stroll, for Pete's sake, what had he been thinking? He took a long gulp of whisky to wet his lust-dry throat. 'We can be in a warm room in ten minutes.'

She laughed, a tinkling erotic sound. 'You think so?'

He grinned back. 'I know so.' In ten minutes they could both be naked and warm and feeling really really good. Why waste another moment? He felt the grin drop away from his lips. Didi could make him feel good, and a lot more—she could help him forget. 'What do you say? Are you game?'

She blinked. 'You're serious. Here?'

'You better believe it.' He lifted his glass to his lips to savour the whisky's aroma.

'You mean we're going to rock up at check-in with no luggage and ask for a room and a "by the way, do you charge by the hour?"' She set her cup on its saucer with a clink. 'How many couples check in to five-star luxury for a quick roll over the sheets?'

'Who says it's going to be quick?'

Her eyes turned a smoky grey, an early morning heatwave haze with a voice to match. 'How many hours do you think we might need, Cameron?' It continually fascinated him; her innocence-in-black-lace routine.

'Whatever it takes.' He polished off his whisky in one long draught. 'As long as we're home before six-thirty.'

She checked her watch, slurped a few mouthfuls of tea, picked up her coat and rose. 'Better get started, then.'

'Ah, a small problem.' He glanced down at himself. Maybe not so small…

She leaned in, her small breasts brushing against his forearm as she whispered in his ear. 'Stay close behind and come with me.'

He reached for her cool slim fingers, entwined them with his. 'I intend to do just that, sweetheart.'

'Hurry.' The urgency in Didi's voice sharpened his anticipation to a razor's edge.

'Going as fast as I can,' Cameron muttered, swiping the key-card for the second time, his free hand still locked with hers.

Finally. He tugged her hand and they spilled into the room like a couple of horny teenagers, tossing handbag and jackets on the floor and not bothering with lights. Only the master lamp cast a muted yellow pool in the room's foyer.

'Didi…' He whirled, pressing her against the door so he could ravish her mouth the way he'd been wanting to since early this morning. His blood pounded into life, roaring through his veins. Already he'd committed her taste to memory, the scent of her skin, the sound of her moan as her mouth opened beneath his.

Their joined hands brushed the front of his jeans; he wasn't sure who'd made the move, didn't care. He took advantage, rubbing her knuckles over his throbbing erection while his tongue dived over hers. This fever of need wasn't anything he'd not experienced before but this strange vicelike grip in the region of his heart was new.

So he'd die of a heart attack in the throes of passion. He'd die a happy man. But he lifted his head, let them both catch their breath. Her breasts rose and fell in rapid succession, hard nipples abrading his chest through their combined layers of worn jersey.

'I want to see if you're as beautiful as I remember,' he muttered, and tugged her T-shirt over her head. Tossed it over his shoulder. Dragged the bra cups down and filled his palms with warm female flesh.

Her skin was rich cream against his darker hands, delicate and fragrant, her nipples pale and tight. Impossible not to taste. He captured one, scraped over it with teeth and tongue.

She hauled in a whimpered breath, tracked fingernails through his scalp. Urgency pinched at his flesh. He wanted those fingers on other, more needy parts.

'And…?'

She tugged his head away from her breast with the palms of her hands and he fell into her eyes. 'You're…' *not what I expected* '…enchanting.'

What was happening here? Was this more than sex?

He thrust the questions from his mind. It would *not* be more. Peeling them both away from the door, he lifted her off her feet and quickstepped them to the foot of the bed.

He grabbed his wallet from his jeans as he toppled her onto the mattress and followed her down, hot, impatient, wild for her. His fingers fumbled with the leather a moment, then closed over the foil package. He held it up in front of her face. 'The only condom I have with me.'

Her hand snapped up to cover his, eyes dark with a wicked promise of approaching turbulence. 'Better make the most of it, then.'

Cameron caught her hand before it slid off his sweat-slick belly. He didn't want to move yet; he was enjoying the feel of her body tucked against his. 'So…you said you've seen it all before.'

'I've always felt an obligation to try and help out where I can. There was a halfway house for those undergoing drug rehab…' She moved her head side to side against his shoulder, her fragrant hair tickling his chin. 'Well, you know how it is.'

He did. And the fact that she did too was a connection he hadn't anticipated. He was still mulling that over when she rolled onto her stomach, tugging the sheet with her, and traced a finger down the centre of his chest.

'But you… You let me believe all you were interested in was money.'

He hesitated. 'For a long time it was. Because growing up

I didn't have it.' He should have moved. He should have known she'd ask questions. And he should have thought before he answered. Even in the semi-darkness he felt the incredulity in her eyes.

'What? Money?'

'Surprised, Didi?' His private smile was humourless. 'Seems we've traded places.'

She was silent a moment. 'You know about my family, tell me about yours.'

His lips turned numb, the black hole that had been his life yawned before him. A life that distanced him for ever from Didi's world. He pushed her hand away. 'You don't want to hear about my family.'

'I want to know what motivates a man to build a centre for runaways,' she said quietly. 'To invest not only money but time and interest. I saw how you were with those kids. Why?'

He shrugged, turned away from those perceptive eyes. But Lizzie's collapse tonight had wrung his emotions dry. He expelled a long sigh. 'Because I keep hoping that one day my sister will walk through those doors.'

'You have a sister?'

His body tensed as the old pain around his heart clenched its fist. 'Listen, can we just drop this?'

'No. Tell me about her.'

He'd already discovered Didi's tenacity and since he'd already opened his mouth… 'Amy. I don't know where she is, or even if she's still alive. The last time I saw her I was eighteen and doing what I could to keep us together, she was seventeen and on drugs.'

'Where were your parents?'

'Dead.' His voice sounded flat and devoid of emotion. Experience had taught him emotion made one vulnerable. He didn't intend to be vulnerable, to anything, or anyone ever again.

'Oh, Cameron. I'm sorry.'

That old cliché. 'Don't be.' He clenched his jaw against a

rising anger that had nothing—and everything—to do with Didi. What the hell would she know with her childhood of opportunities? 'It's the familiar story of drugs and domestic violence.'

'It might help if you t—'

'Leave it alone, Didi. It's ancient history and nothing to do with you.'

Wanting distance, he rolled out of bed and crossed to the window. He didn't need the woman with her sympathy and sad eyes. Instead he watched the reflections in the river, a late train snaking into Flinders Street Station. For the first time in years he desperately craved a cigarette.

But memories of a childhood he kept ruthlessly buried flashed before him. Wanted fugitive, Bernie Boyd had died during a police chase, Cam's mother of a prescription drug overdose a few months later.

His biggest mistake had been confiding all to Katrina, and hadn't she had her moment of glory with the poster campaign? *He's not the man you think he is.*

He would not make the same mistake with Didi.

'Come back to bed, Cameron.'

Her arms slid around his back, her hands splayed over his chest—not provocative or teasing—just…easy. Soothing. He hadn't heard her approach but she was warm and suddenly very welcome. Her hair felt like soft warm rain against his skin. He knew if he looked into her eyes he'd see understanding. She didn't understand of course, but she cared. Perhaps she wouldn't if she knew, but for now it was enough that she was here.

Wordlessly he turned into her embrace.

Where he knew he was wanted.

Where he wanted to be.

He showed her how much with nips and open-mouth kisses beneath her ear, down her throat, while he let his hands glide over the dips and curves. How good they could be together—*were* together.

She responded with little murmurs and sighs. No words. As if she understood he didn't want them. She seemed to know just what he needed, yet how could she? She'd known him a matter of days.

Warmth stole through him like a thief, catching him unawares. He'd been damn rude to her—how long had it been since any woman had shown him anything approaching compassion? And he'd cut her off.

He wanted to hold her again in a fever of passion and have her body once more, apologise, but the strength had drained out of him. So he stroked her hair and simply held her. Within her aura he could forget the dark and live in the light.

As long as he kept his past private, so long as he didn't let emotion get the upper hand, there was no reason they couldn't continue what they'd started.

Didi woke to the pink pearl light of morning, the conversation they'd had before they'd fallen asleep fresh in her mind. She could still feel Cameron's emotional scars as if they were carved into his flesh, and wanted to weep. And comfort.

But when she opened her eyes and turned to him she discovered she was alone. A note written on the hotel's stationery lay on the crisp white pillow beside her.

Good morning, Didi,
I've gone to the hospital to check on Lizzie before I head in to the office...

She frowned. He worked on a Saturday? Yeah, that sounded like him. She read on.

Sleep in for a bit, ring room service and order up breakfast; it's already paid for. I've arranged for a taxi to take you home when you're ready, speak to Concierge. Have a productive day. Cam.

PS I'll feed Charlie on my way, no need to rush.
PPS Thank you for last night.

She basked in the warm glow of his PPS for a few seconds. Then shook it off. *Silly girl.* He hadn't meant last night as in *last night*—the way she wanted him to mean last night—he meant her help at the community centre.

Didn't he?

He'd booked the cab and paid for breakfast. So despite his own problems he'd thought of her well-being this morning. *Don't get used to it.* He was pampering her because he wanted her *productive.*

So she sat up in bed, dialled room service and ordered the biggest breakfast on the menu, since she'd not indulged in that particular luxury in a long time.

She fluffed her pillows, pulled the sheet up to her chin and lay back to wait for her meal. Theirs wasn't a relationship where they shared intimacies of the family kind; at least on his part. It was all about business—he wanted an artist who could deliver a product.

And it was all about sex. Great sex, the hottest sex she'd ever had. With the most attentive lover she'd ever known. But it was still sex without intimacy.

A problem. Because against all her good intentions to adhere to the rules they'd agreed on she was falling for him—her casual no-strings walk-away-when-it's-done lover. Which should *not* mean she wanted to know him better on a personal level. She should *not* want to know more about his family.

A sixth sense told her there was more to the situation than drugs and violence. How to get him to open up—or not—was the million-dollar question. Would it draw them closer or push them apart?

* * *

'Hi.'

Didi's needle slipped, spilling the gold beads she was threading as her heart did a little flutter. Scooping them into her palm, she put them back in their container and looked at him over her glasses. 'Hi.'

She hadn't heard Cameron come in over the sound of the stereo. He was wearing khaki trousers and a casual navy shirt. He looked a little ragged around the edges. Running on the little amount of sleep he must have had, she wasn't surprised. Her heart fluttered again at the reason for his lack of shut-eye. 'How's Lizzie?'

'She's lucky. She's going to be okay.'

Didi nodded. 'Thanks to you.' She studied him a moment. 'Do you always work on the weekend?'

'When it's necessary.' He stared at her a moment with those blueberry eyes, a bemused smile on his lips. 'For days you've had me wondering… Why the pink lenses?'

'Because then everything looks rosy on the greyest of days. Even you.' Smiling at him, unreasonably happy to see him, she took them off, rubbed the bridge of her nose, then stretched her arms up and out and wiggled her fingers.

She'd worked all day. She had spray glitter on her leggings, needle-stab wounds in her fingers and beads from here to Christmas, but she'd made darn good progress.

He wasn't looking at her progress.

He was watching her nipples prickle and tighten beneath her T-shirt. Her nipples hadn't had such a workout since… never, she decided, and lowered her arms slowly. 'Um…so… what do you think?'

'Very nice.'

'You haven't even looked,' she accused. She knew because she'd had her eyes on his since she'd caught him standing there.

'I've looked.' He crossed the room. 'I've been here at least thirty seconds watching you work.'

'Oh.' He'd seen her naked, there wasn't an inch he hadn't seen, yet still she felt the blush bloom on her cheeks.

'Watching and imagining you wearing nothing but those pink glasses and eating apples. Red apples.'

Her blush deepened and she flapped a hand. 'What is it with you and apples?'

He smiled. 'Just a little fantasy of mine.' Still smiling, he held out a slim box she'd not noticed. 'For a hard day's work.'

'Ah-h-h.' She ripped off the paper, opened the lid. An assortment of exclusive, handmade dark chocolates.

'Soft centres,' he said as he plucked one out and slipped it between her lips. 'I promised you chocolate.'

Its decadent cream flowed over her tongue. 'Mmm.' She beamed at him. 'Thank you.'

'You're supposed to share.'

'Of course. Sorry. Which would you like?'

'You choose.'

She checked the guide, then rose. 'Honey myrtle.' And pressed it against his lips. He opened his mouth, closed his lips over her fingers and for a moment…

'Right now I have this image of you wearing those glasses—just the glasses—while I feed you chocolate.'

'Not apples?'

'No. I'd bite it in half—*sharing*—and drizzle your half of the cream between your lips.'

Her eyes glazed over at the image. 'That could work.'

The intercom buzzed and the phone rang simultaneously. 'That'll be our meal,' Cameron said, withdrawing his wallet and tossing it on the table. 'I ordered Chinese. Can you get it? Money's there.'

As Didi paid off the delivery girl she noticed a creased photo in Cameron's wallet. A young woman.

An instant punch to her solar plexus. 'That was quick,' she said as Cameron disconnected, juggling their meal and squinting at the photo and trying not to look as if she was before she flipped the wallet shut.

'One of those pesky call centres,' he groused. 'Don't they have weekends in India? If you're wondering who it is,' he said, relieving her of the food, 'that's Amy.'

'I wasn't prying.' *Much.* But she moved to the table and picked up her spectacles for a better look. 'I've seen this girl…'

She felt the instant tension as Cameron stiffened beside her. 'Where?' he asked sharply.

She struggled to remember. The shape of the girl's face, the hair colour… She couldn't have seen her—what would be the odds? She closed the wallet, put it on the table. She shouldn't have mentioned it. *Stupid.* 'I'm probably seeing the family resemblance.' She smiled at the tight-lipped man in front of her and teased, 'She looks like you on a good day.'

'She'd be thirty-one now—she'd've changed.'

'Exactly.' She shook away the odd feeling and changed the subject. 'Let's eat. I'm starving.'

Ten minutes later they were tucking into sweet chilli roast pork and king prawn combination.

'I've got a fund-raising dinner next Saturday night,' Cameron said between mouthfuls. 'I want you to accompany me.'

The sudden punch of nerves caught Didi off guard. 'Are you sure?' She'd known it was likely. But being seen in public as his partner, however temporary, was something new. She had no idea what type of woman he usually dated, but she knew she wouldn't fit in. She'd never fitted in with the elite. She'd be more of an embarrassment. 'Perhaps it's better if you just go on your own.'

'Of course I'm sure, and, no, I'm not going on my own—I've already paid for two tickets. The money raised is going towards a dozen local charities. You'll want to come—this'll be a good opportunity to talk about your art, mention the gallery opening and make some contacts.'

The alternative would be to chaperone another woman…

There *was* no alternative.

She bit off a corner of bamboo shoot, then nodded. 'Okay.'

On the inside her stomach was churning. How would his business associates view her? Would they know she was only his short-term lover?

And what the heck was she going to wear?

CHAPTER ELEVEN

'I GUESS my sequined leggings and macramé top are out?' Didi murmured, only half joking. She liked the glitzy outfit she'd bought at a recycle boutique. It made her feel happy and it drew looks whenever she wore it. She also knew her taste didn't conform to the conventional fashion trends.

Cameron looked up, his mouth open in astonishment. 'This is a formal dinner, Didi. The "rich and famous" will be there. You'll need to wear something suitable. A dress.'

She scowled down at her half-eaten meal. 'I don't own a dress.' Not any more.

'I told you I'd pay for whatever you need. Leave it with me. My secretary, Chris, knows how to shop and what's appropriate. Write down your dress size and preferences and I'll have her send around some items for you to choose from.'

His condescending attitude sent prickles up her spine and she stiffened. 'I've attended a few of these formal shindigs in my time,' she said coolly. 'You think I don't know what's appropriate?'

He stared at her and she could see him trying to dig his way out of the hole he'd got himself in. 'Of course you do,' he said placatingly. In that same condescending tone. 'But I know you're busy here. I'm just trying to save you some time.'

He had a point. She couldn't afford to fall any further behind.

In two weeks their working relationship would be over.

Their private relationship would be over. A stark reminder that this was a temporary arrangement and she'd be better off remembering that. But a hollow feeling opened up inside her.

'You'll find something we both like,' he went on, oblivious to her inner turmoil. Mr Super Confident twirled his chopsticks through his meal, picked up a prawn.

She needed to retain her independence and some control over her life. Their tastes were light years apart—she'd seen the way he looked at her clothes. But what he liked wouldn't matter in two weeks. 'I still have that cash you gave me. You don't need to fork out any more.'

'That's an advance on your commission. It has nothing to do with this.' He glanced at her, his smile indulgent. 'Call the dress a gift.'

A gift. Wasn't that what men like him gave their mistresses? Oh, how she hated that word. She hated that that was all he wanted from her. She realised she wanted so much more. A chill wrapped around her heart. *Don't you dare cry.* Instead she dared herself to look him in the eye and ask, 'Would that be for services rendered, then?'

His smile disappeared, his eyes locked on hers. 'Didi.' He put down his chopsticks, stood and rounded the table. Crouched in front of her and took her face between his hands. 'You know damn well that's not what I meant.'

She'd never heard his voice so quiet, so firm. It wrapped around her like blue velvet. No, Didi thought, he wasn't at all sure how she'd interpreted him. Maybe she wasn't so sure herself. And when had he become more to her than a casual lover?

He *couldn't* be more; she couldn't let him.

'Hell…Didi.' He smoothed his thumbs over her cheeks. His eyes glinted in the down-lights. 'If I insulted you, I apologise. I want you with me on Saturday night. Only you.'

Her heart melted and a smile tugged at her lips. 'Ah, but

would you want me with you in my sequined leggings and macramé top?'

His eyes flickered, then he blew out a slow breath. 'Can we compromise on this? If Chris organises some stuff for you to look at and you don't like anything…' He rubbed his lips over hers. 'Let's just see how it goes with Chris first. Now…come up here.'

He stood, taking her with him, lifting her higher so that his body bits lined up with hers in all the right places. Their mouths feasted on one another's as he headed for the black rug between the sofas. He laid her down on its luxurious pile, his hands diving beneath her top.

'Do we have a deal?' he murmured against her mouth.

Her own hands got busy with his belt buckle. 'Deal.'

The next few days passed in a blur. During the day Cameron worked at the office. Mostly. And they kept things platonic—well, almost. If you didn't count Monday's lunchtime session in the spa or the interlude in the sky garden. Her exhibition piece was growing, taking shape slowly but surely.

One of Cameron's employees took Charlie. Didi was devastated to see him go, but happy he'd found a safe new home where he'd be cared for. One day perhaps she could have him back. She missed him. *Get used to it*—very soon she'd be missing Cameron as well.

In the evenings they went out for a quick bite or purchased dinner from the numerous takeaway stores nearby. Either way, they walked, taking in the fresh evening air so Didi could stretch her legs after working all day in the one spot. And every night was another magical journey of discovery.

The dresses were delivered to the apartment on Tuesday. A boutique full of beautiful expensive designer outfits. Accessories. Shoes. Any woman would have been beside herself. Didi wasn't any woman.

Did Cameron want to help her decide? she phoned to ask.

No. Anything the lovely Chris chose was sure to be a knockout and he was looking forward to seeing Didi all dressed up on Saturday night. And by the way—had he told her?—Chris had booked her in to Tiara's Spa and Beauty—*the* latest 'in' place—for Saturday afternoon. The massage and hot stone treatment would do her good.

It wasn't the massage she worried about. No hairdresser had come within cutting distance of her hair in a long time. She trimmed it herself with the aid of mirrors. And make-up? She didn't bother with more than the basics of foundation, lip gloss and blusher.

Compromise. They'd made some compromises over the past week and Didi was realising it didn't mean she had to give up her control or her independence. That she could look at a situation from another's point of view, another's needs. But this transformation? She wasn't so sure.

A stranger stared back at Didi in her mirror on Saturday evening. A sophisticated-looking woman in a short black organza dress with kohl-rimmed eyes, siren-red glossed lips and her hair carefully styled to wisp softly around her face. At least they hadn't cut it. She wanted to cry, but the truck-load of mascara they'd applied would probably run.

She wanted to run.

She'd seen something she wished she hadn't while flicking through an out-dated magazine at the salon—a photo of Cameron and a stunning brunette almost as tall as he was. The don't-date-him poster girl? Possibly. The woman on the other end of the mystery phone calls? Again, possibly. How could she compete with that kind of woman?

She could hear Cameron pacing the marble floor beyond. She'd cloistered herself back in her own room since she'd arrived back from her salon appointment. She was now fifteen minutes behind their agreed time.

What would he think when he saw her? Would she come

up to scratch? With no hope of competing with women like that brunette, Didi felt the same insecurities that had haunted her when she'd attended functions with her family.

Turning away from the unnervingly false image, she picked up the tiny red velvet evening purse. She wasn't sophisticated, why was she pretending to be someone she wasn't?

Because she was Cameron's partner for the evening. Tonight she'd try to be the poised cosmopolitan woman he expected. She could play the part for one night. One more week, one gallery opening and their no-strings arrangement would be over.

Cameron knocked on her door. 'Ready?'

Her heart gallumphed. Her hands turned clammy and cold. She primed her lips for a smile, took a steadying breath and said, 'Ready as I'll ever be.'

She got a glimpse of dark eyes and clean-shaven jaw as she opened the door. A whiff of aftershave as she ducked under the arm he'd leaned against the jamb and hurried to the hat stand to grab her new black coat, which was part of the package.

'Hey, what's the rush?'

'We're running late, my fault. Sorry.' Her fingers closed over the soft wool but Cameron took it from her.

'We can run a little late,' he said, his deep voice vibrating along her spine, his breath disturbing the hairs on her nape. 'Turn around and let's get a look.'

She almost forgot her own insecurities when she swivelled on her stilettos and got a look at Cameron in full formal get-up. Oh, my… Damn, he looked good. She almost reached out to finger the bow tie and give herself an excuse to drift her knuckles against his throat, until she saw him staring at her as if he'd never seen her before…and remembered why.

She'd gone for elegant black. As she turned Cam stepped back to take in the full effect. The dress hugged her petite figure like a charm. Tiny straps showed off her creamy shoulders, the waistline was cinched with a sparkly clasp. Its short skirt flared, leaving plenty of thigh to admire. And the arch of her feet in those gold strappy heels made his mouth water. 'You look sensational, Didi.'

She smiled, drawing his attention to her carefully outlined lips and the shimmering charcoal framing her silver eyes. He doubted he'd ever escorted a more beautiful woman, but something about the stunning image niggled at him.

She seemed to pick up on that vibe and the smile disappeared. 'Let's go, then,' she said briskly, reaching for her coat draped over his arm.

'Hang on.' He returned her coat to the stand, fingered the box in his pocket. He'd wanted to give her some token, something to show how he felt about her. Even if he wasn't sure yet what that feeling was. Would she be offended? Only one way to find out. He withdrew the box.

She looked at it, then up at him with wary eyes. 'Soft centres…?'

Her voice was unsteady, the way his knees suddenly felt. 'It's just a little something to wear tonight,' he said, holding it out to her. 'I'm not sure if you're a jewellery girl but figured what the heck, a bit of bling couldn't hurt.'

When she made no move to take the box, he opened it himself. The single teardrop gem winked on its glittering chain.

'Is that real?' she whispered, and squinted closer. 'It looks real.'

'It's an Argyle pink diamond on a platinum chain. You being the creative sort, I thought something simple was probably wise.'

She looked up, met his eyes. 'I don't call that simple or wise.'

And didn't that just about sum up their relationship? 'Wear it for me, Didi.' Without waiting for a reply he stepped behind her to slip it around her neck, unaccountably disappointed that her almond-honey scent had been drowned out by cosmetics and styling lotion and a darker cloying fragrance that on any other woman would have been seductive.

On Didi it was just…wrong. She didn't need heavy fragrance to seduce, all she needed to be was herself. Shaking away the dangerous thought, he stepped in front of her again to see how the stone looked against her skin.

She touched the stone lightly with one finger, but her eyes gave him no clue to her feelings, as if she'd deliberately blanked her expression. 'Thank you. It's the most beautiful piece of jewellery I've ever worn.'

'You're welcome.' He wanted to lay his lips on hers and feel them smile against his as she had last night but the slick red gloss looked more like a shield than an invitation. Instead, he reached for her coat. 'Shall we go?'

The hotel ballroom was all glitz. Crystal and silverware sparkled on snowy cloths sprinkled with colourful foil confetti. Towering floral arrangements spilled their early spring fragrance, mingling with French perfume and hors d'oeuvres being circulated on silver trays.

Cam lifted two glasses of champagne as a waiter passed. Then he saw a tall slim blonde wearing gold leopard-skin lamé as if she'd been born in it heading in their direction.

'Let's find out where we're seated,' he murmured to Didi, handing her a glass and turning away.

'Cam.' The woman caught at his arm. 'You weren't trying to run away, were you, darling? I know you'll want to buy a ticket or three in tonight's raffle.' She swept between him and Didi waving her little box of tickets, then reached up to buss both his cheeks.

He forced a smile. Dominique was in her mid-forties and had been pursuing him for at least five years. 'Evening, Dominique.' He stepped around her to create a triangle. 'I'd like you to meet Didi O'Flanagan. Didi, this is Dominique Le Hunte. She's our fund-raiser extraordinaire.'

'Di-di.' Dominique's latest Botox treatment prevented her eyebrows rising but she tinkled out a laugh. 'What a quaint little abbreviation.' She proffered a limp hand dripping with diamonds. 'Why…what's so terrible about your birth name?'

'It's Dee-aahn,' Didi replied with exaggerated aplomb. 'My sister never could get it right so she said Didi. I'm afraid it stuck.'

Cam smiled privately at the way Didi's lie rolled off her tongue and raised his glass to her with an intimate grin that had Dominique frowning. Or would if she could, he mused.

'Well—*Dee-aahn*—it's…nice of you to…attend.'

'Certainly is. Very nice,' Didi drawled as she gave Cam a smouldering look and took a long slow sip of champagne.

Dominique didn't have a comeback.

Cam cleared his throat to cover a chuckle and signalled a waiter bearing spring rolls. Not many people stopped Dominique in her tracks. But then hadn't Didi O'Flanagan stopped Cam himself in his tracks?

Dominique recovered enough to turn on the charm again. 'So where did you two meet?'

Cam smiled at Didi, remembering the event-filled evening with a certain fondness and said, 'At a function a few weeks back.'

'I was waitressing, actually,' Didi said with dead calm, meeting his eyes as she plucked a roll off the proffered plate. 'Thank you.' This directed at the waiter with a sunny smile.

'Oh…' Dominique laughed uncertainly and glanced at Cam. 'Helping out in a volunteer capacity?'

'Making a living.' Didi bit into her spring roll.

'Making a living?' Dominique echoed faintly.

'I've commissioned Didi to complete an arts project for me,' Cam cut in to curtail what looked like developing into a 'situation'. He placed his hand on her back, cruised it up the black fabric till he found skin. Heaven knew what Didi was capable of under such circumstances. He nudged her forward, excusing them both. 'I think they're about to start seating us and we haven't found our table yet. Catch you later, Dominique.'

'Rich bitch,' Didi muttered beneath her breath. 'Your friends—'

'They're not my friends. They're mostly business associates. It's important to project the correct image at these events.'

He felt her spine stiffen beneath his hand. 'Yeah, and haven't I heard *that* before.'

'I—'

'Do you have friends, Cameron?' She stopped mid-stride to look up at him. 'And I don't mean bed partners.'

A muscle in his jaw ticced. 'Yes, of course I do. That's our table.' He prompted her forward.

But how many could he name? He realised he'd been too busy making his mark in his new life without any links to his past to form any lasting friendships.

Mouth-watering food was served on elegant dishes, the wine flowed, the speeches were made. Didi sat opposite him conversing easily with the people around her, as if she'd been born to it. Which, he had to constantly remind himself, she had.

But every time he looked at her it was like looking at someone else. And when their eyes met—there it was again—that vulnerable, sad look in her eyes as her smile dropped away. Just a glimpse before she snapped her gaze to Lady Johnson beside her and *with a smile* renewed their conversation.

He fingered the stem of his wine glass and watched her. She was easily the most beautiful woman in the room, but she wasn't his Didi.

His Didi.

It steamrolled over him with a force that made his heart thud harder and his muscles cramp and his hand tighten on his glass till he thought it might snap. They had one more week. He didn't want their relationship to end yet. She was like stepping into spring sunshine after a long cold winter. He wanted to bathe in that warmth a little longer. What would she say if he suggested renegotiating their arrangement, extending it a little?

He didn't get a moment to ponder that further because it was time for the lucky door prize. 'And the winner is…Didi O'Flanagan,' the MC announced. 'Dinner for two at the Candle-side restaurant. Come on up, Didi O'Flanagan.'

Cam watched her lay her napkin on the table and make her way to the stage, her short skirt flaring around her upper thighs. Those silky thighs had rubbed along his only twenty-four hours ago. And again he felt that overwhelming sense of ownership and pride.

And imminent sense of loss.

'And no second guesses, ladies and gentleman, as to the lucky guy sharing the evening with our lovely winner.'

She took possession of the tickets, held them high, then grinned at Cam. The necklace he'd given her winked in the lights. He could only nod, his throat constricted, his chest tight. Couldn't manage a smile. The noise seemed to dim, the crowd faded to black and all he could see was Didi.

But she wasn't Didi. She was dressed and styled like a woman he might have dated a few weeks ago if he hadn't met her. He didn't like the changes; he wanted the old Didi back. The girl with the offbeat fashion sense and spiked hair.

As she watched him her hand fell to her side, her smile faded. He saw her step off the stage and walk back to the table, chin high. But she didn't sit down—she swiped her purse from the table and headed to the Ladies without looking at him.

Cam excused himself from the table and caught up with her as she exited a few moments later. She stopped short when she saw him.

The sheen of moisture in her eyes damn near killed him. 'What's wrong?'

She shook her head. 'Nothing.'

So she wasn't going to talk. 'I've had enough,' he said. 'How about you? You want to skip dessert?'

She gave a half-nod. 'But you've spent so much money…'

'I don't give a flying fig about the money.' He took her hand, rubbed his thumb over her knuckles. 'We can splurge on that ice cream in the freezer if you want. We'll grab your coat and escape before anyone else sees us.'

'Cameron… Is that what this is all about?' she asked in a small voice.

He frowned and kept walking, tugging her along beside him. 'Is *what* what this is all about?'

'You don't want anyone to see us together?'

'No, I don't.' He squeezed her hand. 'I just want to go home.'

CHAPTER TWELVE

DIDI hugged her arms as they rode home. Even in her new wool coat she felt cold. Cameron had openly admitted he didn't want to be seen with her. She might look the part tonight but he knew it wasn't the real deal. Unlike that glamorous woman she'd seen on his arm in the magazine.

How could she hope to measure up to that poise and sophistication? Once again she didn't fit. She'd never fit in with the rich crowd. Up on that stage she'd been linked with him publicly and all he'd done was frown.

She'd fallen in love with a man who didn't love her.

Yes, she was in love, time to admit it. When was she going to learn? When was she going to stop letting her heart be broken?

'Would you like that ice cream?' he asked as they entered the apartment. 'Or coffee?'

She kept walking, her stilettos clacking over the marble. 'No, thanks. I'm going to bed.'

All she wanted to do was scrub the gunk off her face, strip out of the dress and hide under the quilt. Alone. But time was running out. Very soon she *would* be alone. Permanently. Because she'd never let this happen again. She closed the en-suite door, kicked off her shoes and reached for her make-up remover.

When she opened the door ten minutes later Cameron was sitting on the edge of the turned-down bed, his shirt unbuttoned, his feet bare. Waiting for her. Yes, he wanted her in the bedroom, just not in public.

His gaze tracked her progress, but it wasn't the look of a man who only wanted sex. For a moment he looked as if he really cared in a deeper, more intimate way.

And it hurt. Because now it seemed she was only seeing what she wanted to see. She'd lost the ability to be objective. And damn it all, she was going to give him what he wanted, because she wanted it too. For the next few nights she'd take what they could make together and store the memories in her heart.

'Didi.' He rose and came to her, touched her cheek with such tenderness she wanted to weep. She let him unzip her dress, tug the straps over her shoulders. It fell to the floor with a soft flutter of air. The blunt tips of his fingers fumbled at her back as he unclasped her bra, drew it away. Then her black lace panties as his palms slipped beneath the elastic and tugged. Over her hips, down her thighs.

Fast or slow, he made love-making an art. With one flick of his finger, one brush of his lips, he knew how to tease and arouse, how to soothe and seduce.

'This is how I want you,' he murmured, tracing a damp path down her body from neck to navel with light nips, fleeting open-mouthed kisses. 'No cosmetics to conceal your inner glow, nothing to hide your naked beauty. Just Didi.'

He knelt before her, his eyes following the path his mouth had taken while his palms massaged slow circles over her hips. The diamond he'd given her burned into the flesh above her breasts as if he'd set it alight with his gaze and she knew then that she'd never take it off.

The lump in her throat made it impossible to speak. She needed to remember his words were just that—words. To pretend they didn't flow into her heart, filling it until it felt ready to burst.

To *not* let her imagination leap ahead to happy-ever-afters as he lifted her against his hard warm body and laid her back on the fine cotton sheets.

To *not* notice how his heart thudded against hers as if they beat as one when he stretched out beside her.

His hands were big, his fingers roughened, but he handled her as if she were made of the most fragile glass. Somehow his trousers were gone, his satin-steel erection sliding hotly against the soft flesh of her belly as he eased on top of her.

His mouth covered hers. He drank her in and reason ebbed away, longing flowed in. He tasted of rich dark wine and spice and summer. But summer was impossibly far away and out of reach so she reached instead for the arms that held her, curled her hands around his rock-hard strength and thought only of the moment.

He slipped like silk inside her. Longing turned to need, and need to urgency. Yet even in passion he paid homage to her with a reverence she'd never experienced.

When he sent her soaring she touched the stars, and he was right there with her. It was a long slow slide back to sanity.

To reality.

To the man who couldn't wait to take her home because he hadn't wanted to be seen with her. Once again her not-so-smart mouth had got her into trouble. Dominique had pushed all the wrong buttons and Didi had just had to react, hadn't she?

She just bet that woman on his arm in the picture would know how to work a room, what to say, how to say it. Feeling vulnerable, she pulled the sheet higher to cover her breasts. 'I saw your picture in a magazine at the salon today.'

'I hope it was my good side,' Cameron murmured against her temple while his fingernails traced lazy circles on Didi's upper arm.

'You were with a woman.' *Tall, dark. Stunning.* 'Was it Kathryn…?' She felt a quiver of tension run through him.

'Katrina.' He spoke through stiff lips.

'Ah, of course. *Katrina*. Perhaps you should've taken *her* to dinner.'

Tension tightened his hand and he pulled it away from her arm. 'Don't do this, Didi. It was over with her a while ago.'

'Is she the woman who left the poster?'

A long, telling silence. 'She's out of my life.'

From the photos she'd seen of the two of them the woman was not unlike his sister in looks, Didi thought. Did he even realise that? 'Ah, but are you over her?'

'What do you think?' Irritation roughened his voice as he stared at the ceiling.

A politician's answer—not an answer. Her heart—she had to hold the cracked pieces together. Jay hadn't been honest about his previous partner. A month into his relationship with Didi—they'd even picked out the engagement ring and booked the church…

'What if she changed her mind, Cameron? What if she wanted you back, what if her poster game was a ploy for your attention?'

'No. Why would she do that?'

'Because she's not over you?'

'That's b—'

'The phone rang today,' Didi went on. 'And whoever it was hung up when I answered. It's not the first time. Call it woman's intuition but I know it's a woman.'

Another silence. 'She's over me.'

'Perhaps not, if she thought you'd met someone. Maybe she wants you back because she can't bear the thought of you with someone else.'

'You're wrong. For a start she—' Cameron bit back the words that sprang to his tongue. That Kat, whose father had the top job of Prime Minister firmly in his sights, would have nothing to do with a man whose father had been a criminal wanted over two states.

The sins of the father… His hands tightened into fists, his blood ran like a chill wind through his veins. Beyond the grave and still screwing with his life.

He couldn't tell Didi. He'd confided in Kat and look where that had landed him. The risk of losing this woman who brought the freshness, warmth and promise of spring into his life was too great a risk. He wanted her with him a little longer—was that selfish?

'She what, Cameron?'

'She's getting married.'

He turned his head on the pillow to impress that fact upon her. To look at her…while she stared at the ceiling. Which allowed him a smile when she might not have appreciated it. 'What about your ex?' he said quietly. 'What happened with him?'

She continued to gaze upward for a long silent moment. He thought she wasn't going to answer him but then she said, 'He was good-looking, wealthy, educated at the right schools—a real ladies' man. I didn't know it at the time but he was on the rebound. Then his ex changed her mind…and they lived happily ever after. End of story.'

'I'm sorry, Didi.'

'Don't be.' She turned her face to him, eyes wide in the dimness. 'I'm over him. I don't do serious any more.' She resumed her study of the ceiling.

Moonlight etched her profile in silver, the pert nose and kissable lips, the curve of her breasts outlined against the sheet. Like fairy folk she was made for moonlight. Or maybe moonlight had been made for her.

Then a wispy cloud drifted past, a gauze curtain dulling the image and taking his smile with it. Like the way their relationship was headed. He wanted to hold that curtain back for one more moment…another day, another week. A year. Ten years.

How long would this infatuation last?

If that was what it was. It felt more like… No. He refused

to acknowledge anything deeper. As she'd said, she didn't do serious, neither did he. But how long would it be before Didi wanted more than an affair? A man with his past, his inability to lay his heart on the line and trust, couldn't give her that.

Whatever they had, it would all end in a matter of days. And that would be the wiser course, he thought. But he couldn't stop himself reaching out to brush her hair off her brow, to gently close her eyelids with his fingers. 'I was the luckiest man there tonight,' he whispered. 'You were gorgeous.'

Her eyelids fluttered against his hand and she turned to him, eyes wide. 'But you couldn't wait to get me away.'

'Only because I wanted you all to myself.'

'You mean you weren't embarrassed?'

'Embarrassed?' He took a moment to figure it out. Was *that* what it was all about? He reached for her hand on the sheet between them, brought it to his cheek. 'Ah, sweetheart…no. *No.* Not on your life. I was *sorry.* I pushed you into something that made you uncomfortable. I tried to make you into someone you're not—with the best of intentions—and that was my mistake.'

She blinked. 'Thank you. For telling me.'

But she knew he hadn't answered all her questions and he hated the deception. It was there in her quiet gaze and the emotional distance she'd put between them.

Didi didn't have time or the emotional energy to think about Cameron and their relationship for the next few days. Instead she poured everything into her work. The piece was coming together beautifully, just as she'd imagined when she'd planned it.

She knew Cameron was busy with preparations for Saturday night's opening, which was perhaps why she saw very little of him, until he slipped into bed beside her at night.

They made love. Sometimes he was warm and tender, at

other times it was with an urgency that blew her away; almost as if he didn't want what they had to end. But he never mentioned it, so neither did she. After all, they'd agreed she would walk away at the end, no strings, so she had to assume that hadn't changed. Perhaps if she didn't have the opening coming up she'd have left earlier because it was tearing her apart inside.

He took her to the gallery one evening and showed her the renovations he'd made to the old building. Her Before the Temptation was to be on display, earlier pieces were going to be offered for sale with work from other unknown artists he wanted to support. And then there was the wall where her commissioned piece would hang.

Excitement mingled with a sense of surrealism. Could this really be happening? He'd invited Melbourne's rich and important people. To see *her* work. To launch *her* career. The press coverage was going to be huge.

She'd sent her own invitation to her parents and one to Veronica and Daniel, but had already received an inability to attend from Veronica by return mail. Would her parents treat her with the same indifference?

On Wednesday morning she needed more beads. She stepped out of the building onto the busy footpath and into sunshine where spring was putting in an early appearance. Two trams rattled past, ferrying commuters. Didi rolled stiff shoulders and began walking.

Until she caught sight of the girl she'd seen before near the apartment building. Hard to mistake the six-foot brunette and she was wearing the same velvet jacket she had worn before. And as on those previous occasions, her face was averted and she was hurrying away, disappearing into the swirl of pedestrians.

Didi pivoted on her heel and followed the woman for a few minutes, caught up with her as she was turning into a shopping mall. Her pulse kept time with her fast pace. She had to be right, had to… Didi's hand grasped velvet. The woman jerked, turned. Startled blue eyes met Didi's and she knew she'd been right. 'You're Amy.'

Her eyes darted behind Didi.

'It's okay. I'm Didi and I'm alone. He doesn't know.'

Amy stared at her. 'How do *you* know?'

'He carries your photo in his wallet.' Didi nodded. 'I've seen you near the apartment. I'm surprised he hasn't seen you too.'

'It's been close a couple of times.' Amy twisted her hands around her bag strap. 'He's still got my photo?'

'He wants you in his life, Amy.' When she just stood there, Didi continued. 'You've rung the apartment.'

Amy nodded as tears filled her eyes. 'Then I just chicken out. And he's nearly caught me outside the building…more than once. I turn away, then wish I hadn't.'

Didi slid her arm through Amy's. 'Let's find somewhere to talk…'

'Cameron puts a message in the missing persons column in the paper every month. That's how I know his phone number,' Amy said, stirring her coffee.

'So why haven't you contacted him?'

She stared at her cup. 'He'll think I'm after his money. I was a drug addict… Did he tell you?'

Didi scooped the froth off her cappuccino and watched her. 'Yes.'

'I've cleaned up my life. I've even got a job—only a sales assistant—but I'd like to study some day. I'm saving up.'

'Doesn't the fact he's put an ad in the missing persons tell you anything? He doesn't care about your past. He'd help you. He's set up a centre for kids and there's a new gallery opening this weekend. And you know why? Because he thinks about you. All the time. Let me help.' Didi reached out and covered Amy's hand. 'I'll arrange for you to meet; somewhere neutral if you like. Give me your phone number.' Didi pulled out her mobile.

'You won't tell him? Until I'm ready?'

'No. He doesn't even have to know it's you he'll be meeting. Let's make it Sunday.'

'Sunday?' Amy paled, her hand tightening on her cup. 'That's too soon.'

'No. It's not. He's been looking for you for too many years. I need your word, and I need your phone number.'

Amy nodded. 'Okay. Might as well get it over.'

She gave Didi her number, Didi stored it in her phone, then slipped it back in her bag. 'Remember, he loves you. Now, let's you and I get to know each other.'

'Calm down, you look fantastic and everything's under control,' Cameron reassured her as they headed into the gallery.

It was early, no one was here yet, but in half an hour the place would be full. Full of people who would be looking at her work. Influential people. Judging her creativity. Analysing her style and probably comparing it with Sheila's.

Bats were flapping their wings in her stomach; she'd kill for a glass of water. Or something stronger. She wiped her palms down her thighs as they entered the gallery. 'Oh…'

On the feature wall. *The Eternal Flame. Artist: Didi O'Flanagan.*

She couldn't help it; she rushed over and traced her name with a finger, tears springing to her eyes. 'I can't believe it.'

'Believe it,' said the deep voice she'd become so familiar with.

She took a few steps backwards for the full effect and looked at it through someone else's eyes. Vermilion silk threads leapt from the background of black silk. Living flames insinuating themselves in an abstract yet intricate design around silver filigree and smoked driftwood.

A glance around showed her smaller pieces amongst other artists' works. Her Temptation piece hung by itself on another wall.

'You'll be taking a lot of orders tonight, I guarantee it. Congratulations.'

'You've done a wonderful job with the displays. Thank you. For everything.' Their eyes met. This was it. Soon it would be time to say goodbye. Her commission was finished, their time was up. Why did the happiest night of her life have to be the saddest?

Cam saw the emotion in her eyes but, hard as it was to keep from responding, he wasn't saying anything yet. Later tonight he hoped to talk her into staying on longer. Perhaps, just perhaps, he could even think about taking their relationship to a new level. Although what that new level might look like was still unclear.

She looked stunning, as unique as her art. Like a model in a fashion magazine. Leggings in fabric of a black and white geometric puzzle reached to mid calf. She wore a sleeveless T-shirt in a similar pattern topped with a macraméd concoction of thin strips of grey leather and burgundy wooden beads. A heavy necklace of similar beads in dark red, black and ivory hung to her waist. Five wooden beaded bracelets adorned her arms. She had silver glitter in her spiked hair.

And he knew she wore his diamond necklace hidden next to her skin.

Two hours later he watched her talking animatedly with an art critic while photographers snapped pictures. She'd spoken to a throng of journalists. He'd heard her being touted as an emerging star in the art world. People were buying; not only her works but others. Champagne flowed as artists he'd supported celebrated.

'She's talented,' a female voice said behind him to another woman beside her.

Pride swelled inside him. Of course she was.

'Yes,' the other woman replied. 'She dropped off the social scene a few years ago. There were rumours…I heard she was virtually stood up at the altar.'

Cam stiffened, tempted to turn around and demand to know it all.

'Really?' The woman's interest was clearly piqued by this information.

'Such a shame; she was so looking forward to setting up house and starting a family. She was devastated. You know who she is, don't you? James O'Flanagan's daughter.'

James O'Flanagan? Didi's father—her family—was up there with royalty amongst Sydney's elite?

Shock slammed Cam mid-chest. His entire body felt as if it were losing structure, his foundations collapsing around him. How could he not have realised? He should have connected the name.

And it changed everything.

Bernie Boyd's son and James O'Flanagan's daughter…impossible. His hands balled into fists in his pockets. The press would waste no time digging up the dirt on him, tabloids would have a field day, and Didi's reputation as an emerging artist would be ruined—the public were an unforgiving lot.

Not to mention what James himself would have to say.

Cam didn't know the man personally but the way he'd treated his daughter was beneath contempt. At least Veronica had sent her apologies; she had a prior engagement, which apparently took precedence over her sister's special night. Her parents hadn't even acknowledged her invitation and Cam knew she was disappointed. What did that say about them?

He shuddered to think what the news about his background would do to the new career she'd fought so hard for. Here was Cam about to suggest their relationship continue. Unthinkable now. As if James O'Flanagan would approve of a live-in relationship for his daughter with the son of a criminal—hell, did O'Flanagan already know?

And Cam couldn't offer her anything more. Didi might not judge him the way Katrina had but she hadn't been totally honest about who she was either—what else hadn't she told him?

She hadn't told him she wanted a home and family some day.

And she deserved it—but he couldn't give her that, not with his background and his inability to commit. Better to get tonight over with as soon as and as sensitively as possible.

Feeling as if she were dancing on clouds, Didi floated out of the elevator then twirled around and planted a kiss on Cameron's mouth. 'Wasn't it wonderful? Spectacular? I'm a success! They're publishing an article in *Textiles* magazine *and The Age.* A TV interview, three more commissions—*huge* commissions—and every piece sold!'

Cameron smiled against her lips. 'I never doubted it. *You* were wonderful.' He kissed her again, his arms tightening around her. 'Spectacular.'

She wanted to linger a moment more but it seemed Cameron had other ideas because he broke contact and stepped back. 'Why the mysterious expression?' she asked.

'I have a surprise.'

'Am I going to like it? You look kind of…' Sad. Troubled. Now that she thought about it, he'd been quiet most of the way home. Probably because he hadn't been able to get a word in.

As he opened the apartment door the scent of flowers drifted out. She stared in disbelief. Bowls of roses covered every available surface. 'Oh… You arranged all this?' Her heart slammed against her chest as she took in the dining room. The finest dinnerware gleamed, two candles flickered in the centre of the table, their glow reflected in the night-darkened window. A bottle of champagne cooled in an ice-bucket. Dreamy Frank Sinatra love songs wafted from the stereo.

Romance, she thought. Who knew that Cameron Black knew how to do romance? Anticipation flickered along her veins like fireflies as he pulled out a chair.

'Sit,' he told her as he took a crisp napkin from her plate. He set it on her lap, then uncovered the silver dishes. 'I knew you wouldn't have time to eat at the gallery.'

'You were right,' she said, eyeing the supper. A plate of cold Italian antipasto, smoked salmon and capers with lemon wedges. A green salad. Two fluted glasses filled with a rainbow of exotic fruits, jelly and cream.

Again her stomach was jittering, her heart racing. A man didn't go to all this trouble unless he had something important to say. Did he?

He popped the cork, poured the bubbly and handed her a glass before sitting down himself and raising his own. 'To your success, Didi.'

His eyes, she thought, such emotion in his eyes. Anticipation fizzed inside her like the champagne bubbles tickling her nose. 'To *our* success. Your gallery—the whole complex—is going to help so many people.'

With their gazes spearing each other across the table they took a sip, set their glasses down. She waited, breathless for him to say something more.

He forked some antipasto onto her plate, then his own. 'What are your plans now, Didi?'

She blinked. *Her* plans? That wasn't what she'd expected to hear and the bubbles in her system deflated a little. A lot. She'd hoped he'd suggest some plans that included both of them. Together. 'I…um…I'm not sure yet. It kind of depends…' She waited for him to take her cue.

He bit into a cherry tomato, chewed a long time. 'Stay on here a few more days if you want to think about it. Unwind before you find somewhere else.'

Her heart stopped. Literally stopped. She was surprised it started again because it felt as if he'd sliced it open and her blood seemed to have drained into her feet. How could he sound so…detached after what they'd shared over the past three weeks?

What had she expected? It was over. *When the time's up I walk away, no complications on either side.* The deal—she'd said it herself. And meant it. How could she argue now?

'Thank you. But I'll be looking for somewhere tomorrow.' Her voice seemed to be coming from outside her. On the stereo Old Blue Eyes was singing about only having eyes for you, dear. Cameron couldn't have made a worse choice in music if he'd tried.

His eyes didn't meet hers as he said, 'There's no rush.'

'Oh, I think there is.'

He reached out, touched her fingers. 'It's been fun, hasn't it?'

'Fun.' She remembered their first kiss. *It was fun, Cameron.* Her own words mocked her.

'I've enjoyed our time together.'

'Yes…' She pulled her fingers away. He let her.

'Didi. The trick is not taking these kinds of arrangements too seriously.'

'You're so right. If you'll excuse me, I feel a migraine coming on. I… Thank you for…' she waved a trembling hand over the table '…this.' Somehow she made herself stand. 'If you don't mind, I'll need to sleep it off on my own. I'll just grab my stuff…'

Clutching her toiletries and fisting hot tears away, she closed the spare bedroom door behind her, leaned back against it. What had that poster said? *He's not the man you think he is.* She still didn't know what Katrina had meant by that, but she'd been right: he wasn't.

He was more.

And somehow that was worse.

It was over.

CHAPTER THIRTEEN

CAM braced his arms on the table, mashed his lips together and forced himself not to react visibly in any way as he watched Didi disappear down the passage. But inside…

Inside, some black beast was using Cam's heart as a punching bag. He had to clamp his hands to the table top to stop himself from going after her and telling her what this evening's supper had *really* been about.

Forget the rules they'd made, he'd been going to say. To hell with the three-week agreement. He wanted more, a lot more, and he knew she did too.

Okay, so he didn't do long-term—there'd be no harm in exploring where their relationship might go, right?

Until he'd learned who she was.

Pushing up, he extinguished the candles, killed the music, then scraped the barely touched supper into the bin. He figured neither of them would feel like eating any leftovers from the evening.

He sloshed more champagne into his glass, then took it out to the sky garden to watch the stars. Her big night ruined by this stupid idea of supper. A mistake of gigantic proportions. It could have been a night to celebrate success if their three-week arrangement on the side hadn't happened.

If falling in love with her hadn't happened.

He shook his head, blew out a long breath. For a man who didn't do commitment that was one hell of an admission.

His heart cramped with pain. And guilt. Because his loving her would be the worst thing that could happen to her, and it was all his fault. A man with his background wasn't good enough for Katrina, daughter of a future prime minister. He'd never come up to scratch for someone like James O'Flanagan's daughter.

She must never know.

He hurled his glass against the wall, watched it shatter. Like the pieces of his heart. The heart he'd sworn to keep intact.

He rolled out of bed at five a.m. How could he rest with the knowledge that she was leaving? How could he sleep with her scent on the pillow? Shaking his head to clear the memory of that fragrance against her skin, he saw yesterday's discarded clothes still on the floor—typical Didi. He was about to scoop them up and put them in the clothes hamper…but that wasn't going to work any more. She'd have no use for the hamper now.

It would be best all round if he stayed away today, he thought as he cleared away reminders of last night in the kitchen. He was still holding the candlesticks and wondering what he could do about the roses when Didi put in her appearance.

'Morning.' Her voice betrayed little of the emotion he'd seen last night. Tight, polite. Civilised. As if they were strangers.

And she had to work bloody hard at it, he thought. Her lips were a thin slash in a white face, her eyes shaded by her pink-tinted glasses.

Because everything looks rosy on the greyest of days. Even you.

'Good morning.' His own voice, tight and formal. He set the candlesticks on the kitchen bench with exaggerated control.

He must remember: *James O'Flanagan's daughter. She needs a career boost, she doesn't need you.*

She took juice from the fridge, poured herself a glass. 'I'm packing my stuff. Is it okay to store what I don't need here until I can make other arrangements?'

'Fine.'

'And my Temptation piece, you will make sure it comes back safely, won't you.'

Ah-h-h… 'Didi… Temptation was sold last night.'

She spun around, her eyes flashing fire. 'It was *not* for sale.'

'I'm sorry. The gallery assistant didn't know. It fetched a tidy sum of money.' And named a five-figure sum.

'Money had nothing to do with it.' But her voice calmed some and he could see her working the figure through and coming up with *Wow.* Still, she said, 'You had *no* right. *No right at all,* to let that happen.'

'The gallery's profits from the sale will go towards a good cause.' He turned away, busied himself wiping down the kitchen sink while he let her think about that. 'I'll be out of your way most of the day so you can take your time.'

'You will be home this evening, won't you?'

He turned back to see her eyes dart to his then away. Wary or concerned? Or something else…

'I can be,' he said, cautious. 'Why?'

She lifted a shoulder, taking an interest in the bottom of her glass. 'It's just I've got that free candlelight dinner. We may as well use it before I go. The table's booked for seven p.m. I'll be busy till then so I'll meet you there.'

Part of him wanted to leap at a second chance, another part warned him that leaping into anything remotely connected with Didi was very unwise at this juncture. He stayed where he was. 'I'd like that.' It was too easy to step closer, to breathe her in. 'We don't have to be strangers.' Friends. Only friends.

She rinsed her glass, busied herself drying it. 'Give me a call when you're in town, then.'

'In town?'

'I'm going home. To Sydney.'

It shouldn't hurt. He shouldn't feel as if he'd been sliced and diced. She was cutting ties, not flesh. An hour's flight away.

A world away.

'Didi, your art, the gallery…' *Me.*

She put the glass away, folded the tea towel precisely and hung it on the rail. 'The beauty of what I do is I can work anywhere. I'll continue to display my work in your gallery, if you want it.'

'Of course I do.'

She turned around, her back against the sink, hands spread either side along the counter top—the counter top where they'd shared that first skyscraper-demolishing kiss. Her eyes met Cam's and they were clear and direct for the first time this morning. 'It's time to talk with my parents. We have issues to resolve…I'll be staying with them a while.'

'You didn't tell me who your father is.' He could hear the accusation behind his own casually spoken words.

'No.' And her voice revealed her own surprise that he knew.

'I heard it mentioned. Last night.'

She nodded slowly and those clear eyes pierced his, searched his. Challenged his. 'I guess we both have our secrets, Cameron Black.'

Then she walked away and he had no choice—no bloody choice—but to let her go.

Didi packed what she needed to take to Sydney. The rest she put into boxes and stored them where Cameron had put them before she'd arrived here. When she was done, she rang Amy and arranged to meet her at the Candle-side restaurant at six forty-five p.m. Then she let herself out of the apartment and walked. Anywhere. Everywhere. Until it was time to play the last scene.

* * *

When Cam arrived home to dress for dinner he found the place empty. Since she'd told him she'd meet him at the restaurant, he showered, dressed and arrived at precisely seven p.m.

As he stepped inside candles of every colour, size and shape imaginable illuminated the restaurant, giving it a cosy ambience. He didn't see Didi.

'Did you have a reservation, sir?' A neatly pressed waiter appeared with a couple of menus.

'I'm meeting Ms O'Flanagan. She doesn't seem to be here yet.'

The waiter nodded. 'Right this way.' He led Cam to a row of booths along the back wall. 'Here we are, sir.'

'No…this…' His voice disintegrated as familiar blue eyes so like his own looked back at him. Not dulled with drugs and depression and lack of interest as he remembered, but smiling and clear and alive. His heart spun a circle inside his chest, and somewhere deep inside him an ache that had embedded itself there for fourteen years dissolved.

'Hello, big brother.'

He slid into the booth before his legs crumbled beneath him. 'Amy.' His voice barely rose above a whisper. 'How…?'

'Didi set it up.' Amy poured a glass of water from a pitcher, set it in front of him.

His hand shook as he reached for the glass and lifted it to numb lips. He took a long slow sip to steady himself before he spoke. 'I don't understand.' How long had Didi known and kept it a secret from him? 'Doesn't matter,' he muttered, and slid along the seat to crush his sister against him. To inhale fresh citrus shampoo instead of stale booze and dope.

'Where *is* Didi?' he asked finally, still holding Amy, unable to let go.

'She stayed long enough to make sure I didn't run out on you.'

'She was here?' Cam looked about him, hoping to catch a glimpse of her.

Amy nodded. 'She's seen me outside your apartment. She

caught up with me the other day and we had a long talk.' She twined her fingers with his, her eyes glinting in the candlelight. 'Now you and I are going to talk. Starting with the last time I saw you…'

'You love her, don't you.'

Cam's fingers tightened on his coffee cup. 'It's not that simple, Amy.'

'Yes. It is.' Amy's piercing blue gaze met his. 'You love someone you don't give up on them. Ever. You never gave up on me when you could have turned your back and walked away from a hopeless case.'

'This is different.' He stared into his coffee. 'Our relationship was only ever temporary.'

'So she says. You—'

He shook his head. 'She and her family have issues they need to sort out right now. She needs space.' But his heart was stirring to life in a way he'd never felt before. Was he ready to lay that heart on the line again?

Didi watched the reunion scene from a discreet distance through the restaurant's windows. In the dim candlelight Cameron was so focused on his sister, she knew he wouldn't notice her. But she could watch him for one more moment. A last glimpse through blurry eyes before she tore her gaze away and hurried to the waiting taxi outside.

Three hours later she was standing outside her parents' Rose Bay mansion with two bulging suitcases. She punched in the security code and the high wrought-iron gates swung open on smooth oiled hinges. The panorama of lawn and paved driveway stretched in front of her like a marathon course.

Head high, Didi. She'd done what she'd set out to do. She was a success. There should be a trumpet fanfare for her return, or at least two people waiting on the steps with open arms.

So why did she feel like a little girl again trying to win her parents' approval?

The porch light winked on but the house was in darkness as she rolled her suitcases up the drive.

She rang the bell, heard it echo down the hall. A neighbour's dog barked and the sounds of night stirred in the nearby rose bushes.

Digging out her old key, she fitted it to the lock and let herself in. The door opened with its well-known scrape of wood against wood. She hoped they hadn't changed the security code as she tapped it in but no ear-splitting noise eventuated.

Familiar scents assaulted her nostrils. Mum's French perfume and the smell of old carpet. The Ming vase still sat on the antique rosewood table in the hall.

Nothing had changed.

Everything had changed.

She dragged her cases upstairs, hesitated at her parents' bedroom door. The familiar gold rose-sprigged quilt but the paintwork was new. She wrote a quick note, left it on the bed, then headed to her old room.

Everything was as she'd left it. Pink. It was like stepping back years and that feeling of suffocation with it. *No.* This time it would be different, she told herself, shaking it away, unzipping her case and dragging out her toiletries.

She was going to work here—in Sydney. The only contact with Cameron Black would be through email when she had pieces to deliver. Apart from that, she would not think about him, ever again.

Bathroom ritual complete, she climbed into bed…

The next thing Didi was aware of was daylight and her mother watching her with tears misting her grey eyes. Her complexion was smooth as ever, and only her mum's hair could look as if it had been salon-done first thing in the morning—even if it had a few more streaks of silver than the last time she'd seen her.

Her own eyes filled. 'Mum.'

'Didi. Is everything all right? You're not in any kind of trouble, are you?'

'No. I should have let you know I was coming, but it was…kind of sudden.' She pushed up, ran a hand over her own tousled hair. 'I had thought I might see you and Dad on Saturday night.'

'Saturday night, dear?'

'You didn't get my invitation?'

'We just got back from the airport a short time ago. We've been up to Hayman Island for a couple of weeks. What invitation? Oh, Didi…' Her voice dropped to a whisper, her eyes widened. 'Not…'

Didi waved a hand. Clearly her mother thought she'd been fool enough to fall in love and be dumped again. 'No, Mum. Nothing like that.' She swung her legs over the bed, optimism flooding through her as she realised her parents hadn't come to her special night because they hadn't known. 'The gallery opening. I was commissioned—extremely generously—to do the focal piece of artwork for a new gallery supporting local artists. Did Veronica tell you?'

'She mentioned something about your work. And that you were living with a man.' Only a glint of disapproval in her eyes. 'At a very exclusive address.'

Ah, that made it okay, then, Didi thought, resentment burning beneath her breast. A man like Cameron Black with his money and power would always be welcome here.

Not to her, he wouldn't. Because she wouldn't let him be.

'We've been waiting for you to tell us,' her mother said. She brushed a hand over Didi's hair.

A simple gesture. Only a mother's love could trigger the emotion that washed over Didi, threatening to drown her. 'I didn't think you'd want to know…'

Her mum smiled. 'Of course we want to know. *You* cut us out of your life, Didi.'

'No.' She shook her head, reached for her mother and was enveloped by the warm familiarity of her slender yet sturdy shoulders. Shoulders she desperately needed, she realised. 'I'm sorry we argued. I needed to find my own niche.'

'We know you did, dear. We'll talk about that later, with your father. Right now I'm more concerned with what's brought you home after all this time.' She leaned back, her grey eyes searching Didi's and pinpointing it with dead accuracy. '*He* did, didn't he? The man who gave you the chance you've been waiting for.'

'Oh, Mum. I made a mistake.' Again. She snapped a handful of tissues from the box on the bedside table. 'This time I really think my life's over.'

Her mum straightened, held Didi at arm's length and drilled her with that familiar don't-be-ridiculous-Didi look. 'That's nonsense. It's just started. You've finally achieved what you wanted. *How* much did you say he paid you?'

Didi smiled through her tears, this time not taking her mother's glare so literally. 'I didn't. But it's enough to live on comfortably for a bit while I work on more commissions. I've got orders for more and…'

'The world's opening up for you.'

She nodded, amazed at her mother's support. She'd taken such different impressions with her when she'd left. Hugged them to her for years.

'Tell you what, why don't you have a shower, dress and come down to the kitchen?' her mum said. 'We'll all have brunch. Rosita should be in shortly.'

'Rosita still works for you?' she said, wiping her nose.

'She does. I'll have her whip up one of those omelettes you always liked.'

'I can't get over the fact that you're taking this new career in art so well,' Didi said, between mouthfuls of fluffy egg mixture. 'You never showed any interest.'

'That's unfair, Didi.' Her mother sliced her toast into neat little squares. 'We were worried you wouldn't get anywhere and you'd be devastated; you were always so intense. So serious.'

'Your words were art was a nice little hobby but what was I going to do for a real job?'

Her father's hazel eyes met hers over the table. 'We were worried you wouldn't get where you wanted. We wanted you to have something to fall back on. Not many people can make a living as artists. You wouldn't discuss it, as I recall,' her father continued. 'The moment I mentioned university it was as if I'd suggested life imprisonment.'

'I wasn't interested in academia, Dad. I wanted to create.' *Come back when you're serious.*

'Yes. We know.' The only sounds were cutlery scraping china. 'So we let you stand on your own feet and waited for you to come back.' Another silence. 'It's taken this long. Always were a stubborn little thing.' Wistfulness laced his gruff words. 'This is your home,' he went on. 'Always was, always will be, for as long as you want. I hope you see that now.'

Emotion was washing through her—guilt, regret. Love. 'I do, Dad. I know I was a disappointment to you. I wished I could be like Veronica, but I just couldn't.'

'Not a disappointment, Didi. A puzzle maybe, but never a disappointment. Until you left. You walked away in anger, and you held onto it. That anger tainted your perception of what family is all about.' He shook his head. 'It was never give-and-take with you, was it?'

'I think I'm learning how to do that now, Dad.'

He raised one bushy grey eyebrow. 'Well, that's good to hear.' He wasn't done, she noted as he set his cutlery on his plate and his elbows on the table. She just knew he was going to—

'Now,' he said. 'About this man Veronica spoke about. Cameron Black, isn't it?'

CHAPTER FOURTEEN

CAM took in the view through the reinforced gate designed to keep lesser people out. Old money. The wealth you inherited and enjoyed and never truly appreciated. And there it basked in all its glory in Sydney's spring sunshine. The James O'Flanagan Residence.

He wasn't impressed. Cam had the assets to build better, and he'd earned every cent of that wealth himself with his own blood, sweat and tears. In spite of the low-life he was biologically descended from.

He'd done a lot of soul-searching over the past long torturous and lonely week. Katrina's prejudiced perception of others was wrong, and dangerous. The people Cam wanted to know judged others by their words and actions, not where they came from.

People like Didi.

She was smart and clever, caring and beautiful, inside and out. One of a kind. And he wanted her in his life.

He sucked in a deep breath. The woman he'd come to convince was somewhere behind yonder stone façade.

But first he had to convince her father. Adjusting his jacket, he gritted his teeth against a sudden turmoil in his gut and buzzed the intercom. An employee, he assumed, answered with a hint of an Italian accent.

'My name's Cameron Black and I'm here to see Mr O'Flanagan.'

No, he wasn't expected, and yes, it was personal. He drummed his fingers against the pillar and waited. And waited.

Finally the gates swung open. He shouldered his bag and followed the smooth paved drive and its neatly trimmed hedge, aware that his movements were being tracked from one of those large glinting windows.

It wasn't the prospect of meeting James O'Flanagan that had his gut cramping, his mouth turning dry—he could face any man on an equal footing. But the thought of facing one small woman had him sweating inside his shirt in the chilly salt breeze blowing off the harbour.

Determination added extra length to his stride. He wasn't leaving until he'd seen Didi and said what he needed to say.

A middle-aged woman with long black hair tied back in a black ribbon showed him to a formal lounge room. She wore black trousers and a plain white blouse. He didn't sit as invited, but stood to attention looking out at a statue of Venus surrounded by never-ending lawn. A blue Sydney Harbour gleamed in the distance.

'Mr Black. Good morning.'

Cam swivelled to face the man with the crisp-edged voice. James O'Flanagan stood equal to Cam's own height with greying hair and a day's worth of stubble. For such a distinguished man he looked remarkably casual in a faded navy tracksuit.

His expression was anything but. Cool astute eyes studied Cam. His mouth remained firm but relaxed; a man in full control of the situation. Unlike Cam, who'd grown unaccustomed to being on the receiving end of such powerful scrutiny—and it all had to do with the woman he'd come to see.

'Cameron.' Cam stepped forward, hand extended, feeling as if he were facing his own execution. 'Good morning.'

James's handshake was brief and firm. 'If you're expecting to see Didi, she and her mother are out shopping at present.'

'It's you I wanted to talk to. My apologies—I didn't inform you I was coming. Frankly, I wasn't certain you'd see me.'

James indicated a hard-backed brocade chair, then seated himself in a silk-covered recliner. 'Why's that?'

Why indeed? Cam sat, smoothing clammy palms over his trousers. He felt a tad light-headed. Must be the early flight coupled with a missed breakfast. And the fact that he hadn't had more than a handful of hours' sleep since Didi had left. 'Didi's mentioned me, I presume.'

'Both my daughters have mentioned you. The question still stands—why did you think I wouldn't speak to a man who's been seeing a lot of my daughter in recent weeks? Some might say he's the one man I *would* want to speak to.'

Cam fought the urge to clear his throat. The sound would be another sign of nerves James would pick up on. 'Didi and I parted…Didi *left* under difficult circumstances.'

For the first time, James's mouth allowed a hint of humour to tease the edges. 'Sounds appropriate—Didi's always been difficult.' He tapped a fist against his chin and the humour disappeared. 'When you say parted, are you talking personally or professionally? I was under the impression you were offering her a permanent spot in your gallery and intended liaising with her on future sales.'

'That's true. I will continue to give her all the support she needs, wherever she chooses to base herself.'

'So it's personal.' Leaning back, he folded his arms, ostensibly at ease, but those cool eyes remained steady on Cam's. 'What has Didi told you about our family?'

Diplomacy, here. 'To be honest, not a lot. During our conversations she told me she felt as if she never fitted in.'

James nodded as if it came as no surprise. 'She certainly didn't fit the criteria for your average child and that's not changed. Did she tell you that at five years of age she cut her mother's imported silk brocade curtains up to make matching dresses for herself and her doll?'

Cam had to smile. 'Curtains were mentioned.' Just not the cutting of them.

'We tried everything. Best schools, overseas with extended family. We suggested uni; she wouldn't discuss it.' He shook his head. 'Never could compromise, that girl. In the end we had to stand back and watch her go. To let her find her own place, make her own mistakes. Damn hard not interfering.'

His eyes drilled Cam's and Cam knew he was referring to their living arrangements—*previous* living arrangements. He nodded. 'Didi makes her own choices.'

'Did she talk about Jay?' James asked.

She was virtually stood up at the altar. The words still rang in his head. 'Jay…'

'It was a whirlwind romance—too serious too fast. They were engaged in a matter of weeks. A couple more weeks he was gone, back to his former girl. Broke Didi's heart.'

A knife twisted in Cam's belly—he'd hurt her too. 'Killed me to see my little girl so gutted.'

Cam nodded. He knew the feeling well. Didi's father wasn't what he'd expected. He genuinely cared about her, and she couldn't see it.

Still, James O'Flanagan might seem like a reasonable guy, but would Cam still be of the same opinion in the next few moments? He took a steadying breath and rose. If he didn't have command of the situation at least he could feel that he was in control of his own body. Except that the floor shifted like quicksand beneath his feet and someone was siphoning the oxygen from the room because it was suddenly airless.

But Cam's gaze was direct, his focus steady as he faced James. 'I need to tell you—'

The sound of women's chattering spilled through the doorway, cut off the moment the two women appeared.

Cam felt it all the instant he laid eyes on Didi—the sexual

zing, as strong as ever, the flash of like recognising like. The quiet simmer of something stronger, something deeper—the foundation on which the rest was built.

She looked impossibly fragile and tiny in black leggings and an oversize windcheater, which had slipped off one shoulder exposing a turquoise bra strap and the glint of platinum chain he'd given her. He could smell her honey and almond scent from across the room.

Guilt rode him hard—that last evening he'd been so cool, so distant and unapproachable. He'd hurt her. He wanted to go to her, drag her into his arms, tell her he was sorry and never let her go, but he remained standing where he was.

Didi had heard Cameron's rumbling voice as she reached the open doorway and everything inside her, every thought, had spun in a thousand different directions. *Why was he here?*

And then she forced herself to peek inside and there he was. Looking at her as if he wanted to eat her up. He wore fawn trousers and a deep blue suede jacket that accentuated his navy eyes. His white casual shirt was open at the neck revealing his tanned throat.

'Hello, Didi.'

Ah, the way he said her name…as if she were special. She knew better but her heart clawed its way up her throat along with a rising humiliation, her green eco-shopping bags slipping from her fingers as the strength drained out of her.

Didi had never been afraid of anything or anyone. Not until she'd met Cameron. Not until she'd fallen in love—really in love. Jay had been a mere rehearsal for the ultimate performance.

She was afraid now.

Afraid of what he might say. Afraid of what she might do. Of what she wanted to do. Even now, after the cool way he'd ended it, she wanted to rush right over and hurl herself into his arms and beg him to take her back.

'What are you doing here?' Pride kept her voice firm and

prevented her from running in the opposite direction. Pride and a fragment of that inner strength she thought she'd lost but managed to grapple back. 'I don't want you here, Cameron, nor do I want to talk to you. Anything we have to discuss we can do via a phone call or email.'

'Didi,' her father rebuked mildly. 'We brought you up better than that.'

'I'm here to talk to your father,' Cameron said.

She reached down, picked up her grocery bags. 'I'm going to put these in the kitchen. Please be gone when I get back.' Somehow she managed to walk away, hearing her mother say, 'Well…give Didi a moment. It's nice to finally meet you, Mr Black. What refreshments can I offer you?'

And Cameron's, 'Thank you, but I'm fine for now. Maybe later.'

Which left Didi with two alternatives. She could hide or she could show him she was managing just fine on her own. *As they'd agreed.* And whatever he had to say to her father…well, it couldn't be worse than what he *hadn't* said to her, could it?

Moments later she stood at the doorway. Her parents were seated, her mother saying something inane about the weather while Cameron stood to stiff attention in the centre of the room, his hands behind his back. He turned the moment she stepped into the room and met her gaze.

'You're still here,' she said.

His posture straightened, something flashed in his eyes. 'I'm not leaving yet. I have something to say.'

'Give the man a chance, Didi, for God's sake,' her father ordered.

Holding her head high, she crossed the room, conscious of Cameron's eyes tracking her the whole way. She stood rigid beside the sofa.

Cam dragged his eyes from Didi's and directed his gaze at her father. 'If you do a background check on Cameron

Black you won't find me. Because my birth name isn't Black. It's Boyd. You may have heard of my father, Bernie Boyd. He was a known criminal and he died during a police chase.'

Silence rushed through the room. But James's expression didn't alter. He knew, Cam realised with a flash of insight. Of course he'd know. A man like James O'Flanagan would make it his business to know. He'd probably known the day after Veronica's visit.

Why hadn't he hunted Cam down?

'You never bothered telling me this stuff—why are you telling my parents?'

Cam turned at Didi's harsh voice. She was clutching her hands to her chest, her eyes grey and sharp, running him through.

'My father had a string of mistresses,' James said as if Didi hadn't spoken. 'He cheated on my mother for thirty years and drank himself into the grave. Does that make me a lesser man? I'd like to think not. I'd like to think I'm judged on my own merits.' He inclined his head. 'The same way I judge you, Mr Black. From what I've read about you, you made your fortune through sheer hard work. My enquiries have uncovered a man of persistence and integrity. A man I can respect and admire.'

Cam unclenched the hands he'd fisted behind his back. 'Thank you. I appreciate that.' The tightness in his chest eased, but only some.

He turned to the white-faced woman before him. He'd loved her the moment she'd voiced her low opinion of him loud and clear that first night. He just hadn't known it then. And she loved him too. She had to, he thought as something like panic skittered through him—his heart recognised hers.

Because love, he knew, was such a fragile experience—for both of them—he took a moment to soothe her with his eyes and spoke with a forced calm he didn't feel. 'Didi, why don't we go outside for a few moments? I'd like to talk with you privately—' he glanced at her parents '—if you'll excuse us?'

James nodded. 'Fine by me.'

'Why would I want to go outside with you?' she shot back in turbulent contrast. But he heard so much more behind the defiance and the stormy emotions in her eyes. Panic, pride. Passion.

'Because if you don't, I'll be forced to propose marriage to you in front of your parents and I really wanted to do that without an audience.'

Her breath hitched, her chin came up and shocked eyes stared back at him as twin spots of colour skidded along her cheekbones. 'You don't do commitment, why would you want to marry me? And you've just tried to convince them you're not suitable husband material.'

Would it always be this difficult with Didi?

Would he want her any other way?

'Maybe I've changed. Maybe I've had time to think about it. About us.' He pinned his gaze to hers, searching for the answer he wanted. Needed. The answer he knew was there. He was barely aware of Didi's parents making their way to the door.

Keeping his eyes on hers, he crossed the few steps separating them and wrapped his hands around her upper arms. 'I'm not asking them to marry me, I'm asking you. Damn it, Didi.' He gripped her arms tighter, gave a little shake. 'Look at the mess you're making of this.'

'Me?'

'Yes, you. You stubborn, difficult woman. I thought I'd ruin your reputation as an artist if people discovered my background and I was associated with you in a personal way. I didn't say what I wanted to ask you on that last night—what I'd planned to ask—because I didn't want to jeopardise your future. You'd worked so hard for success.'

'Yes. And you gave me the opportunity I needed.' She smiled for the first time. Only a tiny smile but it lit him from the inside out, spreading warmth through his limbs and hope in his heart.

He'd missed that smile. He'd missed her mess in the dining room, her clothes on the floor in his bedroom, her quick wit and charming idiosyncrasies. He'd missed her tousled hair tickling his nose as he slept.

'What had you planned to ask me?'

'I wanted to ask you to stay, to continue what we'd started.'

The smile faded. 'You mean our little arrangement. I would have said no.'

In the silence that seemed to stretch to eternity he heard birds, the sound of cutlery rattling somewhere in the house. The sound of his heart splintering into a million pieces. 'Would you mind telling me why?'

'Because it wouldn't have worked, Cameron.'

Desperation clawed its way back, his slippery hold on hope sliding through his fingers and they tightened once more. 'No, it wouldn't. I realised that when you walked out of my life. Because it wouldn't have been enough. Because I love you. And you love me. Which makes marriage our best option.'

A soft choking sound issued from her throat but he couldn't see her expression because her head dipped forward. Taking that as a promising sign—he refused to take it any other way—he grasped her hands and flattened them against his shirt.

'Or we could compromise,' he murmured against the top of her head. 'It wouldn't be my choice, but if we extended our arrangement by, say, sixty years or so… Exclusivity would be non-negotiable, however.'

Didi wanted to stand just like this, safe in Cameron's aura of warmth for ever. Breathing in his scent, watching the way his chest moved as he breathed, listening to his heart. He loved her. He'd let her leave because he thought her career meant more to her than him and he wanted to protect it.

With her palms against his hard-muscled belly, she lifted her gaze from the weave of his shirt to the V of flesh at his neck, his Adam's apple, the tiny patch of stubble he'd missed when shaving. The strong chin and those gorgeous lips. Last of all, she met his eyes, marvelling at the depth of emotion she saw there. Not clouded with denial the way she'd seen them on that last night, but naked and transparent, and, right now, tormented.

'If you think I'm going to live sixty years as your mistress, think again.'

'Di—'

'Shh.' She cut him off with a finger to his lips. 'Not another word. There's a place…' Entwining her fingers with his, she tugged him towards the door.

And what better place than the gazebo at the bottom of the garden where the wisteria perfumed the air and a butterfly chased a gentle breeze over the lawn?

She sat on the wooden seat, patted the space beside her. When he didn't sit, she looked up at him, shading her eyes from the sun's glare. All she could see was his silhouette; she couldn't read his expression and a little quiver of doubt rippled through her. Had she gone too far back in the house?

'Well?' she prompted in a very feminine coquettish fashion she'd never heard come out of her mouth before. 'I've provided the privacy and the place. You mentioned something about a proposal… You've told, you've suggested, but you haven't *asked*.'

He moved out of the glare. His face looked unusually harsh, the lines deeper around his thinned mouth, the sun bleaching the usual colour from his normally tanned skin. His voice was subdued when he said, 'Do you *want* me to ask, Didi?'

'I love the man you are,' she said softly. 'I love the way you've kicked adversity in the teeth and made something of your life despite all its obstacles. I love your compassion, your strength, your caring nature towards others. I love that you took me into your home when you didn't know me, even when I publicly embarrassed you that first night and gave me a chance to shine.

'I love *you,* Cameron Black, Cameron Boyd—whatever your name is, I love you.' She smiled up at him with all that love in her heart shining in her eyes. 'So yes, I want that very much.'

The smile he gave her in return was like the sun itself and she basked in the glow as it spread through her. 'Not quite yet,' he said, placing one foot on the seat beside her, leaning forward so she could smell his fresh soaped skin. 'You exploded into my life like a fireworks display, all noise and colour and energy. I'd never met any woman quite like you. A little pixie with no qualms about taking on the big guns and arguing—vociferously—for your fellow evictees. Losing your job in the process.'

'Pixie, huh?'

His smile widened as he danced his fingertips over her blonde spikes. 'I was absolutely enchanted. Still am. Always will be. But it was more,' he went on. 'You brought the spark that's been missing in my life. You taught me to look at things from a different perspective. We come from different worlds, Didi, and I want you to share your world with me the way I want to share my world with you. I don't want no-strings with you, Didi. I want nothing less than marriage, commitment, the works. But I'll compromise if I have to. If you'll have me.'

Tapping on the booted foot resting on the seat beside her, she smiled up at him. 'So get on with it—ask already,' she whispered.

He crouched in front of her and took her face in his palms. 'I said it before and I'll say it again, and I'll go on saying it for the rest of my life. I love you, Didi. Will you be my wife? You and me together for ever and a piece of paper telling us so.'

'Yes,' she breathed. 'Oh, yes.'

The kiss he pressed to her lips was the sweetest kiss she'd ever known, tasting of sunshine, tenderness and passion. Love. The kind that would last a lifetime. Twining her arms around his neck, she deepened the kiss, wanting to show him his feelings were returned multifold.

Finally, he drew away, pulled a little box out of the inside pocket of his jacket. 'I was hoping you'd say that. In fact I was counting on it.' He flipped the lid.

'Ah-h-h…' A solitaire diamond flanked on either side with two pink teardrop diamonds that matched the one on her necklace. She had to press her fingers to her nose to stop it prickling. 'I couldn't have chosen anything better.'

It winked like fire in the sun as he slipped it on her finger.

She looked at its sparkle of promise, then up at him. At the depth of emotion in his eyes, at the smile curving his lips. She watched as those lips drew closer once more, her heart filled with love and hope and happiness.

Then he was kissing her and her heart simply overflowed. Here was rightness; this was what she'd searched for. A man who could accept her as she was, who valued her work and would work beside her.

And not only did he value her work, he valued her. With Cameron she was someone for whom she would come an absolute first. She fitted in. She belonged. She belonged with him in a way she'd never belonged with her family.

When they finally drew apart and she settled against his side, she asked, 'What would you have done if my father's reaction had been different?'

'I'd have asked you anyway, then figured out a way to get him onside. I was hoping you'd still want me, baggage and all. We complement each other. The people I want in my life don't care about one's family background. I kind of figured you'd be the sort who'd thumb your nose at anyone who'd snub your art on account of who your husband is.'

'Damn right I would. But there's something I want to know and I never got a chance to ask you on that last night. Why did you name the gallery the Irene Black Memorial Gallery? You never mentioned her until your speech at the gallery opening.'

'Irene Black was my maternal grandmother. I can't

condone what she did in disowning her daughter, but she gave me the kick-start I needed in the form of a single lump-sum deposit into my virtually non-existent bank account.

'Apparently she came to watch me one day when I was shovelling cement on a construction site as an eighteen-year-old. She tracked my movements over the months, saw how I was trying to cope with Amy and made contact.

'I only met her that once. She died a week later. Alone. I was robbed of knowing my grandmother. I changed my name to hers in her honour.'

'I'm sorry, Cameron.' She touched the tiny crease that had formed between his brows and kissed the shadows from his eyes. 'But you have family now. Amy. Me. My parents. And, for better or worse, Veronica.'

'Yes.' He nodded, shook off the melancholy. 'Speaking of for better or worse, in your family I guess it's the big white society wedding?'

Not if Didi could help it. She smiled at him. 'What would you prefer?'

'The two of us and a marriage celebrant.'

She felt a grin coming on. 'So we'll compromise. It'll still be the big white dress and wedding cake, but we'll invite only our immediate family and have it here in the gazebo. How does that sound?'

He kissed her lips. 'Perfect.'

EPILOGUE

Melbourne, two months later

'WHERE are we?' Didi's hands curled over the blindfold Cameron had insisted she wear for the drive he'd promised would be short but was taking far too long.

'Patience, Mrs Black, we're nearly there.'

Finally the car slowed and stopped. She could barely wait until Cameron opened the door. Then he swept her up against his chest. She could feel the sun on her cheeks, hear birdsong and someone mowing their lawn, kids shouting and the rrrrch of their skateboards as they sped past.

He stopped.

'What?' she demanded.

'I can't decide where…'

'You always were the sort to take too long to think things over. Enough.'

'And you're always too impatient.'

The outdoor noises faded, the warmth of the sun on her skin cooled and she knew he was taking her indoors. But where?

He stopped again, set her on her feet. 'Ready?'

She dragged the blindfold off. And looked straight at her Temptation. 'You said it was sold. It *was* sold—you gave me a very large cheque to prove it.'

'I couldn't bear to part with it,' he murmured behind her. 'What do you think—should it go here or in the bedroom?'

'You mean…this place is…'

'Ours,' he said. 'Yours and mine. It's home.'

Home. Warmth geysered up inside her.

She spun around, taking in the room with its mish-mash of homey-looking furniture. Furniture that looked vaguely familiar. Furnishings and décor she'd commented on in the numerous *House & Garden* magazines Cameron had taken to reading of late.

She turned to the window overlooking a backyard and cottage garden crammed with a kaleidoscope of colours. A place to breathe, to watch the seasons come and go. 'But we have your apartment.'

'You once said you couldn't bear to live in an apartment.'

'No garden, fresh air, sky or pets. I remember. But—'

He took her hand and led her towards a closed door. 'Come with me.'

When he opened the door Didi saw a modern kitchen with just about every modern appliance ever made. And in the corner—

'Charlie!' Surrounded by four mewling kittens.

'Charlotte,' Cameron corrected as she rushed over to fondle him…her.

'Oh, I've missed you so so much.' She stroked the silky fur, careful not to disturb the nursing babies. 'No wonder I thought he—*she*—was putting on weight. I thought it was my care and attention.'

She stretched up on tiptoe to twine her arms around Cameron's neck. 'She'll always be Charlie to me. Thank you.'

'You're welcome. We have a big backyard that'll accommodate as many pets as you want. Within reason,' he suggested.

She smiled up at him. 'Five's good. Although maybe we

could get a dog some time…' The kiss that inevitably followed was long and lingering. 'Are you sure you want to give up apartment living?' she said when at last he drew back.

'I'm sure. Circumstances change. Now we need somewhere with more space—a place for you to create your masterpieces. A garden for Charlie and her brood and room to grow…'

'Speaking of growing…' Didi felt a naughty smile coming on as she drew him back to the living room with its plump green sofa. Naughty for twelve-thirty on a working day. But then, that was becoming something of a habit lately. She looked pointedly at her Temptation mural. 'If we're going to create our own little masterpiece together…we should get started.' Pulling him down on the sofa she began undoing buttons.

'There's a nice soft bed you haven't seen yet,' he murmured, helping her.

'We'll get to that,' she told him. 'Later.'

And they did.

Much later.

Cameron took the rest of the afternoon off.

* * * * *

Playboy Boss, Live-in Mistress

KELLY
HUNTER

Accidentally educated in the sciences, **Kelly Hunter** has always had a weakness for fairytales, fantasy worlds, and losing herself in a good book. Husband…yes. Children…two boys. Cooking and cleaning…sigh. Sports…no, not really—in spite of the best efforts of her family. Gardening…yes—roses, of course. Kelly was born in Australia and has travelled extensively. Although she enjoys living and working in different parts of the world, she still calls Australia home.

Visit Kelly online at www.kellyhunter.net

For those who dare to believe.

CHAPTER ONE

ALEXANDER WENTWORTH THE THIRD could be a very patient man when he wanted to be.

Take the stock market, the money market, the futures market, *any* market, for example… When it came to waiting for the opportune moment, Lex had been known to exhibit the patience of Job.

If an eight-knot wind was blowing north-north-east off the Cornwall coast, and he had no place to be but on his yacht and nothing to do but set a course and peel a diamond-encrusted bikini off a beautiful woman, Lex could be very patient indeed. Journeys of seduction were meant to be savoured and savour them he did. Frequently.

Yes, indeed. Patience was one of Lex's many virtues.

Unfortunately, his current stock of patience was fading fast, and it wasn't just because he was fifteen hours into a twenty-five hour flight from London to Sydney, with a stopover in Singapore still pending. It was because his temporary personal assistant had a God-given talent for driving him nuts.

Sienna Raleigh was her name; personal assistant and right-hand man her latest trade. She had a doctorate in Renaissance Art, impeccable if somewhat colourful lineage, and a smile that could drop a man at fifty paces. Sienna had been five when they'd first met. Lex had been all of eleven, and her failure to acknowledge his superiority in all things had both irritated and intrigued him. He should've taken it as a warning never to employ her, he thought glumly. He really should've made an effort and crushed her insurgency some twenty years ago, the moment he'd first set eyes on her, he deduced with a sigh. Because he didn't have a hope in Hades of crushing it now.

'Any more stock reports to read?' he asked her.

'You mean apart from the dozens you've already read?' she said, without lifting her gaze from the book she was reading. 'No.'

'Any more newspapers?'

'You've read all those too.'

'Just checking.' He waited a beat. 'What's that you're reading?'

'An airport novel.' Sienna's long-suffering tone served only to amuse him. Clearly the nut-driving worked both ways. 'I'm up to the part where our hero—due to a combination of strength, determination, brilliance, luck, and fortuitous plotting—single-handedly nabs the villains and then walks away from the traitorous yet agonisingly beautiful woman who betrayed him.'

'Sounds reasonable,' he said. 'Keep me posted.' He drummed his fingers on the armrest, flicked through the entertainment channels. Sighed.

Sienna looked up at him from her book, those golden brown eyes with their tiny flecks of green revealing acute exasperation and a refreshing lack of guile. 'Admit it,' she said. 'You have the attention span of a gnat.'

'I do not.'

'And you want my book.'

'No, I don't. Unless of course you're finished with it.'

'I'm not.'

'Because it certainly sounds like the end to me.'

'There's an epilogue.'

'You actually *read* epilogues?'

'Wouldn't want to miss anything,' she said sweetly. 'Attention to detail is what you pay me for, remember? It was in the job description.'

'Wasn't catering to my every whim in the job description too?' he asked. 'I thought it was.'

'Maybe in *your* draft. Your former PA removed all references to slavery before she sent it out.'

'She *was* an uncommonly good PA,' he said on a sigh, and meant every word. 'I still don't understand how she could choose marriage and motherhood over working for me.'

'Unfathomable,' said Sienna a little too dryly for comfort.

'You like working for me, don't you?'

'Lex, I've been working for you for three days and so far it's been bedlam. I've rescheduled five meetings, changed our travel arrangements twice, kept an investment bank president on hold for fifteen minutes, begged your former PA to return on a daily basis, and vowed to shoot you at least a dozen times.'

'What can I say?' he said. 'It's been a slow week. You'll like the set-up in Australia, though. Trust me.'

Sienna ran her hand along the leather armrest and looked around the spacious cabin area as if assessing the benefits of business-class travel, before turning an amused gaze on him. 'Speaking of the set-up in Sydney…I still don't think it's a good idea for us to share a house while we're there. A month is a long time, Lex.'

'It's not a house, it's a business hub,' he said. 'And you'll have an entire wing to yourself and a commute to work of approximately fifty metres. None of my other PAs ever complained of it.'

'None of them are still working for you either. What if I want to get away from you and the work? What if I want to entertain? What if *you* want to entertain?'

'Will you have *time* to entertain?' he countered.

'Who knows?' She stood and stretched, giving him a nose to navel view of an impossibly tiny waist and firmly rounded buttocks. 'I might.'

Not if he had anything to do with it. Which—as fortune would have it—he did.

It occurred to him, not for the first time during these past few days, that Sienna might just have a point. That sharing adjoining quarters with her these next few weeks was going to prove far more of a challenge than he'd anticipated. He and Sienna hadn't seen much of one another these past few years. Different paths, different lifestyles, that was what he'd told his mother and anyone else who'd asked. Childhood friends often drifted apart, end of story, and if there was another reason he'd kept his distance lately, well, that was for him to know and no one else. When it came to Sienna, Lex's body and brain were not in alignment. His brain wanted his role in Sienna's life to be much the same as it always had been. Protector, mentor, occasional antagonist.

His body just wanted her naked beneath him. Hotly responsive. Possibly begging…

'Lex.'

Right voice, wrong tone altogether. Where was the breathless pleading? The dulcet whimpers of a woman with nothing but fulfilment on her mind?

'Alex!'

Whoa! He looked up with a start to find Sienna staring down at him in exasperation as she dangled some sort of report in front of his nose—a prospectus for a Shanghai construction company about to list on the New York stock exchange, to be exact. He'd mentioned the company in passing a couple of days ago but hadn't expected her to follow up on it. 'For me? Aw, you shouldn't have.'

'Think of it as the toy truck every mother in the known universe keeps in her handbag for when she's out and about and wants her fractious toddler to behave.' She fixed him with the queen of all challenging smiles, then picked up her book and settled back into her seat. 'Enjoy.'

'No, really. You shouldn't have. They're heavily invested in the US sub-prime housing market. They're going down.'

'Then see what you can pick up in the fire sale. Isn't that what you do?'

She had a point. She did have a point. But he didn't feel like reading any more. He needed to diffuse some of the sexual awareness currently tying him in knots, and if seduction wasn't an option—and it *wasn't*—then an argument would have to suffice. All he had to do was pick a reason, any reason. Maybe he *should* voice those mostly brotherly instincts and tell her that entertaining another man while living under his roof was out of the question. 'About us living together…'

'You mean about us occasionally meeting each other outside of working hours in common entertainment areas?' Sienna arched a delicate eyebrow and smiled a hoyden's smile. 'And what we should do if the other person has someone else with them?'

Lex smiled back, every sense sharpening beneath his lazy façade. She *did* want to fight. It would be churlish of him not to oblige. 'If you happen upon me while I'm entertaining, I will of course introduce you to my companion and quite possibly ask you to join us, at which point you will in all likelihood refuse and give me one of those looks—yes, that's the one—and take yourself off elsewhere. Does that sound reasonable?'

'Does that scenario work both ways?'

'Well…no.' He loved the way her eyes flashed fire and her chin came up. 'Should *you* wish to entertain, I'll require three days' notice and a thorough background check on the individual, or individuals, concerned. How does that sound?'

'Restrictive.'

Perfect. 'One can never be too careful. Imagine how you'd hate yourself if you were played for a fool by a reporter after an inside story on *me*. You'd be crushed. And I just know that *somehow*—in some nebulous parallel universe accessible only to the female psyche—it would be all my fault.' He shook his head sorrowfully. 'Make that five days notice. I hate being the one at fault.'

'You think I can't recognise a reporter when I see one?' she said with the quirk of an eyebrow. 'With *my* family background?'

'You're right,' he said, conceding yet another strategic point. Not a problem to his way of thinking given that the entire aim of this conversation was not necessarily to win but to fight. Sienna's mother had been many years older and several hundred million dollars wealthier than her artist husband. The press had feasted on the disparity for years, but the banquet had really started with Sienna's mother's alleged suicide. The squandered millions. The faithless husband. The forged will and the missing paintings. Two months after Sienna's mother died, her father had played chicken with a freight train and lost, and the gutter press had started up again. Eventually, thankfully, they'd moved on to newer, juicier stories but Sienna's loathing for the press and her reluctance to step anywhere near the limelight remained. 'Bad example. A reporter wouldn't last five minutes with you. But what say a thief tried to woo you in order to gain access to the complex? Know anything about thieves?'

A fleeting smile crossed the generous curve of her lips. 'People call you a thief, Lex. I know a lot about you.'

He knew what people called him. He'd heard it all before and was prepared to let the insult pass. Actually, no, he wasn't. This time the insult rankled. Time to ramp this argument up a notch. 'I pay for what I take.'

'You pay a pittance for what you take—then you break it down, repackage it, and make a fortune,' she said with brutal accuracy. 'Doesn't matter if it's legal, Lex. To some people's way of thinking, you're still a thief.'

'The technical term is corporate raider.'

'Raider, brigand, pirate...thief.' Her eyes challenged him to explain the difference. Presuming there *was* a difference.

'Those companies have been ruined by mismanagement, overextension, or plain old neglect long before I ever arrive on the scene,' he argued. 'I'm not responsible for that.'

'No,' she said. 'You're right, you're not.' Sienna opened her mouth as if to say more, but closed it again without uttering a word. She opted instead for opening her book and trying to ignore him, but he wasn't about to let her off the hook that easily. He reached over, took the book from her hands and shoved it down the side of her seat.

'Say it,' he said curtly. 'Whatever you were about to say, say it.'

Sienna looked mutinous, not to mention defensive. Lex knew from experience that following orders—his or anyone else's—was not her strong suit. But then she spoke.

'You could save those companies, Lex. Turn them around rather than tear them to pieces.'

'I *knew* that was where you were heading with this. I knew it!' He'd wanted an argument, he reminded himself bleakly. Just not this one. 'It's not that simple.'

'I realise that. But you could save them—'

'You give me far too much credit.'

'—if you wanted to,' she finished. 'You just don't want to.'

'You're right. I don't,' he murmured and felt his shoulder muscles bunch and tighten, and all because of a criticism he'd heard a thousand times before. He'd had enough of this flight. Of Sienna's criticism. Of wanting Sienna in his arms with one breath and wishing her a million miles away with his next. He'd had more than enough of that.

He half rose from his seat, trying to get past her so he could go somewhere else. Somewhere Sienna's measuring, questioning gaze wasn't, but she didn't shrink back in her seat to let him past like any normal person would do. Oh, no, she didn't do that. Now that he'd pushed her to state her case, she wanted a reply. 'This isn't about fixing other people's mistakes,' he said curtly. 'It's about capitalising on them. Darwin's theory of evolution fits the corporate business model to perfection. It's survival of the fittest, the fastest, the strongest, and the smartest. Not to mention the most ruthless.'

'Where's your sense of social responsibility?' she asked quietly.

'With me and mine.'

'Working with you these past few days has been such a revelation.' Her green on gold gaze held him prisoner; she would not back down. 'Just when you think you know a person…'

He smiled mirthlessly. 'What? You didn't think I was ruthless?'

'Not that ruthless.'

'Well, now you know.' He could have brushed past her then, would have if he hadn't made the fatal mistake of dropping his gaze to her lips, those soft, perfectly shaped lips. He leaned down, put his hands on the armrests either side of her and moved in close, until his mouth almost brushed hers. 'Want to be mine, Sienna?' he whispered with more than a lick of temper to his words.

She went perfectly still. As if she'd forgotten how to move, how to breathe. As if he were the predator and she the prey, thought Lex, and felt his body respond to the notion with savage satisfaction. Embracing it, savouring it, as simmering temper turned into a different kind of heat altogether. 'Breathe,' he whispered.

'No.' Her voice sounded thready, uncertain, and the beast inside him purred.

'You'll die if you don't.'

She took a breath and released it raggedly before easing slowly back against the seat, her startled gaze not leaving his. 'Breathing's not the problem here,' she muttered and took another shaky breath. 'I'm on it, see? But I'd rather not be yours.'

'No?' Lex smiled grimly and slid his gaze down her body. At first glance, Sienna's body language backed up her words. Her hands were ironing out the creases in her little pink skirt, smoothing the material down towards her knees as if she would have liked a couple more inches of fabric. Her knees pressed primly together, barring his way, and she'd tucked her legs tightly against the seat, demure-schoolgirl-style. Alas, there was nothing demure about her delicate pink sandals. Those shoes were all grown up.

So were other things about her.

At her throat he noticed the frantic beating of a pulse gone wild.

Outlined against her fitted white business shirt he could see the unmistakable imprint of nipples gone hard.

Sienna Raleigh, childhood nemesis and bane of his existence, was all hot and bothered. By him.

Somewhere down in the purely primal recesses of his being, Lex found the notion deeply, *deeply* satisfying. He pulled back to stare broodingly down at her. That tiny telltale reaction was going to cost her. It was going to cost them both. 'Just when you think you know a person…' he echoed softly.

Sienna was the first to look away.

'Tell me something, Sienna. If you don't like what I do for a living and you don't want to share a house with me for the next month, why the *hell* did you come to me and ask me to train you as a PA in the first place?'

'You could have said no,' she said finally, still not deigning to look at him.

'You have no idea how close I came to saying exactly that.'

'Then you should have!' She speared him with a lightning glance before looking away again quickly. 'I'd have understood.'

No, he thought. You wouldn't have. Not until I'd shown you exactly what I want from you these days. Not until now. Lex smiled tightly as the bonds of childhood friendship warred with the desires of a man well used to taking what he wanted. 'You started this,' he said softly.

'You could have said no.' Her voice was low, stricken. She knew damn well what she'd set in motion. She knew *him*. 'Why didn't you?'

'When have I ever said no to you, Sienna?' He had to

get out of here, now, before he covered her lips with his own and smashed a lifelong friendship to smithereens. 'When?'

Sienna watched through hot eyes as Lex strode down the aisle away from her, her mind whirling as she replayed the events of the last few minutes. How on earth had they gone from good-natured bickering to smouldering awareness to outright warfare in the space of a few heartbeats? Lex was her *friend*. Practically the brother she'd never had. He spent half his life needling her and the other half protecting her. That was what he did. What he'd always done. That was how their relationship worked. How dared he bring his sexuality into play and use it against her? How *dared* he give her The Look.

Sienna knew that look. It had brought countless perfectly sensible, rational women to their knees, desperate for more of him.

Sometimes Lex gave more. Any lover of his could expect a significant initial outlay of his time and attention. Rumour had it they could expect generous access to his money and possessions. Extremely generous access to his body. Unparalleled dedication to theirs.

For a time.

Until Lex had satisfied his curiosity, at which point he was gone, leaving hitherto sensible, rational women weeping in his wake, savagely cursing his focus, his stamina, and the sheer animal beauty of him, right before begging him to return.

Lex was a charming rake—just ask any woman he'd ever taken to his bed. Sienna *knew* that. Accepted it. Despised it. And for the most part ignored it—secure in the knowledge that her relationship with him was different. It always *had* been different.

Until now.

What was he doing messing with a perfectly good friendship that was manageable, mildly acerbic, and, above all, safe? Who in their right mind would throw away twenty years of friendship on a brief bedroom romp?

Not her.

So what if she'd found the full force of Lex's sexuality exhilarating? So what if she'd come closer than ever before to understanding *why* women were willing to accept Lex on his terms—on any terms—and to hell with the heartbreak? That still didn't mean she wanted to *become* one of them. No, no, and no!

Oh, look. He'd found a flight attendant. Now he was smiling crookedly at the woman; murmuring to her. Now she was smiling back. Surprise surprise.

Now Lex turned to look down the aisle towards her, a vision of careless elegance in a miraculously rumple-free business suit minus the tie. What was it about lean, dark-haired, grey-eyed men in charcoal-coloured business suits and snowy white shirts that made a woman look twice, and then—if it was Lex—again? Did his obvious wealth lend him an air of sophistication, success, and sex appeal or was it all just Lex? Would her sudden acute awareness of him disappear if she pictured him standing there in, say, grandfather pyjamas? The ones where the waistband of the trousers resided just below the armpits and the buttons went all the way to the neck. Not the sexy low-slung grey-striped cotton trousers she'd shoved in his carry on luggage yesterday. Now was definitely not the time to imagine him in those.

Oh, dear.

Sienna grabbed for the arm of a passing attendant. 'Water,' she croaked. 'Please.'

'Of course.' The attendant took one look at her and

decided to hustle. Did she look pale? She felt ashen. Did she look ill? She felt as if the world had suddenly tilted off its axis and no matter what she did she couldn't set it right again. She didn't *want* Lex to look at her like that. She didn't want to be one of his conquests.

Did she?

Lex started down the aisle and Sienna quickly looked away and braced herself for his return to a seat that was suddenly far too close to hers for comfort. She tucked her legs against her seat as Lex swept past her. Keep going, Lex, well done, breathe out.

'Good news,' he said as he settled into his seat, his voice casual, as if he'd decided to forget all about their earlier altercation. 'We're landing in Singapore in twenty minutes. We can go into the terminal. Stretch our legs, stock up on airport novels and newspapers. There's an executive lounge area that has internet access. Showers too.'

'So much to do, so little time,' she said, but she was grateful for both the impending stopover and Lex's efforts to put their relationship back on its normal footing. Forgetting all about the upheavals of the last ten minutes was a mighty fine plan to her way of thinking. Being able to get away from Lex for a spell was an even better idea. 'You shop, I'll shower.'

'A good PA would stay by my side and see to my needs,' he said.

She knew the basic philosophy but even so… 'Even in transit?'

'Especially in transit.' Lex smiled grimly. He'd been doing that a lot lately. 'Maybe it's a good thing I *was* prepared to take you on and train you up. Imagine if you'd taken that job with the oil sheik in Dubai? OPEC would never have been the same again.'

'The sheik didn't think I'd make a mess,' she said tartly. '*He* thought I could do it.'

'The sheik was besotted with you, Sienna,' said Lex darkly.

Unfortunately, Lex was correct. It was one of the reasons she hadn't taken the job. The other reason, and it galled her to admit it, had been her lack of experience in all matters pertaining to the business of being a good personal assistant. She'd needed experience. Lex had needed an assistant for a month while he was in Australia. Sienna had no aversion whatsoever to visiting the colonies. Sienna had long overdue personal business she could attend to while in Australia. The entire plan had seemed like such a good idea.

At the time.

'Thank you for agreeing to this, Lex,' she said awkwardly. 'I do appreciate it. Really. And I didn't mean to question your business ethics, earlier. I just…wanted to understand.'

'And now that you do?' He looked wary. Defensive. 'Do you still want to be my PA for the month, Sienna?'

'Yes.' She shoved her newfound awareness of him aside, took another deep breath and collected her scattered wits. 'If you're skilful enough to take bits and pieces of broken companies and put them together in ways that work, then I'm all for it. I was in fix-it mode before. Now I'm thinking salvage. Corporate recycling. I'm all for recycling.'

'Recycling,' he said disbelievingly.

'Absolutely.' She offered up a smile for good measure.

'You've missed your calling,' he told her. 'Corporate public relations needs you.'

Sienna felt her smile widen. This was the Lex she knew and understood. *This* Lex she could handle. 'So what exactly is it that you want me to *do* while we're in transit?'

He stared at her through narrowed assessing eyes and Sienna stared back with as much calm as she could muster. After what seemed like an eternity Lex bestowed on her a smile an angel would've been proud of. He was up to something. Nothing surer.

'Tell you what…' he said graciously. 'I'll shower, you hold the towel.'

CHAPTER TWO

TWENTY minutes later the plane touched down in Singapore and Sienna preceeded Lex along narrow non-descript corridors towards the transit lounge. She felt a lot better now that they were off the plane—more in control of herself and her surroundings. Far more inclined to think that her and Lex's sensually loaded altercation had been nothing more than edginess and boredom on his part and a never-to-be repeated moment of insanity on hers.

Sienna's internal clock told her it was long past her bedtime, but the arrival and departure boards inside the terminal said it was six p.m. and the light outside the windows confirmed it. She was tired, she realised belatedly. Add that to the list of reasons for her strange reaction to Lex. She added it to his side of the equation too. The hours he'd worked during these last few days leading up to the trip had been phenomenal. *And* there hadn't been a beautiful companion in sight. Not for months, according to her godmother, Adriana, who also happened to be Lex's mother. Sienna added 'overdue' to Lex's list of reasons for uncharacteristic behaviour. Wonderful things, lists.

The standard array of shops graced the terminal corridors. Coffee bar, newsagent, chain-store music and books, lotions, potions, and soap… Wait! Soap. Gorgeously scented luxury soap. To use in the shower… Sienna stopped abruptly and Lex all but crashed into her in the process.

'What did you forget?' he said.

'Nothing.' He of little faith. 'I just want some soap.'

'I already have soap.'

'Why is it always about you?'

'It just…usually is.'

'Well, not this time.' Honestly, the man had been thoroughly indulged for far too long. 'The soap is for me.'

'My mistake.' Lex wandered over to the nearest display. 'What kind of soap do you want?'

'I'll know it when I smell it,' she said.

'I see.' His expression said he didn't understand the delights of scented-soap shopping at all. 'What say we forgo your PA training for the next couple of hours and I meet you back on the plane?' But the ancient Asian saleswoman had already made her move.

'Come. Come,' she said, waving them into the shop proper. 'It is good for the man to choose the soap for the woman. Choose now, benefit later, no?'

'No,' said Sienna, but the saleswoman ignored her.

'This one,' she said, and handed Lex a block of soap. 'Ylang ylang and lemongrass. Smell good, no?'

Lex sniffed. Considered. Decided. And all without giving Sienna a second glance. 'No,' he said as he handed the soap back to the woman. 'She's more of a rosehip kind of girl.'

'I am not!' said Sienna.

'Rosehip and vanilla?' said the saleswoman, picking up

another block of soap and offering it to him. 'This one you like?'

'Hello,' said Sienna. 'Over here.'

'Got anything with ginger in it?' said Lex.

'Sandalwood and ginger,' said the woman and passed that one to him as well. 'Also matching body lotion, hand cream, and shampoo.'

'Sold,' said Lex and produced a wallet from his trouser pocket. 'Don't bother wrapping it.'

'How sweet,' murmured Sienna. 'You think we're done here.'

'We are done here.' He strode towards the register. 'You wanted soap. You got soap. And moisturiser, and shampoo. What more could you possibly need?'

This wasn't about need. It was about shopping. Possibly about revenge. 'There's a men's range.'

'No,' he said hastily.

'Oh, yes.' Sienna studied him serenely. If he thought he could treat her like a charity case and pick up the tab for her expenses he was mistaken. She wasn't on the poverty line yet. She could still afford soap.

The saleswoman studied him too. 'So much hurry,' she said. 'Does he have airplane to catch?'

'He just got off one.' Lex opened his mouth to speak. 'He's about to tell you he already has soap,' Sienna murmured. 'Anyone would think he's not a patient man.'

'A man with no patience is like an ocean without fish,' said the woman, and continued to study Lex. 'Why even cast the net?'

'I have fish,' said Lex indignantly. 'I have plenty of fish.'

'Of course you do.' Sienna couldn't quite hide her smirk. Who'd have thought there'd be such joy to be had in a transit terminal soap shop?

'Allspice and lemon thyme?' offered the saleswoman.

Close. There was no denying the man's edibility, although she fully intended to. 'I'm thinking cinnamon.'

'Cinnamon and orange,' said the woman, picking up a nearby block of soap and handing it to her. 'Good choice.'

Sienna took it. Sniffed it. 'I don't know… I'm not sure…' And with devilry in mind she said, 'He may need to try it on.'

'How—?' he began, and then spied the basin and tap. 'No.'

Oh, yes. 'I'd hate to choose wrong. Imagine if the aroma didn't complement your manly essence?'

'Sienna, it's *soap*.'

'How little you know,' she said and reached for his arm, pushing his jacket sleeve up to his elbow before taking his wrist and turning it to expose the inside of his forearm. 'Think of the fish.'

The saleswoman slapped a damp cloth on his skin and deftly wet him from elbow to wrist. 'The soap will slide,' she said.

The soap did slide. And somewhere between elbow and wrist Sienna lost the upper hand and Lex found it.

'Now you rub with your hands,' the saleswoman told her. 'I take the soap.'

Lex's mouth curved lazily and his eyes gleamed. 'I like a firm touch,' he murmured.

He got one and winced, doubtless from pleasure.

'She's so obliging,' he told the saleswoman. 'Really. Ouch!'

'A woman without spirit is like a sky with no clouds,' said the woman.

'Perfect?' said Lex.

'No. Such a sky will never quench your thirst.'

'Isn't that what bottled water's for?' said Lex, and winced some more as Sienna's thumb accidentally encountered another soft spot. 'Easy, sweetheart. You're bruising the goods.'

'Sorry.' Sienna trailed her fingernails lightly down his arm, leaving a row of wavy snakelike tracks in the lather. Lex shuddered ever so slightly and his eyes flashed a heated warning.

'Keep it up, Sienna, and you will be.'

Oh, dear. There it was again—exhilaration, illumination, and a powerful curiosity about what Lex might bring to a sexual relationship—all of it coalescing into a tight ball of sensation deep in the pit of her stomach. Sienna moved to the sink, washed the soap from her hands and stood back to let Lex wash his arm, acutely aware that lathering him in cinnamon soap hadn't been one of her better ideas.

She wasn't six any more; Lex wasn't her indulgent older playmate.

She wasn't a skinny, smart-mouthed fifteen-year-old any more either; Lex wasn't her confidante and protector.

Lex dried his hands and arms with a paper towel and turned towards her, every movement a subtle challenge, and Sienna realised with blinding clarity that those days were over.

He put his forearm to his nose, took a whiff, shrugged, and held his arm up towards her, those knowing grey eyes daring her to play out the scene to completion. Maybe she ought to add 'too easily led' to her side of the equation, she thought wryly, because she knew instinctively that breathing him in was going to cost her control she could ill afford to lose. But she closed her eyes and breathed deeply anyway.

The aroma of cinnamon came first, then citrus, then Lex. The ache in her stomach pulled tighter.

'How does it combine with my manly essence?' he murmured, his voice a low, husky rumble that sounded like sin and burned like the devil.

'Quite well,' she whimpered, her eyes still tightly closed.

'I was aiming a little higher than quite well.' Had he moved closer? Was it his body that was on fire or was it hers? Because something here was burning, nothing surer. Something brushed her ear and she shivered hard. His hair, she thought at first. No, maybe his cheek. His lips… 'Maybe we should try a different soap on the other arm,' he whispered.

Sienna stumbled back a step and opened her eyes and immediately wished she hadn't. There it was again: The Look. And Lex didn't look tired or edgy or in any way bored. He looked focussed and sexy as hell and the reckless hunger in his eyes called to needs she'd never known she had. 'No need to try another one on,' she said, adding a weak smile for good measure. 'This one combines very well.'

'I appreciate the adverbial upgrade,' he countered with a lazy grin. 'But the fact remains that the basic assessment is mediocre. Are you sure you don't want to make me try on another one?'

'It lifts your manly essence into the realms of the sublime,' she practically yelled. 'I am trembling with lust.'

'I think she likes it,' Lex told the lady. 'I'll take a month's worth.'

Sienna fled Lex's company after that and Lex let her. The scent of cinnamon and orange soap and Lex the marauder stayed in her mind and on her hands until there was nothing for it but to shower it off, wash it straight down the drain, and replace it with plain old airport hotel soap and shampoo, never mind the gorgeous goodies from the soap shop burning a hole in her handbag. Even then her mind strayed as she lathered up and scrubbed hard. She imagined a man's hands on her, but not just any man's hands. These were knowing hands, demanding hands.

Lex's hands.

'Why me?' she whimpered. Why Lex? 'Why *now*?'

Oh, there'd been that time on her eighteenth birthday when Lex had commandeered her for a slow dance at the end of the evening and she'd been a mass of nerves for fear he was planning to kiss her, but that had been years ago. Besides, he hadn't. Not on the lips. He'd kissed her temple instead, told her to watch out for Bobby Carmichael's wandering hands, and left with the beautiful blonde events manager that Adriana had hired to oversee the evening.

The beautiful blonde hadn't lasted a week.

Neither had Bobby Carmichael.

Then there'd been that time when Lex had turned up at her flat one morning and the very sweet Aidan Russell had chosen that particular moment to wander out of her bedroom. Lex hadn't liked coming face to face with Sienna's love life, never mind that his own had spanned three continents by then, the ice in his eyes could have frozen the Thames. After about two minutes of stilted conversation, including introductions, Aidan had become visibly nervous.

Aidan hadn't lasted long either.

How many years ago was that? Two? Three? There'd been no one for Sienna since then. Sighing, Sienna added 'long overdue' to her list of reasons for her sudden uncomfortable awareness of Lex's manly attractions and tilted her face beneath the spray. Moments later visions of Lex in the shower with her—with his hands on her—began to assail her. She turned the cold tap on full and concentrated on getting clean rather than aroused, but occasionally an image stuck and when it did it ripped into her with cyclone force. Her body bowed and her skin ached for a lover's touch.

A *lover's* touch, she told herself fiercely. Not Lex's touch.

Any lover would do. There was such a thing as taking the edge off.

And then her relationship with Lex would be the same as it always had been. Sacrosanct.

Sienna emerged from the shower feeling suitably clean but in no way relaxed. The thought of Lex showering with *his* soap and Sienna having to sit next to him on the plane for another eight hours, breathing him in, wasn't a reassuring one to a woman whose body ached for fulfilment and whose mind had remained back in London. If he turned that lazy charm on her again, heaven forbid if he touched her, she was likely to implode. Lex would probably find it amusing. Sienna didn't find the notion amusing at all.

Think, Sienna, think. She'd known this man for most of her life. She knew his strengths and all his flaws. She knew full well that he was only amusing himself with her on account of a distinct lack of anything else amusing at hand. The obvious solution, therefore, was to find something else for him to focus on.

She hit the shops again and bought him a book. An adventure story with ticking bombs and many villains. That'd doubtless keep him occupied for, oh…five minutes. She bought him a book of mastermind sudoku puzzles. That'd hold him for longer. What else? A major crisis of confidence on Wall Street would be good. She skimmed the newspapers for just such an occurrence, but it wasn't to be. What else would a good PA collect for her boss before getting back on that plane?

Probably her composure.

Definitely her wits.

Her resolve to not become romantically involved with old friends, new bosses, or millionaire playboys for whom romance was just a diversion. Which pretty much ruled Lex out on all counts.

The final boarding call came about far too quickly and Sienna stepped gingerly back inside the plane, armed to the teeth with distractions, only to find Lex already seated, with his computer open on his lap. His gaze was penetrating but his smile was the one from their childhood as she tucked her purchases into the webbing of the seat in front of her and her carry bag into the locker above. She settled into her seat and took a tentative breath. No cinnamon or orange. Lex had showered—his hair was still damp—but not with his new soap.

Hallelujah.

Lex shut down his laptop for take-off, his impatience a tangible force, those long, lean fingers drumming rhythmically on the slim machine, his gaze distracted and far away.

'Something I should know about?' she queried, feeling ever so slightly guilty that she hadn't stuck with him during the stopover.

'The breakdown of the Scorcellini assets has come in,' said Lex. 'They're in surprisingly good shape for a company going under.'

'Is this a good thing?'

'It is for them. Means their chances of attracting a rescue bid are higher than I thought.'

'So where does that leave your bid?'

'In need of readjustment.' He shot her a glance. 'You're not going to suggest that I rescue them?'

'No. I have a new approach when it comes to dealings of a financial nature. I won't criticise your decisions.'

'I like it,' he said.

'And you don't criticise mine.'

'You had to go and spoil it.'

'Do we have a deal?'

'No.' He smiled crookedly. 'Criticise away. I may not always like or agree with what you have to say, Sienna, but I still want to hear it.'

Sienna sighed heavily. Now he was being charming. 'Would you want to hear the opinions of a PA you *hadn't* known since childhood?'

'Probably not. But, then, you're not a regular employee, are you? Which means some of the regular rules simply don't apply. I can give you the workload a PA would get from me. I can show you how to do it. But don't ask me to treat you like a proper PA this coming month because I can't.'

'You could try.'

'And I'd fail. I don't look to you for instant obedience, Sienna. I look to you for truth.'

Sienna went all marshmallow-soft inside; she couldn't help it.

The seat-belt lights went off. Lex opened his laptop and started opening files. 'And trouble,' he muttered. 'Trust me, Sienna, you bring that to the table too.'

At five fifty-five a.m., local time, Sienna and Lex stepped off the plane, collected their luggage, cleared customs, and stepped into the arrivals area. Sienna had never been to Australia before. The dress code of the people waiting for passengers seemed far more informal than that of the people at Heathrow. People smiled more and walked slower, the air was warmer and the general vibe felt a whole lot more relaxed.

Or maybe she only thought it felt more relaxed because

she was so glad to finally get off that plane. Lex had focussed on his work for most of the Singapore-Sydney leg of the trip, stopping only for meal breaks. There had been no awkward moments of heart-stopping sexual tension, nothing out of the ordinary at all, not on Lex's part at any rate. But Sienna still hadn't quite been able to relax in his company. Not until they'd left the plane behind.

'The trick to jet lag and adjusting quickly to the new time zone is to stay awake for the rest of the day, local time, and crawl into bed around midnight,' Lex told Sienna as he collected both his suitcases and hers.

'Uh-huh,' Sienna replied with increasing good humour as they strode through the glass doors and out onto the Sydney pavement. Fresh air, heavily laden with exhaust fumes and the promise of a hot summer's day, greeted her. 'It sounds perfectly sensible in *theory*, don't get me wrong. Remind me again when I fall asleep in my soup at lunchtime. How far is it to your place from here, again?'

'Half an hour.' Lex steered the bags towards a waiting limousine, gave the driver the address and opened the back door for Sienna to get in. 'Watson's Bay lies just inside the southern entrance to Sydney Harbour. The land there tapers off to a point, with one side facing the bay and the other side facing the ocean. It's a nice spot. You'll like it,' he told her with a boyish smile that told of his enthusiasm for his latest cubbyhole. He'd always had dozens of special places tucked away in the grounds of his family's estate as a child. Sienna had delighted in seeking them out during her visits, and Lex had always shared them with her with good grace and enthusiasm, just as he was doing now. It had taken her years before she'd realised that Lex was a whole lot more careful about sharing himself with anyone else. He'd grown up wary of reporters and social climbers; people who saw the money and the position in society rather than the man, never mind that the man himself was spectacular.

If she could just think of this Sydney home as Lex's latest cubby rather than the abode of a man who could damage her calm with nothing more than a single heated glance, they would get along just fine. 'And the house?' she questioned. 'The hub? Which side is it on?'

'The bay side. I needed somewhere to put the yacht.'

'Of course,' she said dryly. 'The yacht.'

'There's a housekeeper too. His name's Rudy. He used to be a Navy frigate midshipman. He likes things tidy. Cooks extremely tasty French frou-frou food but you might want to stay out of his kitchen. He's territorial.'

'Pity. I like kitchens.' Kitchens had been her refuge as a child, especially when her parents had been mid-argument, which had been most of the time. She tended to gravitate towards them, even as an adult. A boiling kettle and the fixings for a cup of tea provided comfort and warmth on too many levels to count.

Lex sent her a sharp glance but stayed silent.

'Is the presence of Rudy the former frigate midshipman supposed to be reassuring when it comes to the thought of sharing a house with you for a month?' she said next.

'I figured it would be,' he said mildly.

'What if *he* wants to entertain?'

'Don't dwell on it. I never do. Rudy lives in the apartment over the garage. What he does there is his business.' And at her raised eyebrow he added, 'All I'm saying is that we're not going to be entirely alone in the house, that's all. You might want to factor that into your decision-making process.'

'Thanks. I will.' Sienna chewed pensively on her bottom lip. She didn't want to be contrary or difficult. She just wanted the month to go as smoothly as possible. 'In the interests of exploring all options, have you any idea how expensive the rents nearby would be?'

'Expensive,' he said. 'Watson's Bay isn't a budget area, Sienna.'

'What about housing a little further away?'

'Then the commute will be longer.'

'It's called compromise.'

'I know what compromise is,' he said curtly. 'The business world is full of it. What I don't understand is why you feel the need to make such a compromise.'

'So I'm frugal,' she said lightly. 'Not all of us have deep pockets, Lex. You know I'm not in your league.'

'I also know that parting with a month's worth of high-end rent—unnecessary as it would be—shouldn't really bother you.' Lex's gaze had sharpened; his interest had been piqued. 'Sienna, are you in financial trouble? Is that why the sudden push to become a PA?'

'No! And no. Of course not.' She sent him a bright smile, but she couldn't hold his gaze. She opted instead for staring out the window at Sydney's suburbia. Subterfuge never had been her strong point. She didn't have to see Lex's diamond hard gaze to know that it was boring into her. She could feel it. 'There simply aren't that many advancement opportunities for art curators at the moment, that's all. I figure if I can combine business skills with my knowledge of the art world I might be able to pick up a PA position with a collector or gallery owner. Broaden my horizons.' Find some missing paintings… 'I will confess that a bigger pay cheque would also be most welcome.'

'So you *do* need money,' he said next. 'I knew it. I knew there was something to all of this that you weren't telling me. How much?'

'I *said* my money situation was *fine*. Just fine.'

'I swear you're the worst liar I know,' he muttered, and lapsed into a brooding, simmering silence. Lex didn't know the true extent of her woeful financial circumstances, none of the Wentworth family did, and Sienna took great pains to keep it that way. They'd given her refuge and protection as a child and friendship and family closeness as she'd grown older, but there were some things that Sienna didn't share with anyone. The small matter of her rapidly dwindling financial resources was one of them.

'What does it cost you to maintain that ridiculous mausoleum your mother left you?' demanded Lex suddenly. He didn't wait for an answer, he saw it in the dismayed glance she sent him because he cursed and his expression turned even grimmer. 'If it's draining you of every cent you have, *sell* it. Realise some profit or cut your losses, but get rid of it.'

'No.' There was no defending her emotional attachment to the old summer house set high on the cliffs of southern Cornwall. She didn't even try. 'Are we *done* with the commerce lecture yet?'

'You are *impossible* to help,' he said from between gritted teeth. 'Why can't you just tell me what you need like any normal person?'

'I have!' Sienna glanced over at him again, nothing more than a fleeting stab of desperation and pain, but it might as well have been a sword because it certainly made Lex bleed. 'I need to learn how to be a good personal assistant and you're going to teach me. That's all I want from you. That's all I need. Don't value add.'

'Dammit, Sienna!' Didn't she understand yet that that was what he did? 'I'm asking you one simple question. How much money do you need?'

'You don't understand,' she said quietly.

'The hell I don't!' Lex turned to stare out the window at

the passing suburbs, cursing Sienna's long-dead mother for willing her a keepsake she couldn't keep, cursing himself for not figuring it out sooner. He knew Sienna was touchy when it came to money, knew he shouldn't have pushed her for answers she wasn't prepared to give, but, dammit, why couldn't she just confide in him the way she used to?

It wasn't until the limousine pulled into the circular driveway and stopped at the entrance to his sprawling luxury mansion that Lex made a determined effort to shake his black mood and play the host. He didn't bother pointing out again that it would be far cheaper for Sienna to live here with him than find somewhere else to stay. She knew that already.

The front door opened and Lex felt his lips curve ever so slightly as the dour and imposing Rudy stepped out. Rudy was doing his bodyguard-butler impersonation today—black trousers, a black T-shirt that strained across his massive torso, black wrap-around sunglasses, and an almighty scowl.

Sienna had seen him too. 'Rudy the territorial?' she queried with a glance that held equal parts wariness and apology.

'Yes.'

'You didn't tell me he looked like Steven Seagal.'

'That's because he doesn't.'

'Does he talk like Steven Seagal too?'

'Steven Seagal doesn't *talk*,' said Lex. 'His skills lie elsewhere. Come to think of it, Rudy doesn't talk either, unless he has to.'

'I swear you make some of the strangest decisions when it comes to choosing hired help,' she said.

'So I'm noticing,' he said and stifled a smile as her chin rose defiantly and those remarkable eyes narrowed in silent warning. 'Come on, I'll introduce you.'

Rudy nodded curtly in greeting as they got out of the car, then he headed for their luggage. Sienna followed.

'Sienna, this is Rudy. Rudy, this is Sienna Raleigh, my new PA. Sienna's a little different from my old PAs. She's practically family.'

Rudy's sunglasses zoned in on Sienna first and then Lex. What he thought was anyone's guess. The limo driver began unloading bags from the boot and setting them on the steps. Rudy joined in. Sienna went to retrieve the smaller of her two suitcases only to have Rudy swipe it at the last minute and set it firmly behind him. 'What's she doing?' he asked Lex gruffly.

'Hard to say,' said Lex. 'Sometimes she goes looking for an argument.'

'She picks up that suitcase and she'll get one,' muttered Rudy. 'Inside. Now. There's iced tea, chicken and cucumber sandwiches, and crème brûlée waiting for you in the west-wing drawing room.' The sunglasses zeroed in on Sienna again. 'You eat the crème brûlée last.'

'I knew that,' she said loftily.

'Family, you said,' said Rudy darkly.

'I've known her since she was five,' said Lex.

'Six,' said Sienna.

'And you employed her.'

'Believe me, point taken.'

Sienna stared from Lex to Rudy in indignation. 'What is this? Some kind of boys' own shorthand?'

'Did I mention the handmade French chocolates?' said Rudy pointedly.

'Nice try,' she said. 'But I'm more of an ice-cream person. Now if you'd said you had handmade triple-cream French Vanilla ice cream waiting for me in the west-wing drawing room I'd be there already.'

'There's one in every family,' muttered Rudy.

'I know,' said Sienna agreeably. 'Annoying, isn't it?' She looked up at the house, her expression faintly wistful. 'Thing is, Rudy, I'm not family and I may not be staying here so could you leave my bags by the door?'

Rudy ignored Sienna and looked to Lex. 'She's not staying?' he queried ominously. 'I've laid in provisions for two.'

'Family spat,' said Lex. 'I'll handle it.'

Rudy glanced towards Sienna, who'd abandoned the conversation in favour of making her way towards the front door. 'Does she sail?'

'Like a champion.' Lex had seen to that part of her education himself.

'Her bags will be in her room,' said Rudy. 'I hate clutter at the front door.'

'Don't mind me,' called Sienna. 'I'm moving through the front door and into the beyond. No clutter here. Come to mention it, there's *nothing* here but space and sunshine. What happened to all the furniture? Where's the umbrella stand? The sideboard and the vase full of flowers?'

'It's all right,' said Lex reassuringly. 'She's not serious.'

'You need sleep,' muttered Rudy. 'You're becoming delusional.'

This was a distinct possibility. He'd packed too much work and far too much wanting of Sienna into this day already. It was time to set things back on track.

He caught up with Sienna in the atrium, just inside the doorway looking curious and tentative all at once. 'What do you think of it?' he asked her casually, trying hard to pretend that it didn't matter what she thought. The house was a modern-day masterpiece, all sleek lines and open spaces. Lex hadn't designed it, the previous owners had, but it suited him well and Rudy kept it immaculate. Sienna would like it, he knew she would. She just had to give it a chance.

'It's lovely. Very private. Bigger than I expected.'

'I told you there was plenty of room. South wing's yours,' he said and, heading left, proceeded to show her the guest wing, complete with luxury spa, sitting room, breakfast nook, and four bedrooms. 'Take your pick,' he said. 'It's all guest accommodation.'

He led her downstairs next, to the pool area and gym, tennis court, boat shed, boat ramp, and dock.

'Yours?' she said, glancing towards the yacht moored at the end of the dock, and Lex nodded.

'Sienna meet *Mercy Jane*. There's also a speedboat called *Angelina* in the boat shed for getting places in a hurry,' he told her. 'Rudy maintains both boats and, when I say maintain, I mean he's fanatical about their function and their finish.'

'So...no getting to know the girls,' she said.

'Wrong. Befriend the girls by all means. Just cut your nails, take all your jewellery off first and don't lead them astray. Should you want to go somewhere and should Rudy decide that you're suitably attired, he'll have the speedboat in the water before you can say wouldn't it be easier to take the Porsche.'

'How protective is Rudy of the Porsche?'

'You can have a set of keys to the Porsche,' he told her with a grin. 'Rudy doesn't give a fig about the Porsche.'

He took her back upstairs and showed her the middle section of the house next, otherwise known as the west wing. 'Kitchen,' he said, and opened the door onto a spotless stainless-steel wonder. 'Library,' he said next, and showed her a room containing dark leather lounges, the odd desk or four, and floor-to-ceiling bookcases covering three walls. 'The billiards room,' he said, opening another door and affording Sienna a brief glance of yet another manly entertainment area.

'Is Rudy precious about his felt?' she asked him sweetly.

'You have no idea.' He ushered her through to the formal dining area with its floor-to-ceiling windows and multimillion dollar view of the harbour, the bridge, and the skyscrapers of the city proper. Adjacent to that was the west-wing drawing room where Rudy had set out the food. This room had been furnished with comfort in mind rather than to impress, even though it boasted floor-to-ceiling windows and that panoramic harbour view. There was more in it, for starters. Deep, comfortable chairs, a settee for lounging on, footrests and reading lamps, table and chairs for two, a couple of sideboards…

'Nice,' said Sienna, wistfully eyeing the food. 'Where's the business hub?'

'Third floor. The staircase to the left of the atrium just inside the front door will take you straight there.'

Sienna nodded. Inched her way a little closer to the food. 'Where do you sleep?'

'Same floor as this, north wing.' Lex beat her to the food, poured two glasses of iced tea and handed her one. He picked up a chicken and cucumber sandwich triangle—no crusts—and ate it in a couple of bites before washing it down with tea. He had another, then another, then reached for a chocolate with a pistachio nestling on top of it. Would she stay? Would he be able to keep their relationship platonic if she did stay?

He didn't know.

He still wanted to protect her. Some things never changed. He wanted her to confide in him so that he could fix whatever financial difficulty she was in. She shouldn't have to give up the curator's position she loved for an all-hours job where she'd be constantly at someone's beck and call, even if the pay *was* better. He couldn't stand the thought of it.

The only person whose beck and call he wanted her to be at, he realised grimly, was his.

'Rudy will ask you what you thought of the chocolate, you know,' he murmured. 'Try one.'

'You're trying to win me over with food,' she said.

'Not at all,' he replied, selecting a dark chocolate truffle and letting the taste of it explode in his mouth. 'These are *good*.'

He'd keep.

Sienna ignored the chocolate and reached for a sandwich instead. There was something very virtuous about selecting a chicken and cucumber sandwich in the face of crème brûlée and handmade chocolates. Besides, if she was going to stay here she needed to start building her resistance to items of extreme temptation. Like tempting truffles and ruthless rogues in sexy suits. She needed to start building it *now*.

'Rudy knows I'm not much of one for chocolate,' she said. 'He won't mind if I don't have any. I think it's good to come to an early understanding about such things, don't you?'

'Only if you're bent on declaring war.' Lex smiled in a way she was fast coming to learn was his ruthless pirate's smile. 'Rule number two for all successful personal assistants is to try and get on with the rest of the staff.'

'I'll do my best,' she murmured. 'What's rule number one?'

'Don't annoy the boss.'

Ah. Rule number one was the kicker. 'I'll work on that too. Speaking of which, when do you want to start work?'

'That depends on whether you still want to find alternative accommodation. If you do, then we'd better sort something out today.' He looked at her, his expression watchful, more old Lex than new. It didn't change her awareness of him one little bit, though. Her awareness was here to stay. All the appearance of the old Lex did was increase her confusion and add mightily to the overall appeal of the new. 'It's up to you, Sienna,' he said quietly. 'Nothing you don't want.'

Why-oh-why did he have to play the man of honour *now*? Why couldn't he have stayed the raider of hearts and made her decision on whether or not to stay here an easy one? Sienna looked at the food on tap and that glorious view. She thought of that fifty metre commute to work and the money she'd save by not having to pay rent. She thought of how blissfully *easy* life would be for the next month if only she and Lex could stick to work and friendship and forget all about the sexual curiosity kicking around between them. They'd managed friendship well enough for the past twenty years, hadn't they? They'd managed it without any romantic inclinations whatsoever, for the most part.

Nothing you don't want.

Well, she *didn't* want to become his latest conquest and that was that. Lex would honour her wishes in that regard; she knew he would. He was honouring them now.

'I'm prepared to give this place a chance,' she said awkwardly, and immediately wished she didn't sound quite so ungrateful. Lex was helping her out by taking her on as his PA. He didn't have to. He could afford to employ the best, but instead he'd agreed to train her, *and* he was paying her triple her old wage for the inconvenience. She tried again. 'You have a beautiful house, Lex, with an amazing guest wing and I appreciate the convenience. I'd like to stay.'

'Good.' Lex loaded up a plate with sandwiches, and topped up his tea. 'Get unpacked. Settle in. Go for a walk. Take a look around the bay. I want you in my office, ready to work, at two o'clock.'

'Yessir!'

Lex shot her a dark glance.

'Yessir, Mr Wentworth?'

'God give me strength,' he muttered.

'Well, what do your PAs usually call you?' she asked him.

'Lex.'

'I'll be there,' she said. 'Two o'clock sharp. Ready and willing to learn. You'll see.'

Sienna went straight to the south wing after Lex headed north with his plate of bounty in hand. She found her luggage in the largest bedroom and, mindful of rule number two, figured she might as well stay there. Rudy didn't do the full maid-service unpack of feminine fripperies—he'd simply placed the bags by the bed. Sienna made fast work of unpacking, considering her clothes as she went. None of the items she'd brought along were outlandish, but none of them could be classified as elegant professional secretary garb either. If clothes made the man—or at least reminded him what he was supposed to be doing—she needed to go shopping.

She found Rudy in the drawing room, clearing away the remains of the refreshments. 'You do good sandwiches,' she said by way of greeting.

'What about the chocolate?' he said.

'That was good too.'

His eyes narrowed. 'You didn't have any. No one mentions my sandwiches once they've eaten my chocolate.'

'Good point. Rudy, I have a problem. I need to shop.'

'For what?' he said gruffly.

'A business suit. Dark-rimmed glasses. Possibly sensible shoes, although I may not have the fortitude to carry through on that particular notion.'

He looked at the shoes she was wearing. 'It's a wonder you can walk at all.'

'The shoes are good,' she said. 'The shoes are fine. I've changed my mind about the shoes. But I still need a suit. Trousers maybe. No-nonsense shirts. Corporate body armour. Do you know of any shops nearby that sell that type of clothing?'

'Do I *look* like I frequent women's clothing stores to you?'

'No, but you might have a sister who'd know. Or a female friend who walks past a shop just like that every day on her way to work. You won't know until you ask.' Sienna smiled winningly and got a glower in reply.

'Don't you have other clothes you could wear?'

'Not if I want a constant visual and tactile reminder of the new corporate PA me—which I do. Today,' she added when Rudy grunted and headed for the door with plates and jug in hand. She scooped up the mugs, shoved a chocolate in her mouth and followed him to the kitchen. 'The chocolate is divine,' she said around a mouthful of it.

'Try chewing it next time.'

'I chewed it this time. C'mon, Rudy. I need some local knowledge. Are you sure you don't know anyone who dresses like Wonder Woman when she's not out saving the day?'

'Who?' he said.

'What about one who dresses like Clark Kent, mild-mannered reporter, before he morphs into Superman?'

He shook his head as if baffled.

'I need something to remind me that I'm working for Lex now and that I should just do the job he's paying me to do and not deliberately set out to annoy him,' she snapped. 'I want Lex to look at me and see an efficient personal assistant and not his old family friend Sienna. I need a suit! A no-nonsense, focus-on-the-job, don't-look-at-me-like-that *suit*.'

'Have you always been bonkers?' muttered Rudy. 'Or is this a recent development?'

Sienna smiled tightly. 'It's new.'

'I'll make one call,' he said. 'If that doesn't work you're on your own.'

The call did work, and within two minutes he'd arranged for some woman called Gracie Mae to collect her from the house in ten minutes' time and take her shopping.

'That's Grace to you,' he said curtly. 'She's the publicity officer for the Point Clarence Yacht Club, and mind you show her some respect.'

'You're a sweet man,' she said.

Rudy didn't even attempt a smile. 'You're so wrong.'

CHAPTER THREE

GRACIE MAE and her red BMW convertible pulled up to the steps where Sienna and Rudy stood waiting exactly ten minutes later. She was prompt—no doubt about that, but no one could ever say she dressed down. The woman was all Sophia Loren curves and sexy sophistication, with enough eye-catching jewellery on her person to stop traffic. She smiled languidly and blew Rudy a kiss before leaning over to open the door. 'One day you're going to take me sailing, big man.'

'Only if I lose my mind first.' Was Rudy actually *blushing*?

'I keep telling you there's no need to worry about losing your mind beforehand, sailor. You won't need it.' Gracie Mae turned that knowing smile on Sienna next. 'So,' she said, and gestured for Sienna to sit in the seat beside her. 'Rudy says you need a Wonder Woman costume.'

'I—what?' Sienna turned just in time to see the big man disappear inside. 'Rudy is confused. I need a business suit. Some dark-framed glasses. I need to look the epitome of corporate efficiency and control.'

'Even better. Because frankly, darling, the Wonder Woman look is getting old. You can call me Grace.'

'Sienna.'

'Beautiful,' said Grace approvingly as she drove out of the driveway and onto the road. 'It suits you. Been in Australia long?'

'Two hours.'

'And thinking about work already. I like that. Call me if you ever need a job.'

Sienna liked the woman already. Reaching for her handbag, she unzipped a side compartment and pulled out a pale blue airmail envelope, its folds not sharp and fresh but worn thin and ragged with age. She turned it over and studied the return address. 'Grace, may I ask if you know where Hornsby is? Is it nearby?'

'No, it's one of Sydney's outer northern suburbs. Right now we're skimming the outer eastern suburbs. Hornsby's about three quarters of an hour away by car.' Grace glanced her way. 'You need to go to Hornsby?'

'Not today,' said Sienna with a smile, carefully folding the letter with the precious address on it and tucking it back in her bag. 'I just wanted to know where it was. Is,' she corrected. I'll get there at some stage, but it doesn't have to be today. She'd waited twelve years…a few more days wouldn't hurt. 'Today I'm all about jet lag and business suits.'

'Business suits, business suits…I've seen some recently, but where?' Grace tapped thoughtfully on the steering wheel as they waited for traffic lights to turn green. 'Do you only need the actual suit or do you want the works?'

'The works. Except for the shoes. I already have the shoes.'

Grace glanced at Sienna's shoes. 'There's nothing wrong with your shoes, don't get me wrong. They're perfectly acceptable. But I know where you'll find better.'

'Better is good,' said Sienna. 'Is better expensive?'

'Sweetpea, better is always expensive. Best tell me your budget and we'll work from there.'

'The budget is tight.' Lex hadn't been wrong about her financial situation. There'd been enough money left over after her parents' deaths for her to live modestly and acquire a fine education. But lately the costs of maintaining a crumbling manor house in Cornwall had got the better of her. The roof needed replacing, the wiring was a mess, and her savings were almost gone. Sienna needed to make money, not spend it. 'I need class on a shoestring.'

'Don't we all?' said Grace. 'But I know of a place where you'll find it. We'll go to Georgie's.'

'Georgie's is a boutique?'

'Oh, no, darling.' Grace shot her another one of those fabulous lazy smiles. 'Georgie is an artisan.'

For an artisan, Georgie lived in a fairly downmarket part of town by Sienna's reckoning, what with the graffiti and the neon lights and the men of disreputable intentions littering the street and all.

'Welcome to Darlinghurst, darling. Don't come here alone,' said Grace as she drove into a driveway and spoke into a security intercom set into the wall. Moments later the driveway gates swung inwards and they drove inside. Not a boutique, thought Sienna. A private residence.

'Do we need an appointment?'

'You just got one.' Grace slid from the car and headed for the door, her saunter as high-voltage sexy as the rest of her. 'Let's see what Georgie can do for you.'

Georgie was a remarkable-looking woman with a husky laugh, a penchant for neck scarves, and a dress sense that bordered on lush but suited her to perfection. She and Grace exchanged air kisses, continental-style, after which Georgie ushered them into a sunlit parlour with snow-white furnishings. 'And who have we here?' she said, turning towards Sienna with a warm smile.

'This is Sienna,' said Grace. 'Fresh off the plane from London.'

'Twirl for me,' Georgie told her. And in a hushed voice, 'If I had a face and a figure like that I'd be a millionaire twice over.'

'Working on it,' said Sienna.

'That's my girl,' said Georgie. 'Tell Georgie what you need.'

'I need a suit,' said Sienna readily. 'Maybe some dark-framed glasses. And shoes.'

A tape measure appeared as if from nowhere. 'Arms out,' ordered Georgie. 'Thirty-five perky—twenty-one flat—and thirty-six toned. Sweetcakes, you've got *curves*.'

'I'm aiming to cover them in a cloak of corporate respectability.'

'Girl's got style,' said Georgie and pointed Sienna towards a large Japanese-style screen in the corner of the room. 'You can slip off your clothes behind that while I go hunting. Can you do virginal, darling? Because I'm thinking white.'

'What?' said Sienna, poking her head around the screen.

'Perfect,' said Georgie. 'Back in a jiffy. Grace, will you have tea?'

Georgie disappeared, presumably to look for a business suit, possibly to make tea. Sienna ducked back behind the screen and slowly removed her shirt and skirt. Moments later two scraps of white lace and silk appeared over the top of the screen. Stockings followed. A white garter belt. Not a business suit in sight. 'Uh, Georgie? About that suit…'

'We start from the skin out around here, darling. Put them on and let's have a look at you.'

Sienna hesitated. She was in the market for a suit, not underwear. But the lace was exquisite, the garter belt matched, and lo and behold the lace at the top of the sheer skin-coloured stockings matched too. A girl could never have too many sets of matching underwear and stockings, right? A girl could at least have *one* set. She wriggled her way into them, fiddling with clasps and straps as she went before stepping tentatively out from behind the screen.

'There's the tiniest bit of support in the bra,' said Georgie to Grace. 'See the lift? Turn round, sweetie, and let us see you from the back.' Sienna turned. 'What do you think?' said Georgie. 'Are the panties too modest?'

'Borderline,' said Grace. 'That's what's so clever about them. Is that Chantilly lace?'

'Stunning, isn't it?' said Georgia.

'About that suit,' said Sienna and slipped behind the screen again.

'Keep the underwear on,' said Grace. 'Georgie has a holistic approach.'

As long as Georgie eventually coughed up a suit, Sienna was fine with whatever approach Georgie wanted to run with. 'I'm after something sexless,' she said. 'A disguise, if you will. Body armour. Easy on the va va voom.' She thought she'd been heard when the next thing that came over the top of the bamboo screen was a perfectly plain white cotton vest. Until she tried it on and the va va voom kicked in in spades. The neckline dipped and swooped across the curve of her breasts, framing them in sacrificial-lamb white. 'Is there a shirt to go with this?'

'Front and centre, Sienna dear,' said Grace. 'We won't know until we take a look.'

Sienna stepped out from behind the screen, lifting her arms to her neck and freeing her hair from beneath the collar. 'The hair will have to go up, of course,' said Georgie, coming at her with sewing pins and adjusting the seams and the darts to fit more snugly before crayoning in a new and even more revealing neckline for good measure.

'Uh, Georgie? I was thinking more along the lines of filling this neckline *in*.'

'Nonsense, darling.'

'I don't suppose you have a *mirror* handy?' said Sienna.

Grace shook her head.

'Not even a little one?'

A well-groomed, slimly built dark-haired man appeared with a loaded tea tray, greeting Grace with easy familiarity and sending Sienna a friendly smile completely lacking in sexual interest as he set the tray on the sideboard. Okay, so maybe she'd miscalculated. Maybe this get-up *was* frumpier than she thought.

'Raul makes the *best* tea,' said Georgie, still intent on reworking the neckline. 'He blends it himself. Raul, love, can you bring in the dove grey Armani from rack one room two?'

Raul nodded and headed for the door. Georgie finally crayoned in a neckline on the fabric that she was satisfied with and headed for the sideboard, pouring tea and handing it to Grace with a flourish before turning back to Sienna. 'No tea for you until we're done. The suit Raul's fetching is an elastine-wool blend with the *sweetest* little pinstripe running through it. It's very subtle but I think you could make it work.'

'I like subtle,' said Sienna. 'Subtle is good. And I'm really going to need something underneath this vest. I need to cover my assets, not flaunt them. A business shirt. With a collar. Buttons to the neck…'

'But, darling, *why*?' said Georgie. 'Why not showcase what you've got?'

'I'm having trouble settling into my new job—'

'She's Alex Wentworth's new PA,' murmured Grace.

'I want to be in control.'

'Trust me,' said Georgie. 'In this suit, you will be. What's your shoe size?'

'Seven.'

'Oh, the *envy*,' said Georgie, heading for the doorway. 'I take an eleven.'

Grace took a seat on the pristine white leather sofa, sipped her tea and smiled. 'How are we doing so far?'

'I'm not sure.' Sienna nibbled at the edge of her lip. 'I mean, I love it, don't get me wrong. But not for the office.'

Grace's smile widened. 'The suit will help. Armani never disappoints.'

Armani was a fiend, decided Sienna a few minutes later as she smoothed the suit into place. The fabric was gloriously soft to the touch with an elasticity to it that Sienna had never before associated with wool. The suit was subtle, the skirt modest in length, the jacket cleverly cut to emphasize the vest, the lingerie and the curves beneath without going overboard. This wasn't a clunky corporate disguise. It was sleek efficiency and understated sexuality and, boy, did it feel good. And then Georgie dangled a pair of steel-grey Italian-made stilettos with a three-inch heel over the top of the screen and Sienna's resolve to protest the sexuality of the outfit melted.

'Oh, my,' she murmured. Grace hadn't been kidding about the shoes. Sienna perched on the stool, slipped them on and stepped out from behind the screen only to have Georgie descend on her like a bee on a flower, straightening hems and pinning seams before finally standing back and pursing her lips. 'Slip these on,' she said, and handed her a pair of high-fashion dark-framed glasses. 'Now turn around while I put your hair up.' Sienna turned around obediently and Georgie wound Sienna's hair into a messy knot at the nape of her neck. 'That'll do for now. Now walk out to the next room and come back in as if your boss has just called you into a board meeting. Don't forget to knock first.'

Sienna knocked, but didn't wait for an imaginary invitation to enter. She just sashayed on in and stopped when she reached them, her hands on her hips. Georgie rolled her eyes. But then her sharp gaze roved over Sienna's snugly clad frame and she let out a very unladylike guffaw. 'Girl's got style,' she said. 'My work here is done.'

'It's gorgeous,' agreed Sienna. 'Divine. But I don't want gorgeous. I want sexless.'

'She's so young,' murmured Georgie. 'So misguided.'

'I know,' said Grace. 'Reminds me of myself thirty years ago.' She sent Sienna a rueful smile. 'Bear with me, gorgeous girl, while I dispense a little advice. I've dealt with men like Alex Wentworth for years. Smart, competitive, successful men. Used to getting what they want. The sailing world is riddled with them. And what I've learned is that with those types of men, the best defence is a good offence. A successful businesswoman doesn't hide her sexuality behind some shapeless suit. She wears exactly the type of thing you're wearing now. She wears it with confidence and knows it for a weapon when she needs one.'

'Amen,' said Georgie. 'It's not about how the clothes look—it's about how they make you feel. How do you feel?'

'Powerful,' said Sienna. 'In control.'

'We rest our case,' said Georgie. 'I can have the alterations done and the outfit delivered to you by noon tomorrow. You just say the word.'

'I need a price before I say anything,' prompted Sienna.

'Oh, honey, you've got that businesslike attitude *nailed*.'

Georgie laughed again and named a figure that would have kept a bottle-a-day drunkard in single-malt Scotch for a year. 'Listen to me,' said Georgie. 'I'm practically *giving* that suit away. The cost is in the lingerie and the shoes. I'm throwing in the glasses and my expertise for free.'

Sienna hesitated. Thought of the roof back in Cornwall that needed replacing. Thought of how long it had been since she'd bought new clothes.

'Fully tax-deductible, of course,' said Georgie. 'As are the dry-cleaning costs.'

Great. A suit that required maintenance. She could add it to the list.

'Think of it as an investment in your future,' said Grace.

There was that.

What to do? She really should resist. This get-up was so very wrong for a day at the office with Lex. And yet, perversely, she wondered what his reaction to it would be. Sienna paced and preened while Grace and Georgie made small talk and left her to her thoughts. The shoes were going home with her, no question. So was the lingerie. As for the suit…

'I'll take the lot,' she said. 'Do you take Visa?'

Grace dropped Sienna back at Lex's mansion just on a quarter past one. Sienna waved her goodbye before trying the door handle, only to find the door locked. She buzzed the intercom with a chirpy SOS and then spoke into it for good measure. 'It's Sienna. I'm back.'

'The joy,' said Rudy's voice through the intercom, but he came and let her in and she beamed at him for his effort.

'No Wonder Woman outfit?' he said. 'Shame.'

'Grace and Georgie convinced me to trade up,' she said sweetly. 'The suit of destiny is being delivered tomorrow.'

Rudy stared at her impassively.

'You look tense,' she told him. 'You should have come shopping with us. Ironed out a few of those kinks. That or indulged in them. It's very therapeutic. Did you know that Grace has crewed in the Sydney to Hobart yacht race six times?'

'Yes.'

'And that she's got her hands on an Alliaura Supercat and wants to put it through its paces? Of course, for that she needs a crew. I told her to give you a call, what with one good turn deserving another and all that. The feeling is that you owe her.' Sienna made her way through the atrium and started down the corridor towards her room before stopping and turning back as if she'd just remembered something. 'When's your next day off?'

'Tomorrow,' said Rudy with a scowl.

'I must be a mind-reader.' Sienna's smile deepened. 'I told her that too.'

In the absence of The Suit, Sienna made do and changed into a lightweight skirt and a plain shirt before making her way up the stairs to the business centre at ten to two. Lex was already ensconced behind a glossy blackwood desk, a computer screen off to one side emitting a never-ending stream of stock prices, and another computer screen directly in front of him. He'd changed into different grey trousers and a white business shirt. He'd rolled up the shirtsleeves and left the top couple of buttons undone. If she looked in the top drawer of his desk she'd probably find a tie.

'Rudy said you went shopping,' he murmured, his gaze not leaving the screen, his fingers moving swiftly over the keyboard.

'Rudy was correct,' she replied, forgoing a chair in favour of perching on the edge of his desk. 'Where do I start?'

'With the Scorcellini bid. See if you can get Scorcellini Senior on the phone. Someone bought up three per cent of their stock in the time it took us to fly here. I want to know who. After that I need you to get hold of the last quarter's results for Zintex, Westshelf Mining, and Orion Transport.' He stopped typing and looked up at her, his gaze moving to her outfit as he leaned back in his chair. He took his time with the perusal, his eyes moving leisurely over her curves and turning her insides to mush before finally meeting her gaze. 'Rudy says you went shopping for a business suit.'

'That was the plan,' she said. 'All part of the new me.'

'So did you *get* a business suit?'

'Oh, yes. It's being delivered tomorrow. It needed a few alterations.' She sent him a smile. 'The new me was quite a revelation.'

'There's really nothing wrong with what you have on,' he said next. 'The skirt's a little short for the office, strictly speaking, possibly a little too bright, but your shirt is modest and blends in just fine. Those bone colours always blend. Team it with a pair of dark trousers and you'd have the perfect PA attire.'

'Really?' A smart man would notice a slight curtness in her voice, the tiniest narrowing of her gaze, but Lex didn't seem to. 'Something wrong with colour?'

'In fact,' he said, leaning back in his chair, a picture of dishevelled corporate elegance and power, 'why don't we keep the dress code around here modestly informal and I'll let you know in advance when I want you to don a suit? It's good that you have one, don't get me wrong. But you probably don't need to wear it all that often around here.'

'Don't mind me,' she said smoothly. 'I'm just experimenting with clothing that'll help me keep my mind on the job.'

'Good thinking,' he said. 'Rule three of successful personal assistanting the world over is to dress appropriately. In your case, given your very fine natural assets, I'd even advise toning down a little.'

'Toning down,' repeated Sienna, her voice deceptively pleasant. 'Really?'

'Just a little,' he said. 'You need to give your future employers a constant reminder that you're not available to them on anything but a professional level.'

'I see. You don't think that coming to an understanding about such things at the beginning of my employment would be enough?'

'Depends who's employing you.'

'Tell me something, Lex. Have you ever changed your workplace clothes in order to tone down the effect *you* might have on your employees?'

Lex smiled ever so slightly. 'No.'

'No.' It was okay for *him* to look distractingly fetching. She, on the other hand, had to blend. Grace was right. With men of his ilk the *only* defence was a good offence. 'Well, thanks for the wardrobe advice. I'll try and keep it in mind.'

'Your desk is over there. Yell if you can't find anything.' Lex eyed her warily, as if expecting her to bite. 'Was it something I said?'

'Why on earth would you think that?'

Lex's eyes narrowed and Sienna took it as her cue to get off his desk and on with her work. She was halfway to *her* desk—another beautifully polished blackwood confection accompanied by a black leather chair—when he spoke again.

'Sienna?'

'What?' He probably had another list of things for her

to do. She probably should be sounding a little more obliging. She'd never had a problem with who exactly was in charge of any given workplace situation before. She was a hardworking, co-operative, non-confrontational employee, open to direction and ready to learn. At least, she hoped she was. 'Yes?'

'I've never seen you in a suit.'

'So?'

'I'm trying to imagine what you'll look like in one.'

Sienna thought of the suit of empowerment and smiled at the memory. Some memories were meant to be savoured. 'It's grey,' she said. 'The accompaniments are white. Nice, nondescript colours. I'm sure they'll blend in here just fine.'

Lex's eyes narrowed. 'What about the cut?'

Sienna smiled again, she couldn't help it. 'You'll like the cut,' she said. 'Armani never disappoints.'

Ten hours later, Sienna yawned and leaned back in her leather office chair, barely managing to focus on the computer screen in front of her. The evening meal had been and gone, exquisitely prepared and presented by Rudy the kitchen whiz. The ten p.m. snack Lex had insisted on was nothing but a distant memory. Midnight had come and gone; it was eighteen hours past her usual bedtime. Most normal people would have surrendered to tiredness by now, but the New York stock exchange had just opened for the day, Lex was still working at breakneck speed, and Sienna was attempting—unsuccessfully—to keep up with him.

'Got any money?' said Lex.

'Not any more,' she replied sleepily. 'Why?'

'The share market's moving. Give me ten thousand pounds now and by the end of the day's trading I'll give you back twelve.'

'Sounds wonderful,' she muttered. 'Use your money.'

'You want to stay awake, don't you? I guarantee that if we use your money rather than mine, you'll stay awake.'

'I don't want to stay awake.'

'Where's your sense of adventure?' he cajoled.

'I had a big day. I'm all out.'

'Okay, I'll accept five thousand,' he said.

Money. Always money. Maybe if she stopped trying to hoard what little she had left and started investing it instead, it might grow. It wasn't as if Lex was a novice when it came to working the stock markets. Maybe she'd learn something. Like how to turn a little bit of money into a whole lot more. Wouldn't that be handy? 'All right,' she grumbled. 'Five each. If I go down, so do you.'

His eyes took on a lazy gleam. 'I love equality. Pull up a chair.'

A minute later they were huddled around the computer screen and Lex had his money and hers riding on a hunch that zinc shares were on the up. 'What else is on the up?' she said.

'Energy and electricity,' he murmured and shot her a crooked grin with more than its share of lazy sizzle in it. 'Seriously.'

'Let's put five thousand each on that too,' she suggested. 'I spent a small fortune today on a suit I'm never going to wear. I need to recoup.'

'You spent *how much* on a suit you're never going to wear?'

'Okay, I *might* wear it. Never say never, right? I'm just a little hazy on the when.'

'Yes, but…*how much*?'

'What are those stock prices doing?' she said, trying to distract him.

'Dropping,' he said.

'What?'

'Look at you,' he said in admiration. 'Wide awake.'

'What does a good PA do when she wants to brain her boss with the hole punch?' she muttered.

'She resists.'

For that Sienna was going to need distance. And being cosied up next to Lex, elbow to elbow and knee to knee, simply didn't provide enough. Sienna pushed back her chair and stood up, smothering a yawn with her hand before stretching out the kinks in her back. 'You're on your own, rogue trader-san. I'm going to bed. Wake me in the morning if I'm rich.'

'And if you're not?'

'Hide the hole punch.'

CHAPTER FOUR

SIENNA made it to her bedroom, shimmied into her nightgown, crawled into bed, and slept hard for the rest of the night. Somewhere around sun-up she started to rouse, and toss and turn in the unfamiliar bed as her mind skipped backwards to another big bed in another lake-sized bedroom, and to the people that had populated it. Her mother, porcelain pale as she stared down at the shattered pieces of a broken vase. Her father roaring. Ranting.

'Stupid passionless bitch.'

Never mind that he'd been the one to throw the vase.

'Who are you to tell me what I can spend and where I can go? Who are you to tell me anything? Stupid crone.'

Sienna tossed and turned some more, needing sleep, not getting it. Her mother hadn't been a crone. Her mother had been beautiful, inside and out. Beautiful, and kind, and completely in love with the brooding, black-hearted bastard she'd married.

'You!' Sienna heard her father say savagely as she fell back into fitful slumber, only this time he hadn't been speaking to his wife. 'Get out. Out of my sight!' And as the drawing-room door had closed on her father's rage and her mother's frozen features, 'You're just like your mother.' A smile then, a smile just for Sienna. 'Pathetic, cowering, and weak.'

Sienna woke again at seven, startled into wakefulness when the bedside alarm buzzed into action. She certainly hadn't set it. Presumably Rudy the former frigate midshipman had.

'Man's got a death wish,' she muttered, groping for the clock and fiddling with its bits until it fell silent.

Not a good night's sleep, all told. Not one of her happier memories, although there were plenty worse. Plenty worse.

She contemplated rolling over and ignoring daylight completely in search of less fitful slumber, but if she did that Lex would doubtless come knocking and that would be bad. Lex was dangerous enough as it was; no need to hand him his ammunition on a plate. So it was legs over the side of the bed and a heave-ho as she hauled her protesting body upright. She pushed her hair from her face and finally coaxed her eyes open.

Ah, yes. The *other* lake-sized bedroom. The one she fully intended to exchange for a smaller model at some stage during the day. Sienna had become adept at avoiding her childhood memories. It was either that or be crushed beneath the weight of them.

If her more recent memory served her correctly—and it usually did—the en suite was approximately fifty metres away, somewhere to the south. Sienna got there eventually and took her time in the shower, emerging a whole lot cleaner and slightly more awake.

A hike to the cupboard garnered underwear, dark grey trousers, and a button up white cotton shirt. If Lex wanted her to dress down, Sienna would deliver. For a time. It would make the impact of the suit all the sweeter if she ever did decide to wear it.

Sienna dressed fast, accessorised with some pretty leather sandals and a dainty bead necklace in brown, black and beige, and figured that if she looked any more nondescript she'd disappear altogether. She power-walked back to the bathroom to apply a light dusting of make-up, and then hiked over to the bedroom door and along the never-ending hallway towards the kitchen. There would be absolutely no need for her to use the downstairs gym at any time during her stay, she decided happily. There was more than enough exercise to be had from traversing this house.

No one was in the kitchen, the vast dining room, or the drawing room. The library stood empty, so too did the billiards room. Sienna looked towards Lex's wing of the house but decided against going in search of him there. A man was entitled to his privacy. Someone—probably one of his former women—had once told her that he looked his absolute best between the sheets of a king-sized bed. Sienna didn't doubt it, but she didn't exactly want the image engraved on her brain either.

She went back to her room and collected her sunglasses and ventured downstairs with every intention of exploring the garden or maybe even heading out for a stroll. She hadn't asked what time Lex wanted to start work this morning—she'd simply assumed they'd start around nine like most normal office workers. Knowing Lex that probably wasn't the case. Lex had probably started work around six and was already in the hub wondering where she was.

Wrong.

Lex was swimming laps of the pool, his stroke smooth and powerful as he cut through the water with seemingly effortless ease. Sienna watched a little longer, wondering how she could have ever seen him as anything but the ruthless marauder he was. Smart. Sexy. Driven. Until yesterday she'd thought she was immune to him, but no. The rapid acceleration of her pulse at the sight of his sleek brown body suggested otherwise.

Sienna breathed deep, trying to push the attraction away, out of her body, out of her brain. She didn't want it, couldn't handle it. Couldn't handle him. Not if he really did decide to pursue her. Time to stop staring, and fretting, and go and explore the garden before Lex stopped swimming and Sienna started swooning.

The pool gate opened with a click and closed with a clatter, and Sienna strolled leisurely down to the jetty and along it, enjoying every bit of this peaceful, pretty spot amidst the chaos of a major city. Trust Lex to find it and own it. Trust him to know how to enjoy it.

The jetty rocked gently with the footfall of another and she turned and watched as Lex strode towards her, his hair all wet and mussed, a beach towel riding low on his hips and the rest of him splendidly naked.

Sienna couldn't remember the last time she'd seen Lex's near-naked self. Ten years ago? Longer? She'd called him scrawny once—she remembered that. It had been the day of his fifteenth birthday. He'd pushed her off the catamaran they'd been sailing and refused to let her back aboard until she'd flattered him half to death about the potential of his scrawny, yet surprisingly strong physique.

He wasn't scrawny now. Sienna stared at the stupendous example of raw masculine beauty heading her way—it was impossible not to. Lex's potential had been well and truly realised.

So much for not wanting an image of him without a

whole lot of clothing taking up space in her mind. Because this one was here to stay.

'I like your sunglasses,' he murmured when he reached her. 'Although those lenses aren't nearly dark enough for you to be looking where you're looking.'

Oh. She dragged her gaze upwards past the washboard stomach and sculpted chest, over deliciously broad shoulders and finally found his face. 'My mistake,' she said. 'Nice towel. Great towel.'

He sent her a marauder's grin. 'How'd you sleep?'

'Like the dead.'

'How do you feel this morning?'

'Like the walking dead.' Sarcasm dispensed, Sienna considered the question. 'Not too bad, all things considered. Did I really buy ten thousand pounds' worth of shares last night?'

Lex's smile widened. 'You really did.'

Which meant that Lex had probably seen exactly how much money she had in her account. He'd been sitting right beside her—he had to have seen her meagre bottom line although he'd made no comment. He probably thought it was her working account. No need to mention that it was her only account. 'Do I still *have* ten thousand pounds' worth of shares?' she asked tentatively.

'No, you have eleven thousand seven hundred pounds in cash. We could have realised more but I bailed early and went to bed.'

'You're forgiven.' Hard to be cranky with a man who'd just made her seventeen hundred pounds richer.

'I hate to sound like a broken record,' he said, 'but you'd tell me if you were having money troubles, wouldn't you?' He sounded earnest. He looked earnest. Sienna adored him for his persistence even as she cursed him for it. But she wasn't about to tell him her money woes. If Lex knew of them he'd want to fix them for her and that was out of the question. The trick lay in making him *see* that helping her was out of the question. Sienna leaned her forearms against the jetty railing and stared down at the water, searching for the words that would make him understand. Finally, she thought she had them.

'The thing is, I can accept your helping to train me as a PA because I know that if you turned around tomorrow and wanted to become part of the art world I'd do the same for you. I can accept your hospitality because I can offer mine in return, albeit on a somewhat more modest scale. Maybe you can teach me more about this day-trading caper. Maybe that's an option I need to explore. But I won't take financial help from you, Lex. If I did we wouldn't be equals any more. And I need to be.'

Lex came to stand beside her elbow to elbow, only instead of leaning forward he leaned back against the railing and looked the other way. Once upon a time, Sienna might have leaned her shoulder into his and drawn comfort from that small contact, but not this time. Lex's touch no longer seemed comforting and familiar. It made her as nervous as a skittish kitten who'd never been touched. What would it feel like to be gentled by Alex? She didn't know. She wanted to know.

'If I needed five pounds and you had it in your pocket would you give it to me?' he said reflectively.

'Of course I would.' She knew where he was going with this. 'If you asked it of me. But answer me this. If you knew there was a good chance that you'd never be able to repay me...would you ask me for it?'

'Sienna,' he began, and then stopped abruptly to run his hand through his hair before turning to glare at her.

'At last he walks a mile in my shoes,' she murmured.

'They pinch.'

'You lie,' she said. 'They fit you just fine. Which is why you won't be offering to take care of my financial worries any time soon.'

'I hate it when you're right,' he grumbled. 'Especially when it feels so wrong.'

Lex headed for the yacht and stepped lightly aboard her, before turning to offer Sienna a hand across, expecting her to follow. Which she did. His thumb at her wrist was warm and rich with sensual promise. Sienna's heart tripped and she let go of him fast. 'What happens if you fall in love with a rich man and marry him?' he muttered gruffly. 'I can tell you now that he'll want to take care of you financially.'

'Marriage isn't for everyone,' she said carefully. 'It's not for me.'

'I thought you might have grown out of that particular notion by now,' he said lightly.

'Nope.' Maybe she *had* been carrying the intention never to marry around since childhood, but it still seemed to fit her just fine.

'What about children?' he said next. 'You love kids. Don't you want any of your own?'

'Maybe.' Maybe there were certain flaws in her plan of no commitment. 'Maybe I'll have to just commandeer yours every now and again, and, anyway, I thought men like you liked your women free of commitments.'

'Not always,' he murmured.

Not a lot she could say to that reply. Maybe it was time to change the subject. 'May I come with you when you take *Mercy Jane* out next?'

'You may,' he said, his eyes lightening with the all too familiar promise of adventure. 'You have to see this city from the water. Preferably at dusk. Watch it come alight.'

She'd watched it come alight last night, from the windows of the work hub, and marvelled at its beauty. It would be even more spectacular on the water—Lex was right. 'Sounds wonderful.' It sounded downright romantic, actually. Which, given the way her body had reacted to his nearness this morning, wasn't such a good idea. Lex opened the hatch and disappeared below. Sienna made her way to the helm and started to admire all the nautical bells and whistles. 'I thought I had a lead on those missing paintings a while back,' she said idly. 'A pretty little pond scene turned up in a private collection, origin unknown. I really thought I'd found the Monet.'

'And?' Lex's voice floated up to her.

'It *was* a Monet. Just not my Monet. If I could just *find* it…'

Lex reappeared in the hatch staring up at her, his expression guarded. 'Then what? Then all your financial worries would magically disappear?'

'That's the plan.'

'Even if you do find the paintings, how are you going to prove that they're rightfully yours?' Lex said next, with irritating logic. 'The current owner might have the records to prove that they were purchased in complete good faith.'

'Not the Monet.' Sienna shook her head adamantly. 'The others, maybe, but the Monet was mine. It was a birthday gift from my mother. She even let me choose it from the catalogue. She would never have sold it without telling me.'

Lex eyed her steadily. 'But your father might have. He was perfectly capable of fencing those paintings and spending the change no matter who they belonged to.'

'I know,' she said quietly. 'But I think that if he'd fenced them or sold them outright, word of them would have surfaced by now. People would have seen them by now.' Two Picassos, a Rembrandt and a Monet—they were hardly insignificant doodles. 'If nothing else there would be innuendo about who had them. Rumours. Whispers.' And Sienna would have heard them. She hadn't chosen a career as a curator on a whim. She wasn't aiming to work as a PA for a wealthy collector on a whim either. If someone had those paintings squirrelled away, someone *somewhere* would know of them. It was simply a matter of moving in the right social circles and keeping her ears open. 'No, the more I look for them, the more I think that my mother put them somewhere. For safekeeping.' So that Sienna's father wouldn't do exactly what Lex had just suggested. 'She just...died before she could tell anyone where they were, that's all. One day, *one* day, I'll find them.'

'And when you do? What'll they give you that you don't already have? Wealth? There are other ways of acquiring wealth.'

'Not just wealth,' she said defensively.

'What, then? Happiness? Closure? What?'

When they'd been younger Lex had been as enthusiastic as her about going on a treasure hunt, but as he'd grown older his attitude towards the missing paintings had changed. He'd long since stopped seeing them as a challenging puzzle, and he'd *never* viewed them as a miracle cure-all. These days he considered her continued search for them nothing but a waste of time.

'Maybe closure,' she said quietly. Her mother's death. Her father's...indifference. Somewhere amongst all the venom and passion and sheer destructive force that had been her parents' relationship she still clung to the fragile belief that her mother in particular had had space in her heart for Sienna as well. 'Maybe I do see them as some sort of proof that my mother thought about me before she died. That she tried to provide for me. That she cared. About me.'

Lex sighed heavily, his hard-eyed gaze softening. He didn't say what she knew he was thinking. That if Sienna's mother had *really* cared for her she would never have taken her own life.

'Don't equate those paintings with your mother's love, Sienna. It's not healthy,' he said quietly. 'Mary loved you. Dearly. That's the way I remember it. Maybe that's the way you should remember it too.'

'I do.'

Sometimes.

'I just don't want to see you spend a lifetime searching for paintings you may never find,' he said. 'Maybe if you stopped looking back so hard you'd be more inclined to see those things that are right there in front of you.'

'Like what? A way to solve the current financial crisis I refuse to admit to having?' she countered. 'I'm on it. Reality has been dissected and rearranged with an eye to fiscal improvement. Why do you think I'm here? Which reminds me, what time do you want me to start work in the mornings?'

'Nine is fine. I usually start a few hours earlier to catch the end of the day's share trading in the US but there's no reason for you to start then. I break at seven-thirty or so for breakfast and head back up to the hub at around nine. That's the general schedule.'

It was a punishing schedule by anyone's standards, particularly when he worked late into the night as well.

'Rudy normally serves breakfast in the drawing room,' continued Lex. 'This being his day off, he's prepared all our meals in advance and left them in the fridge. Each meal has its own shelf. According to Rudy you're to serve breakfast in the drawing room and clean up afterwards.

Lunch is served in the drawing room as well and the clean-up procedure still applies. The evening meal is to be served at seven sharp in the dining room. Rudy trusts you know how to use a dishwasher and specifically told me to tell you not to mix meals.'

'Is that so?' she said airily.

'They're calorie balanced. Vitamin and mineral balanced too, for maximum uptake. Nutrition is another one of Rudy's little specialities.'

'The man's a genius,' she said. 'Of course, there is a school of thought that allows you to balance calories, vitamins, and minerals by the *day*. Which means you could, theoretically, choose food from all three shelves at every meal. Rudy would never know. Come to think of it, if I served the meals, *you'd* never know.'

'For some unknown reason Rudy took the time to write out the day's meal menu and leave it on my desk,' Lex told her with a grin. 'He's very thorough.'

'Isn't he just?' The cur. 'You do realise that I'm going to have to tweak *something* about those duties he left for me to do. It's an ownership thing.' Sienna didn't wait for Lex's answer. 'Where would you like your breakfast served, Skipper? Out by the pool? Down here on the boat?' She sent him a conspiratorial smile. 'We could be really rebellious and eat breakfast in the kitchen. I'm good at that.'

'Rebellion?' he queried. 'So I'm noticing.'

'Eating meals in kitchens,' she corrected. 'From the fridge. You should try it some time, rich man. Take a walk on the wild side.'

Lex joined her on the bridge, his eyes telegraphing the promise of a very wild ride should she choose to take it. 'You think I don't walk on the wild side?'

'*I've* never seen it,' she said, moving aside to give him room to move and her room to breathe.

'Then you haven't been looking,' he murmured. 'Would you like to?'

'Eat breakfast in the kitchen? Yes. I'm all for it.'

'That's good.' His eyes had darkened. 'But it's not exactly wild behaviour, now, is it? Now, if I were to come up behind you and put one hand on the wheel and my other hand low on your stomach and pull you back towards me you'd probably find it unexpected,' he whispered against her ear as his movements mirrored his words. 'Hopefully you'd find it pleasant. But it's not wild behaviour. It's just normal behaviour.'

'Ah…Lex? Not for us.'

She didn't know which sensation affected her more, the heat of him at her back or the gentle pressure of his hand at her stomach. But together they set her aflame. Need warred with apprehension, both of them fierce, both of them demanding a response. The compromise was to close her eyes and stand very, very still.

'A man might breathe in the scent of the woman he held in his arms and put his lips to the skin on her neck, but that wouldn't be wild behaviour either,' he murmured as his lips brushed her ear.

Sienna gasped. There was no air left for breathing. Nothing but heat that threatened to engulf her. 'It wouldn't?' Because, as far as she was concerned, her body's reactions were getting very wild indeed.

'No. Not until you turned in my arms and put your hands to my chest and gave me your lips would things get out of control.' Sienna trembled in his arms, she couldn't help it, and Lex groaned and pressed her more firmly against him. 'I've been thinking about what happened between us yesterday, Sienna. I've been thinking about it a lot.'

'I'm surprised you found the time, what with your work schedule and all,' she said, trying to sound unaffected and failing miserably. All she could feel was Lex at her back and all she wanted was more.

'What can I say?' Amusement laced his voice. 'I'm a man who can multitask. I can also,' he said as his lips grazed her neck, 'recognise a problem when I see one coming. You and I, Sienna, have a problem. The only question is…what are we going to do about it?'

'I'm for ignoring it completely and hoping it'll go away,' she said fervently.

'You see, that's where we differ,' he murmured. 'I'm more inclined to find out how big our problem is. What say you, Sienna? You want to find out once and for all how wild this is likely to get?'

She really did.

She knew she shouldn't.

'Turn around,' he whispered.

Sienna turned around.

Hot colour rode high on Lex's cheeks as he stared down at her with eyes that held more than a hint of her own turmoil at the changes taking place in their relationship.

'You know what to do next,' he murmured.

Sienna started where Lex's towel left off, trailing her fingers over his stomach, ridiculously pleased when his breath seemed to catch in his throat and his stomach muscles clenched beneath her touch. His hands rested lightly on her hips, his feet were slightly parted, and she stepped in between them as her palms absorbed the pleasure to be found from tightly budded nipples amidst the damp tickle of chest hair. She lingered a while, learning the feel of him, delighting in the tremors that ripped through him. 'It's not so wild,' she whispered.

Lex covered her hand with his and guided her hand to the back of his neck. 'Yet,' he muttered and bent his head to hers.

Sienna didn't stop to think. She didn't want to think, just feel and taste and take. His lips were firm as she'd thought they'd be. Warm as she'd always known Lex to be. Gentle, as she knew he could be. Nothing she didn't want, but Sienna wanted more. He'd promised her wildness, he'd deliberately sown the seeds of her need for it. Sienna parted her lips and tasted him with her tongue, a leisurely slide along the join of his lips, a request for permission to enter. She expected consent but instead he pulled back.

'Be very sure,' he said gruffly. 'I'm not playing, Sienna.'

'Yes, you are,' she said, her gaze firmly fixed on his mouth, but right now she didn't care. 'You always do.'

'Not always,' he murmured, and set his lips to hers. They parted readily beneath his, soft, willing, following him effortlessly into a kiss that shattered his composure into a million tiny pieces. Lex had known need for a woman before. The sharp end of desire, the wanton side of willing. Known it and revelled in it, but nothing like this. Not like this. He slid his hands over the lush curve of her bottom, drawing her closer, needing her closer still. Sienna gasped and her arms came up to twine around his neck as she pressed against him and all the while her kisses destroyed him. Deep and drugging at first, until she pulled back for an open-mouthed exploration involving the barest brush of lips and tongue and an innate sensuality guaranteed to send him mad. He had her pinned against the ship's wheel with her thighs cradling him and her legs wrapped around his waist before she could do anything more than gasp. Another minute and he'd be carrying her down to the cabin and stripping her naked. Two seconds after that and he'd be buried inside her if he didn't slow this insanity down.

He broke free of her kiss, eyes closed as he fought for control. 'Don't move,' he muttered as she shifted slightly in his arms, framing his hardness even more snugly within the V of her legs. 'Sienna, please.'

She stilled immediately and Lex opened his eyes cautiously, only to close them again at the baffled mix of hurt and confusion in her eyes. He'd started this seduction, not her. And for all his considerable expertise in the area he didn't have the faintest idea how to finish it. 'I don't want to—' But that was a lie. 'I didn't mean to—' Also a fabrication. 'I'm not—

'Interested,' she said raggedly. 'For God's sake Alex, how many times do you think you need to say it? I get the point.'

She really didn't.

'Let me go,' she said, starting to pull away, all sharp elbows and panicked squirming. She was scared, he realised. Of him. 'I'm done with walking on the wild side.'

He released her reluctantly and watched her scramble across the deck and leap from the yacht to the jetty, her cheeks flushed and her eyes glittering suspiciously.

'I knew this was a bad idea. I *knew* it. Twenty years of friendship gone in a heartbeat and for what?' she said from the safety of the jetty. 'One stupid kiss! I valued our friendship, Alex. I needed it.' Tears threatened to spill from Sienna's eyes and Lex prayed they wouldn't fall. He'd rather slit his own throat than make her cry. She looked away, looked out over the harbour, and her chest heaved. 'Now what do we do?' she said brokenly. 'How are we supposed to get past this?'

'Sienna—' But she'd already turned away and started walking down the jetty towards the house. 'Sienna!' Louder this time. Sienna's steps faltered, but she didn't turn around. 'This wasn't some meaningless game of seduction, so if that's what you think you can stop it right now! I needed to touch you, needed to know what we'd be like together, and so did you.'

She still didn't turn around.

'Do you really think I'd throw twenty years of friendship away on a *whim*?'

Sienna's footsteps quickened.

'Goddammit, Sienna. *That was not a stupid kiss!*'

This time Sienna ran.

By the time Sienna reached her bedroom door and had shut it behind her she was breathing hard and heavy with the tears she wouldn't let fall. Panic had set in; fear of the passion Lex had conjured from her so effortlessly had mixed with an overwhelming sense of loss and the combination left her screaming inside. There had been no gain as far as she could see. Only loss, the loss of Lex who had been the one constant in a life full of loss, and she buckled beneath the weight of it. She put the heels of her hands to her eyes and leaned against the wall, striving for some semblance of calm, some interpretation of events that would help her find her way through this mess. Lex had touched her, invited her to kiss him, and she had. That had been her first mistake. Her second mistake had been in getting so caught up in Lex's kisses that she hadn't noticed that Lex hadn't been lost at all.

Lex had still been capable of coherent thought.

Lex, the supremely experienced seducer of women had reduced her to putty and then stopped. He'd had to ask *her* to stop. He'd stripped her down to her soul, but Lex had only been playing.

Footsteps sounded in the hallway. Not the loud clack of shoes on polished wooden floorboards, but the muted thud of a barefoot male. The thuds came closer and stopped at her door, replaced by impatient hammering. No prizes for guessing who it was.

'Go away, Alex.'

'No.' One word, quiet and implacable. 'Let me in.'

'Why? So you can kiss me senseless again just to see if you can make me want you and then stop? I don't think so. Once was enough.'

'I'm not going to kiss you senseless and stop,' he said tightly. 'I'm trying to repair the damage I've just done to the relationship I value above all others.'

'That's very sweet of you,' she said. 'Maybe later. I'm a little busy right now.' Busy trying to stem the flow of hurt from the gaping hole in her heart. 'Now go away.'

'For heaven's sake, Sienna, we were on a boat in broad daylight in full public view. Would you rather I *hadn't* stopped?'

'I'd rather you hadn't started,' she muttered darkly.

'You were just as curious as I was, Sienna.'

'Yes, well, consider my curiosity satisfied. Considering your ability to start and stop at will, I'm assuming your curiosity has been satisfied as well.'

'For the last time, I did not stop because I wanted to! Do you have *any* idea how hard it was to pull back from you? If we'd been anywhere else but on that deck we wouldn't be arguing right now, I'd be buried inside you!'

She didn't want to hear that. She did *not* want to hear that.

'You and I have a problem, Sienna. You *liked* being in my arms—you loved it. And I sure as hell intend to have you there more often. You're worried about ruining our friendship. You should be more worried about where this attraction is headed given what you already mean to me. This isn't a little problem, Sienna. It's goddamn huge.'

CHAPTER FIVE

HUGE.

That was one word to describe the workload Lex set himself and, by default, Sienna over the next four days. Exhausting was another word Sienna could have used if she'd had the energy for speech. She struggled to keep up, but she simply couldn't seem to stay alert come mid-afternoon no matter how many energy shakes Rudy set in front of her. By ten in the evening she was asleep on her feet. Rudy had begun to glower at Lex and make pointed remarks about bringing in additional help if the workload was set to continue on this way. Rudy had left the number for a temp agency on her desk. Sienna wasn't sure if he thought she needed to start looking for another job or if she was supposed to bring in help in order to do this one.

The tension between her and Lex wasn't getting any better. Something had to be done. Somehow, she had to make him see that working them both to death wasn't a particularly smart move when it came to finding a way through the wreckage their kisses had created. It was eight p.m. on a Thursday evening and Lex hadn't called it a night yet. Lex was gearing up for Thursday morning in London, but Sienna had had enough.

She shut down her computer, tidied her desk and shoved the to-do pile in her in-tray. Tomorrow would come around soon enough. She sauntered over to his desk and leaned her rear against the edge of it until she had his reluctant attention.

'I'm clocking off,' she told him sweetly. 'From now on I intend to work for you from nine till say, eight, on a daily basis, with an hour's break for lunch and another hour for dinner. I think that's more than reasonable. Anything over that you're on your own. If the work you want done doesn't get done in that time I suggest you employ additional help or find someone who *can* get everything you want done in a day done. Good luck with that.'

Lex sat back in his chair, his eyes narrowing. 'If you weren't coping you should have said something earlier.'

'I thought you might at some stage come to your senses.' Sienna smiled, sharp as a blade. 'But no. By the way, I'm heading out for a while. Don't wait up.'

He didn't like that.

'Oh, and Lex? You know that problem we had? The one where I had this irresistible urge to test your sexual prowess and find out what all the fuss was about?' Sienna leaned forward, in his face, deliberately confrontational. 'I'm over it.'

Sienna took refuge in the stainless steel wonder of a kitchen after that. It could have worked for her except that Rudy was still there.

'You want supper?' he said.

'No. And I have no idea what Lex wants so don't bother asking. I'm off duty. Possibly on strike. Depends who you talk to.'

'Took you long enough,' he said gruffly and Sienna looked up, startled. She hadn't been expecting support, but now that she had it she might as well take full advantage of the moment.

'Rudy, I need to explore your fridge. Possibly your freezer. Some people look to alcohol for fortitude and stress release, but not me. I need ice cream and I need it now.'

But Rudy was shaking his head. 'You'll need to go out for it. Do you good.'

He was absolutely right. 'Which way to the nearest ice-cream parlour?' There was a string of shops a mile or so back down the road; she remembered them from the drive from the airport. 'Out the driveway and turn right? Can I walk there?'

'Not on your own,' said Rudy.

'Can I take a ferry to somewhere with ice cream?' There was a ferry terminal not far from the house. She'd seen it from the jetty.

'No,' said a familiar voice from the doorway of the kitchen. Lex, looking tousle-haired and brooding and lethal enough to make a big jungle cat think twice about taking him on. 'Rudy, can you get *Angelina* ready? Sienna and I are heading out.'

Sienna ignored him completely. 'What about chocolate?' she said to Rudy. 'I've changed my mind about needing ice cream. Chocolate works just as well for millions of women the world over, right? I'm willing to give it another shot.'

Silently, Rudy removed a domed lid from a silver tray sitting in the middle of the counter. A dozen perfectly presented milk chocolate truffles of varying darkness sat on a white paper doily. He left without another word. Probably to go and make ready with *Angelina*. Sienna leaned forward and eyed the truffles intently. She picked one up, nibbled at the edges. It was creamy and nicely textured, sure enough. But it wasn't cold.

'Face it,' said Lex. 'They're not your weakness.'

'Weakness can be cultivated,' she said curtly. As could resistance to grey-eyed workaholic bosses from hell. Sienna was living proof of it.

'I know this ice creamery on the edge of the water,' he said next. 'Forty-six different flavours. Rows and rows of toppings.'

'Only forty-six? How pedestrian.' She smiled at him none too sweetly for good measure. 'I'm not going anywhere with you, Lex. This evening's plan revolves around getting away from you. I happen to think it's an exceptionally good plan.'

'They make waffle cones on the spot as you order.'

Nice touch. 'What was that address again?' No reason why she couldn't find her own way there.

'Hard to say. I only know how to get there by boat. I could of course *show* you how to get there by boat.' He picked up a truffle and ate it with obvious enjoyment. 'They have a person sitting there making mini Bombe Alaskas. I hear they're superb.'

Bastard.

'C'mon, Sienna. I'm trying to make amends here,' he said.

'For working me so hard?'

'It was either that or haul you into my arms again. I thought I was giving you time to get used to the idea of entering into a relationship with me.'

'What you were giving me was grief.'

He shrugged and sent her a crooked smile. 'Only a little.'

At least they were talking about the problem. She wanted to talk about it, Sienna realised belatedly. She badly wanted to understand what was going on in Lex's head. Why he'd chosen to set them on this course rather than stay on the one they'd been travelling along for years. She nibbled again at the chocolate. Sighed. Bombe Alaska it wasn't. 'I still don't understand how you can want me all of a sudden after a lifetime of never looking at me like that.'

'I looked,' he said. 'You just never saw me. You didn't want to see me.' He smiled grimly. 'You still don't.'

She couldn't deny it. Any time her thoughts about Lex had strayed from ones of friendship she'd slapped them down and kept them down. There was the small matter of self-preservation to consider. 'I know the kind of women you prefer, Alex. They're beautiful. Smart. Rich. You can have any woman you want. Why me?'

'You're beautiful. Smart too, except when it comes to relationships with the opposite sex. When it comes to those you're so scared of entering into the same sort of destructive relationship that your parents had that you'd rather not risk your heart at all. I've watched you, Sienna. No one gets close to you. You cut away anyone who tries. Even me. You're doing it now.'

He was right. She wouldn't wish the twisted love her parents had shared on her bitterest enemy. She didn't want it. Went to great lengths to protect herself from ever getting close to a relationship like that. Lex wasn't her father. He wasn't controlling, bitter, or malicious. But Lex's power to make a woman incandescently happy one day and leave her weeping the next had shades of her father's behaviour in it. Too much of her father in it.

'Has it ever occurred to you that one of the reasons I don't want to get involved with you is that I've watched you play at relationships for years as well?' she said earnestly. 'You leave destruction in your wake, Alex. You walk away the minute you get bored, and the women you leave behind are devastated.'

'They're not that devastated,' he said. 'Most of them feel

the loss of my money and the status that comes with it far more than they feel the loss of me.'

'Oh, Lex.' She shook her head. 'You don't seriously believe that?'

'Happens I do,' he said curtly. 'And might I just add that whenever you start mentioning *all* my women I start picturing a cast of thousands. There haven't been that many.'

'Oh, Lex.' She shook her head again. 'All right. Have it your way. I'll downgrade the number of women you've romanced to *plenty* but then I'm standing firm. You might recall that I've seen a fair few of them come and go.'

'And you might recall that you've known me for years. Average *plenty* out over that time and I bet I can get you down to *not excessive*. Okay, so I've enjoyed my share of female company. I don't deny it and I certainly don't regret it. Because here's the thing, Sienna. I've never entered into a relationship without the hope that I might find what I'm looking for. I've never left one while that hope was still there. Can you honestly say the same?'

She couldn't.

'You want to know why I kissed you?' he said with a twist of his lips. 'It's not because I'm some nefarious playboy intent on yet another conquest. It's because I've been looking for years now for a woman who understands me, fascinates me, and continues to fascinate me on every level. But none of them ever do. I keep circling back around. To you.'

Sienna watched in stunned silence as Lex ran a hand through his hair and glared at her for good measure.

'I have no promises for you, Sienna. You and I together might be the worst combination possible, and given your attitude to commitment it probably will be, but there's no other way through this for me. So here I am. Laying myself wide open and risking twenty years of friendship in the hope of forming a deeper relationship with you.' He looked away but not before Sienna had glimpsed a vulnerability she'd never seen in Lex before. 'You're not even going to let me in, are you?'

'Lex, I—I don't know.' She didn't want to. Self preservation screamed at her to tell him to stop this madness before it began, but this was Lex, and she couldn't bring herself to speak the words that would drive him away from her. She might not be able to give him everything he wanted from a relationship, but surely she could give him something? Enough to make him see that this woman he spoke of…this fascinating woman he kept circling back to simply didn't exist. There was only Sienna, and the Sienna she knew would never be able to hold a man like Lex, even if she wanted to. Which she didn't.

Maybe it *was* time to explore the attraction that pulsed between them. An affair with Lex would be passionate. Exhilarating, for a while. And then it would be over. Passion spent, minimal damage done, and if they were really lucky they might be able to salvage something by way of friendship at the end of it.

'Bombe Alaska, you said?' she said at last.

'Yes.' He glanced back at her and the sudden fierce hope in his eyes caught at her, dismayed her.

Pleased her.

'You'd better not be joking.'

'I never joke about ice cream,' he said solemnly. 'At least, not around you.'

To call *Angelina* a mere speedboat was to do her a grave injustice. Sienna didn't know boats the way Lex knew them, but she knew enough to realise that *Angelina* wasn't simply a ready means of transport for around the harbour.

Angelina was a sleek and luxurious power ride, built for the specific purpose of giving whoever was at the helm a great deal of pleasure. Lex took his pleasure where he found it and always had, even as a boy. He took his pleasure now, skimming the beautiful craft across a smooth expanse of glistening water and leaving a trail of foaming white-wash in their wake.

She knew this man, his reckless smile and his quicksilver ways, his temper and his gentleness. Before too long she would know more of him. Lex wanted it. Curiosity demanded it. Her body willed it. She wanted her hands on him; she wanted his hands on her.

Knowing hands. A lover's hands.

Lex's hands.

Sienna had seen him at the helm of a boat many times before, but she saw him through different eyes tonight. His effortless command of the craft wasn't unusual—her reaction to it was. His innate sensuality had always been there—this time she allowed herself to respond to it, focus on it, revel in it.

'Call it a hint or call it a last-ditch effort to stop myself from turning this boat around and heading straight for the nearest bedroom,' he said huskily, 'but you'd see a lot more of the sights if you tried looking at them.'

The sights. Right. Sienna spared a glance for The Coathanger bridge and the Opera House. Very nice. But her gaze soon slid back to Lex's profile and then to those long tapered hands manoeuvring the craft so expertly through the water.

Lex sighed heavily. 'You're not paying the slightest attention to your surroundings,' he said and stepped away from the helm. 'And you think *I* have a short attention span. Here, you steer.'

It was no hardship taking a turn at the wheel of a craft like this. No hardship at all. Sienna even managed to turn her attention to her surroundings for a while now that she had to concentrate or risk driving them into the path of an oncoming ferry. That was until Lex gathered up her wind-blown hair and tucked it expertly under a cap, his fingertips brushing her neck before setting his hands to her shoulders.

'Better?' he whispered.

Sienna figured a whimper was as good as a yes.

'Turn to port, we're almost there.'

Definitely a good thing. She needed to be somewhere with noise. People. Alternative forms of temptation. Her attention was *bound* to be diverted once ice cream had been placed in her path, right?

Wrong.

For once in her life frozen dairy delights simply couldn't compete, no matter how delicious. And it *was* delicious. Lex had to finish half of her Bombe Alaska for her, a tragedy of the highest order, except that somehow the combination of Lex and ice cream became temptation of the highest order instead. Lex's lips would be cool from the ice cream; his mouth would taste of it.

When Lex stopped walking to lean against a big wooden jetty post and finish off the last of her ice cream, Sienna left common sense behind and let temptation take hold. She stepped up close, took the ice cream dish from his unresisting hands and set it on top of the post before dropping her cap to the deck, and setting her lips to his.

Cool, just as she'd known they would be. Firm, just the way she wanted them to be. He shuddered when she ran her tongue along the seam of his lips, but he didn't pull back, not this time. This time he opened for her, twining his hands in her hair and taking her deep into uncharted territory. By the time she remembered where they were and broke the kiss, she was shaking hard and Lex was cursing, sailor fashion, his grey eyes signalling a fast-approaching storm.

'What the hell was that for?' he muttered.

'You were eating my ice cream,' she said defensively. 'What did you expect? Restraint?'

'A *warning* would have been nice. Or privacy. Definitely privacy.' He dumped the ice cream in a nearby bin while she retrieved her cap. She was setting it back on her head when he grabbed her hand, and headed for the boat, his long, purposeful strides forcing her to hustle to keep up with him.

'Where are we going?'

'My place. Your place. The workplace. Home. We're done with sightseeing.'

An independent woman might object to his high handedness. A feisty woman would remind him that he could at least *ask* her if she wanted to see more of the harbour before handing down declarations from on high. Sienna just looked at him and smiled a reckless smile.

'Here's the plan,' he said tightly once they'd boarded *Angelina*. 'You sit in that seat and you take in the sights. You do not move and you do not speak. You do not *look* at me until we reach the house. Are we clear on that?'

'Crystal,' she said.

Sienna became a creature of sensation on the way back to the hub. The wind on her face and the throbbing rumble of the engine as *Angelina* sped across the water. The rising tension coursing through her body on account of Lex's nearness and the realisation of where this was all heading. The lazy rhythm of the ocean's swell as they approached the outer harbour. The sudden loaded silence as Lex cut the throttle and steered the speedboat gently into place beside *Mercy Jane*.

It didn't take long to secure the boat. It didn't take long for Lex to walk her to her room. Once at the door he shoved his hands in his pockets and leaned against the wall. Watching. Waiting. Waiting for her to make the next move. But she didn't know how.

'Invite me in,' he murmured.

'It's your house.'

'It's your room.' His eyes were dark and promised heaven if only she would take a chance on him. 'I need to hear the words, Sienna. Invite me in.'

If she took this final irrevocable step towards intimacy there would be no going back to the easy friendship they'd once shared. When it finished, and it *would* finish, that would be the end. She made one last valiant effort to alter course, knowing in her soul that it was already too late, that this way lay heartache. She'd been stepping towards it ever since she'd first kissed him. 'We're friends.'

'Bonus,' he said.

'I'm your employee.'

'That definitely adds a little something,' he murmured.

'This is never going to work.'

'How do you know?' he said silkily. 'Until you try?'

Sienna fumbled for the door handle, turned it, and watched as the door opened silently. Tension clawed at her. Her body railed at her to forget her fear of failure and abandonment and to hurry.

'You know, this might come a lot easier for you if you just stopped *thinking* the moment through and just let it *happen*,' he murmured.

She took a deep breath and turned to face this man she knew so well in so many ways and not at all in others.

'When have I ever hurt you.' he said quietly, and clinched the deal, right there and then.

'Come in,' she said raggedly and held the door open for him.

She followed him in and shut the door behind her. She tried to smile but she was too nervous. She wasn't a virgin, but this was Lex and he made her feel like one. She took a breath and a step towards him. Another breath and he had her backed up against the door as he lowered his head and captured her lips with his.

He'd been expecting resistance, possibly token, possibly not. He'd expected hesitation, a physical manifestation of her earlier words. He didn't get any. What he got was warmth and softness and a quiet invitation to take a little more. He deepened the kiss and she let him. He trapped her between the wall and the circle of his arms and she let him do that too. And then she fisted her hand in his shirt and pulled him towards her as her kisses turned ravenous, instantly catapulting him into a world where nothing existed but blinding desire and the desperate need for more.

There was a bed here somewhere, Lex was sure of it, and he headed in the general direction of it amidst frantic kisses and the escalating need for flesh on flesh. She tugged his shirt free of his trousers and started in on the buttons, from the bottom up. He started on her shirt buttons from the top down. They tangled somewhere in the middle amidst laughter and curses and all the while her kisses fed his soul. Lex's shirt went, so did hers. He set his lips to her breasts the moment it was gone, demanding a response and getting one as she whimpered her pleasure and arched into teeth and tongue.

'Alex!' His name ended on a half-sob, raw and needy, equal parts command and surrender.

He lifted his head and met her gaze in wordless acknowledgement of a force far greater than the sum of its parts, and then he was unzipping her trousers and removing them along with her panties and Sienna was doing the same for him, her movements every bit as frenzied as his own. Sienna, with her quick smile and contrary ways. Sienna, who drove him mad and challenged his thoughts the way no one else could. Sienna, who made his body burn with a need so hot and fierce he could have rivalled the sun. Soft, so smooth and soft, as he slid one hand into her hair and the other hand down her body. So damned responsive, the hand in her hair becoming a silken fist, part binding and part capitulation as he set his lips to her collarbone, her neck, the edge of her jaw…

Needing her abandoned response. Getting it.

'Alex, please!'

He wanted to please, he really did, but his body demanded instant gratification; no foreplay, none of his usual finesse. He wanted inside her, needed it more than he needed to breathe. This wasn't the casual recreational love-making of an adept; this was possession in its purest form.

He tumbled her down onto the bed in a tangle of arms and legs. Sienna's eyes were closed, the corner of her lower lip caught between her teeth, making the colour there flee. He wanted in, into her mouth, into her body before she drew blood; his blood or hers.

Lex got his wish; lips against lips, tongue against tongue as he sheathed himself deep inside her with a single smooth thrust.

One stroke, two, before Sienna's inner muscles began to contract around him, and then she was coming apart in his arms and he was following helplessly in her wake, feeding her abandon, revelling in it, matching it.

Enslaved by it.

CHAPTER SIX

SIENNA gulped down ragged breaths as her body recovered from its lightning trip to the stars. Lex was somewhere off to her left, sprawled on his back, his chest bellowing as he too struggled for breath amidst spasms of deliciously masculine laughter. Heaven only knew what he was laughing *at*. Wild monkey sex that had lasted less than two seconds, perhaps? The indelicacy of their current positions? The way he'd barely had to touch her for her to come apart in his arms?

All of the above?

'Here's the plan,' she said, her eyes tightly closed as she groped for a pillow to cover her face and hide her utter mortification at the speed of her surrender. 'If you take your shirt and your trousers and *leave* there's a slim chance I might be able to convince myself that this never happened.' Sienna hit softness with her palm and dragged the fluffy pillow across her eyes and her nose, leaving only her mouth free for talking. 'So….you know…don't let me keep you.'

More laughter from Lex and then movement from him. The mattress dipped but he didn't seem to be getting off the bed. No, it felt a whole lot as if he'd rolled over towards her and propped himself up on his elbow. Which meant that he was in all likelihood staring down at her—and there she was with her legs open and her limbs trembling, stark naked, in the lamplight. Oh, dear God!

Forget her face, the pillow was needed elsewhere. Breasts, no! Lower. No. Lengthways to cover both those areas. Sienna positioned the pillow for maximum coverage, hugging it tight, her eyes still firmly closed in an increasingly futile attempt to deny reality.

'What are you *doing*?' said Lex as he removed the pillow from her clutching arms, never mind her attempts to keep it.

Sienna eased one eye open and shut it again quickly at the sight of smooth supple skin encasing perfectly sculpted muscle. 'Pretending I'm not here?' she ventured.

'Sienna, look at me,' he murmured and she opened her eyes to find him staring down at her with an intensity he usually reserved for billion-dollar deals. 'Don't you think it's a little late for that?'

'Not at all,' she said fervently. 'I'm willing to give it a whirl.' Anything to ease her embarrassment at the speed of her capitulation. 'I, ah…I'm sorry I rushed you.'

'It wasn't that rushed.'

'You lie.'

'All right,' he said. 'I concede that we may have been somewhat hasty. But that's easily rectified.' The gleam in his eyes turned wicked. 'Touch me.'

'Again?'

'You didn't really think we were finished here, did you?'

'I was really, really hoping we might be.'

'No, you weren't,' he whispered and proceeded to show her why.

Round one should have taken the edge off his hunger, thought Lex as he set his lips to Sienna's shoulder, her collarbone, the soft curve of her breast. Unfortunately, it hadn't. Sienna only had to touch him for his hunger to become insatiable. She only had to gasp and arch into his touch for need to overwhelm him.

When she rolled him onto his back and set her lips to his chest he nearly launched them both off the bed. When she trailed her fingers up his thigh and slid her mouth even further down his body Lex knew he had to do something before this lovemaking session went exactly the same way as the last. Not that fast and frantic didn't have its place, because clearly it did, but a man had his reputation to think about, not to mention the woman in his arms. A modicum of restraint wouldn't go astray. Civilised sex. Languid sex. Surely he could manage that?

Sienna's palm skated across his erection and her tongue touched the tip, and all thoughts of civilised behaviour came to a groaning halt. Lex shot out from beneath her, cursing, half laughing, as he rolled her over and pinned her face down against the bed, one hand on the small of her back as he half straddled her to stop her turning over and reaching for him again. Better, much better, as he slid her silky hair to one side and nipped the back of her neck. Sienna moaned and tried to turn around but he wasn't having that. There was the small matter of control. Lex had it. He was keeping it.

'Here's the new plan,' he whispered. 'Close your eyes, think of England, and we might just manage the minute-and-a-half mark this time.' Lex ran his hand up Sienna's spine to the base of her neck and back down again until he reached the delightful vicinity of her bottom. He took his time exploring the curve of her buttocks, the slenderness of her waist, her buttocks again, this time with the accompanying scrape of teeth. 'There's no rush. I'm not going anywhere.'

Sienna whimpered but it wasn't with pain. She bucked beneath Lex's ministrations but it wasn't to dislodge him. There was no later, not yet. There was only now. Digging her fists into the sheet, Sienna gave herself up to it.

'Relax,' he whispered while his hands and teeth raised goosebumps on her skin. The soft abrasiveness of the sheet beneath her cheek felt like sandpaper compared to Lex's mouth on the curve of her hip. Another whimper escaped her.

'Shh.' A long, languid stroke of her back with his hand. The rasp of his leg against hers. A kiss between her shoulder blades. He soothed her even as he drove her body higher.

And then he was rolling onto his back and taking Sienna with him, her bottom nestled against his hardness and her shoulder blades digging into his chest as he parted her legs and slid his hand possessively over her hips.

'Relax.'

But Sienna's body wouldn't let her.

He entered her around about the time he set his fingers to her centre. He slid his other arm around her waist at exactly the same time as he started to move. Controlling everything; every caress, every sensation until Sienna was almost blind with the need for release. 'Alex, please! I can't see you. I need to see you. Touch you.'

'Later.'

'Now!' Sienna strained in his arms, her nails digging into his forearms. 'Let me turn around. Alex, please!' She was almost there, almost there…

'No.' His voice sounded husky, strained, his breath a warm caress that whispered through her hair. 'Close your eyes, Sienna. Close your eyes and feel.'

Sienna closed her eyes, cursing him for his control and her lack of it.

And then she slid her hand down his arm, past where his fingers pressed firmly against delicate flesh and on to where their bodies joined. Slickness and heat as Lex surged into her, his body tightening beneath her questing fingers.

'That wasn't quite what I meant,' he muttered unevenly.

'I know.' She'd thought to undo him but it was she who came undone, arching her back the better to take him deep inside her as she began to climax.

Moments later, Lex followed.

Lex bit back an oath as his body twitched and softened in the aftermath of ecstasy. He lay on the bed on his back, with Sienna next to him, also on her back—this time minus the pillow. He considered the lack of a pillow an improvement, of sorts. The baleful glare Sienna slanted his way wasn't an improvement at all.

'You *restrained* me,' she said accusingly.

'Only a little. It was supposed to slow things down.'

'Well, it didn't!'

He'd noticed. Lex hoped he didn't look smug. He certainly felt smug. The passion and abandon Sienna had brought to their lovemaking made him feel like a king. Maybe a pirate king. 'Got any rope?'

Sienna's fist shot out and caught him in the gut.

'Oomph! Guess not.' Lex began to chuckle.

'Not funny, Alex.'

'Illuminating, though.' He reached down and entwined his fingers in hers in case she decided to thump him again.

'You asked me to touch you and then you *stopped* me. Again.'

'You can probably touch me *now*,' he offered. 'But I'm making no promises where future lovemaking is concerned. Every time you touch me I lose control.'

Sienna looked away and Lex discovered that he far preferred her glare.

'Say it,' he said. 'Whatever you're thinking, say it.'

'I don't know what to say,' she muttered. 'I don't know the rules of this game.'

'It's not a game.'

'I don't know the rules for one of those either. I'm working for you, living in your house, friends with you, and now I'm your lover. I've never had a relationship quite this complicated before.'

'It's not that complicated.'

'You,' she said with a tremulous smile, 'are a cockeyed optimist.'

'I'm thinking that's just another term for visionary.'

'Fool,' she said, but her smile grew firmer. 'I need some rules, Lex. I need my own space and a way of knowing when you want me to be your PA, when it's okay to be your lover, and when you want me to just be your friend.'

Lex sighed and ran a hand through his already dishevelled hair. He'd known this would come. Sienna never had been one to stop analysing a situation long enough to simply go with it. 'All right, guidelines.' He didn't think it was quite the time to mention that he'd never been this neck-deep in complications before either. 'The main guideline being that the work gets done. There's no office politics to worry about because working for me is only a temporary arrangement and no need to be discreet because no one else is working with us. That takes care of our employee-employer relationship. As far as our platonic relationship is concerned it's business as usual. Any time you need your own space just tell me and I will do my utmost to make sure you get it. When it comes to lovemaking why don't you just consider me at your disposal for the foreseeable future?'

'You're very decisive,' she said.

'It's part of my charm.'

'There's no going back for us, is there?' she said a touch wistfully.

'No. But look on the bright side—and I really wish you would—I don't see why we can't happily mix business and friendship with pleasure.'

She sat up and glanced down at him, her eyes satisfyingly appreciative as her gaze swept over his body. 'I'm pretty sure the work will get done,' she said. 'It's not as if our lovemaking takes up a lot of time…'

Ow! 'Mind the ego, Sienna. Lucky for you it's healthy.' Alas, not that healthy. 'Was that a complaint?'

'Not at all.' Sienna reached for her clothes. 'Although…'

'Was it a challenge?'

'Would you like it to be?' Sienna's slow-burn smile sent a shaft of heat straight through him. 'A man like you needs to be challenged every now and then, don't you think? Keeps you humble.' Clothes in hand, she headed for the bathroom with a sensual sway to her stride that Lex heartily approved of. 'Now, if you don't mind, I think I'll take a shower and get some sleep. My boss is a slave-driver, I have a huge day of work ahead of me tomorrow, and I need to be refreshed enough to get it done before I can go sailing with my lover tomorrow night.'

When the bathroom door closed firmly behind her, Lex sat up, his grin wide and his thoughts anything but humble as he reached for his trousers.

Sienna wanted more of him.

CHAPTER SEVEN

SIENNA worked her behind off for Lex the following day and together they cleared the backlog. She managed to hold the memories of their lovemaking at bay, concentrating on the work, sticking fast to the notion that the work had to be done before they could play. No touching, no distracting him, no undressing him with her eyes when he was watching, and above all no remembering the pleasure he could bring to her body.

And if the dampness and warmth between her legs was a constant reminder of Lex's possession and if her inner muscles rippled every so often in remembrance of him, well, she'd kept that to herself and turned her attention to counting ferries on the harbour instead.

At five past six Lex swivelled around in his desk chair and stole her breath away with a single look. 'Come sailing with me,' he said.

So here they were, as the sun set lower and the night crept in, taking turns at the wheel as they chased the wind in search of speed. *Mercy Jane* skimmed effortlessly through the water, responding obediently to Lex's every command, and he rewarded the little boat by making her fly. Sienna rewarded her own obedience to the demands of the day by slipping inside the circle of Lex's arms and letting the breeze caress her face as her body grew pliant and her need to undress him grew fast.

One ferry. Two ferries. Two ferries and a hydrofoil…

Sex with Lex had been breathtakingly good and she couldn't deny her need for more of it. No wonder his girlfriends wept when he left them. No wonder they begged and pleaded with him to stay. But he never had, he never did, and Sienna wasn't fool enough to think that this time would be any different. He saw, he conquered, he moved on. That was just his way. The trick to getting through these next few weeks would be to never take him seriously. Never give her heart to him so that when the ride ended she would remember it with joy.

So that when the ride ended she would not weep and she would not beg.

She could control this overwhelming need for more of him. She *could*.

'A good PA would do something about acquiring dinner,' she said, desperately trying to ignore her body's demands.

'A gentleman would have taken care of dinner reservations already,' he replied. 'A gentleman would have packed a picnic hamper and a bottle of champagne.'

'Gentlemanly behaviour is all well and good, don't get me wrong,' she murmured. 'But I'm woefully easy, I'm not dressed for dining out, and I know full well you didn't pack a picnic hamper. All I want is the champagne.'

'You'll find some in the fridge below.'

'Perfect.' Sienna looked towards the approaching inlet: a sheltered cove with a tiny strip of secluded beach. Five more minutes, she told herself firmly. Five more minutes and you can touch him some more.

'Sienna,' he said tensely, and the raw desire in his voice

and the unmistakable hardness pressing against her left her in no doubt that she wasn't the only one practising restraint right now. 'Maybe you need to go and find that champagne now.'

'And maybe you need to find us a parking spot,' she muttered as she slipped from his arms and headed for the hatch.

By the time she'd found a couple of non-breakable champagne flutes and popped the bottle Lex had dropped anchor and joined her in the galley. 'How many glasses of this stuff do you think we'll need?' she said and quickly dropped her gaze when his eyes met hers, wickedly knowing.

'In order to replace an evening meal?' he said. 'A few.'

'How about in order to slow our lovemaking down?'

'A few.' His smile was pure rogue. 'Maybe we need to go back up on deck for a while and enjoy the sunset. Kick back and relax. Make small talk.'

'Small talk?' she murmured. Big ask given the shimmering promise that filled the air. But she made her way back up on deck and settled down port side, with her legs dangling over the side of the boat and her champagne flute beside her, and prepared to watch Sydney come alight. Raucous screams sounded in the distance, a cacophony of unexpected jungle sounds. 'What was *that*?'

'Monkeys. We're next to the zoo.'

'Oh.' Monkeys. Handy. No need to worry about the odd cry of ecstasy what with all those monkeys around. 'So…' she said. 'Come here often?'

He smiled crookedly and sat down beside her. 'Only if I'm in the area.'

She wanted to ask him who he came here with, but figured the list would likely be long, illustrious, and thoroughly demoralising. Small talk. Small talk… There wasn't a lot about Lex that she didn't already know. 'How's your mother?' she said.

The look Lex sent her was faintly incredulous.

'You said you wanted small talk,' she reminded him.

'Not about my *mother*. She's well, by the way. Says to remind you that you promised to visit her when you get back. She'll want to know how I treated you. She'll be hoping you'll say I treated you well.'

'Mothers and their expectations.'

'*I'll* be hoping you'll say I treated you well.'

'*I'll* be wishing I was paddling up the Amazon,' said Sienna dryly. Adriana Wentworth had served as a mother figure and confidante on many occasions. This would not be one of them. 'Maybe I'll go home by way of Dubai. Find another sheik in need of a PA. That could solve a multitude of problems. You'll probably be ready to move on by then. I may have come to my senses. There's probably no need to mention our current arrangement to your mother at all.'

'What makes you think I'll be ready to move on?' he said lazily, but his eyes were sharp. Lex at his most disarmingly dangerous.

'You always do.'

'That again,' he said.

'Face it, Alex. You enjoy women. And they enjoy you. It would take a rare woman who could get your undivided attention and keep it.'

'You're rare,' he said.

'Not that rare.'

'I don't know whether to be insulted on my behalf or yours,' he muttered. 'Why can't you take me seriously, Sienna? What are you so afraid of?'

Of never measuring up. Of never being worthy of anyone's love. Of not being able to keep it. 'The usual,' she said finally, avoiding his gaze in favour of staring at the Harbour Bridge instead. 'You were right about me, Lex. I don't find it easy to let people in. Even you.'

'What are so you afraid I might find in there?'

Sienna picked up her glass, but didn't drink from it. Instead she played with it, cradling it loosely between both hands, her hands between her knees so that if the boat rocked and the champagne in the glass spilled it would fall into the water. 'Nothing you want,' she said quietly.

Alex fell silent at that and together they watched as the sun lost its battle for supremacy over the sky and moonlight took its place.

'Drink up,' he said finally and touched his glass to hers before draining his glass in one long swallow.

'What am I drinking to?'

'I'd say to us, but I'm not sure you'd raise your glass,' he said somewhat dryly. 'We could always drink to the prospect of long and languorous lovemaking.'

'So we could,' she said with the tiniest of smiles. 'Here.' She picked up the bottle and sloshed more bubbles into his glass. 'Have another.' Lex's smile grew lazy and intent and Sienna's pulse began to quicken. 'Cheers.' She finished hers for good measure.

'Sienna?' Even his husky murmur could set her to trembling these days.

'What?'

'Maybe you should have another one too.'

Lex's lovemaking had lost none of its intensity. Sienna expected passion and he gave it freely. She expected heat and he burned her up with it. But she hadn't expected tenderness and he gave her that too. She could feel it in the way he undressed her, and in the sweetness of his kisses.

Lex wasn't just sating a fleeting hunger, he was laying himself wide open, revealing kiss by kiss all that he was.

Passionate. Gentle. Patient. Playful.

Sienna's first orgasm built slowly and lasted for ever.

There was nothing inside him she didn't want more of.

CHAPTER EIGHT

ON HER first free Saturday Sienna took the opportunity to escape the hub and head for Hornsby, by way of a ferry at first, followed by a train. From Hornsby station she continued on foot. She had a map and two good legs, it was a beautiful day, and she needed the exercise. Rudy's cooking was a little bit too good at times. Sienna was seriously contemplating having to become better acquainted with Lex's downstairs gym after all.

After twenty minutes spent walking in a south-easterly direction she found the street. Five minutes after that she found the house, a neat brick house with a red-tiled roof and a tiny, tidy garden filled with chrysanthemums.

She fumbled in her bag for the letter, wishing not for the first time that Elsie had included her phone number with her address. She'd tried looking in the phone book and ringing the directory, but there had been no E Blaylock listed at the address on the envelope. Then again, Elsie had left Sienna's mother's employment to go and look after her ageing sister. Maybe the phone number was in her sister's name.

Elsie Blaylock. Kind-eyed, grey-haired Elsie. She'd been housekeeper to Sienna's family for the first eleven years of Sienna's life. Closest thing to a grandmother Sienna had ever had.

Hesitantly, Sienna looked at the letter again. She'd found it last year amongst a box of bills and paperwork pertaining to the sale of her childhood home. Some twelve years ago now Elsie had given her address as 42 Aldersley Road, Hornsby, Sydney, Australia. This was the place. All she had to do was walk up that path to the door and knock, but still Sienna hesitated.

She should have written. Elsie would be in her seventies now, or thereabouts, and might not even remember Sienna. Calling on her in the hope of a clue to the painting's whereabouts was ridiculous. Calling on her because Sienna was desperate to sit and talk to someone else who'd borne witness to the travesty that was her parents' marriage was ridiculous too. And yet…

Maybe, just maybe, Elsie *would* remember her, and offer her tea, and start to reminisce. Elsie hadn't forgotten Sienna in the letter she'd written. It was a pleasant letter, a chatty letter that told of Elsie finding her sister's health much improved, and of her belongings finally arriving and of how hard it was to squash two lifetimes' worth of memorabilia into the one household. It spoke of scorching summer days and desert-dry gardens and a hope that all was well in Cornwall. Elsie's sister kept finches, Elsie had told Sienna's mother. Sweet-natured little birds with striking markings and a busy way about them. Elsie was growing quite fond of them but finches weren't children. You couldn't hug them. Elsie had asked about Sienna. Elsie had said that she missed the little girl terribly. Her last sentence directed Sienna's mother to give Sienna a big hug; a big bear hug from Elsie.

Sienna couldn't ever remember getting that hug.

Maybe, just maybe, she would get it now.

She opened the knee-high wooden gate and followed the path to the door. Taking a deep breath, she fisted her hand and knocked on the security door.

No one answered.

She knocked again.

And again.

Nothing.

She hadn't thought past getting here. She hadn't thought about what she would do if no one was home. Sighing, Sienna trudged back up the garden path towards the little gate. Maybe she could leave a note in the letterbox with her phone number on it.

'You're after Margaret?' said a light and friendly voice. A neighbour, studying her from the other side of the adjoining fence. A neighbour who looked to be about Sienna's age, with a lively, curious face.

'Er, no,' said Sienna. 'I'm looking for Elsie. Elsie Blaylock. This is the address I have for her, but I don't know…' Sienna shrugged and put the envelope carefully back in her handbag. 'The information is old.'

'I don't know that anyone named Elsie lives there,' said the neighbour, frowning. 'That's Maggie Cameron's place.'

Could Maggie Cameron be Elsie's sister? Possibly. Sienna had no idea of Elsie's sister's name. 'Do you know when Maggie might be back?'

The woman shook her head. 'No.'

'Do you know how long she's lived here?'

'Longer than me,' said the woman. 'And we've been here ten years. Do you want to leave a message with me for her?'

And say what? Hello, my name is Sienna Raleigh and I'm trying to track down an old friend and a bunch of missing paintings? What if it wasn't Elsie's sister at all?

'No. I'll call back another time.' Maggie Cameron. Maggie Cameron. With any luck Maggie Cameron's phone number would be in the phone book and Sienna would be able to call the woman rather than turn up on her doorstep unannounced. Call her and explain.

Another week went by and Lex watched, unsurprised, as Sienna gradually worked the rhythms of his household around to her liking, taking to big business as if she were born to it and to Rudy as if it were her mission in life to annoy him. Lex didn't interfere because it was perfectly obvious that Rudy enjoyed her baiting and could more than hold his own. Rudy kept making triple cream vanilla ice cream and giving Sienna the tiniest taste before tasting it himself, deeming it highly unacceptable, and giving the rest of it to the next-door neighbour's Rottweiler.

When it came to their personal relationship Sienna seemed happy to spend her spare time with him, happy enough to share his bed or for him to share hers, but true intimacy with Sienna eluded him. He'd known that breaking down Sienna's barriers to intimacy wouldn't be easy. He'd been counting on their years of friendship to make it easier for her to trust him, easier for him to win her love, but when it came to love it seemed Sienna trusted nothing and no one. Whenever he tried to talk of a future beyond their time in Australia he repeatedly hit a wall so solid and so high that he didn't have the faintest idea how to climb it.

He didn't want to push. He knew he shouldn't push. Patience was the key.

Unfortunately, patience had been a little hard to come by of late. He'd turned to his work, knowing it for a distraction, nothing more than a convenient excuse to avoid focussing more strongly on what he wanted from Sienna.

Soon there would be a reckoning. Soon he would push for something Sienna did not want to give. But not yet. Not yet.

When it came to Sienna's work ethic, Lex couldn't fault her. Sienna learned fast, surpassing seasoned personal assistants with her appreciation for the nuances of negotiation and her ability to recognise what was important and what was pure ploy. If he hadn't had other plans for her he'd have offered her a permanent position and a pay rise by now, but he did have other plans so he kept his praise to a minimum. Sometimes, though, praise simply had to be given.

'You really were wasting your talents as an art curator,' he told her bluntly after she'd fielded yet another urgent phone call from Scorcellini Junior about Lex's latest bid.

Scorcellini Junior had a good head for business but he didn't have his father's experience and he didn't hold the majority stake in the business. Sienna had the younger man's measure. She also, thought Lex wryly, had Scorcellini Junior completely charmed. 'If they'd had any sense they'd have made you a museum director.'

'Flattery will get you everywhere,' she said with a smile.

'I meant it. You're good at this. See if you can set up a meeting with both Scorcellinis for Monday. The son is going to have to fall in line with his father's wishes on this one and the sooner he does, the better for everyone.'

'Your territory or theirs?'

'Mine. Wear your suit.'

'Er, Lex? You might want to rethink the suit strategy. You don't quite know what you're asking.' Sienna glanced towards the door as it began to open, her smile turning into an outright grin as a scowling Rudy stomped into the room.

'The quiche is cold,' said Rudy darkly. 'It was made to be eaten *hot*. When do you think you might get to it?'

'Blame Lex,' said Sienna the traitor, happily feeding him

to the watchdog. 'I was good to break for lunch an hour and a half ago.'

'Blame Scorcellini Senior,' said Lex. 'He's had second thoughts about the opposing rescue bid. Seems we're back in the game.'

'I'm very happy for you,' said Rudy, in no way mollified. 'Perhaps if your personal assistant could let me know of any future schedule changes in *advance*?'

'Rudy, my sweet,' said Sienna, in no way cowed. 'The minute he *tells* me in advance, you will know.'

Rudy shook his head, clearly disappointed with Lex and Sienna both. 'I'll bring the lunch plates up.'

'I'll help you,' said Sienna, stretching her arms above her head before getting to her feet. 'What?' she said, at Rudy's offended look and Lex's amused one. 'I need a break. You need a break. Even Rudy needs a break. Look at him.'

Lex looked at him. 'What's wrong with him?' Apart from the scowl.

'How on earth is he going to make decent ice cream with a frown like that? Not that you need to keep trying,' Sienna told Rudy magnanimously. 'Grace is coming round at six-thirty this evening with a no-fail ice-cream recipe. We're going to commandeer the kitchen while she shows me how it's done.' Sienna gave Rudy her very best smile. 'Feel free to watch.'

Lex eyed the shaping battle appreciatively. Nice shot, straight over Rudy's bow.

'We might make use of the billiards room as well,' said Sienna. 'I hear Grace is quite the grifter. Apparently an old sailor taught her how to play when she was a child. Mind-boggling, really. Grace being so elegant and refined and pool being such a ballsy game. Wonder what she'll wear?'

Direct hit. Rudy turned and strode from the room

without another word, with Sienna following in his wake, turning to wink at Lex as she left. 'We'll be right back with the food,' she said. 'You just keep right on working.

'Tell me, Rudy…' Sienna's voice floated back to him from the atrium. 'Do you play nine ball?'

Sienna followed Rudy into his kitchen, her thoughts only marginally taken up by the food Rudy had prepared for them, never mind how delicious it was guaranteed to be. Most of her thoughts these days were tied up with Lex. Lex's lovemaking, Lex's smile, his patience with her when it came to matters of the heart, and his ability to compartmentalise his life. The latter was really beginning to annoy her. Walk into that hub and Lex the lover became Lex the driven corporate raider. He did not push for any kind of physical intimacy at all within their working environment. Not even the brush of his hand against hers as he passed her some paperwork.

He could have given her *some* small physical contact, the rotter.

Because the only thing his noble restraint in that direction had done was make her want him more. Every time she went near the man her pulse raced and her body remembered the feel of his hands on her. Whenever he sat back and ran a hand through his hair as he stewed over figures that weren't to his liking she wanted to wrap herself around him and tell him not to worry, that wealth and the acquiring of it, although useful, were nowhere near as important as getting naked and making love to her.

Lex *knew* how to have fun. He and Sienna had had a lot of it over the years. But apart from when they were making love, he seemed to have lost the knack for it. He wasn't the carefree and impatient charmer she knew. The Lex of the past few days had been sombre and watchful to the point that she wondered what on earth was wrong with him. Maybe it was the Scorcellini bid. Maybe she'd simply never seen that part of him that could concentrate long and hard enough to see a difficult project through. Lex's companies made millions every year. He worked hard. She knew that already. But she hadn't realised that he had to work quite so hard to make it happen.

'Does Lex always work like a navvy?' she asked Rudy as she watched him load up two lunch trays with more delicacies than either she or Lex could possibly eat.

'No.'

Rudy the conversationalist. 'I mean, I know the Scorcellini bid is a big one, but Lex doesn't usually take all this work on himself, does he? He does have other employees who could do a lot of this work for him? Back in the London office?'

'Yes.'

'So why doesn't he let them?'

'If you ask me—and I really wish you wouldn't—he's making work for himself,' said Rudy reluctantly. 'A man usually does that when he's trying to avoid another far more difficult problem.' Rudy pinned her with a stern look. 'The way I read it, that problem is you.'

'You're right,' she said. 'I shouldn't have asked.'

But Rudy was on a roll. 'It seems to me that you're not deliberately messing with his mind. It seems to me that he wants something from you that you can't give. Normally he'd move on and source whatever it was he wanted from some other place. Given that what he wants this time might well be you and he can't actually get you anywhere else, he's probably feeling thwarted. He hates being thwarted.'

'Geez, Rudy. Can you go back to single-word sentences soon?'

'Yes.'

'Possibly not that soon,' she said, and Rudy sent her a long-suffering glance in reply. 'So, ah, given that your analysis is largely correct, what do you think I should do?'

'Simple. Either give him what he wants or leave. These trays are ready to go up.'

'Not simple,' she said darkly. 'What if what he wants wouldn't be good for him? What if he could do so much better?'

'I've always found him to be a very good judge of what's good for him,' said Rudy.

Sienna bit her lip.

'Have a little faith,' said Rudy gruffly. 'The man knows what he wants. Always has. Why not try giving it to him? Now about those trays…'

'Can you take Lex's up? I might take mine to my room. There's something I need to do.'

'Pack?'

'No.' Sienna smiled faintly. 'Not yet, anyway. I need to change clothes, that's all. And I have an idea.'

'Try and make it a good one' said Rudy.

Once in her bedroom Sienna nibbled at the food Rudy had prepared and hastily gathered together the items essential for her transformation. She reapplied her make-up and pulled her hair back into a sophisticated chignon before donning the corporate image, layer by increasingly gorgeous layer. The shoes came last and made her three inches taller and somehow a whole lot curvier. Jewellery she kept to the minimum—the Cartier watch Lex had given her on her twenty-first birthday; a pair of diamond earrings that had belonged to her mother. One last swipe of her lipstick and she was ready to go do business. She picked up the tray, grimacing at how much food was left on it, never mind that Rudy had overloaded it in the first place. Nerves never did leave a lot of room for appetite. Rudy would scowl at her. What was more he'd mean it.

Rudy was back in the kitchen, working on something floury, when Sienna took the tray back. He looked up as she carried it across to the counter and set it down. 'I wasn't as hungry as I thought,' she said somewhat defensively, but Rudy didn't even spare a glance for the tray. His eyes had widened fractionally; a muscle twitched in his jaw. He ran a floury hand across his mouth and Sienna was almost certain he was hiding a smile in there somewhere.

'What do you think of the suit Grace helped me buy?'

'I'm speechless,' he said.

'You usually are,' she reminded him. 'C'mon, Rudy, I need an opinion.'

'Where's the shirt?'

'The shirt was an optional extra we decided I didn't need. I invested in a vest instead.'

'Try wearing it.'

She pointed to the tiny strip of white showing just inside the suit lapels. 'I am.'

'Has your *employer* seen you in this suit yet?' asked Rudy. There was that smile again, only this time he didn't bother to hide it.

'Not yet. I'm just on my way up.'

Rudy nodded and began to clear the bench. 'Tell him I'm on my way *out.*'

Lex was on the phone, deep in conversation, when Sienna walked into the hub, but that didn't stop him from losing the power of speech entirely for a good thirty seconds. He swallowed hard, cleared his throat and forced himself to look away from the vision office fantasies were made of. 'About those terms…' But that was as far as he got for he made the fatal mistake of looking at Sienna again as she leaned over her desk and checked something on her computer. He closed his eyes and brought all his considerable will power into play as he forced his mind away from her hourglass figure and back to the call. 'Sorry, Stuart. Something's just come in that needs my attention, so I'll make it quick. You know I prefer to do business with you, but if you can't give me at *least* market rate I'll have to go elsewhere. Shave another half a percent off your lending rate, we have a deal.' He only half heard the other man's hasty reassurances that the lending rate was in fact negotiable. He'd never doubted it for a moment. 'Good. Fax it through. I'll get back to you. Fine.'

He swung around and put the phone in its cradle. Sienna had moved from her desk to her usual place, perched on the edge of his desk. Usually her sitting there while they prioritised the workload didn't bother him. The difference this time being that the little grey suit she was almost wearing did everything to emphasise her sexuality and nothing to cover it up.

'I thought you might want to take a look at my suit *before* the Scorcellinis came to visit,' she said with an easy smile. 'Just in case you figured it wasn't suitable.'

'It's…' Words failed him.

'Grey?' she supplied helpfully. 'Subtle?'

'Well, it's grey,' he said. Subtlety was a stretch. The skirt length was modest, true, but those shoes gave the outfit a whole new meaning. As for the cut of the jacket…

'It's comfortable too,' she said idly. 'And soft. Feel it. It's also very empowering.'

'So I see.' He reached out and ran a finger down the lapel

of her jacket, deliberately skimming the skin where lapel met Sienna along the way. 'So I feel.' What the hell was she wearing beneath that jacket? Some sort of white linen corset? He didn't know but beneath the linen peeked snow-white lace. Office fantasies had never really been his thing. Until now. 'Take it off.'

'No, that would be stripping.'

'Okay, leave it on and *I'll* take it off for you,' he offered. 'No stripping required on your part at all.'

'Alas, I would still be naked. Where's the empowerment in that?'

'I'd probably be on my knees by the time you were naked,' he offered. Nothing but the truth.

'You're right. That does sound vaguely empowering,' she said with a slow smile that lit him through. 'I'll think about it. What else do you have for me this afternoon?'

'There's work to be done here somewhere.' He was sure of it. 'But it can wait. I think you need a demonstration of what you're likely to encounter if you ever wear that suit to work for anyone *else*.'

'Sounds taxing,' she murmured.

'I'll try and make it brief.'

'That *does* seem to be your forte.'

He took it on the chin. Nothing he didn't deserve. But he didn't intend to deserve the speedy tag a whole lot longer. 'About that suit…' he said with a smile that felt predatory and probably was.

'Gorgeous, isn't it?' she said artlessly. 'I couldn't resist.'

'You do realise what a suit of that nature will bring you in an office situation? Which is—by the way—nothing but trouble.' It was time for a demonstration. 'It'll start something like this. You'll be called into the boss's office and told to close the door behind you. There's your first warning.'

'I see. Thanks for the tip.'

'Sienna,' he said softly. 'Close the door.'

Slanting him a long glance, she slid from her perch on the edge of his desk, sauntered across to the door, and closed it. By the time she was done, Lex's mouth had gone dry and his body was harder than the Rock of Gibraltar. But he didn't rush things, not yet. The best seduction—just like the wooing of a torn and tender heart—required patience.

'The next thing that boss will do is use some vague and possibly work related excuse to bring you within arm's length,' he said mildly. 'You'll do it because you're used to doing what this man says. You'll wonder if this is about the work, you'll be beginning to think that it's not, but you'll want to give him the benefit of the doubt. Don't. Stay out of reach.'

'Got it,' she said, leaning back against the closed door with more than a hint of knowing challenge in her gaze.

'Sienna,' he said softly. 'My desk needs tidying.'

'So it does.' She walked towards him with a sway in her step that tested his self-control to the limit. 'If you could just move your chair a little to the left I'll do it now.'

Lex shifted his chair fractionally, and gestured towards the desk.

Sienna moved in, her legs brushing his as she bent over and began to tidy.

'That pile of quarterly reports, top right hand corner,' he said. 'They can go.'

Sienna had to lean far over his desk to reach them. It seemed only fair that he steady her with a hand to her behind, which, as fortune would have it, lined his thumb up exactly with the seam of her skirt. She gasped and looked back at him, her eyes several shades darker than they had been. 'Wouldn't want you to fall,' he murmured.

'Is this the part where I turn around and slap you?'

'Yes. Now is definitely the time. Use the hole punch. Cause a scene. Leave.' The skirt material was soft against his palm, the flesh beneath promised to be softer still. Lex forced himself to breathe, to wait, to think.

'What happens if I don't leave?' she asked.

'That would be seen as encouragement. You should avoid this at all costs.' Lex slid his hand lower and lifted it again to its original position bringing the material of her skirt with him, hiking it higher. She wore stockings. Suspenders. He couldn't see any panties. Lex bit back a groan.

'Where do you want these reports to go again?' she said huskily.

'Top left-hand corner.'

'I see.'

Lex needed to. He inched her skirt higher still, until her panties came into view, snowy white to match the suspenders and the stockings. Modestly cut. Demure enough to drive a man mad. He traced the edges, let his thumb skitter over her mound and felt her buttocks tense beneath his hand. He did it again and Sienna gasped.

'Could have been worse,' he murmured. 'It could have been my mouth.'

Sienna spun around about the same time Lex surged forward. He had her bottom on the desk and her legs wrapped around him at about the same time she grabbed his shirt and set her lips to his for a kiss that gave new meaning to the word wanton.

'I'm sure Grace said this suit would empower *me* rather than you,' she muttered between more of those wild kisses. 'Something's wrong here.'

'You're letting me take charge,' he muttered. 'You want to wear that suit and drive a man mad, you have to own it.'

'Believe me, I own it. But you're absolutely right. I'm working this all wrong.' Her thoughts didn't run to absolute domination. She didn't need a lot of control. Just some. 'Take a seat, Alex. The one you just vacated.' Sienna punctuated her statement by removing his hands from her and pushing him away.

Lex grinned and held his hands up in a gesture of surrender as he took a step back. 'Hot in here this afternoon,' he said conversationally. 'You'd be far more comfortable with that jacket *off*.'

'There you go again,' she said. 'Taking control.'

'Habit.'

'Sit.'

'Say please.'

'If you don't sit I'm afraid my suit will have to go back in the cupboard, never to be seen by you again,' she threatened sweetly. 'And that would be a shame.'

It seemed he agreed. He sat down in his executive chair, bold challenge in his eyes, every sinuous line of him a temptation. 'Now what?' he said in a voice that promised her whatever she damn well decided to take. A shiver of anticipation ran straight down her spine and into her loins.

'Now I straighten up your desk.' She did so, papers top left, hole punch on top of them, his telephone a fraction to the right, his computer screen a hue or two brighter. 'There.'

'I like my notepad slanted a little to the left,' he said.

'I'll keep that in mind.' Sienna turned back towards him, her fingers playing with the front button of her jacket, darkly pleased when his gaze followed the small motion and his expression turned intent. 'You're right. It is hot in here.'

Lex wisely kept his mouth shut as Sienna shrugged out of her jacket, lined the shoulders and the cuffs up, and folded it carefully before setting it on the edge of his desk.

She leaned against his desk, as was her wont to do, with her hands either side of her and her fingers curling over the edge, and arched an eyebrow in silent query. 'You said there was work to be done. You usually have a list of things for me to do,' she prompted.

'I would if I could *think*,' he said huskily. 'But your vest has driven every last bit of blood from my brain.'

'You like?' she queried. 'I was a little unsure of it myself. I wanted a business shirt but they wouldn't give me one.'

'Have mine,' he said. 'Have it now.'

'Thank you. That's very sweet of you. But, no.'

'It's no trouble.' He had half the buttons undone already.

'Alex,' she said softly. 'Keep it.'

His fingers stilled. The buttons stayed undone, but he sat back in his chair, his eyes dark and hot. 'Now what?'

Sienna didn't know. Control was all well and good, but now that she had it she didn't quite know what to do with it.

'The thing about power,' he said silkily, 'is that you have to know how to wield it.'

'You're right.' Sienna regarded him wryly. This suit was proving more trouble than it was worth. And it was worth plenty. 'Thing is, I don't actually want power very often. Equality will do fine.'

'That again.'

'I know it's a stretch for you.'

'Only sometimes.' Lex's eyes narrowed. 'And might I just add in my defence that the only time I ever *have* dominated you, you liked it.'

True. Very true.

'Sienna—

'Shh. I almost had it.' The compromise of the century. Yes, there it was, all shiny and bright, but did she have the fortitude to go through with it?

'Lex, would you mind dropping by my desk some time this afternoon?' she said with what she hoped was an air of command. 'I have something for you.'

'I'll drop by now,' he said.

'Fine.'

Lex's lips twitched but he got up and headed for her desk. Sienna started walking towards it too, anticipation warring with a hefty dose of apprehension at what she was about to take. And what she would surrender.

'Take a seat,' she said. 'My chair will do.' It didn't have armrests like Lex's office chair. Armrests would be a hindrance to what she had in mind. She waited until he was comfortably settled before heading on over to straddle his legs, and ease her way onto his lap, her skirt riding high and her suspenders and panties in full view, should he eventually choose to look past her cleavage. Her body felt boneless, her skin hungered for his touch. Lex's eyes when they finally met hers held a passion and a promise guaranteed to drive them both to the edge of madness. 'You may put your hands back where you promised your mouth,' she said next.

He did as he was told, cupping her thighs so that his thumbs brushed the V between her legs. 'It wasn't a promise,' he said with a marauder's smile.

'It should have been.' She finished unbuttoning his shirt and pushed it from his shoulders, delighting in the silkiness of his skin and the hardness of the muscle beneath. She took a ragged breath and put her lips to his ear.

'Alex,' she ordered huskily. 'Dominate me.'

Alexander Wentworth the Third was not a man to take tasks lightly. He gave them his all. He paid attention to detail, to the little things that should not be forgotten. He liked to excel.

He started with the row of white buttons on her vest, taking it slow as he ordered Sienna to kiss him.

Lightly.

Tease me.

Sienna was very, very good at taking orders.

And then the vest went and Lex grinned wolfishly at the full impact of Sienna wearing delicate white lace and a smile just for him. The lingerie would have to go, of course, but for now he chose to work around it. The swell of her breasts demanded his attention; the swelling in his trousers demanded hers. The scrape of her nails along the hard ridge of his arousal. The scrape of his teeth along the lace at her breasts. An indrawn breath. A shuddering sigh.

It wasn't enough.

He wanted her on the desk so he carried her there, tenderness warring with his need to possess her.

Need won.

Dominate me.

He could play that game. There was no denying he knew how. But he didn't want subservience from Sienna and never had. He wanted her to argue with him when she thought he was wrong, chide him, fight with him, make peace with him.

He wanted her to love him.

'Hold all my calls,' he murmured as he sank to his knees in front of her. 'Tell them I'm busy. Tell them whatever the hell you want.' He parted her legs and pressed a kiss to her panties, right before he tugged them to one side with his fingers. 'Now, put your hands in my hair and keep them there.'

CHAPTER NINE

BY SIX o' clock that evening Sienna's desk was clear of everything, including her. She felt sated, dominated, and well pleased with the way the afternoon had progressed, but there was no escaping the fact that they'd neglected the work, or that as a result Lex's desk was currently overloaded with work that only he could do.

'You may as well go,' he said, looking back at his desk with the distracted expression Sienna had come to associate with calculations that contained far too many zeroes. 'I still need to finish up a few things here. Go make ice cream with Grace. Bring me up some later. Torture Rudy. Have fun.'

'You work too hard,' she said.

Lex smiled fleetingly and rubbed his temple. 'Only sometimes.'

'Only a lot.' Sienna perched on the edge of his desk and regarded him solemnly. 'Why don't you come down for a break around seven-thirty? We'll be in the billiards room by then, emasculating the felt.'

'Have you confirmed what Grace will be wearing?'

'No idea.'

'What will *you* be wearing?' murmured Lex, his eyes darkening as he scanned her suit.

'A smile.'

'Good choice,' he said. 'What else?'

'I haven't decided yet.'

The intercom cracked to life and Rudy's gruff voice filled the room. 'Grace is at the door,' he said. 'Who's letting her in?'

Sienna leaned over Lex's desk and pressed the intercom. 'Rudy, would you? I'm just finishing up here with Lex. I'll be down in a minute.'

'You're getting very good at giving orders,' Lex murmured as she broke the connection. His words were directed at her, she was sure of it. But his gaze was on the swell of her breasts, lovingly encased in virginal white and cloaked thereafter in the softest of grey.

'What can I say? I'm feeling very empowered.' Sienna grinned at his continued distraction and took a deep and undulating breath just because she could. 'Man, I love this suit.'

'You're also getting extremely good at manipulating events to your liking,' he muttered, finally lifting his gaze to hers.

'That's just natural aptitude. Is Rudy cooking tonight?'

Lex shook his head. 'It's his night off.'

'So if he could be persuaded to join Grace and I in the kitchen—as our guest—would that be a problem for you?'

'As in how strong a hold does the English class system have on you, Lex?'

Sienna nodded.

'Not that strong. Rudy's a good man. He cooks for me and looks after this place because it suits him. He maintains the distance between employer and employee because that suits him too. He knows he's welcome at my table; he's sat at it before. I've sat at his. Ask him to join you by all means. Just don't be surprised if he refuses. He's uncomfortable around women as a rule.'

'He's not uncomfortable around me.'

'That's because you're at war with him. Retaliation gives him something to do.'

'You're a good man, Alexander Wentworth the Third.' She leaned towards him and brushed his lips with hers. 'Work fast.'

He captured her lips again for a kiss that quickly turned hungry. He cursed and sat back in his chair looking pained. 'Sienna, I need another hour before I can finish up here. Or four.'

'I know.' Sienna sighed and dropped a kiss on his hair before heading for the door. 'Do your work. I can entertain myself. Come down when you can. I can wait.'

Barely.

Sienna's watch told her that Grace was ten minutes early. Her prolonged bout of afternoon lovemaking with Lex made freshening up before she met up with her guest a necessity. She would poke her head around the kitchen door and beg some time, she decided as she headed down the stairs and into the atrium. How much time depended on the vibe in the kitchen. It would also depend on not giving Rudy the opportunity to leave.

'Grace, I'm so glad you could come over,' she told the older woman when she reached the entrance to the kitchen, trying to decide whether half in the doorway and half out was better than mostly out or mostly in. Neither would hide her general state of dishevelment for long. Rudy stood on the fridge side of the kitchen counter and appeared to be pouring Grace a glass of champagne. Grace stood on the other side of the counter wearing a red chiffon shift with a plunging neckline, slimline navy trousers, and high-heeled pumps in the exact same blue as the trousers. 'Are you sure you're ready to make ice cream, though? You look much too elegant to do anything so mundane.'

'Gorgeous girl, I am wearing the perfect ice-cream-making attire,' countered Grace. 'Ice-cream making is a seriously glamorous endeavour. At least, it is when I do it. You, on the other hand, don't look dressed for cooking at all. You look like you've just walked in from a hard day at the office.' Grace's smile deepened. 'Nice to see the corporate image in play.'

'I'd like to take the corporate image out of play if you can give me a few minutes to change clothes and freshen up,' Sienna said hastily. 'Would you mind if I left you in Rudy's care a little longer?'

'Not at all,' said Grace, but that was only half the equation as far as Sienna was concerned.

'Rudy?'

'Go,' said Rudy gruffly.

'Darling man,' she said, and left before he could change his mind.

Sienna made it to her room with every intention of taking the fastest shower she'd ever had, followed by slipping into a casual shirt and pair of trousers, and thereafter returning immediately to the kitchen. But she remembered Lex's touch as she removed her suit and began to unclip her stockings. She remembered the appreciation he'd finally got around to showing for her lingerie and her hands paused as she let the memories take her over. Making love with Lex was like flying naked into the sun; a body burned hotter and brighter with every passing moment until heat finally ripped it apart. In that incandescent moment Sienna was his and only his. Nothing else existed. There was only Lex and her hunger for him. No one else's lovemaking had ever come close. She doubted anyone's ever would. He had her measure—body, soul, and mind. If she allowed it to, the thought of him could fill every last piece of her with longing.

Was this what it felt like to love?

Was this what her mother had felt for her father? Was that why she'd taken her life when their marriage had fallen apart?

Hadn't there been *any* love left over for anyone else?

'I would have had love left over,' she muttered as she came to her senses and continued to strip down to skin and head for the shower. 'I would have had love for my child no matter how badly that child's father had betrayed me. I wouldn't have let him have it all.'

She didn't intend to let Lex have it all now.

Did that make her less in love with Lex than her mother had been with her father?

Or more?

It was all too confusing. Trying to relate her feelings for Lex with what she knew of love from the example set by her parents was a guaranteed recipe for heartache. Far better to simply admit that she had no idea how a functioning adult relationship between two people who cared for each other worked and get on with the process of finding out.

Sienna soaped down fast, taking full advantage of the calming scent of sandalwood and ginger that teased at her senses. Grace was waiting, Grace and Rudy, and there was no time for an out and out analysis of love right now. No time for memories, heartbreaking or otherwise.

Sienna never had been able to afford to live in the past. She didn't particularly want to think about the future. There was only the present.

* * *

'The secret to handling a man like Alex Wentworth,' said Grace as she sampled her ice-cream-making efforts and gave a nod of approval, 'is to keep him guessing.'

'No problem there, considering I have no idea what I want from him,' replied Sienna with a frankness born of French champagne on an empty stomach. 'Except the sex. I'm completely sold on that.'

Grace had brought the champagne along for the evening and insisted on it being an accompaniment to their ice-cream-making efforts. Sienna was currently contemplating the merits of adding Grace's ice cream to France's finest and turning it into a spider. Rudy was nowhere to be seen—he'd fled the minute Sienna had returned, which was probably for the best, decided Sienna. 'Rudy would die if he saw the mess we're making of his kitchen.'

'Rudy's not here,' said Grace. 'I swear it's enough to give a confident woman a complex. Did you know he designs ocean-going yachts? He's having one built now—eight point two million dollars' worth of clean lines and luxury specifications. I've seen the plans.'

'Who's financing it?'

'Rudy and Alex. Apparently they plan to venture into the yacht-building business together if this one's a success. I've seen a lot of boats in my time, Sienna. This one's a winner. I'd order one myself if I could afford to.' Grace's expression grew dreamy. 'A woman could do a lot worse than to sail the world on a boat like that with the right man at her side.'

'Is Rudy the right man?' queried Sienna and Grace smiled wryly.

'He could be. If I could just get past his shyness.'

There was that. 'The trick to handling a man like Rudy,' said Sienna, 'is to make him feel needed. Are you hungry?

Because I'm starving.' She headed for the intercom and pressed the buzzer. 'Rudy, are you there?'

There was a brief pause followed by the crackle of static.

'No,' said Rudy's voice. The wit.

'Grace and I are thinking of ordering takeaway for dinner. We need guidance.'

'No, you need a phone.'

'Or we could throw a little something together ourselves. You don't mind if we use a few of the ingredients in the fridge, do you?' Grace crossed to the fridge, opened the door and began pulling out fixings. Sienna listed them as they landed on the counter. 'The prosciutto, the veal, the mascarpone…looks like we're going Italian. Grace wants to know if you're doing anything with the roasted pine nuts and pumpkin?'

'Out of my fridge,' he said curtly. '*I'll* cook the dinner.'

'Rudy has graciously offered to cook for us,' Sienna told Grace. 'Shall we accept?'

'He's such a gentleman,' replied Grace, shutting the fridge door and resuming her position propped against the counter. 'Of course we accept. But only if he lets us help with the preparation and clean up, and only if he helps us eat it.'

'Grace is going to be your able-bodied assistant and you are hereby officially invited to join us for dinner,' translated Sienna.

'I'll cook,' he said. 'That's all.'

'Sorry, Rudy. It's a package deal. You're either all in or you stay out of the kitchen. Grace wants to know if you're saving the kipfler potatoes for anything special. Hang on.' Sienna grinned at Grace, who had yet to even find the kipfler potatoes, let alone decide what to do with them. 'Grace wants to know if you have any pink sea salt.' Grace was sipping champagne and watching with dry amusement as Sienna banged a couple of pots down on the bench for chaotic effect. 'I don't suppose you have a little white apron she could use?'

Dead silence at that and Sienna wondered if she'd overplayed her hand.

'Tell her she does not need an apron.' Did Rudy's voice sound gruffer than usual? Hard to tell over the intercom. *'I will cook the meal.'*

'Perfect. See you soon. I'll make a start on the hors d'oeuvres, though, shall I? I'm thinking champagne spiders but I'm in a quandary.' Grace was laughing silently as Sienna closed in for the kill. 'One scoop or two?'

Fifteen minutes later the stainless-steel state-of-the-art kitchen had been restored to order and dinner was taking shape beneath Rudy's watchful gaze as he guardedly let Grace loose on his precious ingredients. He'd declined the champagne, with or without the addition of ice cream, but accepted a beer and even allowed Sienna to put some music on. She'd chosen a classic mix of American jazz divas because Grace reminded her of one, and some early Rolling Stones because it ought to be familiar to a shy former frigate midshipman.

'How much longer before dinner?' queried Sienna, glancing at the clock. Ten past eight. She glanced at the ceiling.

'About fifteen minutes,' said Rudy dryly, following her gaze. 'Another quandary?'

'Yes.' Lex had said he'd join them when he was done. He hadn't joined them, ergo he wasn't done. But she wanted him to be. 'Think I should go and tell Lex we're almost ready to eat?'

'Yes,' said Rudy.

'He had a lot of work to get through,' she said with a twinge of guilt. 'He said he'd be down when he'd be done.' Lex's foremost stipulation regarding their current living and working situation was that the work had to get done, regardless. He might as well have been talking to the moon for all the attention she'd paid to his request.

'Then we'll send a dinner tray up,' said Rudy.

'You're right,' she said to Rudy. 'I shouldn't disturb him.'

But deep down inside a battle began raging. Because she wanted to disturb him. She wanted to march upstairs and demand he come downstairs and eat with them. Not for his sake, she realised with brutal honesty, but for hers.

She wanted his reassurance that he hadn't forgotten her so quickly. That even when he worked he held the thought of her close. She didn't know where it had come from, this constant need for reassurance as to his affections, this constant need for his attention. She remembered her mother behaving exactly the same way with her father.

The thought terrified her.

'I'll set the table,' she said, dredging a smile up from somewhere. 'For three,' she said next. 'And I vote we eat in the dining room.'

'You loathe the dining room,' muttered Rudy, shooting her a sharp glance. 'You never set foot in there if you can avoid it.'

'I will confess to being somewhat daunted by its formality,' she replied airily. 'It's not a relaxing room. Tonight, however, you and Grace will be there and I'm feeling relaxed enough and contrary enough to make that rotten room work for me.'

'Candles help,' offered Rudy and reddened when both Sienna and Grace stared at him in astonishment. 'You'll find them in the middle left-hand drawer of the sideboard.

If you want them, that is—it makes no difference to me. Cutlery's in the top drawer. Glassware is to the right.'

'The man buys candles,' Sienna murmured, and to Grace, 'Did you know he was a romantic? Because I didn't.'

'I suspected he was,' replied Grace. 'The strong, silent, creative types often are.'

'Maybe you should offer him another beer,' said Sienna. 'Maybe he'll suggest a moonlight sail.'

'I'm all for it,' murmured Grace. 'Maybe I'll offer him *two* beers.'

Rudy sent the pair of them a level, thoughtful stare, and Sienna just knew that retaliation wasn't far away. 'Right, then. I'll be in the dining room making it habitable if you need me. Not that you will.' She had to pass by Rudy on the way out. She couldn't resist stopping and laying a hand on his shoulder, her expression as solemn as she could get it with thoughts of Grace trying to tempt Rudy into even more romantic behaviour running through her mind. 'Good luck, sailor. Make us proud.'

Grace eyed Sienna's retreating form with a mixture of affection and concern. She didn't know the younger woman particularly well, but she knew enough about womankind to know that something was on Sienna's mind. One didn't need to be a telepath to predict what that something might be.

But first things first.

'At ease, sailor,' she said to Rudy with a disarming smile. Never mind the nit-picking, Rudy had shown a surprising sensitivity to Sienna's increasingly reflective silences. Woeful social skills aside, he'd been surprisingly adept at keeping the mood festive when Sienna's smiles had faltered. Grace liked that about him. She liked a lot of things about this man. 'I may have suggested that second beer, but that doesn't mean you're obliged to drink it. I can recognise a no as well as the next person.'

Rudy looked down at his hands and Grace suppressed a disappointed sigh. For a moment there she thought she'd seen a wanting in his eyes, a heated need that had made her hopeful. Not confident, but hopeful.

And then he looked up and speared her with his bright blue gaze and there was no mistaking the desire in his eyes this time. 'I'll have another stout,' he said gruffly.

Grace's movements weren't always languid and sexy. Grace could move fast when she wanted to. Where the *hell* was the stout?

'Bottom shelf of the drinks fridge, a couple of rows in.' This from Rudy.

'Got it.' Phew! Right. No need to rush. Breathe in, breathe out. Where the hell was her poise? She straightened up, turned around, and tucked a stray strand of auburn hair only marginally streaked with grey back where it belonged. The ground trembled beneath her feet, but she made it to the bench and set the beer directly in front of the only man to ever take her breath away without even trying.

'Thank you,' he said with a slow, sweet smile that promised heaven if she didn't die of asphyxiation first.

'You'll let me know when you want another one?' she croaked.

'Maybe once we're on the boat. We need to have dinner first.'

Dinner. Right. 'Yes.' Grace had temporarily lost track of her surroundings, but recognition was coming back fast. Dinner. Here. With Sienna. The increasingly melancholic Sienna. Grace looked to the ceiling, much as Sienna had done earlier, and narrowed her eyes. 'What about Alex?'

'What about him?' said Rudy.

'The man has to eat some time this evening. He may as well do it with us. Besides, Sienna wants him to come down. How do we go about getting him here? Does coercion work?'

'Not usually,' said Rudy.

'Bribery?'

'With what?'

'What about prompting a spot of self-reflection about what a work-obsessed, neglectful ass he's being?' she suggested.

'That might work,' said a voice from the doorway, and Grace looked up, embarrassment warring with pleasure at the sight of Lex entering the room. He looked freshly showered, shaven of jaw, and altogether as dangerous to womankind as his reputation suggested in his white dinner shirt and formal grey trousers. Sienna had her work cut out for her with this one, no doubt about it. Good thing the girl was up to the task. 'Evening, Alex. How lovely to see you again.'

'Always a pleasure to see you too, Grace,' he said dryly. 'How did the ice cream turn out?'

'It needed champagne.'

Lex looked to Rudy for clarification. Rudy shook his head. 'Your personal assistant turned a perfectly good glass of French champagne into a frothing, bubbling mess.'

'Ah, yes. The Spider. It's one of Sienna's specialities. She usually uses ginger beer.'

'She's a culinary heathen,' said Rudy. 'Next thing you know she'll be eating spaghetti from a tin.'

'Only when sitting in a tent,' said Lex. 'You should see what she does with marshmallows. Where is she, by the way?'

'In the dining room, setting the table,' replied Grace.

'She did wonder about setting a place for you too, but I think she decided against disturbing you.'

'She could have disturbed me.'

'She does disturb him,' murmured Rudy, sotto voce.

'Excellent. I do like a man who isn't all about the work. Tell me, Alex. Do you always dress for dinner or is this a special occasion?'

'I always dress for ice cream,' said Lex, and Grace beamed at him.

'I swear you've all gone ice-cream mad,' muttered Rudy. 'Can someone please tell me what is wrong with chocolate?'

Sienna found the candles and the cutlery in the sideboard and began to collect up the pieces she needed. The tableware, like everything else in the room, screamed of subtle elegance and no shortage of money. Maybe that was why she never felt comfortable in here, she thought wryly. Maybe the visual confirmation of Lex's wealth rammed home her relative lack of it just that little bit too hard.

Give away most of your money, Lex, so I don't feel inferior.

Drop everything and pay attention to me. Only me. To hell with the work and to hell with anything you might want.

Love me and all my insecurities and maybe one day, some day, I might be brave enough to love you back.

'Aren't you the prize?' she muttered to herself as she lay three sets of cutlery in place and turned to go and get side plates from the kitchen.

She wasn't alone. Lex stood leaning against the door frame, his smile warm but his eyes sharp. 'I wouldn't say prize, exactly. Sometimes I can get downright neglectful of the people who matter to me the most.'

His generosity shamed her. 'I wasn't talking about you. I was talking about me.'

'Ah. Self-reflection,' he murmured as he started towards her looking elegant, confident, and dangerously unpredictable. 'Nasty beast. I had a little moment of it myself not fifteen minutes back, when I looked at the clock, looked at the work, and realised that I'd rather be down here with you. What prompted yours?'

'Silver-plated forks.'

'Kinky. Care to elaborate?'

'No.' Sienna busied herself by looking for matches to light the candles with. She found them in the same drawer she'd found the candles. 'Did you get your work finished?'

'Not all of it.'

Not what Sienna wanted to hear. 'Lex, I'm sorry about interrupting the work today. I shouldn't have done it. I should have left the personal things—relationship things—for later. I know it wasn't right of me.'

'Did you hear me complaining?'

'Well, not *then*,' she said. 'But what about now? You said there was more to do.'

'I've sent half of it to the London office,' he said. 'It'll be done overnight by someone else and faxed through ready for me tomorrow morning. London works when we sleep. It's one of the benefits of being in different time zones. Relax, Sienna. The work will get done.'

'My mother used to do this,' she said faintly.

'Do what?'

'Ask for too much. Want more of my father's time. Always more.'

'For heaven's sake, Sienna, you are not your mother!' Lex swore fiercely and regarded her bleakly. 'You're *you*, and I've never known a woman to ask for less. So if you want something of me, *ask*. And watch me try and move heaven and earth to see that you get it.'

Not like her father. So not like her father.

'Would you care to join us for dinner?' she asked tentatively, knowing the moment for yet another tiny victory over the past on her part. 'I think it's going to be fun. Lots of fun. It involves—'

'You,' he murmured.

'—a meal,' she countered, 'which Rudy and Grace have generously prepared, followed by an hour or two unwinding in the luxury billiards room to your right and drinking the rotgut of your choice—'

'Cognac,' he whispered with his lips to her ear as his arms came around her, wrapping her in warmth. 'It's called cognac.'

'It's also likely to involve you sending Rudy and Grace out on a mission to collect some obscure bottle of wine that you don't actually want shortly thereafter. They'll use *Angelina* for transport, possibly *Mercy Jane*, and I really don't think we should wait up.'

'And then what?'

Sienna smiled and surrendered to the moment and to the urge to wrap her arms around his neck. 'Then I guess we go to bed.'

They made it through dinner and billiards and cognac. They saw Rudy and Grace off on the *Mercy Jane*. They made it to Lex's room, with its Italian leather sofas and its big plush bed. They managed to get naked and into the bed and thoroughly entwined in each other's arms. And then they slept.

Sienna woke the following morning to Lex entering the room bearing a tray with two steaming cups of what smelt like coffee on it. He wore a white business shirt and tailored trousers and couldn't have signalled more clearly if he'd shouted that work was on his morning agenda.

'What time is it?' she said sleepily.

'Twenty to six,' he said cheerfully.

'That would be why my eyes don't want to work.' Clearly there were some kinks in this sleeping-in-each-other's-beds business that would have to be ironed out. 'Do you always wake up this early?'

Lex nodded.

'And this cheerful?'

'Usually.'

'Ugh.' Sienna closed her eyes at the injustice of it all. 'You're a morning person.' She, on the other hand, was not.

'You think you've got problems,' he said and she reopened her eyes to find him setting the coffees on the bedside table beside her and then propping the tray against the wall. 'I used to be a lover of some repute. I didn't deliberately cultivate that reputation, mind, but I did grow fond of it. There were certain standards I felt obliged to live up to, and live up to them I did. I never took a woman to bed only to fall asleep. It simply wasn't done.' He sighed heavily and took a seat on the side of the bed. 'And then I took up with you.'

'It might not be me,' she protested, the smell of coffee rousing her to action. She sat up and tucked the sheet firmly around her before propping her pillow against the bed head and leaning back against it. 'You've never actually shared a house with a lover before. Maybe it takes the need for sex on a nightly basis right out of you. Not that I'm complaining, mind. I like to sleep on occasion. You can call me Maverick.'

He handed her the coffee in his hand with unconscious courtesy and reached for the one on the table.

Sienna took a sip and grimaced, not at the flavour, which was perfect, but at the temperature of the brew. 'Hot.'

'I know it's early but I have to go upstairs for a while,' he said. 'I need to resource the capital for this bid and most of it's coming from Wall Street. Two hours on the phone, three at the most, and then I'll be able to hand almost all of the work over to the London office.'

Oh, yeah. The bid. Sienna rubbed her hands over her face and tried to move smoothly from sleepy bed partner to efficient PA. 'You want me to come up now too?'

Lex smiled as he strode towards the door. 'Normal time is fine.'

Which meant nine. 'I'll be there. Ready to work. Possibly clothed. You'll see.'

CHAPTER TEN

'MARRY me,' murmured Lex a week later as they lay sprawled together on the lounge in the drawing room eating home-made French frou-frou food and watching a remake of *Pride and Prejudice* on the television. It was after ten on a Friday evening, maybe after eleven, and Sienna was wearing pyjamas in the form of a grey singlet top and baggy white cotton trousers. Lex's pyjama bottoms were pale blue and white striped and his chest was bare. The day's work had been done, they were well into the play part of the evening. Mr Bingley had just proposed to Jane. Sienna was undeniably happy with her lot.

At least, she had been until Lex had uttered those two little words guaranteed to make her tremble, and not in squirming anticipation. She looked from Lex to the TV screen and back again. No need to panic. Maybe he was just having a little fantasy interlude with one of the Misses Bennetts. Maybe he was playing the film critic and attempting to distil the theme of the story down to two words that started with something other than P.

But then he looked at her, his eyes dark and his expression brooding, and spoke those words again.

'Marry me.'

'What?'

'You heard.'

'Yes, but—' Lex looked away and Sienna felt her heart constrict. 'You're serious.'

'Yes. That's also all you have to say to make this happen, by the way. *Yes*. I particularly liked the way the very sweet Jane Bennett just said, "Yes, yes, a thousand times, yes". Not a *but* in sight. Makes a man feel wanted.'

'Keep watching,' she said. 'You might pick up a thing or two about delivering a successful marriage proposal. There's usually mention of love. Ardent love, tempered by the utmost respect. These words are often delivered with an appealing lack of confidence, possibly even a very sexy stutter. Even if you are as rich as Croesus.'

'You've seen this movie before,' he said.

'Oh, yes.'

'You do realise that both the book and the screenplay were written by women.'

Sienna eyed him narrowly.

'I'm just saying…'

'Your chances of hearing that *yes* are so very low right now,' she told him darkly.

'But there is a chance of it,' he said with no little satisfaction. 'We've established that the offer is sound.'

'Lex, I—' She didn't know what to say that wouldn't hurt him.

'Would it help if I told you how much I love you?' he offered quietly, and when she met his gaze she realised that, although his smile was teasing, his eyes were deadly serious. 'You were right. I may have overlooked that part earlier.'

Sienna ducked her head as tears pricked at her eyes. Served her right for asking for something she didn't know what to do with. 'How can you be sure that this isn't just infatuation?' she said shakily.

'Because I love being with you. Always have, always will. Because I know you. Because there's a place for you inside of me and I want you there.'

Siena closed her eyes.

'Sienna, do you love me?'

It felt like it. If the pain in her heart was anything to go by. Her tears began to fall in earnest.

'Would it be so bad, being married to me?'

'No.' Sienna shook her head and wiped her eyes with her fingers, grateful for the curtain of hair that shielded her face from view. Until gentle fingers tucked her hair behind her ear. She heard Lex curse softly. 'I'm sure you'll make some woman very happy.'

'Why not you, Sienna? Why can't I make you happy?'

'What if it doesn't work?' She knew their time in Australia was coming to a close and that she would lose the closeness to him that she craved once they were back in England, but she wasn't ready for this. Not marriage. Not that. Never that. 'What about your wealth? And my lack of it?' What about her inability to commit for fear of failing him? 'We're just not *equal*, Alex. And I need to be.' Sienna knew exactly what happened when monetary inequality soured a marriage. When *any* type of inequality entered a relationship, for that matter. When one gave more than the other. When one loved more than the other. She knew what came of that.

Hope died first. Then courage died. And then the will to live...died.

'I know you're thinking of your parents, Sienna,' said Lex urgently. 'I know their marriage was a disaster, but it was the exception, not the rule. It doesn't have to be like that. It *wouldn't* be like that. We could be happy together. I know we could. All you have to do is believe in yourself and the things you bring to this relationship.'

But self-belief had never been Sienna's strong suit. 'I don't bring much.' A bundle of insecurities and an old stone house in Cornwall that needed more money spent on it than it was worth. 'You could do so much better.'

'Dammit, Sienna, I don't want better. I want you!' Lex pulled away to stare at the screen. So did Sienna. Mr Darcy currently held court, burning it up with his brooding glances, but he had nothing on Lex. When Lex decided to sizzle and brood he could set the drapery on fire.

'All right,' he said after a fraught twenty seconds of silence. 'Do you concede that, apart from the disparity in our wealth, that we're well matched? That we're quite capable of holding our own with each other intellectually, morally, and—' his eyes took on a decided gleam '—sexually? That to all intents and purposes we are equals in those areas?'

'You're playing with words, Lex.'

'I'm taking that as a yes,' he said. 'For my part, I'm willing to concede that I do have much healthier self-esteem than you, and far fewer abandonment issues. However…I'm willing to wager that, give or take a decade or two, you'll finally figure out your own worth and realise that I'm not going anywhere. Problem solved.'

'In a decade or two?'

'I'm a patient man.'

Bemusement began to spread through her. This conversation had taken a distinct turn for the surreal. 'There's still the small matter of your wealth and my lack of it,' she reminded him. 'How do you plan to even that out? Become the philanthropist and give away all your money?'

'I'd really rather not,' he said dryly. 'Although I do know this woman who needs a few hundred million in order to believe in her own worth enough to take a chance and commit to the man who loves her. I could always give it to her. No?' He'd seen the refusal on her face long before she thought to voice it. 'Hell, Sienna. It was worth a try. All right, so we find another way to improve your finances.'

'We're talking a *lot* of improvement,' she said. 'How do you propose I become a megamillionaire overnight?'

'I didn't say overnight,' he said. 'Realistically speaking, I think you need to look at a somewhat longer time frame than that. I'm thinking that with your rapidly growing business acumen and occasional guidance from a very interested party that you could get there inside a decade.'

'I'm having a thought,' she said.

'Does it involve lottery tickets?'

'No.'

'Games of chance?'

'No.'

'Felonious acts?'

'No,' she said, rolling her eyes. 'Maybe I just need to find those paintings. Maybe if I did that, then everything else would fall into place. Money. Self-confidence. Everything.'

'No.' The teasing light in Lex's eyes had disappeared, replaced by a weariness she didn't often see in him. '*Enough* with the paintings, Sienna. You need to stop pinning your hopes on them, devoting your life to looking for them. You need to find some other way to put your past behind you. That train's not coming.'

She knew it. In her heart she knew it. And still she clung to the thought of them the way a dying man clung to the thought of a miracle cure. 'How do you know?'

'Because my mother's been looking for them for the past twelve years on your behalf,' he said curtly. 'She's had Scotland Yard looking, private galleries, private collectors, private investigators, you name them, she's had them looking for those paintings. Adriana's investigation force spans the globe, but she's never heard a whisper. Not one. They're gone, Sienna. All the way gone.'

'She's been looking for them all this time?' Sienna whispered. 'For me?'

'She knows what they mean to you, Sienna. We all do. I'd love for her to find them for you. I'd love for you to find them so that you could rewrite your past and find some comfort there. But I also need to believe that there's a way for you to move forward without those paintings. With love,' he said quietly. 'With me.'

'I can't,' she said quietly. *Pathetic cowering weakling.* 'I'm so sorry, Lex. You're the finest man I know. Generous, and beautiful, and…beloved. But I just can't.'

Sienna slept badly that night and she slept alone. Surrounded by space, bereft of warmth, she dreamt of loss and of loneliness. Of Lex and a life without him. She lay there in the half light of dawn, her pain a living thing as she remembered the desolation in Lex's eyes when she'd refused his offer of marriage and the hollowness he'd left behind when he'd stood and left the room without another word.

The one person in her life who'd never once let her down and she'd refused everything he had to offer because she would not allow herself to believe that someone like him could want someone like her.

Pathetic cowering weakling. Her father's words haunted her. Cut at her.

Defined her.

At seven-thirty Sienna abandoned all pretence of sleep, pushed back the bedcovers, and headed to the west-wing breakfast room, praying that Rudy had delivered the coffee already and that Lex would be nowhere in sight.

The coffee was in evidence, she could smell it before she'd even entered the room. One down. But Lex was there too, and why wouldn't he be? It was his coffee. His house.

'Morning,' she said, wishing herself far, far away. Wishing that she could somehow turn back time and make everything all right between them. Because it wasn't all right. It was all wrong. And she had no idea how to proceed from here.

He'd showered and shaved this morning, but that was where his concession to orderliness ended. His olive-coloured T-shirt was an old one. His steel-grey workman's trousers had seen better days. The colour matched the colour of his eyes. His eyes made her nervous.

'Morning,' he said smoothly. 'Sleep well?'

She hadn't and he knew it. She figured it for one of those rhetorical questions that didn't need an answer. 'You look dressed for dirt,' she said instead.

'Rudy and I are heading to the boatyard soon. We're building a boat together.' He regarded her with those watchful, measuring eyes. 'You're welcome to come along.'

'No. I—no,' she said awkwardly, heading for the coffee. The sooner she had coffee in hand, the sooner she could leave. 'Thank you. I just—no.' How on earth was she supposed to extricate herself from his life when she was so deeply enmeshed in it?

'You think I'm going to let you go, don't you?' he said mirthlessly. 'Just like that? Just because of one minor setback in our negotiations? I thought you knew me better than that, Sienna. You should have known that come this morning I'd have another offer on the table.'

Sienna fumbled with the coffee pot, cursing as it sloshed over the rim of the cup and onto the floor. Rudy would not be pleased. She set the coffee down and reached for a napkin.

'Leave it,' he said curtly.

She left it. Which left her standing there clutching a napkin in one hand and a coffee in her other. 'What kind of offer?' she said hesitantly. She couldn't deal with another marriage proposal right now. She really couldn't.

'I still want you by my side,' he said. 'That's non-negotiable as far as I'm concerned. Marriage is somewhat more negotiable. We don't necessarily have to marry, although I will reiterate that I would prefer to. It's easier on the children, wouldn't you agree?'

'Children?' she echoed.

'Ours,' he said blithely. 'As for the paintings, I'm prepared to throw considerable time and resources into helping you look for them. Maybe you *will* turn up something that my mother has missed. I figure I can take a month off work, starting from when we leave here, to help you look for them. With all that I am. All that I have. If you really think those paintings will make a difference to your past and to our future, then I'll help you look for them.'

'Lex—'

'Think about it.' He came to stand in front of her and leaned down to press a light kiss against her unresisting lips. 'That's all I'm asking you to do. Just think about it.' His smile turned rueful. 'Think about it and don't say no.'

Sienna thought about Lex's latest offer all the way back to her room. She should have realised that he would find a way to reopen negotiations. That he would come up with what sounded on the surface like a wholly reasonable compromise—one that nonetheless moved him inexorably closer to getting what he wanted. She'd been watching him in action all week with the takeover bid. At the end of last week she'd have bet money she couldn't afford to lose that the Scorcellinis would decline his offer. But they hadn't. Lex was good at negotiating his way through difficult situations. At turning 'no's into 'maybe's and 'maybe's into 'yes's.

At making people believe.

She *wanted* to find a way to overcome her fears. For Lex. For herself. She badly wanted the scars of her past to stop determining her future. She wanted to understand what had made her mother so fragile that she'd taken her own life. What fundamental flaw pushed a person down that path? What flaw inside her father had made him treat his wife and child so badly? What flaw inside *her* had made them leave her without a second thought? Only someone who'd lived through those years with her parents would know the answers to those questions. Someone who'd lived in the house and witnessed it all. Someone like Elsie.

Elsie had left her too, but Sienna didn't want to dwell on that.

With a little more effort she might be able to find Elsie and talk to her. About the paintings. And about the past.

She needed to see if Maggie Cameron of 42 Aldersley Road, Hornsby, had her phone number listed in the directory.

She did.

Moments later, with Elsie's letter in hand, Sienna had dialled the number and started to pace. The phone rang once. Twice. Five times.

'Hello?' said a woman's voice she didn't recognise. The accent was Australian. The voice sounded elderly. Maggie Cameron, she presumed.

'Hi,' said Sienna hurriedly. 'Ah, hello. I'm not sure if

you can help me, and I do apologise for disturbing you if you can't, but I'm trying to find a Mrs Elspeth Blaylock.'

There was a long pause, and then the woman spoke again. 'Who is this?'

'Sienna. Raleigh. Elspeth used to work for my family in Cornwall years ago. I'm in Sydney at the moment and I have your current address written on the back of one of her letters. I got your name from your neighbour, and your number from the book…' Sienna closed her eyes and cursed herself for not being better prepared. 'Her name's Elsie. Elsie Blaylock.'

'Yes, dear. I know. This is Margaret, her sister. But I'm sorry, Sienna. Elsie passed away some twelve years ago. You might remember that she came home to look after me? Turned out that she was the one who was ill.'

'I'm sorry,' Sienna mumbled. 'I'm so sorry. I didn't realise.'

'You're Mary's girl,' said the voice.

'Yes.'

'The one who used to sit in Elsie's kitchen and make pastry snails and butterflies.'

'Yes. That's me.' Sienna fought back unexpected tears. 'I'm so sorry to trouble you. I just thought…well…it would have been nice to see her again, that's all.'

'Elsie would have liked that you called her,' said her sister. 'She used to talk about you all the time. She'd have packed you up and brought you back here with the rest of her belongings if she could have. She never could countenance the way your parents treated each other. Or you, for that matter. "Such a dear little thing," ' she used to call you. "Such a dear and loving little girl." '

Sienna's vision blurred. She could feel herself clutching the letter in her hand; she just couldn't see it any more.

'I swear she used every trick in the book to try and convince her doctor to let her go to Mary's funeral, but she was far too ill to travel by then,' said the voice. 'She had to make do with sending a card. She wrote you a letter too, as I recall. Fretted over it for days, but finally it went in the post.'

'I don't remember receiving it,' Sienna said shakily. 'I don't remember much about those few months at all.'

'Ah, well. You were so young, see? Such terrible things to happen to someone so young. I wouldn't fret one little bit over not remembering that letter. Elsie wouldn't want you to fret,' said the voice. 'She'd have been so pleased that you called. She'd have loved to see you again.'

'I—thank you,' said Sienna. 'I'd have loved to see her again too.'

Sienna ended the call on a wave of emotion. She placed the letter gently on the bed and turned to stare unseeingly out at that million-dollar harbour view, her arms wrapped around her waist, holding her feelings in, keeping others out. She was still standing there when Lex walked in some time later. It could have been one minute later, it could have been ten. She glanced at the clock. Ten past eight. Make that closer to twenty minutes. She gathered herself together with a start. 'I thought you and Rudy were heading out?'

'We are. But Rudy invited Grace to meet us for lunch. She wants to know if you'd like to join us. She thought she could drop by and pick you up on the way.' Lex's sharp gaze went from her to the letter on the bed. 'May I?' he said.

Sienna nodded.

He crossed to the bed and picked it up, scanning it fast. 'You called her?'

'Yes.'

'To ask her if she knew anything about the paintings?'

'More or less.'

'And?'

'She's dead. I spoke to her sister.'

'What did her sister have to say?'

'Nothing much. Nothing about the paintings. She mentioned a letter…a letter Elsie wrote to me after my mother's death. I think I'll try and find it. Not because there'll be anything about the paintings in it because I doubt there will be. But I'd still like to find it.'

'Want some help?' he said quietly. Different offer from his earlier one. Same unwavering support.

'Yes.' It was that or walk away from him and she couldn't do it. She just couldn't do it. 'Will you come to my house in Cornwall with me when we get home? My mother's belongings are there, up in the attic. That's where Elsie's letter will be—if my father didn't throw it out.'

'I'll come,' he said gently.

'For a month?'

'Yes.'

'And help me look for the paintings?'

'If that's what you want.'

Sienna nodded and looked away. She didn't deserve this man. Not his support. Not his love. 'Tell Grace I'll give her a call later,' she said shakily.

'You'll come to lunch?'

'Yes.' He gave so much. She gave so very little back. She could at least join him for lunch. She'd be fine by lunchtime. 'Excuse me. I'd better go and have that shower.'

She left him standing there as she made her way to the bathroom, shed her pyjamas and stepped beneath the spray of a showerhead set to stinging. She felt the tears she'd been holding at bay start to swallow her and she let them come, silent, choking sobs of despair. The water wasn't hot enough; the water didn't burn nearly as much as the pain in her heart. She wanted it steaming, scalding.

The shower door opened abruptly.

Lex.

He saw her face; he saw her tears. 'We'll go to Cornwall,' he said abruptly. 'Paintings or no paintings, you can find your way through this, Sienna. I know you can.' He stepped into the shower beside her, fully clothed, and held her while she wept.

CHAPTER ELEVEN

THE coast of Cornwall in the summertime could be picture perfect, what with its hidden coves and tiny villages nestled atop rugged grey cliffs. Cornwall in February, on the other hand, could be bleak, windswept, miserable and bitterly cold. It was February now, and the attic in Sienna's crumbling manor house didn't afford quite as much protection from the gale that had blown in as she'd have liked. There was a roof. There were damp stone walls all around her and a window that didn't quite fit its rotting wooden frame any more. There were boxes.

A whole row of damp and mouldy boxes that Sienna and Lex had yet to look through.

'I think your roof leaks.' The mildness of Lex's delivery was a masterful example of frustration kept on a very tight leash. He'd said very little about the sorry state of the house. His eyes had said plenty though. He was gearing up for a reckoning, an offer to fix things, probably a health and safety lecture. She didn't want to hear any of it. 'And I think I've found a box of condolence cards,' he added.

Sienna clambered her way over the refuse of her mother's life until she reached Lex's side. She stripped off her gloves and tucked them under her arm, straightened the woollen beanie hat on her head, delved into the box, and opened up one of the cards. Bingo.

'Where do you want them?'

'The kitchen.' It was warmer in the kitchen. Soothing cups of tea could be made in the kitchen. There was gin in the kitchen and a girl never knew when a shot might come in handy.

They'd been home two days, during which time they'd opened up the house, aired the rooms, and shopped for groceries in the village. For all his wealth and the pampering that usually went with it, Lex seemed to be enjoying living life in the rough. He fitted, whether it be up here in the attic with cobwebs in his hair or naked in her bed rousing her with kisses and caresses she was powerless to resist. No Rudy, no pampering, no trappings of wealth. He didn't need them. He fitted *her*.

Two hours later, Sienna sat at the kitchen table with the woodstove throwing welcome heat and the ancient light fittings throwing as much light on the situation as they could, aided in their task by the bronze-based lamp Sienna had brought in from the dining room.

'How old is the wiring in this place?' murmured Lex.

'Older than the ark,' she said dryly. 'And before you nobly refrain to comment any further on the state of the wiring, yes, it needs replacing. It's on the list.'

'That would be the list on the side of the fridge,' he said.

'Yes.'

'That's a long list.'

'I live for challenge.'

Lex's gaze slid to the piles and piles of musty, water-stained condolence cards on the table in front of them and then to the number of cards still in the box. 'This is a good thing.'

'Here's one from your aunt Sophie,' said Sienna. 'With

Deepest Sympathy… I think I like the simple cards best. The ones that stay far, far away from promises of heavenly bliss and a better place.' Sienna did better with this task when she concentrated on the myriad ways the greeting card companies portrayed death rather than the names and handwriting of the people who had known and loved her mother.

'I like this one.' Lex held up a card with a picture of an English bulldog in an armchair on the front. 'It's from the secretary of the Cressingdon Rotary Club.'

'It *is* a nice change from lilies,' said Sienna. She glanced down into the box and sighed. 'Anyone for gin?'

'Gin will make you morbid,' he said.

'I'm already there. I'm hoping gin will give me the fortitude to keep going.'

'Have some ice cream instead.'

'I would, but a certain yacht-building, frou-frou cooking *fiend* has spoilt me for all other ice cream but his.' Sienna sighed heavily. So much for Lex doing remarkably well living without the trappings of wealth. Sienna was having withdrawal symptoms. 'I miss Rudy.'

'Half of these haven't even been opened,' muttered Lex. 'This one's a letter. Looks like it's from your father. It's addressed to your mother.' His gaze met hers, wary and concerned. 'Want me to read it?'

'No, I'll do it.'

Lex handed it over reluctantly, as if he could sense her sudden dread. 'Sienna, you don't have to do this.'

But that was where he was wrong. 'Yes,' she said quietly. 'I do.' More than ever she wanted to understand her parents' love-hate relationship. Dissect it, understand it, be free of it.

'I'll put the kettle on,' said Lex.

'Thanks.'

The kettle had boiled and Lex had made instant coffee for them both by the time Sienna had worked her way through both pages of closely written prose. 'Anything interesting?' he asked as she set the letter aside and he set the coffee in front of her.

'No. Nothing to do with the paintings, at any rate. My father was explaining why he'd been bedding one of my mother's acquaintances. Apparently my mother drove him to it. She wasn't earthy enough. Passionate enough. He called her a porcelain doll and just as cold. It was a hurtful letter. He'd written it that way deliberately. I'm glad she never read it.' She picked up her coffee and sipped, grateful for the bracing hit of caffeine on a body that was running low.

'That's not how I remember Mary,' said Lex. 'Beautiful, yes. With porcelain skin. Gracious and graceful and sometimes a little reserved around people she didn't know. Sometimes there was a sadness about her, but she wasn't cold.'

'No.' Sienna slid him a grateful glance and a watery smile. 'She wasn't cold at all. He didn't love her, not properly. Not the way she should have been loved.' She tossed the letter aside and reached for the next envelope. 'He didn't love anyone.'

'Do you know much about your father's background, Sienna?' said Lex gently.

'You mean the starving artist living in his garret and the beautiful heiress who discovered him and then proceeded to fall in love with him?' Another condolence card not from Elsie. 'I know enough.'

'Adriana once told me that your father's mother had died giving birth to him. And that he'd been raised by a father who'd found solace in a bottle and given little thought to feeding or clothing the boy who'd killed his wife. Your father grew up hard, Sienna. He grew up without love. Hate and envy had a very strong hold on him. One he couldn't shake.'

'Is that supposed to make me understand why he did the things he did?'

Lex shrugged and sent her a rueful smile. 'Does it?'

'No,' she muttered and reached for another card. 'He was so…destructive. The more she gave, the more he hated her. If he didn't love her, why couldn't he have just let her be? He never let her *be*. He broke her. And then he killed himself because he couldn't live with what he'd done. I don't *understand*.'

'Maybe you don't *need* to understand,' countered Lex gently. 'Maybe knowing that you're not like him is enough. Because you're not like him, Sienna. Or your mother, for that matter. You're stronger than they were. You're the strongest person I know. You kept going, never mind the wounds they inflicted on you with their neglect. Your resilience amazes me, your willingness to believe the best of people humbles me. After all you've been through you still look for sunshine, even after the bleakest of moments. Why do you think I fell in love with you?'

Sienna felt her insides melt at his words. She'd spent most of her life feeling abandoned and confused. Scared of intimacy. Scared of turning out like her parents: over-dependent or abusive, suicidal, take your pick. But Lex didn't think she was any of those things. He thought her strong.

The notion staggered her. Her, strong.

They found Elsie's letter towards the bottom of the box. In it Elsie poured out her love, concern and regret that she wasn't able to attend the funeral. She offered advice on whom of Mary's friends and family young Sienna could trust and turn to for advice. Adriana Wentworth's name was at the top of her list. She spoke of Margaret, her own sister, and said that if ever Sienna phoned or came to visit and Elsie wasn't there, then Margaret would take care of her. She told Sienna never to forget that there were people who loved her and that all Sienna had to do was reach out to them and they would be there. She wrote not a single word about Sienna's father even though he'd still been alive at the time. Elsie had been with Mary for twenty years. She'd known that young Sienna would find no comfort there.

There was no mention whatsoever of Elsie's own illness.

The letter made Sienna's eyes water and her heart fill with gratitude towards an old woman who'd tried to steer a young girl through the aftermath of her mother's death from half a world away. Sienna looked up to find Lex staring at her, his jaw clenched and his eyes shadowed. 'There's nothing here about the paintings,' Sienna told him with a weary smile that she couldn't make stick. 'It's just advice to a young girl who's just lost her mother. Good advice,' she added faintly as her eyes filled again.

'Sienna, you don't have to do this,' said Lex gruffly. 'I don't give a damn whether we find these paintings or not. It's you I care about. And I hate what this is doing to you.'

'Hey, people pay good money for therapy like this.' Sienna tried for lightness and almost succeeded. 'I'm saving a fortune here.'

'You're hurting,' he said. 'And watching you hurt and not being able to do anything about it is killing me.' He stood up, paced the room, back and forth, back and forth. 'Let's get some air. Take a wander around the grounds or a walk along the cliffs.'

'In this weather?' She'd been watching the wind pick up and the rain come down all afternoon, wondering if today would be the day that the roof on this place finally gave up the good fight. Judging by the rattling of the windows and the whistling of the wind there was a very good chance it might be. 'It's a nice idea, don't get me wrong. It's lovely along the cliffs, but right now it's raining *pellets* out there and they're coming down sideways.'

'Exploration is not weather-dependent,' he said, striding to the kitchen door and opening it, only to be driven back a step by an icy north easterly that set china rattling and envelopes flying. 'I see your point,' he said, leaning his shoulder into the door in order to push it closed again. 'You can show me round the inside of the house instead, point out all the things that need fixing or replacing.'

'Are you going to offer to have them all fixed or replaced?' she said, eyeing him as sternly as she could, given that this was the man who loved her and thought her strong.

'I was thinking more along the lines of bypassing the offer altogether and moving straight onto the fixit side of things.'

'You donning a carpenter's belt is an appealing picture,' she said. Very, very appealing. There was something about a handyman multimillionaire who loved her and thought her strong that pushed every one of her buttons and then some. 'But I think I'd rather you gave me your thoughts as we went around as to whether this place was worth fixing up at all. A very clever man once told me to sell the place and cut my losses if I couldn't maintain its upkeep. Maybe it's time I took his advice.'

He looked at her, his expression wry. 'Sienna, no. Some things you have to let go of. The sins of your parents is one of them. They're not your sins. The need for a bunch of paintings to make you rich enough that you can marry me is another. But if you love this house, keep it. There's a solidness here that's worth building on.' He looked around the long-neglected room. 'Maybe you need to investigate the possibilities of taking on a business partner who can provide you with the capital you need to restore this place properly. You could look to opening up the place to paying guests at a later date, if you wanted to. A sympathetic business partner would be amenable to any number of plans for this place, including retaining it as a summer house for the occasional benefit of himself, his life partner, and their offspring.'

Sienna left her seat for the sole purpose of finding a better one on Lex's lap. She put one hand to his heart and her other to his cheek and dropped a gentle kiss on his lips, a kiss that inevitably turned hungry. 'Where exactly might I start looking for this wondrous-sounding business partner, do you think?'

'Oh, you wouldn't have to look far.'

'You're a good man, Alexander Wentworth the Third,' she whispered, twining her arms around his neck and positioning her body for maximum points of contact, never mind their bulky clothing. 'Why don't I start by showing my potential new business partner the master bedroom?' It was warm up in her bedroom, she'd had a fire going in the hearth all afternoon to ward off the chill. 'We can tour the rest of the house later.'

Lex's touch had always brought pleasure and need to Sienna, but this time it brought with it so much more. His touch infinitely gentle as he peeled away her layers of clothing until she was as vulnerable and as naked as the day she was born. His movements hurried as he shed his own clothes thereafter. As if he thought she might change her mind and turn him away, but there was no turning away from this. She couldn't bear to turn away.

She could see their reflections in the gilt-edged mirror

over the mantelpiece, Lex so dark and beautiful, every leanly muscled line of his body drenched in perfection, and herself so pale and slender in comparison. She'd inherited her mother's porcelain skin. She had her father's eyes. Her father's words came back to haunt her only this time she tried pushing them away. I'm not pathetic, cowering, and weak. I'm not!

'Tell me what you see,' he murmured, and she shook her head.

'No.'

His smile grew rueful as his gaze met hers in the mirror. 'Want to know what I see?' He didn't wait for an answer. 'I see a six-year-old girl in a pretty pink dress, with a ribbon in her hair halfway up a tree staring down at me and asking me if I'd ever been to the top. I see a twelve-year-old girl so pale and withdrawn she almost broke my heart, and then she saw me heading her way and smiled and broke my heart all over again. I see an eighteen-year-old woman-child in a pale blue dress who trembled in my arms and made me feel like a king. I see the generous and loving woman who holds my heart, and I see our future and it's bright with love and riches that have nothing to do with money. Tell me you see it too.'

I'm not pathetic cowering and weak. I'm not! She repeated the litany over and over in her mind but she wasn't there yet. She still couldn't bring herself to take that last step. Sienna turned her back on the mirror and the picture they made and drew his head down towards hers, praying that it would be enough, that he would not turn away from her. 'I see only you.'

The eye of the storm hit at around midnight, rattling the windows and the roof and funnelling icy gusts of air down the chimney, sending the cinders flying. Lex got up to check the fire, Sienna got up to go upstairs to the attic and check on the roof.

'No,' said Lex when she declared her intentions. 'It's not safe up there right now. It'll have to wait until the storm passes. Check it tomorrow. Get some local roofers in to look at it tomorrow. They can put together a quote on the replacement cost while they're there.' Not a man to cool his heels once a concession had been made, Lex. Not a man to take no for an answer and leave it at that. She loved that about him. She needed that from him. 'Come back to bed,' he murmured, his eyes darkening. 'I guarantee I'll make it worth your while.'

'I have a better idea,' she said, with every intention of taking control of this lovemaking session right from the start, and, what was more, *keeping* it. 'Why don't you let me make it worth yours?'

The view from her bedroom windows the following morning wasn't a pretty one. Long-neglected trees had lost branches, the dovecote lay in pieces on the ground, and the stable roof had fallen in and taken part of the stable wall with it.

'It could have been worse,' she murmured as Lex came to stand beside her. 'I could have had a horse.'

'True,' he said. 'There's something sticking out of the wall.'

There *was* something sticking out of the wall. Some sort of thin wooden-pallet-sized container. Probably just insulation. One tiny little patch of insulation. In a stable wall. Sienna looked harder. Then she looked at Lex to see if he was thinking what she was thinking. His eyes were narrowed, his brow furrowed. 'Want to go down for a closer look?' he said finally.

'I think so,' she said, trying hard to emulate Lex's calm. Paintings came in pallet-sized thin wooden containers these days. Rembrandts didn't, to be sure. But some did.

'Now?' he said.

'I think so.'

'Yes,' he said next. 'I think so too.' And matched her, speed for speed, in his rush to get dressed.

'There's a Monet in my stable wall,' said Sienna some ten minutes later as they stood amidst the rubble and stared at the thin wooden box sitting snugly between the outer stonework wall and inner stable-box lining.

'No, there *might* be a Monet in your stable wall,' countered Lex calmly, though if ever a box looked as if it contained a couple of paintings, this was it. As a child he'd adored the excitement and anticipation of a treasure hunt. As a man he still enjoyed the hunt, but the stakes here were too high and he wasn't talking about a bunch of priceless paintings.

He thought he'd been so clever, agreeing to help her look for the missing paintings. It had bought him time to show her what a life with him would be like, given her more time to get used to the idea of marrying him. It had kept her by his side. Somewhere along the way Sienna was supposed to have come to the conclusion that she loved him enough to marry him anyway, and to hell with the paintings.

But she hadn't.

He'd never really expected to *find* the paintings.

He didn't know whether he wanted to find the paintings now. They would make her wealthy in her own right, true enough. They might help her reconcile her past—he didn't really know how that was supposed to work, other than Sienna thought it would help. If finding the paintings gave her the confidence to marry him, good.

If a small part of his brain protested that if Sienna really loved him she wouldn't let herself *be* deterred by financial inequality or a traumatic past, well, he tried to ignore that particular philosophy in favour of working with the one on the table.

'Let's pull it out,' she said, suiting actions to words, but the box didn't move. 'Lex, help me pull it out.'

Her excitement was infectious. Her suppressed impatience conjured up his own. The sooner they knew what was in that damned box, the sooner he could deal with it. He added his strength to hers, but the box was wedged in tight. 'Got a crowbar?' he said. 'And a hammer?'

'All that sort of stuff used to live in the tack room,' she said with an air of dismay as she turned to survey the rear of the stables. 'The good news is that the tack room is still intact. The bad news is that the entrance door is blocked by wreckage from the roof. It's that door on the far left. But there's a window.'

The window proved the way in and shortly thereafter Sienna armed with the hammer, and Lex with the crowbar, headed back towards the box.

Halfway there, Sienna began to grin. Then she began to laugh. 'Does this feel somewhat surreal to you? I feel like Nancy Drew.'

Lex did not feel like Nancy Drew. Lex felt a lot like a tack-room door, one whose world was about to come crashing down around him. But he anteed up and set the crowbar to shifting stones with as much goodwill as he could muster. Minutes later the thin wooden box was free and Sienna lowered it gently to its side on the ground.

'How do you want to do this?' he said.

'Carefully. Maybe there's a latch or a lock. Maybe it'll just swing open.'

But there wasn't and it didn't. The box, if it was a box, had been nailed shut tight. 'I vote we loosen one of the sides with the hammer and then pry it off with the crowbar,' he said. 'Carefully.'

Sienna nodded and he set to work. The join came loose reluctantly but finally Lex had made enough of a crack to lever the claw of the hammer into it and loosen one side of the box. He wedged the crowbar deep into the centre of the crack so that one solid push would pop the side entirely and knelt there, looking to Sienna kneeling in the dirt on the other side of the crate, her clothes dusty and her eyes shining with hope.

'Hey, Nancy,' he said softly, holding out the crowbar towards her. 'Your turn.'

Sienna leaned across and closed her hand over his. Her hand trembled. 'Together,' she said.

'All right.'

Together they pushed on the crowbar and watched the side of the box pop free. Lex looked at Sienna and she at him. 'I can't look,' she said in a shaking voice.

Lex didn't want to. The contents of that box held the key to his future, his and Sienna's, and he hated being at its mercy. 'Together,' he said gruffly.

'All right,' she whispered.

And together they leaned down and peered into their future.

Lex sat back up first. Sienna stayed looking, looking for what he didn't know because there was nothing to see.

'It's empty,' Sienna said in a small voice, and the stricken look in her eyes made his heart bleed and his stomach clench.

'Yes.'

'They're not here.'

'No.'

'There's nothing here.'

'I don't care,' he said fiercely, and at her continued dismay, 'I don't care. The only reason I gave a damn whether those paintings were here or not was because you gave a damn, and because you have it fixed in your head that a marriage between us would fail without them. Well, it *wouldn't* fail, Sienna. The difference in our financial status carries as much weight as we decide to give it, and I give it none. *None!*' Her eyes were huge and she made as if to speak, but he wasn't done yet. 'And if you would just stop *thinking* about our circumstances for a moment and start *feeling* your way through all this, you might just decide that you don't give a damn about the money side of things either.' He looked down at the empty crate and something settled inside him, something bleak and bitter to fill the growing hollowness. 'I can't do this.'

She scrambled to her feet, her hand outstretched towards him, but he couldn't have her near him, didn't want her near him, not now. His need was too strong and so was his despair. 'Alex—

'No!' He backed away fast. 'No, Sienna. I'm sick of watching you dodge commitment to me in favour of wallowing in your past and pinning your hopes on a bunch of paintings we may never find.' He made it to the door without stumbling. He almost kept walking, he needed to keep walking, but there was one last point he needed to make. 'Why can't you pin your hopes on me?'

Sienna watched helplessly as Lex strode away from her, dashed hopes mixing with despair and self-disgust to form a cocktail of rioting emotions. The one that surfaced first was anger. Not at Lex, no, not at Lex. This anger was directed squarely at herself. At her past and her stupid, senseless inability to let go of it. She stared down at the pallet on the ground and the hammer and crowbar lying next to it. The hammer wasn't big enough, she decided, and the crowbar wasn't quite right either. There was an axe in the tack room, maybe that would do the job. She found it a couple of minutes later, and with carnage in mind headed back to the pallet, her anger building with every step she took towards it. She kicked the box for good measure, stamped on it, and finally she raised the axe over her head.

'Hi, Daddy,' she said. 'I hear you in my dreams, in my head, and I'm sick of you. You hear me? I'm sick of listening to you. This is for being a husband no woman deserved.' Down went the axe and bit deep into the box. Wood splintered, but not enough. 'And this is for being a father no child deserved.' Thud went the axe. Crack went the pallet.

One down. But there was still her conflicting feelings for her mother to deal with.

'I'm sorry that you never knew love the way I know it. I'm sorry that you chose the wrong man to give your heart to, but you didn't have to let him break you,' she said, and let the years of anger and grief at her mother's final betrayal begin to build inside her. She started in on the sides of the box this time, swinging the axe in a wide sideways arc, sending the pallet skidding across the dirt. 'I don't care if I never find those bloody paintings, you hear me? I don't want them any more. I don't need them any more. I don't need you.' She set the axe aside and dragged the half-ruined pallet upright to rest against what was left of the wall. She picked up the axe again, hefted it, found a solid two-handed grip. 'I'm very, very angry with you. This…' She raised the axe high. 'This is for leaving me.' And with a frenzy of blows she smashed that box to hell and back.

When she was done…when her breath came in great gasping heaves and sweat stung the corners of her eyes…she dropped the axe to the ground and wiped her face with the sleeve of her shirt, well satisfied with the destruction she had wrought.

'I'm through with you,' she muttered, kicking at a corner chunk of box for good measure. 'Both of you. I won't let you destroy the love I've found.'

And turning her back on the wreckage of her past, she went in search of a future bright with love and filled with riches that had nothing to do with money and everything to do with belief.

She found him on the cliffs, looking every inch the brooding, scowling thief of hearts that he was. He watched her approach but he gave her nothing. Why would he, thought Sienna with a growing sense of panic, when all she'd done lately was reject everything he offered? Too scared to accept his love. Too wrapped up in her past to see the pain she'd been causing him.

But she saw it now. And she wanted it gone.

'I wondered if I'd find you here,' she said as she came up beside him.

He looked at her in silence and the hopelessness and despair in his eyes tore at her soul. The Lex of her childhood had never lost hope. There'd been nothing he couldn't do. *She* had been the child of despair and lost dreams, but she wasn't a child any more. She was a woman. A loving, caring woman, and if the man she loved beyond measure had lost hope, then he would just have to accept some of hers. 'We didn't eat breakfast. I thought you might want a cup of tea, or coffee. Or something.'

'No.'

'Or we could go into the village and have breakfast at the bakery. I hear the pies are very good.'

'No.'

'I'll find something in the cupboard,' she offered next. 'Tinned baked beans on toast. Don't tell Rudy.'

A twisted smile. Not much, but it was something.

'Alex, I have an apology to make. I was hoping to make it over breakfast or at the very least over a cup of coffee in the kitchen, but I'll make it here if I have to. I'll make it anywhere, and I'll make it short. I'm sorry I hurt you with my refusal to believe in your love for me, or in mine for you. I'm sorry it took me so long to realise that all the love I've ever dreamed of was right there in front of me and that it was mine for the taking if only I dared to believe. I didn't mean to hurt you. I never want to hurt you. I'd rather cut out my own heart than trample yours.' Sienna took a ragged breath and straightened her shoulders. 'I know it's a lot to ask, but if you haven't given up on me…if you still want me for your wife…I'd like you to ask me to marry you one last time.' She was trembling by the time she reached the last word. 'If that's what you want.'

'I have no ring,' he said roughly.

'I don't need a ring.'

'I don't have pretty words.'

'You do have pretty words. You can string together the prettiest, most persuasive words I've ever heard. But the ones in your heart are the only ones I want to hear. They're the most beautiful words of all.'

A smile began to bloom in Lex's eyes, a teasing light that chased away the darkness and always had. 'About that bended-knee thing…'

'Alex,' she said warningly. 'We can talk about control issues later. Preferably when we're naked. I love it when we do that. But right now would you mind a great deal if you just got on with your proposal?'

'I can do that,' he said, and his eyes grew vividly intent as he took her hand in his and lifted it to his lips. 'Ready?'

'Ready.' Finally ready. Love had graced her life and she didn't ever intend to let it go.

'Marry me, Sienna,' he said quietly. 'Marry me and fill my heart.'

'Yes,' she whispered joyously. 'A thousand times, yes.'

EPILOGUE

Sydney, Australia—a good day for a christening

'LOOK at her,' cooed Grace, a vision of nautical elegance and sophistication in navy blue trousers, a lightweight cream-coloured tunic, and a red and gold silk scarf tied around her neck just so. A pair of practical navy-blue deck shoes completed the outfit and gave notice to all who sailed these waters that the lady had plans to come aboard. 'Isn't she just the most gorgeous thing you've ever seen?'

'She certainly is,' said Sienna admiringly. She'd opted for white shorts and a deep red T-shirt made from the softest jersey, and she too had traded heels for something with a little more grip. Practical white tennis shoes graced her feet, and her fingers were bare of everything but a dazzling white diamond on her left-hand ring finger, which Rudy could remove over her cold dead body. No scarf for Sienna, just a floppy-brimmed hat and sunglasses. Newly purchased sunglasses, sourced by Georgie and dark enough so that a woman could look where she would and no one would know. No one but Lex, that was. Lex always seemed to know when she was admiring him.

Sienna smiled and raised her hand in greeting as the

sleek and graceful eight-point-two-million-dollar baby, currently manned by a skeleton crew of two—one of whom she'd just been admiring—came slowly in to dock at the Watson's Bay private jetty where she and Grace waited. Engine-powered for the moment, the yacht would unfurl its sails for the first time ever once the current skipper had picked up the rest of his crew and made for open water. Sienna could hardly wait to get on deck and feel her go.

'What did they call her?' she asked Grace. She'd been remiss. She'd been too busy admiring other things on board that there boat to notice her name and now it was half hidden by the jetty.

'Rudy named her.' Was Grace *blushing*? 'Ask him.'

'I will,' murmured Sienna, enjoying the moment even more once she'd made out the words written in slashing black scrawl on the side of the bow. 'Oh, I will.'

The engine purred as the craft slid ever closer towards them. Lex was there, leaning port side, hand outstretched to help them board. First Grace's beach bag and an overstuffed picnic hamper, then Grace herself, followed by Sienna. Lex grinned, the black bandana keeping his hair in check reminiscent of a somewhat more piratical age. Pirate looked good on him. Always had. Love looked good on him too.

'Grace,' he said, 'gorgeous as always,' and brushed Grace's cheek with his lips.

Sienna's welcome was somewhat more lingering. Clearly his pirate attire had gone to his head.

'Later for you,' she murmured as her body tightened in response to Lex's caress. 'I have to go and pay my respects to the skipper.' She waited until Rudy had cleared the jetty and turned the yacht around and pointed her towards the Pacific, but that was all the reprieve the big man was going to get from her today.

The bridge area gleamed white in the sunlight; the boat wheel a matt-finished masterpiece of low-gleam stainless steel. Below, she would doubtless find an engine room fitted with all the latest in radar, sonar, and communications equipment needed by the intrepid ocean-going sailor as well as a luxury galley, entertaining area, and bedrooms.

'Grace tells me you were the one who named her,' she said airily by way of greeting. 'Dangerous move, what with you being such a romantic and all.' Rudy scowled. Sienna's smile widened, she couldn't help it. She'd missed the big man, missed his gruffness and his cooking. Definitely his cooking. 'Unfortunately, in all the excitement of watching the yacht slide up to collect us, Grace clean forgot to tell me what it was. I'm afraid I was too busy admiring her beauty to notice her name. I do hope I'm not turning into, you know, a male.' Sienna beamed at him for good measure. So far Rudy had been running true to form and hadn't said a word. 'So about that name…Is it romantic? Does it involve chocolate?' Sienna looked up at the shiny new rig; this really was the most beautiful craft she'd ever crewed on. Not that she'd actually *done* any crewing on her yet. 'You didn't call her *Truffle*, did you?'

'She's called the *Gracie Mae*,' muttered Rudy gruffly, ears reddening as he stared straight ahead.

Yes, she was. Sienna smiled at the sky. There wasn't a cloud in it. 'Because she's fast?'

'Because she's all I've ever wanted,' the big man said simply, and she closed her eyes and breathed in deep and thought Grace a lucky woman. Almost as lucky as Sienna.

'That's so sweet.'

'I hear your nuptials are to be here in Australia,' he said next.

'Yes.' Sienna opened her eyes and turned to smile at

Rudy, who was eyeing the high set solitaire diamond on her ring finger with wry resignation. 'No,' she said, pre-empting his request for her to take it off.

'Figured as much,' he said, with the hint of a smile. 'Grace is beside herself at being asked to be your matron of honour.' He cleared his throat. 'I found a giant Bombe Alaska recipe the other day. It needs tweaking, but I figure I can have it sorted by your wedding day. If that's what you wanted for a cake.'

'Rudy, that sounds brilliant.'

Rudy nodded, once, and that was that. Wedding cake sorted. 'Mr Wentworth,' he said in a louder voice. 'Ready on the mainsail. The spinnaker's yours,' he said to Sienna. 'Let's get moving.

'C'mon, my beauty,' Sienna heard him whisper coaxingly as she headed for the foredeck. 'Don't be shy. You've shown them your quality. Now let's show them what you can do.'

Gracie Mae's crew played until well after noon, but finally they slowed and dropped sail and settled down to the business of refuelling their bodies. Grace's picnic basket was a treasure trove of goodies and the galley fridge had been fully stocked. There was home-made triple-cream vanilla ice cream in the freezer section of that fridge. With chocolate chips. Sienna didn't eat it first. She had to make her way past the sandwich platter first. The salmon, rocket and cream cheese with dill on sourdough. The king prawn and Thai salad wraps. And the strawberry, watermelon, rockmelon and lemon mint kebab chasers.

Only after she'd done full justice to the *Gracie Mae*'s maiden feast did she turn her attention to ice cream.

'Rudy, you've outdone yourself,' she murmured after savouring her first taste. 'This is fabulous. I especially like the chocolate chips.'

'They're not chips,' said Rudy. 'They're shavings.'

'Oh. Shavings.' She caught Lex's smirk and hid her own smile. 'Well, they're very good. Mind you, it could do with a little something…more,' she said, eyeing the magnum of champagne Rudy had seemingly conjured out of nowhere.

'Eyes off,' he said. 'This is for *Gracie Mae*.'

'Really?' Sienna winked at Grace. 'Hog.'

'The *boat*,' said Rudy.

'I knew that.'

'There's one in every family.' Rudy's voice was long suffering, but the corners of his eyes had crinkled.

'It seems to me,' said Sienna artlessly, 'that this "smashing of magnums over the bow of the boat" business could well scratch the finish. And that would be a shame. It seems to me, that a lady such as this one would prefer us to pour some bubbles into a fine crystal flute and tip it gently over her bow as everyone aboard her raises their fine crystal flutes full of champagne and whatever other additives seem to be on hand and drinks to her as well. But don't mind me. Just a suggestion.'

'You didn't seriously think that would work, did you?' murmured Lex from behind her, holding two champagne flutes towards her as Rudy headed above deck with his magnum in tow. Lex carried two more champagne glasses in his other hand. 'There's more champagne in the fridge.'

'Watch and learn,' she said with a slow smile guaranteed to drop a man at fifty paces. 'When are you going to make an honest woman of me?'

'Whenever you set the date,' he murmured. 'How long did you say that dress was going to take, again?'

'Six weeks. The dress will be ready in two. We're waiting on the shoes.'

'Couldn't you just choose a different pair of shoes?'

'Not according to Georgie.'

'You mean Georgie of business-suit fame?'

'That's the one.'

'I stand corrected,' he said fervently. 'By all means, wait for the shoes. Feel free to get her to design your entire trousseau.'

'She does have a holistic approach to these things,' said Grace, coming up and deftly commandeering two champagne glasses from Lex. She plucked another from the galley cupboard. 'Wedding plans aside, we seem to have a slight problem with the christening arrangements. Rudy can't quite bring himself to risk the finish.'

'Well, who would?' Sienna smiled innocently.

'He wants us all up on the foredeck,' said Grace as she headed for the hatch.

'Be right there,' said Sienna.

'What? No ice cream?' said Lex as she swiftly set the lid back on the container and set it back in the freezer.

'Not this time. This is Rudy's big moment and I want to do right by him. No ice cream.'

They stood on the foredeck with blue sky above them and ocean below, and nothing on the horizon but more sea and more sky, and filled five glasses to the brim. Lex began the toasts.

'To the best-laid plans,' he said.

'To dreaming the dream,' said Rudy.

'And following your heart,' said Grace.

And then it was Sienna's turn. She looked to Rudy and to Grace and saw love at play, vivid and strong, never mind that it had found them so late. She looked to Lex, her patient Lex, with his quicksilver eyes and his marauder's soul that had so completely captured hers. He'd showered her torn and tender heart with the sweetest kind of love and she savoured every moment and knew it for a gift, such a priceless, treasured gift, and she gave it back in turn. From her heart back to his, and round and round again. She lifted her glass high and touched it to the others.

'To those who dare to believe.'

* * * * *

The Italian Boss's Secretary Mistress

CATHY
WILLIAMS

Cathy Williams is originally from Trinidad, but has lived in England for a number of years. She currently has a house in Warwickshire, which she shares with her husband Richard, her three daughters, Charlotte, Olivia and Emma, and their pet cat, Salem. She adores writing romantic fiction and would love one of her girls to become a writer—although at the moment she is happy enough if they do their homework and agree not to bicker with one another.

CHAPTER ONE

IT WAS not yet seven-thirty and Gabriel Gessi was already at his desk. It was his daily routine. Half an hour running on the treadmill at his gym, half an hour scything through the empty pool, a quick shower, a shave and then on to his office, already charged to face the onslaught that constituted his average day. The only interruptions to this brutally physical routine came in the form of his frequent trips overseas, although, even then, he would try his level best to kick-start his working day on a physical high.

The past three months had not seen him deviate from this punishing routine, even though the accustomed high had been marred by a succession of irritations that he really should not have been expected to handle. Even though they concerned him.

Gabriel Gessi inhabited that rarefied world of the supremely wealthy and, as such, was not accustomed to dealing with life's minor irritations. His adrenalin rush came from the aggressive cut and thrust of deals and acquisitions, not from the more prosaic set-backs that dogged most people's working lives.

Set-back number one had come in the form of the temp who had sailed through the interview process under the successful camouflage of an efficient working girl but who, after one week, had turned out to be a ditzy emotional wreck who spent the majority of her two weeks sniffing discreetly into a handkerchief and muttering lame excuses about boyfriend problems.

Gabriel had no time for females with boyfriend problems and even less time for females who cried. He had had to get rid of her and thereafter had followed a catalogue of mediocrity which had left him gritting his perfect white teeth in frustration.

He couldn't imagine how the incompetents who appeared in front of him could ever have been fortunate enough to find gainful employment and yet, by all accounts, they had.

He had seen off the last one the Friday before with an audible sigh of relief. She, at any rate, had lasted longer than the expected fortnight, but he reckoned that that had only been because he had swallowed his irritation and, with laudable patience, tolerated her annoying tendency to cower whenever he spoke and to address him so quietly that he'd constantly had to tell her to speak up. Whenever he'd told her to speak up, she'd invariably jumped and spilled something. Coffee. Water. Her cup of tea. Something of a liquid nature had always seemed to be around waiting to be nudged accidentally over, which, in turn, had rendered her even more incapable.

The whole thing had been extremely trying and Gabriel was overjoyed that his life was now going to return to normal.

For the first time in three long months, he had actually strolled through the smoked glass doors of his very plush four-storied offices without a scowl on his face.

Rose would be back today. Life could return to its normal smooth course, leaving him to get on with the process of running an empire without having to worry about the tiresome nuts and bolts.

Of course it was not yet eight and, even though he half expected her to demonstrate her enthusiasm to be back at the helm, he did not reasonably expect her to appear, like him, at the crack of dawn. She would, after all, probably still be recuperating from jet lag. A flight back from Australia was enough to throw even the most seasoned traveller, and Rose was not a seasoned traveller. Even though a fair percentage of his business was founded on the leisure industry, including a range of exclusive hotels scattered all over the world, her knowledge of foreign shores was limited. In the four years she had worked for him, she had only travelled with him a handful of times and, even then, only to Europe. He hadn't minded. He needed her back at the office anyway, in his absence, making sure that things were ticking over.

In that quiet time before employees started arriving, time which he usually spent going through the emails which would have been forwarded overnight, Gabriel instead swivelled his leather chair round so that he was facing the huge window, staring out at a skyline that was cluttered with the busyness of the concrete jungle, but still oddly beautiful against the crisply blue May sky.

The past three months had showed him how much he relied on Rose. She was well paid but he contemplated giving her another pay rise. Or maybe a company car, although he couldn't imagine her driving to work. Who did? He, personally, either took a cab or else was driven in by his chauffeur, sparing him the horrors of the London traffic. But she might be able to use a car if she ever wanted to get out of London.

Briefly, Gabriel wondered whether she ever did. Despite his occasional prodding, he realised that he knew precious little about her personal life. She had a talent for deflecting unwanted questions that would have guaranteed her a career in the diplomatic service.

Did she even have a driving licence? He vaguely assumed that everyone did, but maybe not.

Wrapped up in the lazy perambulations of his thoughts, he was only marginally aware of time passing and not at all aware that it was nine until, reflected in the glass pane through which he was still staring, he saw her standing in the open doorway that separated his office from her working area.

For a few seconds he was aware of an unusual slam of emotion, then he glanced at his watch and swivelled round.

Rose involuntarily drew in a deep breath, releasing it very slowly. It steadied her nerves. Even when she had been coming in every day, seeing him every day, he still had, had he but known it, an oddly destabilising effect on her. Something about his sheer, overpowering physicality.

Three months spent away intensified the effect to the point that she felt faint, even though her face remained as pleasantly unrevealing as always.

'It's nine o'clock,' Gabriel said, scowling. 'You normally get in by eight-thirty.'

The brusqueness of his tone released her from her immobility and she walked towards the chair positioned in front of his desk and sat down. 'I see you haven't changed, Gabriel,' she commented dryly. 'Still avoiding all the rules of common politeness. Aren't you going to ask me about my trip to Australia?'

'No need. I gathered from your emails that you were having a whale of a time. You've changed. You've lost weight.'

Rose couldn't help it. She blushed as his blue eyes gave her the once-over.

She fought to remember what her sister had said about getting out of the rut she was in, tearing herself away from her hopeless infatuation with a man who was a health hazard when it came to members of the opposite sex.

But he was just so sinfully sexy. It was impossible not to

feel her toes curl in her sensible flats as she drank in the sensuous curve of his mouth, the powerful beauty of his features, the daunting perfection of his body.

'Yes, I have,' she admitted steadily, looking down at the letter on her lap and nervously smoothing her fingers over it. 'It was hot over there. I lived on salads. I'm sorry you had such a problem with my replacements,' she said, changing the subject because those amazing eyes of his were boring holes through her. 'I honestly thought that Claire was going to work out or else I wouldn't have recruited her. What exactly was the problem?'

Gabriel, however, was still reeling from the transformation, not sure that he liked what he was seeing. Gone was the comfortably plump Rose, last seen in a practical navy-blue suit and white roll-neck sweater. In its place was a very slim Rose, showing off a surprisingly eye-catching figure in a tan and black checked skirt that actually revealed a bit of thigh and a figure-hugging black three-quarter length T-shirt that revealed breasts that would be more than just a good handful. The only sensible thing about her were her flat ballet style shoes.

'I never knew you had legs,' he mused aloud.

'Of course I have legs, Gabriel! How do you think I manage to get from A to B? On wings?'

'But you've always hidden them before…' He moved swiftly from chair to desk and perched there, staring down at her assessingly. 'And very attractive they are, too. But you might want to observe a little more decorum in the office.'

Rose's mouth dropped open in outrage at his openly sexist remark.

'What have you done to your hair? Have you done something to your hair? It looks different.'

'I haven't *done anything* to my hair, Gabriel, aside from

having it trimmed, and shall we leave the subject of me behind just for a moment…?' She fiddled with the letter, not quite knowing how she was going to give it to him without having to sit through the torturous process of watching him read it.

'Why? I'm fascinated by the transformation. I thought you were going over to help your sister with her new baby. I had no idea you were going for a complete make-over.'

'I *did* go to help Grace!'

'And in the process decided to go on a crash diet, cut your hair and lounge around in a bikini all day so that you could go brown…?'

Rose counted to ten and wondered what exactly she saw in a man who was as arrogant as they came and saw nothing amiss in barging through every warning red light she was giving off without a second's thought.

'Have you ever been in the company of a newborn, Gabriel?'

'Now that's something I've always tried to avoid…'

'Thought so, because if you had you would know that screaming newborns and tanning on loungers are two things that don't go hand in hand.'

'Surely your sister didn't expect you to look after the thing the whole time!'

'It wasn't a thing. It was a baby. A beautiful little boy. They called him Ben.' Her voice softened as she remembered the feel of that small, wriggling, plump body in her arms, a sensation that had kick-started her determination to change the rut into which she had comfortably sunk. Grace, two years older than her, had been so blissfully happy. Next to her, Rose had had an ugly vision of her own life and its sad limitations and she hadn't cared for what she had glimpsed. In two years' time she would be twenty-eight, the same age as her sister, but would she be cradling a newborn infant with a loving husband by her side if she continued doing what she was doing—working flat out for a man who didn't have a clue she existed aside from her role as his capable secretary? Or would she be the eternal career girl who spent her life improving her house and bettering her lifestyle with nothing to show for it in the end? Well, nothing worth having, anyway. A certain wistfulness crept into her voice as she told him about her experiences in Australia. Grace's husband, Tom, was an orthopaedic surgeon and had needed his nights to be free of interruption so that he could get enough sleep to enable him to operate safely. Hence, Rose's input had been more than just a luxury. She had done her fair share of waking up during the nights, settling the baby back to sleep after his feed, but she had enjoyed every minute of it.

Gabriel was hardly listening to her spiel about the baby. Babies would doubtless eventually come for him—he was, after all, half Italian—but for the moment he couldn't care less about the antics of some undersized human being on the other side of the world.

He was far too engrossed in the nut-brown creature sitting in front of him. The nut-brown creature with the abundant breasts, to which his eyes were repeatedly drawn.

At the risk of appearing pathetically lecherous and feeling an unwelcome stirring in his loins, Gabriel removed himself back to his chair and tried to focus on what she was saying about baby Ben and the crazy inaccuracy of his baby clock. He had never seen that soft look in her eyes before, and he suddenly frowned.

'I hope this trip hasn't put ideas into your head,' he said, interrupting her in mid-sentence, and Rose blinked.

'Sorry?'

'Trip? Ideas? Your head?'

'I don't know what you're talking about,' Rose told him bluntly.

'I'm talking about my perfect secretary suddenly deciding that the time has come for her to dip her toes into motherhood. All that baby business can prove contagious sometimes. I know that for a fact.'

'Oh, really, Gabriel…' Rose felt a cold anger sweep through her and she had to make a big effort to keep her voice level. 'And how would you know that?'

'I have two sisters and a brother and both my sisters have children, roughly the same ages. I have it on good authority that other women are often afflicted by maternal feelings the minute they get too close to a newborn baby…'

Rose looked at that dangerously sexy face and was unsurprised at his dismissive tone when referring to babies, parenthood and all that that implied. He was a man to whom settling down would be a notion best left on the back burner for as long as was humanly possible. Why complicate a perfectly satisfactory life, having any woman at the click of a finger, by choosing one woman and then, to compound the error, having a child? A screaming, demanding infant that would put paid to all thoughts of mobility?

'I don't intend to be trying motherhood any time soon,' Rose said coolly. 'I believe it's necessary to have a serious partner before a woman takes a step like that.'

In that one sentence Gabriel had more insight into Rose than he had ever had. He had always assumed that there was no man on the scene but only because she had never mentioned one and women generally couldn't help mentioning the men in their lives. Now it was confirmed and he was quietly pleased.

'And there's no man in your life at the moment?' he risked,

pressing on in the face of her obvious reluctance to prolong the subject.

Rose flushed and wanted to kick herself for the revealing crack in her armour. She had managed to keep their relationship on a strictly business level by making sure never to reveal anything about herself. She had instinctively known that the more he knew about her, the more dangerous her silly infatuation with him became. He could charm the birds from the trees and without really trying he could easily have sussed how she felt about him had he known anything about her private thoughts.

Of course it no longer mattered. She was forgetting that in the heat of the moment. The realisation gave her the strength she needed and she smiled nonchalantly.

'They come and go,' she said airily. 'You know how it is. I'm between chaps at the moment.' The small white lie was worth every penny just to see the incredulity in his eyes and she smiled demurely, daring him to voice his shock that she might actually have a life outside his corporation. 'Anyway…' she fingered the letter nervously '…now that I've told you all about my trip to Australia, there's something I need to give you…' She stretched forward and placed the white envelope on his desk and a sudden rush of sickening nerves flooded through her in a tidal sweep.

But she reminded herself that she was absolutely doing the right thing. She had talked it over with Grace and just voicing her thoughts had been sufficient to make her realise what she needed to do, how badly she needed to escape the powerful net Gabriel had spread around her over the years to the point where he was always somewhere in her head, whatever the time of day or night, whoever she might or might not be with. It was dangerous and getting more so with each passing day. In another four years' time her emotions would be so tethered to him that she might well find herself crippled by her own inability to find a suitable mate without resorting to unfavourable comparisons.

He was looking at the letter warily, but he eventually took it, ripped it open and quickly scanned the contents. Several times. Obviously thinking that he had misread something. Finally, when her nerves were on the point of totally shredding, he said, very softly, 'What's going on here, Rose?' Shock and disbelief flared in his deep blue eyes and Rose automatically cringed back, her normal assertive crispness abandoning her in the face of his concentrated, focused energy.

'It's my letter…of…of resignation…'

'I know *what it is!* I can read perfectly well! What I *don't understand* is why it's staring me in the face!' The pleasant anticipation with which his day had optimistically dawned, when he had contemplated the satisfaction of his life being returned to normal, now seemed like a distant thing of the past.

First of all, she had strolled in way later than she normally would have, sporting a changed look that would have had every man's head reeling in appreciation as she strode through the office and, as if that hadn't been bad enough, she had flung a resignation note down on his desk with all the preliminaries of someone who could not give a damn.

Gabriel, in addition to feeling rage and bewilderment, was assailed by a sense of bitter betrayal.

'I just feel…'

'I mean, *no warning!*' he said, interrupting her harshly, waving the sheet of paper about in an accusatory fashion. 'You stroll in here at God only knows what time…'

'Eight-forty-five!' Rose objected. 'Fifteen minutes before I'm technically due to start the working day!'

Gabriel chose to ignore her input. 'And suddenly you're telling me that you're walking out on me!'

'I'm not *walking out on you.*' Rose cleared her throat and willed herself to meet his eye. 'You're being melodramatic...'

'Don't you dare accuse me of being melodramatic!' Gabriel bellowed, leading her to fear that in a minute the rest of the office would come hurtling through the outside door to see what the commotion was all about. He stood up and placed both his hands squarely on his desk, every muscle in his body rigid with threat. He couldn't have felt more shocked by her resignation than if he had walked into his office only to find a gaping hole waiting for him instead.

'I let you go to Australia,' he thundered, 'at massive inconvenience to myself...'

Rose, unwilling as she was to wave any red flags in front of charging bulls, was not about to let Gabriel get away with implying that she had cleared off for three months and left him in the lurch. In fact, she could count on the fingers of one hand the number of times she had not been available for him. She had worked late more evenings than she cared to remember, had eaten takeaway food in front of her desk way after the rest of the workforce had departed, had cancelled friends at short notice so as not to let him down.

'I arranged a perfectly good stand-in for you in my absence,' she pointed out quietly.

'You arranged to have an emotional wreck take over! A woman who spent the duration of her appointment to me on the brink of a nervous breakdown! Not my idea of a perfectly good stand-in!'

'And the rest of them?' Rose hung on to her temper with difficulty.

'Useless. Surprised they could find jobs anywhere. Can't imagine what that agency was thinking, having them on their books.'

'Maybe you should have looked at the pattern,' Rose murmured under her breath but not so softly that Gabriel didn't hear exactly what she said.

'What are you trying to say?' he roared and Rose jumped and glanced nervously over her shoulder.

'Nothing!' she said placatingly.

Wrong move. If anything, her attempts to soothe had stoked his anger even further and he shot out of his chair and moved round the desk to where she was sitting, pressed back against the soft tan leather, hands clenched on her lap.

'Well!' He leaned over the chair until his face was thrust aggressively into her line of vision. Rose flinched.

She had known that her letter of resignation would not meet with a favourable response. She was good at her job and over the years Gabriel had become accustomed to her. They worked together in perfect harmony, often barely needing to verbally communicate in order to understand what the other meant. Unlike the secretaries he had had in the past, Rose had never been afraid of him. She had witnessed his rage at some piece of incompetence or other presented to him by one of his employees and had always managed to deflate it, usually by ignoring it altogether.

Her unflappability, she knew, meant a lot to him. And Gabriel would not appreciate the huge change to his routines which her resignation would engender. His private life might be colourful and ever changing but he liked his working life to be ruthlessly ordered and part of the order, she knew, was her predictable presence.

'I'm waiting!'

'I'm not going to say a word until you…stop leaning over me, Gabriel. You're making me feel…*threatened*…'

'What do you think I'm going to do?' Involuntarily, his eyes raked over her breasts, noticing the hint of cleavage he could see in the deep V of her T-shirt. When she didn't answer, he pushed himself away from her and raked his fingers through his black hair in frustration.

Rose instantly felt her breathing get back to somewhere near normal. 'Every one of those temps couldn't have been hopeless, Gabriel.' He glanced at her over his shoulder and their eyes met. 'You intimidate people. You probably intimidated them.'

'Me? Intimidate people?' He resumed his position, perched on his desk so that he was staring down at her. 'Maybe, occasionally,' he admitted reluctantly. 'But in the world of business, you know that a little intimidation can be a very handy tool. Is that why you're leaving? Because you just don't like working for me?' Gabriel frowned, trying to make sense of the incomprehensible. She had been happy enough with her work when she had departed for Australia. Now, here she was, suddenly keen to head off to greener pastures.

Not that they existed. As far as Gabriel was concerned, she was on to a damn good deal working for him. Salary wise, she would be hard pressed to match it at any other company in London. Probably in the country, for that matter.

He wondered what that sister of hers had said to her about her job in London. Holed up in some rural retreat in the outback, she had probably been keen to encourage Rose into a similar situation, maybe dump the fast pace of city life in favour of something a little more laid back.

'Has that sister of yours tried to persuade you that leaving London is a good idea…?' He frowned as the pieces of the puzzle began reforming in his head. 'Don't tell me that you're stupid enough to consider moving to Australia!' Shock mixed with something else ripped through Gabriel like a jolt of electricity. 'Just because your only living relative happens to be there! And what if she decides to move somewhere else? What if that husband of hers gets a transfer to somewhere even more unlikely? Do you pull up your roots and follow them?' He snorted with disbelieving laughter.

'If I'm that stupid, then why the fuss if I leave?'

'Stop fishing for compliments, Rose.' Gabriel began pacing the room and Rose watched his restless progress out of the corner of her eye until he was back behind his desk, reclining back in the leather chair so that he could look at her with accusatory disapproval. 'You know I value what you do for me. I don't need to say it. Are you planning on going to Australia?' For some reason he found that he didn't care for the thought of that at all. He tried to imagine her forging a life in the outback, stuck in the middle of nowhere. But then, she wouldn't be forging it on her own, would she? Hooded blue eyes took in the now slim figure in front of him, her skin bronzed and glowing from three months spent in the sun, her brown hair shiny with copper highlights and falling in a thick, blunt bob to her shoulders. No, some Neanderthal outback rancher would be all too happy to play caveman to her. That thought made his teeth snap together and he frowned at her.

'No,' Rose informed him wearily. 'I'm not planning on moving out to Australia and I know you value what I do here.'

'Then why?' He gave one brief scathing glance at the offensive letter lying on his desk. 'One polite paragraph is all I deserve after being an exemplary and generous boss to you over four years?'

'I didn't think you would like flowery speeches. And there

was nothing more to say, anyway. I really am leaving because I think there are still things out there left to do and I can't do them while I'm working here, even though, yes, you've been a very generous boss.'

'Things left to do?' Gabriel frowned.

'I…yes…'

'What things?'

'A business course, as a matter of fact…' Among other things, she thought, such as developing a life of my own, a life that included finding a suitable mate, settling down, having a family, doing all the things most women dreamed of from a young age.

'You want to do *a business course?*' He made it sound as though she had just revealed a secret yearning to fly to the moon.

'As a matter of fact, I do!' Rose tilted her chin up defensively, her normally serene face flushed with sudden annoyance that he found it so incredulous that she should have ambitions outside the ones he so kindly allowed her. 'I left home at eighteen,' she snapped, revealing yet more of a life she had previously been keen to keep under wraps, 'to look after my mother and when she passed on I did a secretarial course, took a series of temporary jobs just so that I could get sufficient funds together to put myself through a really good intensive course… If you recall, I came to *you* as a temp…and ended up staying here permanently…'

'You never said…' Gabriel murmured, reading the dismay on her face as she contemplated her outburst. So his cool, calm, level-headed secretary had fire burning inside. Of course he'd suspected that from the very start. 'What was your sister up to while you were looking after your mother?' he asked curiously, sidetracked by that window into her private life.

Rose looked at his devilishly handsome face and tried to

wriggle back to her secure guarded territory but he was having none of it. After a few seconds of thick, expectant silence, she shrugged and looked away. 'Grace was at university and then she met Tom and everything got…very hectic for her. So. Anyway, that's one of the things I want to do…'

'And you've checked out these business courses?'

'Well…'

'No point spending time doing a business course only to find that it qualifies you to bounce right back here…'

'Thanks for the tip, Gabriel. I'll make sure I'm very careful what sort of course I sign up to.'

He was looking at her thoughtfully, so thoughtfully that her antennae pricked up, waiting for some passing remark which she suspected she wouldn't like.

'Naturally, I'll work out my notice,' she ventured into the lengthening silence. No response. She plunged on, wondering whether this silent tactic was designed to make her feel guilty. He certainly wouldn't be beyond using every trick in the book to get her to stay, if that was his goal, especially now that he had a benchmark for comparison after three months of unsatisfactory stand-ins. 'I intend to take just a couple of months off after I leave here, enjoy the summer…maybe even go abroad somewhere…and then the course will start in September…'

'And it never occurred to you that we could discuss this…? Maybe arrive at a conclusion satisfactory to both of us…?'

'Not really. I mean…'

'Why not?' Gabriel was in there like a shot. 'Because underneath it all, you have a problem with working for me?'

'Of course not!' The last thing she needed, not that it mattered, was to leave Gabriel with the ego boosting impression that he had an effect on her.

'Then why didn't you come and discuss your dilemma with me?'

'I really only thought about it when I was in Australia,' Rose admitted. 'I had time to think out there and to realise that I needed a change if I was to advance my career…'

Gabriel, struggling with the prospect of a litany of incompetent secretaries cowering and ducking for cover every time he raised his voice, mentally cursed her absent sister once again for introducing strife into his otherwise perfectly uncomplicated working life.

'And I agree with you,' he told her suddenly.

'You do?'

'Of course I do.' He leaned back, linking his fingers behind his head, and surveyed her with an expression of sympathetic understanding that she had never seen in evidence before. 'You're young. You're clever…' He allowed the throwaway compliment to sink in. 'You want a career beyond taking orders from me. Not,' he felt compelled to add, 'that I haven't given you your fair share of responsibility. In fact, considering your original duties were filing, typing and fending calls, you've come a long way. But that's by the by…'

Rose tried to keep up with this surprising twist. Not that Gabriel wasn't unpredictable. He was. She just hadn't anticipated any such reaction to her resignation because, really, how many ways were there to react to a resignation letter? And so he was now accepting it. Why feel disappointed with an outcome she knew was inevitable?

'I can understand your drive to go further… After all, I am a perfect example of someone who has been there, someone who was driven to better himself…'

'I don't plan on dizzy heights…'

'Did I ever tell you that my parents started with nothing?

That my father's business began with dabbling in the rag trade? Just enough money to raise us without too much hardship but not so much that we didn't know from very young the importance of an education and the importance of making the most of our talents?'

'Don't worry, Gabriel, I won't be competing with you on your level in two years' time…!'

Their eyes met in perfect understanding as he appreciated the gentle, teasing irony behind her remark and Rose looked away quickly. He might not have much inside information about her private life but in many ways he knew her better than anyone else ever had and certainly cottoned on to her quirky sense of humour quicker than anyone she had ever known. Even Grace had seemed left behind sometimes.

'If you had told me sooner I would have happily arranged to fund your course.'

'I'm sorry?'

'Day release. Even two days a week. You keep the salary you're at and the only condition is that you train up someone to fill in for you when you're not here. And, when your course is complete, I guarantee you a junior position on the top floor. I was also thinking of rewarding your efforts here with a company car…'

'I'm not sure…'

'So we're back to that *invisible reason* for quitting and since it's nothing to do with what I have to offer by way of benefits, then it must have something to do with me…'

'I told you, of course not!'

'Then why don't you give it a go, Rose…?' Gabriel leaned forward and rested his elbows on the desk. 'I don't want you to go…' His navy-blue eyes swept over her in a way that felt almost like a caress and Rose shivered with guilty pleasure.

I don't want you to go—lover's words. 'I need you,' he compounded the ambiguous intimacy of his previous plea with a husky murmur. 'If the arrangement doesn't suit you, then you can leave me. No hard feelings.' Then he did something he had never done before. He said *please.*

CHAPTER TWO

THE following morning found Rose on the phone, frantically trying to do some research into business management courses. When she had vaguely mentioned her desire for a change in career to Gabriel, she had had no idea that she would have been called to account. Yes, somewhere in the recesses of her mind, she had toyed with the idea of gaining a couple more qualifications, but really her decision to leave had been based on more pragmatic grounds. She had just thought it time to disentangle herself from Gabriel's pervasive influence over her life.

Somehow she had been manoeuvred into the unenviable position of embarking on a course, which she had supposedly checked out in depth. In addition to this technical hiccup, she would now have to set about recruiting someone to fill in for her when she wasn't around.

When she had discussed her situation with Grace, resignation had seemed the most appropriate solution and thousands of miles away, with a warm Australian sun beating down and the thought of London and her job like a hazy dream, she had imagined a clean cut conclusion. Her letter of resignation, some surprise on Gabriel's part and a valiant attempt to persuade her out of her decision, but of course in her head she never wavered. Roll on two years and she could easily see herself in a fulfilling relationship with a mystery man, someone kind and thoughtful, with the sound of wedding bells clanging on the horizon.

She hadn't banked on the reality of actually walking back in to her office, seeing him again for the first time in three months. She hadn't taken into account how devastating his smile could be and she certainly hadn't envisaged her big, powerful boss with his killer looks gazing at her in that pleading manner and begging her to stay.

She thanked heaven that he was out of the office for the day, giving her ample opportunity to begin researching courses. So far only two stood out as worth pursuing as they seemed to offer what she thought she wanted and both were within fairly easy commuting distance. By the time lunchtime rolled around she had arranged to see both towards the end of the week.

Keeping her afloat whenever she contemplated the rapid desertion of her cause was the thought that she had only promised Gabriel *to give it a go,* leaving her the option of walking away after three months if she chose.

She was still at her desk at six-thirty, playing catch-up with all the work she had pushed to one side having spent the morning on the phone to colleges.

She was hardly aware of Gabriel until his shadow on her desk alerted her to his presence, then she glanced up, involuntarily sucking in her breath as their eyes met.

'I guess you missed this…' He raised his eyebrows and grinned. 'Hence the fact that you're still here slaving away while everyone else has gone…' He dumped an assortment of files on her desk. 'A few more bits to keep you busy but you can sort them out tomorrow. One or two problems with that new build hotel in the Caribbean. We need to source a more reliable supplier. Roberts in Barbados should be able to help you with that one.' He moved round to see what she was doing on her computer and Rose breathed a sigh of relief that he hadn't found her scrolling down colleges in the London area.

'This is what I missed,' he murmured with heartfelt sincerity. 'Your efficiency. Knowing that I could leave the office and not return to find things in utter chaos and some bloody incompetent woman weeping behind her desk somewhere.'

Rose clicked off her screen and gritted her teeth together. And that was just what *she* hadn't missed! His never-ending appreciation of her as his perfect secretary.

'Which is why I would like to take you out to dinner tonight.'

Her head swung round as she edged out of her chair, taking care to avoid making physical contact with him in the process.

'I beg your pardon?'

'I'm inviting you out to dinner,' Gabriel repeated, taken aback at her patent lack of enthusiasm. 'You've been out of the country for three months…' He frowned and tried hard to suppress his annoyance at her studiously blank expression. 'There are work matters to discuss and there is no way we would get the concentrated time to discuss them in the office.'

'Well…'

'If I don't bring you up to speed with things, you'll find yourself left behind and the last thing I need is to have to set aside yet more time during the working day to sort things out.'

'Of course,' Rose said politely. 'I'll just fetch my jacket.' She logged off the computer, aware of his eyes following her every movement, and was self-consciously aware of her body as she stuck on her black linen jacket, a recent purchase that was just right for the fairly warm late spring weather.

Along with her change in shape had come a change in wardrobe. Out had gone the frumpish size fourteen clothes she had once hidden behind and in their place was an array of size tens, clothes with shapes and textures and colours she had never really been able to carry off before.

'I'd rather we weren't too late, though,' she said, bending down to scoop up her handbag which was on the floor by her desk. 'I still have unpacking to do. And you needn't worry about me falling behind with my work. I intend to spend the weekend at home with some of the files making sure that I know exactly what's going on with all our accounts.'

'Right.'

'Where are we going to eat?' Rose glanced down at her working clothes. 'I'm not really dressed for anywhere too fancy.' And Gabriel didn't really do cheap and cheerful. Not because he was a crashing snob but because he never really had any need to. She should know. She had booked enough restaurants for him in the past to realise that gingham tablecloths and bare floorboards were not his style. Something a little wicked stirred inside her.

'I know a very good Italian,' she said, pausing to look at him. 'And it's close to where I live so I can get home relatively quickly once we're done…'

'Fine.' Gabriel was already regretting his invitation. It had not been meant as a working dinner, despite what he had said, and he now felt as though he had been pushed into a corner, forced to gear everything towards business when really he wanted to unwind and, if he were honest with himself, find out a bit more about the woman who had gone to Australia and returned completely changed.

'You don't mind, do you?'

Gabriel shrugged. 'One restaurant is as good as another when it comes to discussing work.'

He called his driver to collect them from the front of the

building and discovered that he was only marginally interested in what Rose had to ask about what had been happening in the office during her absence.

By the time they had reached the restaurant a solid forty minutes later, having waged war with the late evening traffic that had reduced some of the roads to gridlock, he was mightily fed up with discussing mergers and acquisitions. He was even more fed up with the interested but impersonal tone of her chatter. He couldn't remember ever having had such a pressing urge to get behind the smoothly calm surface and see what lay there.

'I hope this isn't too casual for you, Gabriel.'

Gabriel narrowed his eyes and tried to work out whether there was a certain insolence in her voice, although when he looked at her she just seemed politely concerned.

'Why should it be too casual?' he asked as they entered the restaurant. It was more of a pub than a restaurant, with after work people milling around by the bar area, while others were seated at wooden tables in small, animated groups. And, to his surprise, Rose seemed to be known at the place. Someone materialised out of thin air, smiling and kissing her on both cheeks before showing them to a table tucked away at the very back.

'Because I know you tend to like more expensive places.'

'Oh, do I?'

'Yep.' She turned to him and smiled dryly. 'Don't forget I book them for you.' She lowered her eyes and slipped into her seat. 'Beautiful women like expensive restaurants, you once said. They enjoy the goldfish bowl feeling, hence you go to places where seeing who's there is half the fun.'

'I once said *that?*'

'You did.'

'I'm surprised you didn't accuse me of being shallow.'

Rose shrugged, glanced at him and glanced away. 'Each to their own. Besides, I work for you.'

'That's never stopped you from speaking your mind.'

Rose flushed and remained silent. Yes, she had always spoken her mind, had never been scared to disagree with him and he had allowed her to be as open as she felt. Was that one of the reasons why her emotions had become involved, even though she had tried desperately hard to rein them in? He might be a hard task master, with almost zero tolerance of anything that smacked of laziness or stupidity, but he was also the fairest man she had ever met and willing to listen to anyone's opinions, provided they could be backed up. It was an immensely persuasive side of his personality and one to which she had been exposed for four long years.

'Is this your local?' Gabriel asked, changing the subject. He looked around and, after a few minutes, his gaze finally rested on her. 'I didn't imagine that this would be your kind of place.'

'Why is that?' Rose answered with asperity.

'Because…it's pretty noisy.'

'And I'm more of a library kind of person?'

'You're putting words into my mouth, Rose.'

'I'm tired.' She was grateful for the waiter's interruption, placing her order without bothering to look at the menu. 'Why don't you fill me in on what's been happening? I know a bit from your emails, but if you give me some details it'll be easier for me to catch up.'

'That Australia flight's a long one,' Gabriel said, avoiding the subject of work, which seemed unutterably boring just at the moment. 'I can understand why you're tired. And I expect you miss your sister as well, hmm…?'

'Yes. Of course I do. Although they're planning on returning to England to live some time next year. Both of them feel it's time to come back home now that baby Ben is on the scene.'

Their food arrived and Rose was amused to see surprise register on Gabriel's face as he noted the quality of the dishes. He looked up, caught her eye before she could look away, and grinned.

'Now I'm going to get a sermon on the foolishness of people who pay over the odds for a meal they can easily get somewhere else at half the price…'

'No, of course not.'

'I would come to places like this if it weren't for the fact that clients and women expect more elaborate entertaining.'

'I can understand the clients, but maybe you need to mix with a different kind of woman.'

'Why do you say that?'

'Say what?'

Rose, who had not really been paying much attention to what she had been saying, looked up to find his midnight-blue eyes fixed on her. Weren't they supposed to be talking about work? Wasn't that the whole point of them being here?

'I've never really known what you think about my… women…but I guess you must have had opinions on them over the years. After all, you've met them all…'

'Not really…' Oh, yes, she had opinions on them! Beautiful, empty-headed, utterly unthreatening. For a long time she used to wonder how a man as dynamic and astute as Gabriel could ever be interested in the stereotype of the blonde bimbo. Yes, she could understand his need to have a beautiful woman on his arm. Like attracted like, after all. But wouldn't he have been more challenged by a woman who had something to say for herself? Then gradually she had realised the simple truth, which was that he didn't *want* to be challenged. He got enough challenge with his work. What he wanted was docility. When he eventually decided to settle down, he would doubtless want that same docility from a woman who would be content to serve him, have his children and patiently stand by while he worked all the hours God made. Behind the passion and seduction of his work, he would require a soothing, calming domestic life.

'Is that why you're looking at me with such disapproval?' Gabriel asked and Rose caught herself with a little start. While she grappled with the dilemma of working out how to lead the conversation back into safe waters, Gabriel seized the moment to press her for an answer.

'Was I?'

'Oh, yes. Your little mouth was pursed tightly with disapproval!'

Rose glared at him and he grinned back at her, knowing very well that his description would have got under her skin. It wasn't like him to tease. Up until now she had rebuffed every effort he had ever made to move their relationship on to a more cordial basis and he had obligingly backed off, but something had changed and, although he couldn't put his finger on it, he knew that he was rather enjoying the change.

He smiled down into the glass of wine he was cradling in his hand. She had stuck to water but, with a driver waiting patiently for him outside, he had decided to have a couple of drinks.

'What you do in your private life is entirely up to you.' Rose heard the primness in her voice with mounting irritation. 'If you choose to go out with women whose IQs are in single figures, then that's your business!'

'Ah. I never took you for an intellectual snob,' Gabriel murmured in an infuriatingly meek voice.

'I am *not* an intellectual snob!' Rose defended hotly.

'And how,' Gabriel continued with pseudo-thoughtfulness, 'can you condemn women who like having money lavished upon them unless you've been in that position before?' He paused. 'Have you?'

'No, but…'

'I mean, how do you know that you wouldn't enjoy being taken to the finest restaurants? Having pearls and diamonds bought for you? Being flown to Paris or Venice for the weekend?'

'I don't recall booking too many flights to Paris or Venice for weekend jaunts,' Rose said tartly. Gabriel had no problem in spending vast sums of money on gifts for the women who came and went in his life but setting aside time for them was an entirely different thing. He rarely had time off and when he did he invariably went back to Italy to visit family. She should know. She didn't think he had ever booked a flight himself.

'You know what I mean,' Gabriel said irritably.

Torn between abandoning the conversation and standing up for herself, Rose took the plunge and for once set aside her determination to keep her thoughts to herself. 'I don't *have* to have expensive things bought for me to know that it wouldn't be what I wanted. My parents both instilled in us a healthy awareness that money doesn't buy happiness.'

'Oh, I know that money can't buy *happiness,*' Gabriel agreed readily. 'At least not happiness of the lasting kind, but it can buy fun…'

'Depends if you think fun is having a six-month fling, dusting yourself down and moving on,' Rose muttered.

'I take it *you* don't think it is…'

'This is a ridiculous conversation. Weren't we supposed to be talking about work? Apparently, I need to be *brought up to speed* just in case I get left behind.'

Gabriel knew damn well that his comment had been totally

unjustified, but hell, he had invited the woman out to dinner only to find that she had no desire to go so apologising wasn't on his list of priorities. Nor was discussing work. He couldn't think of anything duller than discussing acquisitions, profit and losses, breakdowns in supply and demand with one of his hotels, not when the alternative was so much more interesting.

'There's no chance that you'll get left behind, Rose,' he said placatingly. He nodded to the waiter to clear their plates and when another glass of wine was offered he looked enquiringly at her dubious expression.

'Please don't tell me that that nasty concept called *fun* also includes the occasional bit of alcohol…' That, he was pretty sure, would really get her bristling, and it did.

'Of course I have a drink now and again! I do have a *life* outside work, Gabriel.'

'Tell me about it.' He was in there like a shot, having dispatched the waiter to bring them a glass of wine each. Large. 'No boyfriends with lavish spending habits—that would be unhealthy and bad for the soul…'

Rose opened her mouth to respond and then shut it. Instead she gave him a wry look. 'The devil finds work for idle hands, Gabriel. I feel very sorry for those poor girls if you were like this with them.'

'Like what?' Gabriel asked piously.

'Barbing them.'

'None of them would have been equipped to handle it.'

'Or maybe you respected them more…' Rose insinuated quietly.

'Don't be bloody ridiculous. Is that what you really think? That I don't respect you? Or are you just fishing?' When she didn't answer, he raked his fingers through his hair and gave her a brooding, frustrated look. 'They were bloody useless, the lot of them. I meant it when I said that I needed you, Rose. I do.' His magnificent blue eyes flicked over her and he added, wickedly, 'Need you and want you…' He watched slow colour infuse her cheeks.

Rose, accustomed to his brilliance, his impatience and his temper, which was seldom directed at her, was thrown off balance by his flirtatious charm, something which she had always assumed was abundant but reserved for the women he dated. She didn't like it. It made her feel vulnerable and uneasy and she stoically hung on to her composure and managed to say, without any inflection whatsoever in her voice, 'You think you do, Gabriel, but no one is indispensable, least of all a secretary.' She sipped her wine and eyed him over the rim of her glass.

'Don't underestimate yourself.'

'I'm not. But I'm not about to think that your working life will grind to a halt if I'm not around.'

'Maybe not *grind to a halt,*' Gabriel admitted. 'But run considerably less smoothly. I've spent the past three months finding that out.' He was amused to realise that she had never voiced her opinions to him about the women in his life. He also realised that, without using so many words, she had managed to imply distaste with how he conducted his private life. Belatedly it occurred to him that she had widely overstepped the mark with her smugness and she had got away with it. How did that follow when he prided himself on being a man who knew exactly where to draw his verbal boundaries? Healthy criticism on the work front was fine. In fact, to be encouraged! His personal life was, however, his own business and not up for discussion. He chose to disregard the little voice in his head telling him that he had solicited her opinion. It was not really fair now if he castigated her for having one because he didn't like it.

She had moved on, though. Was defining the role of secretary and why it was a position relatively easy to fulfil. Sounding like a member of the Personnel department giving advice to a prospective interviewee.

Gabriel grunted non-commitally.

'Basically,' she concluded, 'if I'm to be successful recruiting someone, then you need to tell me exactly what you're looking for.'

'Recruiting someone?'

'For the days when I'm at college.'

'How many days would that be?'

'I…I'll be able to tell you that by the end of the week and I can start recruiting in a few weeks' time.'

'Naturally, you will have to continue managing sensitive clients and anything that might be of a confidential nature.' He signalled for the bill and contemplated the dispiriting prospect of a never-ending train of incompetent girls scuttling around, trying and failing to keep up with him. 'The key quality I'm looking for is an ability to function without behaving like terrified little rabbits every time I speak.'

'We've been through that,' Rose said patiently. She glanced at her watch and realised that it was a lot later than she had imagined. And they still hadn't touched upon all that work which apparently she needed to be filled in on. 'We haven't got down to discussing work,' she pointed out.

'And now you have to go? Or else you might turn into a pumpkin?' He frowned and tapped in the pin number for his card. 'I'll drop you back to your house.'

'No need. I live within walking distance.'

'Nonsense. I would never let a woman walk back to her house at night.'

'I do it every single day, Gabriel! Do you think I take taxis to and from work? The bus stops just down from here and I walk to my house quite safely, no matter how dark it is.' She didn't really know why she was bothering to protest because Gabriel always did what he wanted to do. Right now he wanted to play the gentleman and drop her back to her house.

'You need a car,' he said abruptly.

Rose stopped dead in her tracks and looked at him with her mouth open. 'I need a *what?*'

'A car. A company car. The fact that you haven't got one has been an oversight on my part.'

'You must be desperate to hang on to me,' she said wryly, 'if you're now offering me a car…'

'It's not exactly unusual for a PA to have a company car.' He held open the car door for her to slide in. 'Where do you live?'

Rose gave his driver the directions. Today was proving to be a day of firsts for her and she was uneasily aware that a number of them didn't sit well with her. This was the first time Gabriel had managed to crash through her carefully maintained barriers. No, they hadn't shared confidences over a bottle of wine but he had seen her professional mask slip and that wasn't good. It was also the first time he had flirted with her. Or at least spoken to her in that velvety, amused voice that she had only ever heard him use occasionally on the phone to one of his women. It was also the first time they had shared a meal together in a restaurant, just the two of them with no particular work agenda driving the occasion. None of these firsts did anything to soothe her frayed nerves at being back in his company after three months.

It was odd but it almost felt as if a door between them had opened. Over the years she had managed to cope with her feelings for him by being very careful to make sure that their roles were defined. He was her boss, a man she respected, got along well with but ultimately a man who gave her orders which she was obliged to follow. Over time, as they had grown into one another, his orders had stopped resembling orders but she had never deluded herself into thinking that she was anything to him but a very useful tool.

Some of the things she had been requested to do, as far as she was concerned, went beyond the bounds of secretarial duties. Presents for some of his girlfriends, flowers at the end of an affair, bookings for restaurants. She had done them without argument, however. She had never volunteered an opinion and he had never asked her for one. Tonight, some of those barriers had been eroded and Rose felt like a snail suddenly deprived of its protective shell.

Just thinking about it made her skin tingle and she was relieved when, after just a few minutes, the car pulled up outside her house. She pushed open her door, smiling a very hurried thank you, and was only aware that he had followed her up to her front door when he reached down to take the bundle of keys out of her fingers.

'My mother always told me to see a lady to her front door. You're trembling.'

'It's a little chilly out here.' Rose watched his long fingers as he turned the key in the lock. 'I think I must have become accustomed to the milder weather in Australia.' He handed her back the keys and their fingers brushed. 'Well—' Rose planted herself in the doorway and stared at him in a no nonsense manner '—goodnight and thank you once more for the dinner. I'm sorry we didn't get around to discussing work-related issues. Perhaps I could check your diary for the next week or so and slot in a convenient time for us to go through the problem areas…?'

'I'll leave a note about which files you need to check on

your desk and you can have a look at them some time during the day, when you get a free moment.' He placed one foot in the doorway but Rose didn't notice. She was too busy frowning and trying to work out why he had invited her out if the work issue could have been solved by way of a note on her desk.

'You could have told me that in the first place, Gabriel!'

'True,' he was quick to admit. 'But I really wanted to discuss the matter of your temporary replacement with you.'

'I won't be starting my course until September, in all probability! There's no urgency for the interviewing process to begin as yet! We're only in May.'

'The end of May,' Gabriel said darkly. 'Before you blink, we're in July and you know how normal life stops in summer with people clearing off on holiday. After the fine examples of the possibilities on offer, I would say that the interviewing process needs to begin sooner rather than later.'

Rose released a frustrated sigh.

'Have you a problem with that?'

'No. Not at all. You pay my salary. How can I have a problem with that?' She smiled to make a joke of it, but there was no answering humour in his eyes.

'In other words, what I pay you buys your compliance even if you don't agree with what I'm asking you to do.'

His remark was so close to what she had only been thinking herself minutes earlier that she blushed and looked down, to see where his foot was firmly planted.

'I'm beginning to think that all this talk about wanting to move forward your career and being held back professionally by working for me is just so much nonsense…' He wedged his foot a little more firmly through the doorway and leaned against the door frame, arms folded, his expression one of calculating suspicion. 'I smell mutiny in the ranks and experience has taught me that mutiny usually arises from personal grounds...'

'You're being over-imaginative, Gabriel...' She licked her lips nervously and wondered where he was going with this one. 'If I had...any personal problems with working for you, I would have told you...'

'Would you?' He pushed himself past her, taking her by surprise. 'Money can buy loyalty, but loyalty that's only skin-deep, and that's no good to me.' He turned to her and Rose was forced to marvel at the speed with which he had managed to get inside her house and was dwarfing its small confines.

'Can we discuss this in the morning?'

'Why? You know, it's actually only a little before nine. You'll recover from jet lag quicker if you try and maintain your normal waking times. And anyway, if there's an underlying problem I want to hear about it.'

'I told you...' She hoped that she was the only one who could detect the desperation in her voice.

'I would never have stopped you from saying what you thought...' Gabriel said slowly, his eyes raking over her embarrassed face. 'And I'm insulted that you would think me such an autocrat that you might be scared to voice your opinions in case I sacked you...or cut your salary...'

'Of course I didn't think that!'

Gabriel could spot a sincere answer when he heard one. Anyway, he was pretty sure she knew him better than to think that he might really try to control her with her pay cheque, but she had given him pause for thought. Starting with her letter of resignation and ending with remarks which, in a way he couldn't put his finger on, carried the ghost of criticism in them. Something in the tone of her voice and the lowering of her eyes had pricked his curiosity. Curiosity was an untapped emotion for Gabriel. The frenetic pace of his work life got his adrenalin flowing but he had been in the game long enough for uncertainty and nerves to have disappeared. He ran his empire with the confident hand of a master horseman controlling the reins of his animal. And there was no woman who incited his curiosity. Interest, yes, lust, definitely, but curiosity, not at all.

So he was like a dog with a bone now, especially since he had long ago formed very preconceived notions of his efficient secretary, notions which were in the process of being dismantled.

'Why don't you make us both a cup of coffee…?'

'No!'

'Because underneath all the *yes, sirs* and *no, sirs* and *three bags full, sirs* you can't really stand to be cooped up with me for any length of time?'

That was so far from the truth that Rose burst out laughing and after a while Gabriel grudgingly allowed his bunched muscles to relax.

'Okay. Maybe a quick cup of coffee. I wouldn't want to keep your driver waiting.' She headed towards the kitchen, mentally adding another *first* to the stack already piling up. A first for Gabriel coming inside her house. She knew that he had gone outside to tell his driver that there would be a wait. She intended to make it a short one. By the time he came back, the coffee was made, black, no sugar, as he liked it.

Rose was sitting at her kitchen table and had placed his mug conveniently at the opposite end.

'So, talk to me,' Gabriel commanded, sitting down.

'When do you want me to start interviewing for someone? Would next Monday do? Or sooner?'

'Explain your remark about obeying me because of the money.'

'I'm sorry I said that. I didn't mean it.'

'How long have you thought that way? Since you started working for me? In the last few months? Only since you got back from seeing your sister? When?'

Rose nearly groaned aloud. 'It doesn't matter, Gabriel.'

'It does to me. Now tell me what it is that you have disagreed with? You can talk to me. You'll find that I can be very sympathetic. I don't want to lose you and if you've been harbouring any grudges about the way I run things, then now is the time to get it off your chest.'

CHAPTER THREE

THE restaurant in the glass office building, like everything else, was fairly spectacular. It was one of the invisible but very handy perks that came with working for Gabriel. It was open all day, served a staggering choice of first class food and was so heavily subsidised that loose change could buy a hefty enough breakfast to last the day.

Every so often Gabriel, when he wasn't entertaining clients or being entertained by them, would emerge from his glorified sanctum and stroll down for lunch. He did it to *touch base* with his employees. Rose always smiled at that because *touching base* with his employees was a pretty ridiculous notion when it came to Gabriel Gessi. He chatted to them, invited their ideas, and they chatted back. But scratch the surface and it was easy to see the awe that controlled their replies. He wasn't just rich and powerful but he looked the part and that in itself was enough to make most of his employees break out in a light nervous perspiration.

Right now, at two-thirty in the afternoon, the lunch time stampede had come and gone. Over by the windows were two small groups of people—three girls from the kitchens, who were having cups of coffee and doughnuts, and a couple of men who were talking animatedly over sheets with graphs and figures.

Aside from that, it was empty. Perfect conditions for Rose to sip from her mug of coffee and morosely mull over events of the night before.

He had asked her for her opinions and to start with she had had no trouble resisting the invitation. Four years of habit had come to her rescue, saving her from succumbing to the novelty of their situation and behaving in a way that would have been out of character. She had looked at him quizzically, lowered her eyes and paid a lot of attention to her cup of coffee.

He, on the other hand, had stared at her over the rim of his cup, in no particular hurry to go. Then, changing the subject, he had quizzed her about what sort of course she was interested in doing, what qualification would she achieve at the end of it, would she want a job supervising other people or working primarily on her own? Harmless questions that were just what an interested boss would ask, nothing to set her antennae quivering.

When he had asked her about her parents, what her father had done for a living, she had not flinched because the questions had been wrapped up in an intelligent observation about the influences of parents on their children.

'Based on my own parents,' he said, standing up and taking his cup to the sink, 'I should have married years ago. In fact, I'm long overdue for the two point two kids and family dog.' He grinned at her, a self-deprecatory grin that invited her to enter into light-hearted criticism of his rakish lifestyle.

'I can't picture you with two point two kids.' Rose cupped her chin in her hands and stared up at him, noting the way his big, muscular frame dominated her small kitchen. Not in her wildest flights of imagination had she once thought that her letter of resignation, her bid for a life without him, would see her sitting in her kitchen joining him in a cup of coffee as if it was the most natural thing in the world. Talk about plans being derailed! 'I can just about get my head around the dog.'

'What kind of dog?'

'A very big one.'

'Because I'm six foot two?'

Well, of course, that comment invited her to look at him and for a few seconds her heart seemed to stop beating. Six foot two of pure blue-eyed, black-haired alpha male.

'You'd better go,' she said abruptly, standing up.

'I will, in about fifteen minutes. I told Harry to go and fill the car up instead of just waiting and he won't be back yet.'

'Why did you do that?' Rose said in dismay. Now that she was on her feet, she couldn't decide whether to go across to the sink and risk an awkward situation with them both there, squashed side by side into an impossibly small space, or else ignominiously sit back down. In the end she clicked her tongue and turned on her heel, out to the sitting room cum room where everything was done, from television watching to out of hours work to reading the newspaper on a Sunday morning before she walked down to the bakery to buy her weekly treat of croissants.

'Because,' his voice came from behind her, 'it beat the hell out of sitting in the car waiting for me in the dark.'

'He could have turned the light on and read!'

'Provided he remembered to come equipped with a book.'

Rose shot him a long-suffering look, which was water off a duck's back, and sat down. 'Harry always travels with a book.'

'How do you know?'

'Because I once asked him how he tolerated having to drive you places and then wait, sometimes for hours, until you finished whatever meeting you might have been in.'

'You've been having long conversations with my chauffeur?' His tone of voice implied that she had been hiding some dirty secret from him, something which he had only just unmasked, much to his horror.

'Occasionally we walk to the bus stop together if we happen to be leaving at the same time. And there's no need to look so staggered, Gabriel. People do have lives outside your corporation.'

'I know that!'

'Well, stop acting as though whatever happens outside your little world doesn't exist.'

'I don't live in a *little world,*' Gabriel grated.

'Of course you do.' She tidied up the criticism by tossing in a generality. 'You're bound to, really. Anyone in your position would. Running a corporation as huge as yours, having to dictate to other people most of the time, snapping your fingers and knowing that you'll be obeyed. It's not the real world.'

Gabriel's eyes narrowed on her. 'I'm a petty dictator?'

'No, of course not! That's not what I said at all!'

'I give orders, I snap my fingers and expect obedience. I suppose the next step is to issue the royal command that all my subjects kneel when I walk by!'

'I'm sorry if I offended you.'

'You haven't *offended* me,' Gabriel said coolly. 'You work for me and as my employee you are entitled to an opinion and I appreciate your opinion. I only wish you had had the guts to tell me a little sooner instead of scuttling around like a mouse, smiling and obeying and harbouring unpleasant resentments.'

Rose's mouth fell open and she stared at him in horror. 'I wasn't *harbouring resentments,*' she denied, her face turning a deeper shade of red.

'No?' Gabriel felt as though he had been struck a blow

beneath the belt and he didn't like the feeling. Underneath the guise of the man who worked hard and played hard, was a man of exceptional self-control. Right now he could feel his iron control shifting and it was a very unpleasant sensation. Especially considering that the woman was no more than his secretary. A valued member of his team, yes, but still a member of his team and nothing of any worth personally to him.

'No…if I had any problems working for you…well, I would have told you…I wouldn't have *scuttled around like a mouse…*' That description hurt because she could see how he would have arrived at it. She came in, she did her job, she went home. Her own confusing emotional vulnerability as far as he was concerned had made her a more silent person than she was by nature, but how was he to know that? What he knew was a quiet, efficient woman who did her job but never said anything that might have expressed any feelings that were unrelated to work. A highly competent scuttling mouse. And, three months ago, a plump little mouse.

Not for the first time, Rose was besieged by images of all the women he had dated. In her head, they marched past in a long, beautiful procession. She had met them all, or at least most of them because he would often arrange for them to meet him at the office when he had finished work, only he rarely finished when he promised and so they would sit in her office, long legs crossed, their perfect faces blank with boredom as they stared around them or tried to make small talk. Blonde, brunette, red-haired—Gabriel showed no favouritism. His only criteria was that they were gorgeous and intellectually undemanding.

Sometimes Rose would spot an item of jewellery she had bought on his behalf. A diamond bracelet, a necklace, maybe a Hermes scarf, which always went down a treat because it was somehow a little more personal than an item of jewellery, or so they imagined, unaware that Gabriel would have had nothing to do with the choosing.

She looked at him now and saw herself through his eyes. The plump mouse scuttling quietly around, doing his bidding. Little wonder she had become his perfect secretary! And even less surprising that he had been staggered when she had returned from Australia clutching her letter of resignation and sporting a whole new image. He had turned on the charm and pulled out all the financial stops, but her decision to stay had nothing to do with either of those things.

She was a different woman now. She looked different and inside she had changed. She wasn't going to scuttle any more because she had nothing to lose. She had made her mind up that her life was going down a different path and, if she happened to still be working for him, she was merely biding her time.

She liked the sound of that. *Biding her time.* It gave her a heady rush of courage.

'I have no problem working for you, Gabriel, because I'm not afraid of you. I've worked alongside you long enough to know…'

'How to handle me…?'

'How to gauge your various moods…'

'Which is good.'

Rose took in the smug expression and gritted her teeth together. 'Yes, yes, it is. Which isn't to say that I'm not going to set down a few requirements now that you have persuaded me to carry on working for you, provided it doesn't conflict with my course…I don't want you to forget that I'm going to give it three months and during that time I'll make sure I train someone up who could take over completely from me if I do decide to leave…'

Every inclination in him wanted to inform her that he was not in the market for blackmail, emotional or otherwise, but then he remembered the succession of hopeless temps and bit back the words. He didn't want Rose to leave but, if she did, he wanted to make damn sure that she sorted out someone responsible who could take over from her.

'What are your requirements? I thought I had made the financial deal enticing enough.'

'It's not to do with money, actually…' Rose drew in her breath and looked at him steadily. 'Firstly, I want to have a certain amount of notice if I'm required to work unusually late hours…'

'A certain amount of notice?' Gabriel exploded with disbelief. 'How much *notice* did you have in mind? A week? Two weeks? A month?' He shot out of his chair and prowled around the room, scowling. The hopeful anticipation with which he had awakened that morning had turned into grim faced frustration and was getting worse by the minute. And all because his dependable secretary had disappeared for three months and returned a hell cat. Lord only knew what thoughts that sister of hers had put in her head.

'A day or two would be sufficient,' Rose told him calmly. Her cool cream sitting room, with its small fireplace and its neatly spaced oak bookshelves on either side, seemed poky and cluttered with him in the room. Even when they were having a perfectly normal conversation, he still couldn't obey the laws of common courtesy and sit down politely, hear her out without interrupting, just behave like a normal human being!

'And would that be in writing?' Gabriel asked sarcastically.

'I'm not being unreasonable…'

'No? You mean it's common practice for someone in a responsible job, earning, might I point out, vastly more than the national average, to work to rule unless given notice?'

Rose had seen Gabriel in action before. He was physically intimidating and was not above bullying his opponents into submission.

'I wasn't implying that I would *work to rule,* Gabriel, just saying that, whilst I don't object to working late now and again, you've frequently asked me to stay on at the office, sometimes until midnight, working on documents that have a deadline.'

'*Frequently* is a bit of an overstatement,' Gabriel muttered.

'Whatever. I'm going to be occupied studying and I think it only fair that you respect that.'

'What would you classify these *unusually late hours* you refer to?'

'Anything beyond six-thirty would not be acceptable.' Rose waited for the fallout but nothing came. Instead, he looked at her assessingly and, after a few seconds pause, he shrugged.

'Fine.'

'You don't mind?'

'Well, naturally, it'll be inconvenient, but you're right. You're going to be studying. The last thing I would want to do is distract you from that…' He lowered his eyes. 'You will have to make sure that whoever replaces you is not going to be a clock-watcher.'

'You might find it difficult to locate a temp who doesn't mind staying on until whatever time you decide at the snap of a finger.' *Whoever replaces you?* There was a permanent ring to that statement and it sent a chill down her spine even though it was, of course, precisely what she had wanted in the first place.

'Not if I dangle enough money in front of her…and of

course the promise of knowing that the job might very well be hers permanently, with all the perks that go along with it.'

'You mean you're writing me off already?' Rose said lightly. 'I thought I was indispensable.'

'So did I.'

But somewhere along the line he had changed his mind. Probably when she made it clear that agreeing to stay in the job brought one or two conditions that he found unpalatable. He wanted someone who blindly obeyed, never mind the baloney about encouraging free speech with his employees. He wanted to be able to tell her, somewhere around five-thirty in the evening, that two lawyers would be coming in at six and she would have to stay on until all the nuts and bolts of some deal or other had been ironed out. He didn't want to hear anything about outside commitments and he certainly wouldn't want to give her any notice for inconvenience.

As long as she was quietly and competently invisible, all would be right in his world. Money would flow for her, company cars would be forthcoming. He neither wanted nor needed the hassle of a secretary who insisted on having a mind of her own. And Rose had passed four years obliging him on that count, keeping her thoughts firmly to herself.

'There's more,' she said, going with the motto that *in for a penny in for a pound.*

'Since when did you decide that being prickly was a helpful asset in your career?' The mildness of his tone was marred by a faintly disgruntled edge.

'I thought you welcomed your employees' opinions?' Rose said innocently.

'Of course I welcome hearing what my employees think,' Gabriel said irritably. 'And please do me a favour and don't launch into any long, boring speeches about my little world being so removed from reality that I wouldn't recognise free speech if it hit me in the face.' He looked at her, at her wry expression, and grunted. 'Well, you might as well get on with it. What more complaints have you been nurturing?'

Trust Gabriel to turn the tables, Rose thought, and translate her very valid points as below the belt stabs.

'These women of yours…'

'What women…?' It took Gabriel a few seconds to realise what she was talking about, then he narrowed his eyes cautiously. 'Don't go there, Rose.'

Rose could understand why she was in danger of becoming the Secretary from Hell. She felt a few fleeting seconds of sympathy for him. On top of her sudden demands for a change in her working hours, she was now about to inform him that taking care of his women was not part of her job specification and she would no longer be doing it. If he wanted to order flowers at the demise of a relationship, then he could phone the florist and order them himself. If he urgently needed an expensive token to compensate for cancelled dates, then he could set forth and purchase it himself.

'I need to have my say, Gabriel…'

'Which doesn't include preaching to me about the way I conduct my life outside work. That, I warn you, is way beyond your brief.' The flat, hard expression made Rose suddenly bristle. It was fine for him to ask her questions about *her* private life, to try and eke out information and then voice his opinions on the little he had managed to unearth, but he wasn't about to allow her the same freedom! Three months ago it wouldn't have occurred to her to speak her mind. In fact, the decent part of her knew that she should set him straight and tell him that she wouldn't dream of saying anything about how he conducted his private life, that the changes she had in mind were of a more practical nature, but she wasn't feeling particularly decent at the moment.

'What do you think I'm going to say, Gabriel?' She met his dark, brooding gaze evenly. 'Since you seem to be a mind-reader on top of everything else.'

'It doesn't take a genius to work out what's on your mind,' Gabriel rasped. He was beginning to regret his instinct to hang on to his wonderfully reliable secretary come hell or high water. His wonderfully reliable secretary appeared to have gone to Australia and stayed there. In her place was this forthright bordering on aggressive creature with an axe to grind and himself firmly in her sights as the grinding block.

'Oh, yes?' Rose's voice dropped by a couple of notches.

'You've made it plain that you disapprove of my behaviour towards the opposite sex. You've already said so. Of course, it hasn't crossed your mind that the women I date might actually enjoy going out with me, even if we do eventually break up.'

Rose raised her eyebrows, as if questioning his sanity in even thinking such a thing, and Gabriel glowered at her.

'I show them a good time,' he heard himself say. He wondered how it was that suddenly he was reduced to defending himself to someone whose business it most definitely was not. Or where, for that matter, that feisty look on her face had come from. 'I wine and dine them…amongst other things…' He took some satisfaction that her cool, superior expression was undermined by a slow flush. 'And believe me, Rose, when it comes to *those other things* I give a great deal of pleasure…'

'Lucky old them,' she said, recovering quickly. 'Wined, dined and bedded before being relegated to the history books.'

Gabriel was shocked. So was Rose. Where had *that* come from? She reddened and looked away but she still refused to retreat and apologise. Her sister had given her long speeches about the foolishness of falling for a man who wouldn't notice her if she stood naked on a table and danced till dawn. To him, Grace had warned darkly, Rose was a one-dimensional cut-out and always would be. Her only chance of rescuing her sense of self-worth would be to take the pay cut and leave the job.

Well, she hadn't left the job yet but she was still going to be a *woman of substance who was not afraid to speak her mind.*

'I *beg your pardon?*' Gabriel said in a shell-shocked voice, which would have been funny if she could feel anything under the rising tide of mortification.

'You heard me, Gabriel.'

'Where did you get language like *that* from?'

'Language like *what?* I don't believe I said anything obscene? Did I?'

'No, but…'

'That's fine, then!' Her sister's diagnosis of her had been brutally to the point. Rose could out-perform anyone when it came to hard work and skill. Whatever she wanted to do, Grace had said, she would achieve because she was clever and ambitious. *Unlike yours truly,* she had added ruefully. But underneath the brisk, capable exterior lurked a heart longing for romance. Hence her feelings for her boss, which she had allowed to run unchecked for four years. Like a complete idiot. Grace, so impractical when it came to anything involving office work, computers, money and all things electronic, was utterly practical in affairs of the heart. She had never wasted time mooning over unattainable boys at school and Rose was inclined to follow her advice. After all, comparing situations, who was in the better one?

'But actually I don't care what you do with the women who

come in and out of your life. What I care about is how it impacts on mine.'

'And how does it do that?' Gabriel asked with sudden interest.

'Here's how. You meet a woman. You shower her with presents. I buy the presents, usually in my lunch hour or at the weekend. Always in my leisure time, at any rate. Then there are the restaurants that need to be booked. The flowers that have to be sent with the right messages to the right people. Sometimes I have to fend off sobbing women who haven't quite seen your point of view that it was a privilege to have gone out with you and now it's time for them to find the nearest exit door. Sometimes they seem to have been under the deluded impression that you actually *cared about them.*' Her voice implied *poor fools.*

The surprises were piling on by the minute. Gabriel had never sensed any resentment in her when it came to doing what was, as far as he had always been concerned, part and parcel of a good PA's job, namely taking care of the incidentals that he had no time to do himself. Or inclination, if he was to be perfectly truthful. So what was wrong with ordering a few flowers down the phone now and again? Or taking a trip to the jewellers to buy a bracelet? Didn't all women like buying jewellery?

'Are you *jealous?*' Gabriel's voice was silky-smooth and speculative and, in response, Rose could feel her heartbeat quicken, because, and this was a truth she only admitted to herself late at night, when she was alone with her thoughts, she *was.* Whenever she had been in those exclusive shops buying exclusive things, holding up a glittering ruby ring for inspection or twirling a cashmere scarf between her fingers, she had thought, *imagined,* that it was for her.

'Of course I'm not *jealous,*' she said coldly. 'Do you really think…' She caught herself in the nick of time.

'Really think...what?'

'Nothing.'

'No. Tell me. After all, today seems to be a day of revelations.'

Rose looked at him and wondered how he would react if she told him the truth on this day *of revelations*. If he was stunned by the revelations he had had thrown at him today, then he would go into a state of cataclysmic shock if she *really* decided to reveal all!

'All right. As you asked, do you really think that I would ever, *could ever,* be jealous of all those women you choose to date?' Rose laughed humourlessly. 'For a start, they're not the sharpest knives in the block...'

'Who ever said I wanted sharp?' Actually, Gabriel thought, whoever said I wanted to be discussing this? But it was such an unusual ride that he was driven to go along with it. The woman whose thoughts he had never seen was handing them to him now and he was strangely fascinated. In fact, he couldn't take his eyes away from her face, although he reluctantly admitted to himself that that might have had something to do with her physical transformation. 'An intelligent woman is an overrated species,' he said, flexing his arms and then strolling to inspect the books ranging the central fireplace on either side. Though not before glancing at her face to see how she had reacted to his incendiary remark. With gratifying outrage. He decided to continue, curious to see where the road would lead. 'I mean, an intelligent woman will usually end up getting on a man's nerves.' He idly slipped a book out of its nesting place, surprised to discover that it was a first edition and wouldn't have come cheap. An intelligent woman with taste. He shoved the book back in its spot and turned to look at her. 'The endless discussions...the earnestness...the sheer tedium of someone *with a point of view...*' He mimicked a yawn and was amused to see her eyes glitter dangerously. 'Have you noticed how an intelligent woman will always have a point of view and will always bang on about it, even when everyone else has nodded off with boredom?'

'Have you noticed—' Rose was drawn into the argument even though common sense told her that it was ridiculous '—how a bimbo will spout such rubbish that you can end up losing the will to live…?'

Gabriel shot her one of those slow, devastating smiles that made her curl her fists on her lap. Then he laughed out loud. When he had sobered up his blue eyes swept over her and he murmured, with wicked amusement, 'I won't deny they can sometimes spout rubbish but I assure you that when I'm in bed with one of them I never end up losing the will to live…'

Rose drew in a sharp intake of breath. He had pushed himself away from his inspection of her books and for a few heart-stopping seconds she could have sworn that he was moving in her direction, but then he sat down, his eyes lazy and satisfied as he contemplated past conquests. Stupid, stupid jealousy made her feel temporarily faint.

'And then…' she carried on, her voice glacial-cold even though something was raging inside her, 'I suppose I feel sorry for them. You might think that you treat them well, and you do, but what a woman wants goes beyond the things that money can buy.'

'Oh, really?'

'Oh, really. The bracelets and earrings are nice enough but a walk in the park is even better, as is a home-cooked meal and then chatting in front of an open fire or a trip to the seaside on a sunny day…'

'Possibly for *you*…'

'I've had enough conversations with the women you've

discarded to know that they're always more heartbroken than you think they are!' Rose said defensively, aware that she had given away too much in her careless musings. 'Have you any idea how difficult it is to placate someone who's in tears and wondering what they did wrong?'

The conversation, which had been pleasantly challenging, appeared to have taken an ugly turn and Gabriel frowned at her discouragingly. 'I don't know where we're going with this one…'

'You pressed me for an opinion…'

'Which is different from blanket criticism.' He shook his head and tried to get a handle on his self control.

'Only because you don't happen to agree with it,' Rose felt constrained to point out.

'How is it that I never spotted you for the stubborn, opinionated, bloody *maddening* woman you obviously are?' Gabriel grated.

Then you shouldn't mind getting rid of me when I've trained up a replacement, Rose thought, but she kept that to herself. For reasons best known to her, *she* wanted to be the one to leave. That way, she would prove to herself that she was in control, proactive as far as her emotional state was concerned.

She looked down to where her fingers were fiddling uselessly with her jumper and stilled them. But she didn't look at him and she remained mutinously silent, not trusting herself to be discreet when she next spoke. *Opinionated, stubborn* and *maddening* were not easy insults to gloss over with a polite smile and a change of subject.

More annoying than her sudden outburst of frank and open honesty was the prolonged silence that greeted his remark. Gabriel, however much he brought his passion to his work, was formidably controlled in his dealings with women. They never, but never, got under his skin. Rose's calm face lent his annoyance an edge of grinding frustration.

'I have no idea why any of the women I have ever gone out with would have wondered what they did wrong,' he heard himself saying just as he recognised the weakness in saying it. 'It's not as though they don't know from the very start that commitment isn't on the agenda. No one can criticise me for not being fair. The walks in the park, the home-cooked meal and the log-burning fire… Well, I don't do little domestic scenes like that because that would just give them the wrong impression. Actually, I don't think I would *ever* do little domestic scenes like that anyway.'

'Why not?' Rose reluctantly dragged her gaze away from her hands and met his eyes curiously.

'Not me,' Gabriel said abruptly. 'So, getting back to your complaints. No long hours without notice and no additional tasks beyond the call of duty.'

Rose nodded. 'Well, no additional tasks that don't…well, don't have anything to do with work. I'm sorry,' she felt obliged to add because she knew that laying down rules and regulations after four years was a bit of a nerve.

'Anything else?'

'No. That's all. And Gabriel, it's only because I shall need to prioritise my time if I'm to do a course…'

'Let's hope it's worth it.' He stood up and shoved his hands into his pockets and watched as she got to her feet, straightening her clothes. At least *that* reassuringly prim habit hadn't changed!

'It will be,' Rose assured him, walking out towards the front door. 'It'll be hard work but, at the end of it, I'll be able to really start building up a satisfying career for myself. Not,' she hastened to add, 'that I haven't been wonderfully happy working for you.'

'*With* me. And you could have fooled me after everything you've laid at my door this evening.'

They both paused by the front door at the same time. Their eyes tangled, brown eyes clashing with deep blue ones, and Rose had to steady herself by placing her hand flat on the closed door.

'So you intend to have it all, do you?' Gabriel drawled. 'The fast job, the fast car, the kids and the house husband who will stay at home and take care of everything…' He leaned against the door and looked down at her. She was sharp enough to have it all, that much was sure, but until now he would never have thought it interested her. With wry honesty, he acknowledged that he had always thought that *he* was enough for her.

'I don't know about that.' Now that he was on the point of imminent departure, she felt as if she could finally relax. 'I'm too old-fashioned to be happy with the house husband scenario.'

'You see the man as the protector, do you?'

'No, of course not! Well, not in such simplistic terms anyway.' She was mesmerised by the way the half-light in the hallway threw his face into intriguing angles.

'Why? What's wrong with simplistic terms? I agree with you. I'm the kind of man who would want to protect my woman. You'd better be careful, though. Your basic caveman isn't drawn to a woman who's just as capable as he is of hunting prey. Don't pursue too much independence—you might just find it backfires on you.'

'I would never be attracted to a man who was threatened by my independence,' Rose said a little too breathlessly for her liking, but then he *was* very close to her and not just close, but close and giving her his undivided masculine attention. Just in case he saw the jittery spark in her eyes and misinterpreted it, or rather interpreted it too accurately, she thought to throw in, 'And, for your information, I might not be feminist enough to want a house husband, but I certainly wouldn't want a *caveman.*'

'Touché,' Gabriel said dryly. He straightened up and so did she. He had the suddenly consuming urge to touch her, maybe stroke the side of her face. Instead he opened the door. 'But I'm not the caveman you seem to think I am when it comes to women…'

'No? You could have fooled me.'

'You really shouldn't say things like that,' he chided, leaning towards her so that her head was suddenly swimming and she felt as though her legs might buckle under her at any minute. 'I might just be tempted to prove you wrong.'

CHAPTER FOUR

SITTING at the very far corner of the staff restaurant, Gabriel had a bird's eye view of Rose, who was playing with the salad she had taken as though suspecting that something unpleasant might crawl out from under the lettuce leaves at any given moment. He had a feeling that she wasn't even really aware of the clattering of voices on her table. Frankly, she looked as though she was a million miles away, thinking about God only knew what. Maybe the fact that June was proving to be a record breaker as far as soaring summer temperatures went. For the past two weeks the sky had been cloudless, the heat reaching unbeaten highs of early eighties. London was sweltering. People were complaining, as they did whenever the weather did anything unexpected. The parks were a sea of white bodies slowly going red in the relentless sun.

Of course, here in the restaurant, it could have been a fine autumn day outside. The marvels of central air-conditioning, which was probably why the place was packed. Who wanted to leave the comfort of the cool indoors to venture out into the baking sun? The first few days of novelty value had worn off for most of his employees and the fierce heat was not proving to be worth the bother of a tube journey to the nearest patch of green.

Which in turn was why Rose had not noticed his presence, tucked away with a couple of his corporate finance people and one of the company lawyers. They were discussing the minutiae of his most recent acquisition and Gabriel had switched off from the conversation a while back. In truth, he shouldn't really be eating in the staff restaurant at all. A business lunch at the Savoy Grill had beckoned. Nothing that he couldn't delegate to his CEO, allowing himself the bird's eye view he was now shamelessly enjoying of his secretary.

He couldn't quite put his finger on what had changed between them, but something had. Their working relationship when she had departed for Australia had been exemplary. The ideal working relationship, in fact. And then she had returned and he wasn't sure if the physical change in her had kick-started something in him or whether it had been that evening spent with her, first at the restaurant and then afterwards at her house, during which he had caught tantalising glimpses of the red-blooded woman beneath the competent one-dimensional exterior.

Gabriel just didn't know. He just knew that for the past few weeks he had found his eyes straying towards her, noticing the details of her face, like the light sprinkling of freckles on her nose, the way her straight hair seemed to be streaked with a hundred different shades of brown and copper, the contrast of her clear brown eyes and much darker eyelashes.

And her body. He had caught himself thinking about her body at the most inappropriate times. In the middle of meetings. Sitting in front of his laptop in his office at home. On the telephone to a client, when he could look at her through the glass partition separating their offices, look at the way her full breasts were outlined against the flimsy dresses and thin silky cardigans the sheer summer heat compelled her to wear to work. He was beginning to have steamy thoughts about that body of hers which, until a few months ago, had been so properly concealed beneath sensible layers of dark-coloured clothes. Actually, up until a few months ago, he really hadn't been that aware that she had a body at all, at least not in the sexual sense of the word. Now he seemed to spend a good amount of his waking time on the verge of an embarrassing arousal.

To start with he had been amused at his intense reaction to her. And baffled. After all, it wasn't as though he hadn't spent the past four years in her company!

Very soon, though, irritation with himself had set in, at which point his logical brain reached its logical conclusion. He was suffering from sex deprivation. He had been without a woman for a while, at least three months. The last woman he had dated, a model called Caitlin, had been a willing and able playmate but had evidently wanted more than a man who could be relied upon for expensive gifts, expensive meals out, creative sex and not much else. His frequent cancellations had eventually brought about the inevitable showdown and he had been quietly relieved when she had finished with him.

Having diagnosed the problem, Gabriel had set about sorting out a solution with the speed and efficiency with which he addressed all problems. He had simply rifled through his little black book and extracted a name. The woman in question he had met several months previously and had since bumped into her at various social occasions. At each, she had reminded him that she would love a call and, with his unlikely attraction to his secretary causing him pause for uncomfortable thought, Gabriel had cheerfully set the groundwork for an enjoyable and distracting seduction.

Unfortunately, it had failed to work. Their first meeting had taken place at an intimate but lively club, a favourite haunt of

Gabriel's, who liked the live jazz band and the relaxed atmosphere. The flatness of the evening he could only blame on the music, which must have killed the conversation. Meeting two had been at a restaurant, no music and hence no excuse for the fact that he had struggled through the fine food and wine, glancing down at his watch often enough to make him realise that Arianna was perhaps not quite his cup of tea.

Which, he thought now, still left him with the unexpected problem of a secretary he was beginning to fancy. A secretary, he had to admit to himself, who had maintained an enviable detachment ever since that one evening during which she had opened up. She had reverted to being the cool ice queen, but with a sexy little body and a way of flicking a glance at him from under her lashes that made him want to slam shut that damned interconnecting door, grab her and have his wicked way with her on his grand mahogany desk.

Sam Stewart, his company lawyer, interrupted the pleasant daydream that involved some very satisfactory ripping of blouses and yanking down of lacy white bras with a question about the pension trust fund of a company with which they were negotiating and Gabriel surfaced to realise that he had missed most of a very important conversation. He dragged his attention back to the matter in hand, deliberately turning away from Rose, who was now standing up anyway, looking at her watch, straightening her skirt. Getting ready to head back to the office where she would keep her head dutifully down until five-thirty, at which point she would clear her desk and politely bid him good evening.

Later, much later, after an evening spent poring over reports with only some chilled wine and Mozart for company, Gabriel realised that he would have to do something about his worrying situation. Losing sleep over a woman was bad enough, but suffering lapses in his concentration during the day was beyond the pale.

The only solution to satisfying his curiosity, he reasoned to himself, would be to put it to bed. Literally. And the thought of that alone was enough to make his body harden in immediate response.

He made the call at nine-fifteen the following morning. And Rose took it, as he knew she would.

'Shouldn't you be here, Gabriel? I've double-checked the diaries and you're definitely not due for your first meeting until eleven. With the people from Shipley Crew…' Rose had checked the diaries more than just twice. She had checked it and re-checked it roughly a hundred times since she had entered her office, only to find Gabriel conspicuous by his absence.

'Cancel all my meetings for today, Rose. Frank can handle Shipley on his own or he can take Jenkins with him just in case they need any expert advice.'

'Where *are* you?' It was so unlike Gabriel to be unpredictable during working hours that Rose actually felt a physical tingle of apprehension race down her spine.

'At my place.'

'Doing what?' She took a few deep breaths and repeated the question in a less crazed voice.

'Being under the weather.'

'You're *under the weather?* As in *ill?* You're *never ill,* Gabriel!'

'Try telling that to the strep bacteria in my throat.' Which he cleared convincingly.

Rose was torn between thinking that, with typical male lack of stamina, Gabriel had caved in to the simple cold bug with which he was unfamiliar, or else he was really ill. Ill as in *should go to hospital ill.*

'You seemed fine yesterday,' Rose informed him briskly. 'Are you sure you…' she opted for the least worrying option '…haven't got a hangover?'

'I think I'm old enough and experienced enough to recognise a hangover,' Gabriel said.

'Then it's probably just a bug you picked up. There are a few of those flying around. I'll make sure your meetings are cancelled and you can let me know later in the day if I need to rearrange any of the ones you have booked for tomorrow.'

'You'll have to come here, Rose.'

'I beg your pardon?'

'I'll need you to type some urgent stuff up for me.'

'You can't work if you're ill!'

'You know where I live, don't you?'

'I can't come over to your place, Gabriel!'

'Why not?'

'Because…because I have an awful lot to do here…'

'And I have an awful lot to do here. Get a piece of paper and write down my address. And, for God's sake, don't make the journey by bus. Get a cab. I want you here some time before the end of the week.'

'But…'

'I'm keeping strictly to your work to rule, Rose. I'm not asking you to work to an unusually late hour. I'm asking you to have a change of environment for a couple of hours. Now, have you got that pencil?' Without giving her time to lodge another pointless protest, Gabriel rattled off his address and then repeated it slowly to make sure that she'd taken it down correctly. 'Got it?'

'Yes, but…'

'Should take you half an hour to get here, even with a bit of traffic. So I'll see you by ten. I'll make sure the front door's open so you can just let yourself in.' He could have sworn he heard another *but* rising to the surface when he hung up.

Rose stared at the disconnected phone for a few minutes as she tried to get her thoughts in order. She could hardly believe that Gabriel was ill. Ill enough to have taken a day off work. He was always so ferociously energetic that it was hard to imagine him ever being felled by something as small as a bug. She stared at the piece of paper with his address on it. When she thought about actually going into his house or apartment or flat or whatever he had, somewhere posh in Kensington at any rate, she felt physically faint. But what if he really *was* ill? She couldn't imagine that he would take himself off to the doctor's. Heaven only knew if he *had* one!

Sick foreboding made her gather her things together quickly. Whatever disks she might need, her own laptop which the company provided for her free of charge, bits of post that needed to be checked and letters that required Gabriel's signature. Then she rearranged meetings and liaised with a couple of people in Finance who would have to cover for Gabriel at least for the day. She caught a taxi just as it was stopping to let someone off outside the office block.

Nerves kicked in as soon as she had slammed shut the door behind her and leaned forward to give the cab driver Gabriel's address. She could feel her short-sleeved blouse clinging to her as she tried to push down the window so that some breeze could reach her heated face. The knee-length flared floral skirt, which had promised to keep her cool when it had been hanging in her wardrobe, felt horribly constricting in the back seat of a taxi. Everything clung. Even her hair seemed to cling to her skull, making her wish that she had done the sensible thing and tied it back.

When she looked out of the window, she could see that

everyone was as uncomfortable as she was. Red faces, makeshift fans from bus timetables, handkerchiefs wiping backs of necks.

But at least that was where their discomfort stopped. She focused on the black computer case by her side, which was big enough to contain everything, and tried not to think about walking into his domain. She hoped that the surroundings wouldn't be too imposing and that perhaps his thrusting, overwhelming personality found solace in a cottage-style place.

She was wrong. She knew that the moment the taxi stopped in front of an imposing Victorian townhouse in an exclusive crescent which was distinguished by the sheer volume of expensive cars parked nose to bumper outside. She paid the cab driver and asked for a receipt while scanning the pristine row of houses for anything that might look reassuringly unkempt, but no such luck.

The door, as promised, was unlocked, making her wonder how someone as sharp as Gabriel could be so trusting, but as she glanced over her shoulder she noticed Harry sitting in Gabriel's car on the opposite side of the pavement and waved.

Then she was in his...house. Townhouse, she realised, was too unimaginative a term for the place in which she found herself. The floor was a rich dark wood, interrupted, in the hall, by a stunning blue and red geometrically patterned rug and the cream walls, which should have been bland, were a display case for works of art which *looked* horribly expensive.

Rose resisted the urge to peer into some of the other rooms and instead eyed the staircase dubiously.

'I'm here!'

She jumped as his voice surprised her from behind and she spun around to see him standing in one of the doorways, Or rather, she thought, as her heartbeat quickened to a sick-inducing speed, *lounging indolently. Lounging indolently* in a black silk robe which was loosely tied at the front and which appeared to conceal nothing more than bare skin.

Rose nearly yelped. She knew her eyes were round and startled as she made a conscious effort not to stare at the bare legs with their sprinkling of dark hair, the sliver of bronzed chest visible where the lapels of the robe failed to meet. Was he even wearing *underwear?* she thought.

'I expected you a little sooner. Lock the front door, would you?'

Rose was more than happy to do that. Anything to rescue her from the sight of Gabriel Gessi in very little.

He had disappeared by the time she turned back round and she headed for the room from which he had appeared. Spot on.

Rose walked into a room that was striking not because of its size but because of its décor. Deep, rich blues provided a dramatic backdrop for the parquet floor and walls lined with bookshelves. Impressive sash windows were dressed in layers of cream muslin that fell and pooled on the floor and dominating the room was a desk on which all the modern gadgets had pride of place. The computers, one laptop and one full sized, a fax machine, two telephones. And, against the only wall that was not occupied with bookcases or windows, was a long, low couch in a rich Paisley print, the beauty of which was ruined by the pillow and sheet.

Gabriel, she realised, was lying on said couch and had been watching her with amusement as she gawped at her surroundings.

'Blame my mother and sister,' he said, reclining with his hands folded behind his head. 'I wanted lots of white and just enough furniture to fit the requirements of being habitable. Well, don't just stand there with your mouth open. Sit down!'

'Where?'

'Well, there's only one chair available, isn't there? Unless you want to come and perch on the side of the couch here with me?' He patted the couch invitingly and Rose hurriedly went and sat behind the desk. Ready for action. She even pulled out the stack of letters she had brought with her and began sorting them into order of priority, waiting for him to tell her where he wanted to begin. In the meantime, she would not look at him because all that flesh was doing disastrous things to her nervous system.

'Aren't you going to ask me how I am?'

'I'm sorry…' Rose looked at him, flustered. In her haste to avoid staring at him she had bypassed the usual pleasantries and, of course, he would pick up on that even though he himself avoided them like the plague. 'How are you feeling, Gabriel?'

'Terrible.'

'You don't look too bad,' she risked truthfully.

'That's because I'm putting on a brave face. The fact is I've had a helluva night. Very restless. Tossing and turning.'

Rose swallowed. Her thoughts wandered to Gabriel, in a big king-sized bed, powerful, naked body thrashing about. She felt faint. 'In that case, we should finish things here as quickly as possible so that you can get some sleep! It's the best cure there is! Where do you want to start? I've brought the post. I thought you might like to have a look at it…'

'What I'd really like,' Gabriel said, closing his eyes, 'is something to eat. I know it goes beyond your job specification and it's well within your rights to refuse…but I haven't eaten since…hmm…maybe lunch time yesterday…'

'You got me over here *to cook for you?*'

Gabriel looked at her through half closed eyes and wondered whether he should inform her that that particular tone of voice was not at all attractive. Not when he was supposed to be an invalid and she was supposed to be Florence Nightingale. Anyway, what was wrong with cooking for him? He wasn't asking her to rob a bank! He couldn't count the number of women who had been desperate to get into his kitchen and start weaving some magic with one of his frying pans!

'Forget it,' Gabriel said abruptly. 'I might have known that putting yourself out would be unthinkable. I'll do it myself.' He began levering himself off the couch and Rose reluctantly shook her head.

'What do you want?'

Gabriel flopped back down and fixed amazing, sleepy blue eyes on her. It was steaming hot outside. Her clothes were clinging to her even though it was cool in here. Years ago he had had an overhead fan installed and it had been a brilliant idea, even though it only came into its own very irregularly. On a day like this, though, it was so much better than air-conditioning.

'You look hot.'

'I *am* hot.' Rose raised one hand to bundle her hair into a ponytail so that she could fan her neck. Gabriel wondered if she had any idea how provocative she looked, how the movement of her full breasts was very noticeable in what she happened to be wearing.

'You could always strip off…' he allowed a fractional pause '…and change into something a bit cooler. My sisters have random clothes upstairs in the rooms they use and they're roughly your size. You could borrow something.'

'No!' Rose was horrified. She might have altered her look but underneath she was still the same and was frankly horrified at the thought of stepping into someone else's clothes. Especially when it would involve getting out of her own…in Gabriel's house…while he was in it…

'It was just a thought. As far as I know, all the clothes are clean.'

'I know that. And…thank you for the offer but I'm fine. Now, if you just tell me what you want to eat, I'll see what I can do. A sandwich? Or some fruit?'

'An omelette, I think. And toast. Also some coffee, no… tea. Better in ill health, I believe. With sugar.'

'Oh, hang on. I'll just get my pad so that I can write it all down.'

Gabriel grinned. He had always enjoyed her dry sense of humour even though it had been conspicuously absent over the past few weeks when she had been in her Head Down No Nonsense Rose role.

'Think of it as doing an ill man a good deed.'

'Only if you think of it as taking advantage of a good-natured secretary.' Rose exited the room to the sound of his rich chuckle behind her and followed her nose to the kitchen. Like most houses in London, it wasn't a mansion and she located the kitchen without too much difficulty. It was a wealthy bachelor's paradise. Black granite counter tops, chrome double-fronted fridge-freezer with integral ice-maker, coffee-maker that looked as though you would need a degree in electronics to operate it. Nothing looked as though it had ever been used, which either meant that he was rarely to be found doing anything like cooking in his own kitchen or else he had an extremely efficient cleaner.

The frying pan, finally located, was gleaming. It was almost a crime to use it for something as mundane as preparing food.

It was half an hour before she eventually walked back into the study to find him still reclining on the couch. The black silk robe was revealing even more sinfully muscled chest and Rose cleared her throat meaningfully, giving him time to cover himself up, which he didn't. He just sat up, propping himself against the arm of the sofa, which was a band of wood, giving the item of furniture something of a sleigh bed look, a fact she had only now noticed.

'Smells delicious. Where did you find the tray?'

Rose raised her eyebrows questioningly, although it didn't exactly amaze her that he was fairly clueless as to the contents of his kitchen.

'Tucked away in a groove between two of the cupboards. No one would ever guess that it had been used. Along with everything else in the kitchen.' She placed the tray on his lap and averted her eyes as best she could from the enticing glimpse of hard brown skin.

'I don't do a great deal of cooking,' Gabriel agreed, tucking into the food with evident relish. 'In fact—' he paused to look at her '—the last time I ate home-cooked food was…three months ago when I went back to Italy for a week.'

'You can't eat out *all the time,* Gabriel!' Rose was suitably shocked by the thought of that. 'It's impractical, never mind the expense.'

'Why is it impractical?'

'Because…it just is. It's not nutritious.'

'Do you make an effort to cook for yourself?'

'Yes. Yes, I do. I enjoy cooking. I find it very relaxing.'

'Maybe you could come and cook for me now and again.' He saw the expression on her face and bit back his sudden impatience. 'Just a joke, Rose. There's no need to snatch the nearest bottle of smelling salts in case you pass out from the horror of such a thought.'

'I don't cook very fancy food,' she said, trying to pour a bit of oil on troubled waters. A cooped up Gabriel was a dangerous Gabriel, especially now the boundary lines between them had become frighteningly blurred at the edges. 'Not the kind of food you would enjoy eating.'

'I'm enjoying this.'

'Stop being difficult, Gabriel. You know what I mean.'

'Do you know you are the only woman I have ever allowed to talk to me like that? Aside from my mother. And, of course, my sisters, who see it as their duty to keep me in my place.'

Rose grinned at the thought of anyone trying to keep Gabriel in his place. She missed the thoughtful glint in his eyes as he contemplated her, back in her position of safety behind the desk, which dwarfed her.

'What makes you think that you know the sort of food I enjoy?'

Was it her imagination or was he dragging it out with that breakfast? Normally Gabriel worked on full throttle, barely pausing to draw breath. It was unlike him to call her over urgently, only to engage her in chit-chat.

'I don't know.' Rose shrugged and looked down at her fingers, at the pale pink polish which she had applied the day before. She never used to wear nail polish but she did now and she liked the way it looked and the feminine way it made her feel.

'How are you doing with finding a suitable course? Is that all sorted out now?' Gabriel changed tack as dragging the conversation on to a personal level obviously wasn't going to work.

And why exactly he was engaged in this ridiculous charade was beyond him anyway. He felt as fit as a fiddle but despite that had been unable to fight off the driving desire to have her in his territory, have her see *him* in it. Why? Because curiosity was eating away at him? He would have considered himself above sexual curiosity, but clearly not, considering he had concocted a lame excuse for her to come to his house for no better reason that to play games. On a weekday. When he should have been in meetings. Hell, it wasn't as if he didn't work all the hours God made, he decided, squashing his guilty conscience. He deserved a break now and again. And when was the last time a woman had captured his imagination?

'Oh, yes, I think so.' She went pink and stared harder at her neatly painted nails. In fact, if only he knew that her search for a suitable course had led her into some very interesting waters.

'You *think* so? Shouldn't you have signed up by now?'

'Yes. Yes, I have, as a matter of fact.'

Gabriel's eyes narrowed on her embarrassed face. He could smell concealment a mile off and wondered what it was she was hiding from him. Surely discussing something as boring as a business course did not warrant an air of secrecy. For a few enjoyable seconds he toyed with the notion that perhaps his capable secretary hadn't signed up for a business course at all. Maybe she had signed up for a pole dancing course. Now *that* would bring a guilty tinge to her cheeks.

'And?' he prodded.

'It starts at the beginning of October, but I shall have to have a day off for induction some time in September. I'll let you know when.'

'And that's it?'

'What?'

'The sum total of details you intend to throw out at me?'

'There's nothing else to tell you! If you're that interested, I could always bring in the prospectus.' Gabriel, in the wrong mood, could turn being maddening into an art form and he was doing it now, looking at her in a way that made her stomach flip over, steamrollering his way into her private life even though she had spent weeks giving off all the right Keep Out vibes.

'Shall we crack on with the workload?'

Prepared to face a barrage of questions that she would be obliged to dodge like flying bullets, Rose was momentarily taken aback by his change of tack. But she jumped on the bandwagon gratefully and after half an hour her pulse had settled back down to normal, as had her voice.

He had remained on the couch, seemingly unaffected by the incongruity of conducting work in nothing more than a bathrobe, and she had stayed at his massive desk, typing directly on to the computer, punctuating the pattern with little notes in her pad, which she would research and transcribe back at the office.

She looked at her watch once. The next time she glanced at it, it was lunch time. They had been working solidly for over three hours!

'We'll call it a day now.' Gabriel watched as she flexed her fingers and attempted a stretch. 'Come over here.'

'I beg your pardon?'

'Come over here.'

Rose obediently gathered up her stuff, everything ordered and clipped together neatly so that she could move swiftly through them when she returned to the office.

'Sit.' Gabriel swung his legs to one side and patted a space next to him. 'And don't worry, I won't bite…' There was something softly alluring and very, very feminine about her hesitation. It made a refreshing change from women who were as sexually aggressive as men and didn't need an invitation to get close up and personal.

'I don't want to catch anything.'

'You won't catch anything.' How very true, he thought wryly. 'I'm simply going to massage your shoulders, get rid of some of that tension. Come on. Sit. I'm a very good masseur.'

Rose gasped. Her knuckles whitened as she clutched her

wad of papers with horrified desperation. Was he being *serious? Massage her back?* There was nothing *simple* about the suggestion. Not in her fevered mind. She took a step backwards. She thought she might be overreacting. The amused, self-assured expression lurking on his face was giving her an indication of that, but there was no way that he would be laying a finger on her. She took a couple more steps backwards and of course that was when it happened. Sod's law, she thought, as she grappled and failed to retrieve her footing, that the one place that damned low footstool was, the same footstool he had kicked aside to make way for her and the tray, would be right there behind her left ankle. Just the right spot to ensure that she fell in an undignified heap on to the ground, surrounded by her neatly compiled paperwork and with her flimsy summer skirt in hideous disarray. Rose scrambled to gather herself, her face burning with embarrassment, only belatedly registering that, for someone who was supposedly ill, Gabriel had leapt out from the couch with remarkable agility and was now, horror of horrors, bending over her with a concerned expression, bathrobe agape, allowing her a glimpse of boxer shorts.

Lord, but could things get any worse?

Rose pushed herself up and yanked her skirt down, just as Gabriel scooped her up, ignoring her yelps of dismay. There went the skirt. Riding up. Undoing the job she had just done. Exposing so much thigh that Rose was scared to let her attention linger. And his arms around her were like steel, forcing her head against his chest, bare skin because his robe was in as much disarray as she was.

The whole mortifying episode must have taken all of five seconds, but to Rose, it seemed like eternity. Everything seemed to be happening in slow motion until he had deposited her on the couch, at which point it was real time again except she found that she couldn't jump to her feet, the one thing she wanted to do, because he was kneeling in front of her.

'What *are you doing?*'

'Rotate your foot. That was a pretty bad fall. We need to make sure that you haven't twisted anything.'

'I'm fine.'

'If you hadn't been scuttling off like a little scared rabbit, you would never have tripped.'

Rose wanted to smash him over the head with the nearest heavy object.

'If you hadn't been…'

'Hadn't been what?'

'Do you mind giving me back my foot?' He had removed her shoe and was massaging her foot, working his fingers along the soft underside, rotating it with exquisite pressure until she wanted to scream or groan or *something.* 'Nothing's wrong with it! Everything's fine!'

'Hadn't been what?' Gabriel straightened up, which was a more dangerous position because now he was on her eye level and way too close for comfort. She could so easily slide her hand under his silk robe. Four years' worth of fantasies crashed through her like a tidal wave and Rose closed her eyes briefly.

'Well?'

Rose opened her eyes to find that he was even closer to her. And amused. The smile was right there behind eyes that were pretending to be serious and interested. And here she was, desperately trying to fight down the effect he was having on her. *It just wasn't fair!* Four years fighting off a lethal attraction to a man who had now decided that it might be a bit of fun to flirt with her once in a while, when he was between women and had nothing better to do.

Every fibre in her being regretted the decision she had made to stay put for a while longer.

'If you hadn't been flirting with me,' Rose said coldly. 'If you hadn't forgotten that it's totally inappropriate. I expected more of you.'

She had been hoping to shame him. She failed. He gave her a slow, devastating smile.

'Flirting…' He inclined his head to one side as if considering a new found concept. 'You're right. Maybe flirting was a bad idea. Maybe…' his voice was velvety soft and rich with husky sexuality '…I should have just done this…'

For three seconds time stood still. His mouth touched hers with gentle curiosity, then hungry urgency that had her clinging to him, matching his want with hers in equal measure. And it took ten seconds for sickening reality to intrude.

'Don't!' Rose pushed him so forcefully that he stumbled backwards, giving her time to get to her feet and put some distance between them. 'How *dare you?*'

Gabriel stood up, but he wasn't angry. Not at all. And that was even scarier. The expression on his face was as though he had sorted something out in his head.

'I'll *pretend that never happened,*' Rose gritted. 'But if it happens again, then I'm gone! Do you hear me?' She couldn't bear to look at the discarded shoe, but she did, slipping her foot into it and bending to scoop up all the papers, not caring what order they were in. His silence was unsettling. She knew he was watching her and it made the hairs on the back of her neck rise. Would he see? The way her breasts were still throbbing, aching to be caressed? Or the way the dampness was spreading between her legs, honeyed dew begging for his touch? Rose wanted to die a thousand deaths. She would have remained scrambling around on the floor indefinitely but finally she had gathered up the strewn papers and was looking at him with her best ice cold glare.

'Okay.' Gabriel looked down at her. 'It's a deal. I'll pretend it never happened and you can pretend that you didn't want it to…'

CHAPTER FIVE

THE interviewing was not going according to plan. At least not the plan that Rose had germinated in her head, which basically involved finding someone quickly and installing them even more quickly so that in due time, preferably as soon as she had found her feet on her course, she could re-submit her letter of resignation and this time leave with a clear conscience.

Because Gabriel was driving her crazy. True to her request, he had not mentioned a word about *that kiss* but she had still spent the past week in a state of heightened awareness. Big mistake because she was doubly conscious of him. The minute he got within two feet of her, her entire nervous system went into overdrive and she could feel her body tense in dreaded expectation of some casual physical contact.

Of which there had been a fair few instances. More than usual, although she was pretty sure that she was imagining that. A feathery brush of his fingers on her arm when he leant to read something over her shoulder, the briefest of touches when she handed him a cup of coffee or when he sat next to her so that he could go through some detail with her in one of the reports they happened to be working on. Her antennae now seemed to be on red alert and it was driving her crazy.

Try as she might, her body was not letting her pretend that nothing had happened, even if all mention of it was conscientiously avoided. He came close and she felt faint. He casually touched her and her body roared into hot, suffocating awareness. His challenge a week ago, that he would pretend to forget what had happened if she could pretend that she hadn't wanted it, was proving ominously prescient.

Hence her increasing desperation to find a suitable replacement.

And Gabriel was proving frustratingly uncooperative.

'If this woman is to possibly be your eventual replacement,' he'd told her seriously, 'then I have to make sure that I get it right. We're not talking about someone who's going to be around for a few weeks, someone disposable. I need to find exactly the sort of woman I can happily work alongside…'

'Or man,' Rose had pointed out, but Gabriel had shot her one of those looks that informed her right there and then that working alongside the ideal man was not on the cards for him.

They had thus spent the past three days poring over applications and squeezing in candidates whenever Gabriel had a free moment.

Two women, both of whom seemed to fit the bill, had been rejected out of hand by Gabriel, on the spurious excuse that he *just couldn't see himself having a long and problem-free working relationship with either of them.*

'But it would only be for two days during the week,' Rose had mumbled unconvincingly, because in her head she had already slotted her replacement in on a full-time basis, while she went somewhere else to lick her wounds.

'Would it?' he had asked darkly, and she had given him a weak smile.

Now, at five-thirty, they had just seen off the latest in the ever-increasing line and Rose knew, without doubt, that it had been another unsuccessful interviewee.

She hated this bit, when she walked down to the grand reception area in the foyer and did her best to fend off pointed and anxious questions as to whether the interview had been a success or not. This evening, however, it wasn't too bad. Elaine Forbes, number thirteen in the line, was destined to prove true the superstition because her lightweight qualifications had made the business of rejection easier than usual.

Five minutes debriefing with Gabriel and she would be out of the office and ready to begin her weekend.

She arrived back at her office to find him lounging in her chair, feet propped up on her desk, hands folded behind his head.

'Well?' he asked, picking up her pen and twirling it over, 'what did you think of Ms Forbes?'

'I think we can strike her off the list,' Rose told him, skirting round his indolent figure and gathering her various bits and pieces in preparation for going home. She could feel his eyes following her and hated herself for the excited ripple of reaction. She also hated it when he invaded her space. It was much easier to be in his office, because she could leave it and shut the door behind her. Right now, he was focused fully on her and it was difficult to escape the crazy notion that he was doing it on purpose, because he knew it rattled her. It was a thought that had occurred to her previously during the week and whenever it did she always hastened to tell herself that she was being silly, imagining things because of what had happened between them.

'What makes you say that?' Gabriel asked in a surprised voice and Rose paused to give him a jaundiced glance.

'Oh, I don't know, Gabriel. I guess it might have something to do with her staggering failure to master the basic test I set for her to judge how familiar she was with our computer package. Or maybe her lack of speed and accuracy when it came to taking notes on what I was saying.' Rose knew Gabriel well enough to know that he said most things once and expected immediate comprehension. Floundering was not a quality he appreciated and Elaine Forbes had floundered in a fairly spectacular fashion.

'She was remarkably attractive. Did you notice?'

Rose flushed. Yes, she *had* noticed, as a matter of fact. It would have been hard not to. Five foot ten of curves clad in a handkerchief of a skirt and a top that just skimmed her waistline. Long blonde hair and wide green eyes that had sized Gabriel up and clearly not found him wanting.

'I'm not sure what that has to do with anything.' She fetched her lightweight jacket and slung it over her shoulders. It would still be too warm to put it on when she went outside but old habits died hard. She still felt undressed if she left the house without a jacket or a cardigan. Unlike the most recent candidate, who would probably have felt overdressed in anything as mundane as a cardigan. Or cream lightweight jacket.

'Her credentials weren't up to scratch,' she said irritably, irked at the small smile playing at the corners of his mouth as he obviously contemplated the other assets Ms Forbes would bring to any job.

'Which isn't to say that we might not be able to put her on a course, get her up to speed. Provided her attitude is right…'

'And what…' Rose was in danger of snapping, 'would you qualify as *the right attitude?*'

'An ability to work in perfect harmony with me. That is to say, do whatever I want without complaining.'

Rose narrowed her eyes and was about to ask whether he had a problem with her just because she happened to have lodged a couple of small complaints after *four* years when she realised that he was joking.

'Ha, ha.'

'I admit she might not have the required intellect to hold down the job,' Gabriel conceded, 'despite all her other, highly visible assets.'

Rose was getting tired of being baited. 'I really must be off, Gabriel.'

'Not so fast.'

'Well, there's not much left to say on the subject of Ms Forbes. I'm glad we both agree that the person who fills the position will have to have more going for them than long legs, long hair and breasts.'

'I wasn't about to prolong the conversation about the delectable Ms Forbes. I was going to tell you that there are some emails I need to get out today. The interviewing has thrown everything out of sync. So…you'll have to stay on an extra hour or so until we get the workload covered.' He held up his hands as if defending himself from the possibility of a physical attack. 'And yes, I know it probably crashes through your work to rule barrier but I want to remind you of exactly how generous your pay package is.'

'I don't have a problem working an extra hour or two, Gabriel.' *And he knew it.* 'You *know* that! I only have a problem when you ask me to work ridiculous hours and it really only reared its head because, if I'm going to be studying, I'm going to need to prioritise my spare time!'

Gabriel was beginning to wonder how it was that he had never noticed the feisty, challenging side of his perfect secretary's personality. How could he *ever* have found her *soothing?* She was about as soothing as a shark in search of blood! Fortunately he was man enough to tackle any form of shark. And to enjoy the tussle. Right now he was mightily enjoying the sight of her turning pink as her feathers were well and truly ruffled. He also liked the fact that he got under her skin, that under her carefully cultivated cool exterior, the one that had had him hoodwinked for so long, she responded to him. As a man. He was pretty sure that she hadn't been able to relegate that kiss to the back of her mind and that pleased him because he sure as hell hadn't been able to forget it. Just thinking about her cool lips against his, about that instant, that one fleeting moment, when she had opened up and returned the kiss with a fire she was at pains to hide, was enough to make him feel hard. Like an adolescent in the throes of his first crush.

For Gabriel that was a sensation so novel that it was enough to keep him up at night. He suspected that thoughts of him might well keep her up at night too. With any other woman he would have asked, knowing that it was really a very sexy question, especially if he qualified it by saying that the sleepless nights were mutual, but that was the last thing he would have done with Rose. He had no doubt that she would have flung that damned resignation letter straight at him and this time she would have not been open to persuasion.

But he wanted her and he was pretty sure that she wanted him and he had time on his side. Well, sufficient time anyway.

'Of course I know that! But we still have some work to put in here and I'm glad you don't have a problem.' He stretched and rubbed the back of his neck. 'Now, if you want to come into my office, we can start downloading the files we need to have a look at and you have my word that I won't keep you past the witching hour.'

Not so fast, Rose wanted to shout as he disappeared towards his office.

'I'm afraid there's a bit of a problem with staying on tonight,' she said awkwardly, following him in but standing in the doorway, hands in her jacket pockets.

Gabriel, who was leaning over his desk, booting up his computer in preparation, looked up and frowned.

'I thought we'd sorted that one out,' he said abruptly.

'You don't understand. I can't work tonight because I'm busy…'

'You're busy?'

He sounded truly shocked and Rose knew why. Because in all the four years that she had worked for him, she had rarely denied his requests that she work beyond the call of duty. She had put her job ahead of everything. It satisfied her and coincidentally fed her hidden addiction to him. Over the years he must have gained the impression that she had no social life, nothing to distract her from her complete slavish dedication to *him.*

She felt an illicit thrill of pleasure at bursting the bubble.

'I'm busy,' she repeated with a slight nod. 'I could work late on Monday, if it'll keep till then.'

'It won't *keep till then,*' Gabriel said irritably, giving her his full, undivided attention. 'Things at this level don't *keep* indefinitely, Rose. Business doesn't take time out so that we can all have a bit of a rest.'

This was Gabriel at his most coldly sarcastic. It was the voice he saved for when he was well and truly disgusted. He had not scaled the heights by being kind, considerate and retiring. Yes, he was charming and witty and could promote the illusion of being absolutely relaxed, but beneath the velvet glove was the steel hand.

'Well, Gabriel, I'm afraid there's nothing I can do. If you like, I can see whether Emily's free and doesn't mind working late this evening.'

'I have a better idea. Why don't you just cancel whatever it is you were doing? If you were going out with your girlfriends, tell them, from me, that I'll treat them to an evening out next week, wherever they want to go, no expense spared. Call it compensation for putting you out.'

'I'm not going out with my girlfriends,' Rose said eventually. She could almost see his ears prick up.

'No?'

'No.'

'Then what's so important that you can't cancel…?'

'Really, Gabriel, it's none of your business.' But he would make it his business. She knew that. And she didn't know why she was bothering to resist. It wasn't as though she was hiding some shameful secret.

'I think I deserve a decent excuse…'

'I'm going out on a date, if you must know. To the theatre, actually. To see *Les Miserables*. I've wanted to see that for ages. The tickets are all booked and, really, I have just enough time to make it to the theatre. Then Joe and I are going go have a quick bite afterwards. So you see there's no chance I can stay late. I'm sorry.'

'The theatre? Joe? Who the hell is Joe? A quick bite?'

'I have to go or I'll be late.'

'Who is this Joe character?'

'Have a good weekend and I shall see you on Monday, Gabriel!' With which, Rose fled. Not ostensibly. Not to the extent that she was working up a sweat, but moving quickly enough to put a stop to Gabriel's barrage of questions.

She only breathed a sigh of relief when she was in the taxi and speeding to the theatre, and really, really, only relaxed when she was delivered to the theatre and spotted Joe waving at her through the milling crowds.

This was going to be their first date and Rose teetered between anticipation and apprehension. After all, she didn't know him that well. They had met only a couple of weeks previously, a case of pure coincidence. Rose had gone to see one of the colleges on her list and, having set off in anxious pursuit of the business studies department, had ended up in completely the wrong area and knocking on completely the wrong door.

Fortunately for her, Joe had answered it and he had been so nice and so helpful that Rose had found herself opening up to him and confessing her complete ignorance of the further education system, not to mention her utter confusion at finding herself surrounded by so many students, carrying files and laptops, listening to their iPods and generally making her feel like someone from another era.

She had made sure to go to the college dressed in jeans and trainers, in an attempt to blend in, but even her jeans and trainers seemed to be of just the wrong variety, ever so slightly off-key. Rose had poured it all out over the coffee Joe had insisted on buying her in the college canteen.

In the end she had found the right department but, as it turned out, the course wasn't quite what she wanted. So the college was out but Joe, a friend made, was in.

They had exchanged numbers and from that peculiar meeting had blossomed a growing friendship on the telephone.

Rose wasn't sure what would emerge from the friendship but she was willing to follow the road wherever it might take her.

And the evening was a success. The play was good and, over a very late evening meal, they discussed it amongst a thousand other things. She even found herself telling him about Gabriel! Not about her ridiculous feelings for him, of course, but about his annoying, unpredictable ways. In fact, she had to stop herself or risk becoming a bore, and then they chatted easily about Joe and what he did and, before she knew it, it had gone midnight and he was hailing a cab for her.

'I guess this is the time when I ask whether you'd like to risk my company again,' he said, pulling her to one side and kissing her on the forehead. A perfect end to a lovely evening, Rose thought. No pressure for sex, no pushiness. And he was cute too. Blond hair, blue eyes that crinkled when he smiled, and he smiled a lot.

'I think I could see my way to doing that…' Rose couldn't help but smile back at him. 'It's been a great evening out.'

'And we never even got around to discussing what course you've finally signed up to.'

'Oh, and *that's* the most riveting conversation in the world!'

'Absolutely riveting. Don't forget I'm a lecturer. I like to know what it is that you students are interested in.' He smiled again and turned to open the cab door for her. 'So there's no question now. We have to go on another date. Research purposes for me. I'll give you a call on Monday, first thing. I have no idea how much time I'll have to myself on this outward bound weekend of mine. Does this ogre of a boss allow you to use the land line for personal calls or should I call your mobile?'

'Mobile…' Rose said hurriedly, as a mental picture of Gabriel flashed into her head. 'Definitely mobile.'

'In case he ties you to the typewriter and forces you to type a thousand times…*I must never disobey company rules*…?'

'Oh, no. Gabriel's very fair.' It was fine for her to air her moans but she felt hot and flustered at Joe's slight hint of criticism. 'In fact, there's a very low employee turnover rate. One of the lowest in the city. He would…'

'It was meant to be funny, Rose,' Joe interjected gently. 'Now, off you go, Cinderella, before the taxi decides to leave you behind. I'll call you tomorrow.'

He would. Amongst all his good qualities there was a dependability to Joe that Rose knew was just what every woman wanted. If he said he would call, then he would. He was, she went to bed musing, a thoroughly decent man. Not the sort to string a woman along. Not the sort to equate caring with buying expensive gifts. Not a man given to large, extravagant gestures. Definitely not a man who should carry a *Dangerous to Health* warning on his forehead so that women could take note and keep away. And not a man that would make her skin tremble every time he was near.

But there was a spring in her step when she went to work the following Monday. Joe hadn't called but he had sent her a couple of brief text messages, making her laugh with his outward bound stories which he promised to bore her with more fully when they met.

She arrived to find Gabriel already at his desk and, judging from his rolled up sleeves and lack of tie, he had been there a good while. And he did not seem to be in the best of moods.

Rose decided that she wouldn't allow that to deflate her. She fetched him his coffee before making her way into his office and the smile only wavered when he raised his head and frowned at her.

'I'm pleased to see that one of us had a good weekend.'

'Good morning, Gabriel.' She sat in her usual chair, facing his desk, notepad on her lap, ready to begin the day.

He grunted.

'I've brought you your coffee. Is there anything urgent you need me to do or shall I just crack on with the emails from Friday? Don't forget you've got another two ladies to see this afternoon. I've already had the preliminary interviews with them and both seem promising.'

'Cancel them.'

'What? Why?'

'Because one of our places in the Caribbean is behind with some building work and now there's a hold up on some vital equipment, so we're going to have to try and sort this out before the end of the week, preferably before the end of the day.'

'Why the urgency?' Rose was well aware of which particular development this was. There had been ongoing problems with it from day one. The island was very small and very difficult to access. Supplies, in the first stages of building, had been a nightmare to ship across and things had pretty much carried on with that handicap. Gabriel had mentally written the venture off as an ongoing white elephant. It had lost its appeal as a commercial venture, but she knew from the way he spoke about it that he had developed a peculiar fondness for the place. The original structure of a hotel had gradually morphed into a massive villa overlooking the wild side of the Atlantic and the details were more appropriate to a private residence than to a busy tourist spot. Gabriel now nurtured the plan of turning it into an exclusive fourteen bedroomed villa which would be rented for corporate entertaining or else hired by the super-wealthy for the occasional retreat from the rat race.

'There are murmurs of an approaching hurricane. Eileen's sweeping towards Florida but there's a chance it might divert and if it hits us it's going to be fatal for the project. There just aren't sufficient bricks in place to stave off a category four.'

'I'll see what I can do…' Rose privately thought that there was nothing she could do. Time and urgency meant different things out there. The infrastructure on the island, from everything she read in the files, was basic. There were some shops, a school, transport to and from the island. Business was something that happened offshore, largely.

'Good. And, in the meantime, sort out flights for me to get

there. I'll leave first thing in the morning or today if nothing's available for tomorrow.'

'Leave?' Rose looked at him in astonishment. She could feel the blood seeping out of her face and she cleared her throat briskly. 'Leave as in *travel to an island which is on alert for a hurricane?* Where would you stay when you got there? You've been there, Gabriel, and we've both seen detailed pictures of the place. There are no hotels.'

'I could always camp down on the beach.' He stood up and began prowling his office, deep in thought. As he prowled, Rose tried to imagine Gabriel caught up in a hurricane, at the mercy of the elements. The trip to the island was a convoluted one, involving two airports and a boat crossing. What if the hurricane hit while he was in the boat? He would be as vulnerable as an ant in a matchbox hurtling down a waterfall. She shivered and surfaced from the nightmarish reverie to find that he had stopped in front of her. Before she could take evasive action, he was leaning over her, caging her in, his face dark with anger.

'Wake up, Rose!'

'I'm sorry…' She stuck her chin out defensively and thanked the stars that mind-reading wasn't one of his many talents. If it had been, he wouldn't have had much trouble deciphering the dread inside her as she contemplated the foolhardiness of what he proposed to do.

'You're no use to me mooning about the place,' he snapped, thrusting his face aggressively towards hers.

Rose had no idea what he was talking about but, whatever it was, it was a darn sight safer than being accused of being no use to him because she was worried to death.

'You come to work, Rose, and you leave the love struck business behind in the bedroom!'

Realisation dawned and she opened her mouth to protest but then immediately thought better of it. There had been too much entanglement of her private life with her professional one recently and it was time for her to re-define the boundaries.

'Right,' she agreed readily and was treated to an even more thunderous frown before he pushed himself away and strode back to sit behind his desk.

'Cancel everything in my diary for the week ahead. I don't anticipate being out there longer than a couple of days but there's nothing predictable about the weather.'

'It's a ridiculous plan, Gabriel.'

'Thank you for your opinion. That will be all for the moment.' Somehow it seemed all wrong for his perfect secretary to have spent the night making passionate love to a man she barely knew. Because she hadn't denied it and he knew her well enough by now to know that if she was innocent of the accusation she would have denied it vigorously. Despite the change in her appearance, her sense of morality was too ingrained.

What she got up to or didn't get up to was, he acknowledged, a side issue. There were far bigger problems on his plate for him to give even a passing thought to Rose in the arms of a man, but he was finding it hard to rid himself of the image.

'How was your theatre date on Friday?' he heard himself asking. 'Fun?'

'What?'

'Theatre? Last Friday? You were going to see *Les Miserables?*'

'Oh. Right. Yes, of course. It was brilliant. Thank you.' Rose wondered where the change in conversation was leading and decided that it was probably just his distracted way of taking his mind off the enormous problem of how to tackle several hundred thousand pounds worth of incomplete bricks and mortar that was in imminent danger of being reduced to rubble. In truth, he barely looked as though he was paying her the slightest bit of attention.

It was a learning experience to realise that this was the man whose possible brush with any danger whatsoever was enough to reduce her to a state of witless tension.

'Joe was wonderful company!' she added, more to remind herself that there *were* actually normal, genuine, caring men on the planet, men who were far more worthy of her care and attention than the brooding powerhouse sitting in front of her.

Which means what? Gabriel wondered. The mere fact that he was *wondering* was enough to rouse anger at his own weakness. Unlike most men, he had never personally found women to be an incomprehensible species. On the contrary. The women he had wined, dined and bedded had been as transparent as glass. Rose was of a different genetic make up. One minute she slotted nicely into the pre-packaged box in his head, the next minute she had wriggled out and was proving wrong everything he had thought of her. From capable, controlled, private, inoffensive but slightly frosty secretary to sexy, new style, new look, suddenly ambitious woman with a core of fire, to, apparently, vamp who would sleep happily with a man who barely registered as acquaintance on the *How Well Do I Know You?* chart.

Did she really imagine that he wanted to conduct a conversation about her nobody date when he had important things on his mind?

'Is that female speak for *the perfect gentleman?*' Gabriel asked sneeringly.

'I take it that in the world of Gabriel Gessi, being the *perfect gentleman* is considered something of a crime?' Rose asked, bristling.

'Not a *crime.* Just ever so slightly…*dull*…'

'Joe is anything *but* dull, as a matter of fact…'

'There's no need to sound so defensive, Rose! I believe you! I can't imagine you would ever go out with someone as dull as dishwater. In fact, I can't imagine anyone dull would know how to handle you!'

'I don't need *handling.* I'm not a wild animal.'

'Well, you're not most men's idea of submissive either.'

'I am *not* going to get embroiled in this.' She took a few deep, steadying breaths. Until recently she had been submissive enough. At least on the work front. 'I don't want to discuss Joe.'

'You're the one who brought him up.' Gabriel shrugged. Perfect gentlemen didn't usually seduce their women into bed on date number one. So, whatever it was that had constituted their brilliant evening, it probably hadn't been a vigorous romp in the hay, and that was enough to put him in a better mood. 'But you're right. There are more important things to discuss. When you've sorted out flights and transfers, let me know immediately and also I'll need to have an hour or so with the boys in Finance, just to brief them on a few things they'll need to handle in my absence…'

His attention was already far away from the subject of her and her date. Having chipped in with his uninvited opinions, he had now forgotten the matter and was moving on. Typical. He rattled her cage and, while her teeth were still clattering from the shock, he had disappeared off into the distant horizon, leaving her to gather her untidy, scattered thoughts.

'I still don't know what you think you can do over there if a hurricane *does* strike,' Rose said, standing up and once again focused on the dreadful thought of Gabriel caught up in the elements. 'You might joke about camping on a beach but there's nothing funny about the situation, Gabriel.' Her heart squeezed painfully. 'People die in situations like that and it's just stupid to pull a macho stunt and think you can deal with it.'

'Somebody has to,' Gabriel told her seriously, 'and it's not going to be the foreman on the site. My venture, my responsibility.'

'That is *so* bloody typical of you, Gabriel Gessi!' Rose finally exploded from a combination of sickening fear and sheer frustration. 'You think you can handle anything! That you're invincible and *you're not!*' Tears wanted to spring from the back of her eyes but there was no way that she would allow that level of emotion to seep through. 'It's not a sign of *strength* to never admit to being weak!'

'You're worried about me?'

'Of course I'm worried about you!' And, just in case her response was too dramatic, 'Anyone would be!'

'There's no need,' Gabriel said gently. He itched to go over to where she was standing in tight-lipped silence and hold her close against him. For once, he wasn't finding it claustrophobic to have a woman openly show her concern for him. 'The building may not be complete but what's there should be structurally sound. It's taken long enough but it's been constructed to hold firm against the elements, even though the island doesn't lie in a hurricane path. I shall have a solid roof over my head. Only one wing will be exposed to the elements and even that will stand. I suspect the electricity and water might fail if the hurricane hits but, aside from that, I'll be fine.' He grinned. 'Doesn't everyone long to get close to nature? Now I have my big chance.'

Rose looked at the devilishly handsome face and sighed to herself. She did believe him when he said that the structure was solid but, even if it wasn't, she knew that he would probably have gone to the island anyway. In another life, he would have been a Formula One racing driver, enjoying the challenge of dicing with death.

'Of course if you're *that* worried,' he purred softly, 'you could always come with me. Damn good opportunity to see exactly how much more work needs to be done on the place instead of relying on emails and reports…'

CHAPTER SIX

THE more Gabriel thought about it, the better he liked the idea of Rose accompanying him out to the island. He was utterly convinced that, hurricane or no hurricane, neither of them would be in any physical danger and somehow the thought of having her for company was very appealing.

'We would probably be able to make some serious inroads into sorting out the niggles that have been blighting this whole business for months,' he pointed out. 'And having you around would mean that I could work twice as fast because I wouldn't have to do any of the transcribing myself. Four days and I reckon we could have the matter under control.'

Rose looked at him as if he had suddenly taken leave of his senses. 'You're expecting to *work* while a hurricane rages outside?'

'We don't know that the hurricane is going to hit the island.'

'But the weathermen seem pretty convinced.'

'Weathermen are notoriously wrong when it comes to reporting on the weather. In fact, in any other line of work the sheer inaccuracy of their reporting would get them sacked on the spot.'

Rose opened her mouth to protest at Gabriel's vast sweeping assumption but he was already moving on, developing his plans out loud.

'Of course, I realise that with this course ahead of you and the glittering prospect of a bright new career, you might no longer have the necessary dedication to tackle a job that's going to take you out of the country…'

'You know I would never give anything but one hundred and one per cent to the job!'

'Except when it happens to fall at inconvenient times…'

'There will be no one on the island, anyway,' Rose pointed out dubiously. Her knowledge of the place was pretty sparse, confined to the brief dispatches she had read over the months, but mostly she knew of the hiccups in the nuts and bolts of the building work and little else. 'Who do you plan on talking to about what's been going on with the site if there's no one there?'

'Of course there'll be people there! You don't think they're conveniently going to disappear while there's a hurricane watch on because they all just happen to have second homes somewhere else, do you?'

Rose reddened and glared at him. 'I'll go and sort the flights out.'

'Book two.'

Rose paused by the door and stared him down, which was a very difficult thing to do when her heart was thumping like a steam engine inside her chest. 'I'm afraid I just won't be able to make it, Gabriel…'

Gabriel's eyes narrowed. 'It's not this man, is it? Getting in the way of your job even though he's only been on the scene for two minutes…?'

'Of course not!' At the back of her mind, she knew there was absolutely no imperative to defend her decisions but Gabriel's pointed silence accompanied by that infinitesimal raising of his eyebrows was enough to get every self defensive mechanism in her body rearing up into immediate action.

'Joe would never dream of being chauvinistic enough to try and dictate how I conduct my working life…'

'No. I forgot. He's the perfect gentleman.' Gabriel grinned and got a well-deserved glower in response.

'I can't come with you because…'

'It *would* be incredibly helpful…'

'Because…' Rose ignored his velvety interruption '…there's too much to do here, especially as I've had to take a bit of time out with all the interviewing…' The pointless interviewing, she wanted to add.

'I'm the boss. I'm excusing you for the next four days. There's too much to gain, if you accompany me, in terms of speed…'

'You could take Ralph… Surely someone on the board would be better served there with you…' At this point she had virtually jettisoned the sensible argument of how exactly work would be conducted if they were having to shore up the building with sandbags or whatever. Hard to transcribe emails in gale force winds and twenty foot waves.

'Somehow I don't think Ralph would be overly impressed at having to play secretary to me out there. Anyway, I doubt his ability to type is as quick as yours… I just don't get it, Rose… You've never had a problem accompanying me on trips before…'

'Not to storm-battered islands in the middle of the ocean…'

'Which brings us back to those damned over-pessimistic weathermen. Why don't you book the passages over and if you do decide to come I would be very grateful.'

He returned his attention to whatever was absorbing it on his computer screen and Rose, taking the hint, left his office, shutting the door quietly behind her.

Okay, she would book the two passages. He had given her permission to change her mind. The wasted fare would be peanuts to him. Not only could his conglomerate absorb it but he could personally absorb it as well and not even miss it from his bank account.

Everything was booked for first thing the following morning. She had checked on the Internet and gathered that the likelihood of the hurricane sweeping over the island was fairly remote. They probably would be able to get some vital work done.

She paused at the easy way she had assumed herself to be accompanying him.

So, she didn't want to go but he was right. She had never complained before about going with him to meetings, overnighting in the same hotel as him. If she made a point of complaining now and refusing to go, his sly little brain would soon start whirring into action and he would either mistakenly assume that she had morphed into a bimbo whose private life was influencing her professional one or, worse, he would think that she was scared to be in his company.

In the very dark recesses of her mind crept another taboo thought. The notion that the weather might defy the odds and she knew, deep down, that if he was to find himself in any trouble she would want to be by his side.

Where that left Joe, perfect gentleman and epitome of everything a mother would like her daughter to bring home, was a question she would deal with later.

Four days wasn't long and it might well be less, depending on circumstances.

It was what she told herself the following morning as she slung clothes into her pull-along suitcase. Neither of them were taking anything that would have to go into the hold. Too much opportunity with the various changes en route for it to go missing in action. Gabriel would also be bringing his laptop computer, although whether they would be able to link up to a phone line was anybody's guess.

In any event, Rose packed notebooks and pens. The old-fashioned tools were often the best under pressure.

Work kept them busy for the better part of the flight to one of the bigger islands. Rose read the reports at a furious pace. Together they discussed what could be done to shore up the naked part of the site if bad weather struck. When they weren't working, Rose feigned sleep. And then the tail-end of the journey was lost in the confusion of changing planes and finally taking a boat over with the boat man reminding them constantly that they were mad to be undertaking a trip when the weather was going to change. Hurricanes rarely affected that particular spot and the man seemed unnaturally enthusiastic about the possibility of one.

By the time they finally hit their destination, Rose was practically dead on her feet. She had started the day at a little before five and had had very little to eat.

Nightfall on the island, in conjunction with very few street lights, meant that she could barely appreciate the scenery. Not that it made much difference when all she wanted to do in the back of the prehistoric taxi as it bumped its way over the single track road was to nod off and go to sleep.

How did Gabriel manage to keep going for so long without any signs of wear and tear? He didn't even look grubby! Maybe because he had chosen his clothes cleverly.

He was saying something to her now and, in reply, Rose yawned widely.

'Not the kind of response I usually evoke in a woman,' he murmured, to which she yawned again and he patted his shoulder, an irresistible invitation for her to rest her head on it. Which she would, she decided. Just for a minute or two, until she became accustomed to the sticky heat which was quite different from the soaring summer temperatures in England.

She awoke to the sensation of the clanking car shuddering to a halt and her eyes flew open.

Horror of horrors, she'd dribbled! There was a damp patch on his shoulder and when their eyes met, he shot her a crooked smile.

'Don't worry. It's human.'

Rose pretended to misunderstand. 'What is?'

'I actually found it quite sweet, somehow innocent, for you to be resting your head on my shoulder and dribbling ever so slightly.'

Rose's mortification followed her out of the car but, as soon as she gazed at the work in progress in front of her, every hesitant self-conscious emotion fell away.

She was staring at something so ambitious and so impressive, even in its half-finished state, that she gasped aloud.

'Like it?' Gabriel was just behind her, bending down to murmur the question into her ear.

'There's still a way to go,' she said prosaically.

'Coward. Why don't you just admit that you love it? It's an architectural adventure.'

'Who designed it?'

'I did.'

'You?'

'No need to look so shocked.' Gabriel lightly ushered her in with his hand under her elbow. 'You're not the only one with a few secrets up your sleeve.'

Rose was too stunned by what she was seeing to argue the toss with him.

The original gloriously opulent hotel with its sprawling network of state-of-the-art condos, which had been the original plan and which, in fact, was still accessible on the computer, along with all the other documents, had been transformed into what appeared to be three dwellings, either very close together or else linked in some way. Each had its own individual turret and encircling them was a broad patio, still in its primary stage but which, he was telling her, would eventually be weatherproof hardwood.

The land which had originally been intended for the condos would become a nine hole golf course—a very challenging nine hold course, he hastened to add, not for the faint-hearted. A short but killer links course, benefiting from the sea breeze that blew along the coastline.

Right at the moment, the sea breeze was still gentle, although the driver had told them that people had already started leaving the island if they could and, if they couldn't, they were battening down the hatches and preparing for the worst, getting tinned food and bottled water in for the duration.

Rose anxiously tried to work out how secure the structure would be in a raging hurricane. It looked pretty solid and almost completely finished in terms of its final build but, since she had no idea about foundations, she couldn't say for sure.

'Anything that can move has been stowed away safely,' Gabriel said, reading the direction of her concern. 'If the worst comes to the worst, there won't be any flying benches or planks of wood.'

'The sky's so blue…it's hard to think that a hurricane might be on the way.'

'I know, but in this part of the world the weather can change in a matter of minutes. Isn't that right, Junior?'

Junior, the driver, was at least seventy. A very sprightly and knowledgeable seventy. They entered the building to a long, informative monologue on the weather patterns of the Caribbean.

Rose was the first to stop and stare. The façade had been impressive enough, but inside was a fertile imagination in full flight. She had expected square, unfinished brick and cement buildings, maybe with the occasional homage to detail that would distinguish them from the run of the mill. Not so. Black and white tiles were the backdrop for a dramatic water feature that dominated the far corner of the entrance hall. The rooms on the ground floor, Gabriel was explaining to a speechless Rose, would be dedicated to the kitchens, the restaurant and all the various domestic necessities that made a place run efficiently, including a health spa. The floor above housed some of the bedrooms and sitting rooms which could be used by the guests at any time of the day or night. The feeling would be one of a home away from home.

'I don't know anyone who has a home like this,' Rose murmured, taking in the detail in the woodwork and the artistry in the way the place had been designed. 'You thought of this *yourself?*'

'I'm a frustrated architect,' Gabriel said lightly, but when Rose glanced across at him he wasn't grinning. 'Leave the bags, Junior, and you head back to your house. Start packing the corned beef away.' He grinned at Junior, who launched into a protest that was swept aside. 'We've got food. We've got drink. We'll be fine. You can come out when the worst is over.'

Rose was dimly aware of this exchange of conversation as she ventured further into the villa, noting that it was in a far more advanced state of completion than she had expected. So much for her fears for Gabriel as he hunkered down in a building with no roof, missing walls and absent plumbing, at the mercy of the unforgiving elements.

At least here everything was finished. The tiled lobby led through to splendid wooden floors, the windows were beautifully dressed with colonial-style shutters, there was paint on the walls and ceilings. All that seemed to be missing was the water from the water feature that spanned one corner of the entrance hall and the prerequisite plants.

'I had no idea the place was fully operational!' Rose said accusingly. 'Where's Junior?'

'Gone to take care of his family.'

Which just left the two of them. Alone. In the urgency of the travel plans and the hectic nature of the trip, Rose had not paused to contemplate in any real depth what the situation would be when they finally made it to their destination. She'd assumed, in her naïveté, that the hotel would be uninhabitable and they would therefore book into whatever inn was available. But the villa was inhabitable, minus anyone else in it. Her heart slowed and for a few seconds she felt giddy.

'He would have stayed. In fact, he would have brought his wife and three of his daughters to take care of us but that really wouldn't have been fair, would it?'

'Of course not.' Lots of empty rooms and just the two of them. Sharing a meal. Waiting for the impending storm. What if the current failed, as it undoubtedly would? She had visions of the two of them, huddled in a dark room with just one another for company. Not an ideal situation for safe, casual chit chat about work. The giddy spell threatened to become full-blown.

'We'd better go and check the kitchens, see what's there and then we'll sort out sleeping arrangements.'

Outside, Rose could hear the sound of the surf and the little noises of night creatures going about their business. It reminded her of Australia, which was a depressing thought because that in turn reminded her of the fact that she shouldn't be here with Gabriel because, actually, she should have left his employ to seek greener pastures elsewhere.

He was already striding off and Rose hastily followed. She felt tired and hot from the long trip but a shower would come later. A shower and a long rest so that she could recharge her batteries for whatever lay ahead the following day.

They passed through various rooms, all in a state of virtual completion.

'I thought you said that there was a lot of work still to be done, that you needed to be here just in case something happened to the structure if the hurricane struck?'

They had finally arrived at the kitchens, which were equipped but in a basic fashion. There was a fridge, obviously one used by the workforce when they were in the villa, and various other cooking utensils, all bearing the signs of use. No oven but something portable on which to cook very simple meals. A table of sorts.

'All this will go, eventually.' He went to the fridge, pulled it open and was pleased to see some perishables, including cheese, eggs and butter. He knew what would be in the cupboards because he had spoken to the foreman as soon as he had decided to go to the island and had instructed him to stock up. Of course, at the time, he had not known that Rose would be with him.

Gabriel was still slightly surprised that she *was* there, although he knew why. Despite her show of laying down laws, Rose was a perfectionist who was deeply devoted to her job. It was simply the way she was built and he admired her for it. Whatever she did, she would do wholeheartedly. He had appealed to her Achilles heel, namely her sense of duty in sorting out what had been a thorny problem for both of them for a very long time. The villa had had its fair share of setbacks and she couldn't resist his plea to accompany him to the island so that they could sort things out. Unlike most other women, actually *all* the other women he had ever known, the fact that a hurricane might rear its ugly head would not have put her off. She wasn't easily spooked.

And she looked bloody amazing considering she had spent most of the day in various forms of travel, not all of them comfortable. The hair which had started out loose was now dragged back into a pony-tail that was in the process of unravelling but still managed to look sexy and she couldn't have been wearing make-up because her face looked as scrubbed as it had before they started the trip. She was also sweetly disgruntled. And probably hungry.

'What will?' Rose gave him a sulky look and wanted to tell him that she didn't really care, at least not at that precise moment in time.

'You're hungry.'

'No, I'm not. I'm fine.'

'Don't be a martyr, Rose. There's nothing more annoying.'

'Oh, right. I've travelled halfway across the Atlantic because I *thought* you needed me to help you sort out this place and suddenly I'm being a *martyr* and getting on your nerves.'

'I'm going to fix you something to eat and you're going to say *thank you* very sweetly and stop being defensive.'

'All *what* will go...?' Rose asked grudgingly, as she watched Gabriel take cans and packets out of cupboards. Fair's fair, she thought. *She* had cooked for him once and so he could jolly well return the favour, especially considering he had manoeuvred her over here on false pretences.

Gabriel glanced over his shoulder at her and, not for the first time since they had left England, Rose wondered how it was that he could manage to look so fantastic after hours of travel. He wore what looked like linen trousers of some indeterminate colour and, although they were creased, they looked *expensively* and *tastefully* creased, and the dark shirt similarly looked *tastefully* dishevelled. Frankly, it was irritating. Especially when she felt like something the cat dragged in.

'These makeshift appliances.'

'I thought you were building a hotel here, Gabriel. I had no idea you had changed the spec.'

'It is still a hotel. Of sorts. A hotel on a far more personal scale than was originally intended.'

'There's nothing on the computer…'

'You probably haven't caught up with all the paperwork. This place is no longer under the umbrella of the company. It's now my personal baby, so to speak.'

'Your personal baby?'

'Of course, it will still remain a rentable option, but that won't be its primary function.'

'You got me over here on a project that has *nothing to do with work?*'

'You chose to come over.'

For someone whose kitchen was full of the latest in high-tech gadgets, he seemed very adept at making do with the basics and was concocting something on the makeshift stove that smelled very good even though it was the product of some cans and a packet of pasta.

Rose realised that he had broken off what he was doing to look at her and she flushed. 'I thought you needed me on a work level.'

'I do. Things still need to be sorted out here.'

'But it has nothing to do with *work.*'

'What's the use in nit-picking, Rose? There are no planes leaving in a hurry. The bottom line is you're here and labouring over whether you should or shouldn't be is a complete waste of time. When we get back to London, I'll make sure to compensate you financially.'

'It's not about the money,' Rose said stubbornly, but now she felt petty and small-minded. And who was she kidding, anyway? She was curious and interested to see the place he had decided to adopt as his own, curious and interested to have that little bit more insight into the man he was.

'Oh, for God's sake.' Gabriel raked his fingers through his hair in pure exasperation. 'Why don't you try taking a little responsibility here, Rose? You knew the plans had been altered. I assumed you'd read the financial reports and worked out that the whole project had been transferred out of the company and into my own private banking.'

'I…' *Skimmed over the financial report.* She had expected something and so hadn't checked to see if things had altered on that front. 'Oh, you're right. I'm here now. So why don't you fill me in on what made you change your mind about…the purpose of this place…?' Amongst his network of other financial concerns, Gabriel owned a small but elite chain of hotels in offbeat places. This island was perfectly suited for the purpose. Out of the way, not a tourist in sight, small enough to be exquisite but not so small that amenities taken for granted were absent. Tourists, Rose had discovered over years of dealing with their complaints, liked quaint, which was a lot different from uncomfortable. Quaint was the overhead fan with the air-conditioning option, as opposed to a stand up fan with open windows for added breeze.

'I got involved with the project, simple as that.' He brought over two plates of food. Pasta, some sort of tomato sauce smothered in cheese, chunks of bread, butter. It smelled delicious and, when Rose hungrily tucked into it, tasted as good as it smelled.

'You get involved with *all* your projects,' she pointed out. 'This tastes great, by the way.'

'Glad you think so,' Gabriel said dryly. 'Appreciate it, though. I don't make a habit of cooking for women.'

Rose thought that that was stating the glaringly obvious. Home-cooked meals were on a par with domesticity and domesticity was not something he liked his girlfriends to experience. Fun, yes. Excitement, yes. Domesticity, absolutely no way.

'You were telling me why you changed your mind on this project.'

'We ran into problems about two months ago with the design. I sacked the architect working on it and decided to give it a go myself.'

'Because you're a qualified architect?'

'Because I…' Gabriel looked at her, fork in one hand.

'Because you…?' Rose's gaze was curious.

'I have a degree in engineering.' Gabriel shrugged. 'And art was always something I rather…liked… Or is that not a very macho admission…?'

'It's an extremely macho admission.' Rose could feel her mouth go dry as their eyes met. 'Don't you know that there's nothing sexier than a sensitive man?'

'Is that your way of telling me that you find me sexy?'

'It's my way of saying that art is a wonderful thing to be interested in.' She could feel herself perspiring as his eyes roamed over her flushed face. 'I…I know you like art. I just never realised that you enjoyed it in a practical manner…'

'Art was one of my A levels. Along with maths, French and physics.'

'So you could have been a painter…'

'Not quite.' Gabriel shot her a crooked smile. 'I lacked the creativity, but combined with my maths, and later my engineering degree, I discovered it could be quite practical when it came to design. Of course, there was no place for that in the world of corporate business, but it certainly came into its own when I sacked Jones from this project.'

Rose hadn't realised that she had finished eating until Gabriel rose and took the plate from her, ordering her to sit down while he tidied. After all, he pointed out, she was there out of the goodness of her heart.

'So all of this…is your creation?'

'Most of it. What do you think?'

'Well, I suppose we all need to do something in our spare time,' Rose said prosaically as he seemed in danger of letting her interest go straight to his already oversized ego. 'Tell me about it.'

Rose forgot that she was hot, tired and sticky. Gabriel cleared away the dishes while she sat at the table and hung on to his every word. By the time he had made her a cup of coffee, with long life milk because there was no fresh milk on the island, she was living his dream for the project, wanted to see it eventually as a sprawling ranch-style villa that could accommodate all the members of his extended family, and the rest.

She wanted to ask whether his vision included his own family and kids, but that would have been a question too far.

'Tomorrow's a big day,' Gabriel said in conclusion, after Rose had bombarded him with every question under the sun. 'If the hurricane's going to strike, it'll strike within the next twenty-four hours. We should both think about getting some sleep.'

Rose felt stiff when she stood up. 'I shall need to have a wash or a shower. Is everything plumbed in?'

'Plumbed in and raring to go. As I said, the hold-ups have been irritating and lengthy but the basics are in, which is a blessing.'

He had advised her to bring her own towel, which she thankfully had, and her own soap. Also lots of mosquito repellent. There were no beds, just mattresses on the ground, which had been brought in specially for them. The workmen would use them afterwards, Gabriel assured her, so they wouldn't go to waste. And there was also electricity, although he warned her to expect nothing if the hurricane struck the following day. For good measure, candles had been provided.

After this short speech Rose wasn't quite sure what to expect, but the room he led her to was more than adequate. No furniture, but large and airy with an enormous *en suite* bathroom attached to it. As with the rest of the place, barring the entrance hall, the floor was of rich wood. There was even emulsion on the walls and shutters on the French windows that led directly on to the outside porch.

'When it's up and running,' Gabriel explained, 'there will be hammocks here and there on the porch so that people can relax out of the sun but still in the fresh air.'

'Your idea?'

'With a little input from my sisters, who claim to need relaxation more than me as they have children.' He walked into the bathroom and gave it the once over. 'There's no mosquito net,' he told her, lounging against the wall, 'and no air-conditioning, so watch out for insects. You can burn one of those coils—' he nodded in the direction of the ground by the bathroom '—but they're not one hundred per cent effective. My advice is to sleep with the French windows shut. Just leave a crack in the windows open to allow a through draught and you can leave the door open as well. You won't die of the heat. It cools nicely at night. I'll be up early tomorrow. I'll wake you. You'll probably be tired but we might need to start securing things and getting prepared for the worst.'

'Right.'

'Are you scared?'

'Of what?'

'Creepy crawlies? Night time in a foreign place? The threat of a hurricane?'

Rose shrugged and shook her head. Nothing was as threatening as what she felt in the presence of the man leaning indolently against the wall in front of her. The strangeness of the situation was as nothing compared to the sudden, terrifying knowledge that they were alone in this place.

'Brave lady,' Gabriel murmured and Rose thought she could detect an edge of sarcasm in his voice.

'Not every woman likes playing the damsel in distress.'

'Most don't have to,' Gabriel commented wryly. 'They naturally freak out at the thought of insects and thunder storms... Well...' he pushed himself from the wall and strolled past her '...good night. If you need anything...you know where I am...in the room next door...'

'Thanks, I won't.'

And she would make sure to lock the door, just in case he got it into his head that she was really a damsel in distress underneath it all, that she really needed him to check on her to make sure she wasn't cowering under the sheet in fear of the mosquitoes. He felt guilty, she suspected, at dragging her here under false pretences, whatever he said about the fact that she should have known the situation, and guilt might well make a gentleman of him.

She locked the door and then locked the bathroom door as well, although her shower was quick and cold. The plumbing might be up and running but it wasn't a comfortable experience, although she did feel clean and refreshed afterwards.

She had to stick her wet towel half out of the bathroom window to dry naturally, as towel rails had not yet been fitted, and the ground was wet due to the lack of a door on the cubicle. But the mattress, basic though it was, was comfortable and through the open window the sounds of night-life were oddly soporific.

Rose fell asleep quickly. When she woke up, abruptly, with the prickling sensation that something wasn't quite right, it took her a few seconds to orient herself and make sense of her surroundings, and then it occurred to her exactly what was wrong.

CHAPTER SEVEN

WHAT woke Rose was the stillness. The night sounds, she realised after a few unsettling seconds, had disappeared. Living in London had acclimatised her to a certain amount of noise at night and its absence was eerie.

She stood up. She felt remarkably okay, considering bed had been a mattress on the floor. No aches and pains anywhere.

She drew back the shutters and opened the window. Now the silence was deafening. As was the lack of movement. No breeze. Nothing. Rose shivered and wondered uncertainly what she should do. Wake Gabriel? She knew nothing about hurricanes. She might be spooked but what if this was just a feature of the tropics? Lots of noise between six-thirty and midnight and then at—she picked up her watch which she had adjusted on the plane and stuck it on—it was a little after three in the morning—at a little after three in the morning the comforting noises gave way to complete silence.

Without bothering to think about it, Rose stuck on a pair of jeans, one of two pairs she had packed, leaving on the baggy T-shirt she had brought to sleep in. Somehow it seemed urgent that she get to Gabriel, wake him up, even if his response might just be to laugh at her and tell her to go back to sleep.

His door wasn't locked. In fact, it was ajar and Rose pushed it open to see him sprawled in slumber on the mattress on the ground. This would be the only time she would ever get to catch him off guard and she couldn't resist the opportunity. She forgot the elemental fear that had propelled her into his room and tiptoed to stand over him. Awake, he was compulsively fascinating, with his high octane energy and sinful good looks, and asleep he was no less so. The sheet covered most of him but he had obviously felt the heat during the night and worked his way free of some of the covering so that part of one leg was exposed and most of his upper body.

Rose licked her lips nervously, unable to break the spell as she stared down at his, quite frankly, perfect body. He looked very brown against the white sheets. His chest was broad and muscular and the dark hair was almost a little too masculine for her curious eyes. She gulped and looked away, but all that did was bring her gaze into contact with one leg, also muscular, also with that disturbingly masculine dark hair. She decided right there and then that waking him up was out of the question. She would sidle off quietly and her fear would gradually ease off. She was about to turn away when he spoke. Just like that. His voice ever so slightly amused.

'Are you finished staring or would you like a bit longer?'

Rose nearly teetered backwards in shock.

'I…I *thought* you were asleep!' She managed to make it sound as though he had purposefully tricked her into staring at him.

'I was. Until you came in. What's the matter?' He began sitting up, which was a bit of a disaster because more of his body was exposed to her carefully averted, yet still fully aware, gaze.

'I…I know this is going to sound stupid, but I…I couldn't hear anything and I got a little nervous.'

'What do you mean, *you couldn't hear anything?*'

'Outside. No noise. It's spooky.' Rose laughed nervously. 'I know you're just going to tell me to get back to sleep…'

'What I *am* going to tell you is that you need to look away right about now if you don't want to see more of me than you might have bargained for…' He yanked back the sheet a fraction of a second before Rose could avert her startled eyes. It was long enough for her to realise that he wasn't wearing the pair of polite boxer shorts she had expected. He wasn't wearing a stitch. She gave a little yelp and stepped back just as he levered himself up.

She knew that he was saying something to her, something about hurricanes and their behaviour patterns, but all her mind could focus on was the fact that less than five feet away her very sexy boss was dragging on some trousers while she stood with her back to him and tried hard not to imagine what she would see if she turned around.

'…so we need to go outside and check everything,' she heard him finish up. 'Of course, you can stay put in here but two pairs of hands and eyes would be a damn sight more helpful than one…'

Slowly her fuzzy brain clunked back into gear and she looked at him worriedly. 'What are you saying?'

'I thought I'd just made it clear.' Gabriel paused to look at her as he pulled on a T-shirt. He was still getting over the pleasant sensation of knowing that she was staring at him. It had been crazily sexy. And now she was looking at him, all wide-eyed and feminine, after his quip the night before when she had told him in no uncertain terms that she didn't enjoy playing the damsel in distress. He was very tempted to remind her of her statement but he thought that that might have been pushing his luck too far.

Uppermost in his mind was the fact that they had to go and do the checks which he had anticipated doing during daylight hours. Nevertheless he couldn't stop his eyes from straying just that little bit, noticing that her T-shirt, baggy though it was, still revealed the glaring fact that she wasn't wearing a bra.

'The calm before the storm…' He headed for the door and she followed, even more spooked by the fact that he actually looked concerned. Gabriel was not a man to be easily rattled. But he was moving quickly now, switching on the lights in the house, warning her that the luxury of electricity might not be with them for too long.

'We'll circle the place together,' he told her, pausing only once when they were outside so that he could look around him, as though judging the gravity of the situation from tell-tale signs she was not aware of. 'There should be nothing to retrieve, but you can never tell.'

Rose shivered at the tone of his voice and edged a little closer to him.

With no cooling effect from the sea breeze, it was muggy outside and very dark. The lights inside the sprawling house illuminated a small patch just outside the double-fronted doors which led out to the gardens overlooking the sea, but beyond that was inky-black, scarily black. Rose had never seen anything quite like it. She was accustomed to a certain amount of light pollution that came from living in London. Just as she was accustomed to the constant low level noise.

'It's going to happen, isn't it?'

'You don't have to whisper.' He had brought two torches. She had no idea when he had grabbed those, but they were invaluable now as they fanned them along the walls of the villa, both of them moving quickly and finding, to Gabriel's satisfaction, that everything was as it should be.

'Right. Now, inside.' They had covered the outside in a little under forty minutes. 'There's no phone link here yet so I won't be able to check on the Internet for any updates with the weather patterns, but we'll fill some buckets with water and cover them. Come in handy for having a wash in the morning. We'll also start lighting some oil lamps and candles, but no candles where they can be a fire hazard. Think you can manage?'

Rose wondered what he would do if she said *no*. He hadn't brought her over here to look after her. First and foremost, she was his practical secretary, after all!

'Think so!' she assured him briskly.

'Good girl.'

They hadn't made it back to the front doors when the eerie stillness was broken dramatically by a flash of lightning that forked across the sky and was accompanied almost immediately by a clap of thunder that was loud enough to make her ears ring. And then an ominous sound that grew louder as they ran towards the house, hampered by the fact that they had to dodge the usual building debris that was neatly stacked but still an impediment to a clear path.

'Rain!' Gabriel shouted just as it came, in one gusty, raging downpour that was accompanied by the howl of winds gathering speed.

Rose had never experienced anything like it. In under thirty seconds she was drenched. When she looked to her left, she could see the palm trees bending as though some powerful force was trying hard to suck them out of the ground. She had to battle not to be blown backwards.

They slammed shut the door behind them as soon as they were in the safety of the house, and then Gabriel was moving quickly and purposefully, knowing exactly where to go to find the oil lamps. He had obviously given very detailed instructions to the foreman before they'd travelled over and that didn't surprise Rose. He would have considered everything.

'I know you're probably uncomfortable in those wet things, but let's sort out the lamps here and then we can both go and change.'

Even though his attention was elsewhere, Rose was still horribly aware of the T-shirt clinging to her body, outlining her breasts and leaving nothing to the imagination. She surreptitiously tried to flap it into good behaviour but no chance and she couldn't possibly skulk off to change, not when they were clearly facing an emergency situation that needed all hands on deck.

So she did as she was instructed and tried not to stare down at her soaked body and the way her breasts were visible and bouncing under the fine cotton.

From outside came the terrifying sound of strong winds battering at the walls and the distant noises of objects being hurled around outside, obviously things they had missed in their inspection of the grounds.

She was beginning to feel cold in the wet clothes and she had to make a big effort not to let her teeth chatter. Visions of the sea rising up the incline in one ferocious tidal wave did nothing to calm her jittery nerves.

In a God-given stroke of luck, they had finished lighting the last of four oil lamps when the electricity went, leaving them in total darkness save for the watery light from the lamps.

'Right.' Gabriel handed her two of the oil lamps. 'At least these are lit and there are candles in the bedrooms, although these should do for the moment. You okay?'

No. 'Fine. I'm a dab hand at crisis situations like this!'

In the darkness, she was aware of Gabriel grinning at her. 'When all else fails, a sense of humour is all a person needs to keep going. Keep it up!'

'I'll try but I was never good at being a mascot.'

They had found themselves back in the bedroom. Hers.

'You'll need to change and then we should bunk down in one room. Just in case.'

'Just in case what?'

'Just in case this bad weather really kicks in. A strong hurricane can take the roof off a building, although we shouldn't be in too much danger here. But better safe than sorry. If the situation deteriorates, I don't want to have to come looking for you.'

Rose acquiesced quickly. She certainly didn't want to be on her own just now.

'I'll be in with you in a minute. As soon as I've changed.'

She did. Quickly. Into her other remaining pair of jeans and a cotton T-shirt, with her bra safely underneath. Her wet clothes she laid carefully out on the floor although she didn't rate the chances of them drying in a hurry.

The wind was managing to find all sorts of cracks and crevices and the noise was incredible. She almost expected it to sweep through the walls and lift her off her feet, but of course she was safe from that. Even so, it was a relief when she was standing outside Gabriel's room, banging on the door to warn him that she was coming in, relieved to find that he, too, had changed, although into boxer shorts and a T-shirt.

'You're going to be comfortable trying to sleep in *that* get-up?'

'I'll be fine! Shall we get my mattress in?'

'Give me a minute.'

Literally a minute and back he was, having hauled her single mattress into his room and plopped it alongside his.

Now, suddenly, the comforting presence of another body next to hers when the whole world outside seemed to be going mad, didn't seem like quite such a brilliant idea.

'You look green,' Gabriel said. 'Don't worry. The building won't collapse around our ears. You forget that I've overseen everything from the foundations to where the walls go, and that I know quite a bit about the structure of buildings and what makes them solid.'

Rose was quietly relieved that he had misinterpreted her sick look. She was also heartily relieved that the only lighting in the room was from two oil lamps, the other two having been dimmed to their lowest level and placed in the bathroom.

'Do you want anything to eat?' he asked, interrupting the disastrous train of her thoughts and she shook her head.

'Okay. In that case, you definitely need something to drink. Wait here.'

He didn't give her time to argue, not that she was going to. She could feel exhaustion creeping over her, but the sickening anticipation of lying down next to him was a more powerful force and promised to keep her eyes wide open for what remained of the night. She didn't make a habit of drinking but she sure as hell figured that there couldn't be a better time for a glass or two of whatever he managed to rustle up.

It was dark rum. And soda water, both of which were in plentiful supply. The workmen weren't allowed to drink on the premises, he told her, but he doubted that held true when they slept there most nights. He had brought the bottle in along with six plastic bottles of soda water and two glasses.

It tasted great. She drank the first one quickly and the effects were pleasantly immediate. Her nerves were beginning to do a disappearing act. In fact, after her second drink, it felt fine to be sitting cross-legged on the mattress, facing him, chatting about their experiences of being caught up in bad weather. Since Rose had precious little, most of the chat came from him and she was more than happy to listen to him as he talked to her. The deluge clattering down against the walls and on the roof and the angry roar of the wind as it gusted along the coastline were a lot easier to bear after some alcohol.

Eventually, Rose yawned.

'Sleepy?'

'Suddenly.'

'You'll never get to sleep in those jeans, you know, and as soon as you do, you'll wake up because you'll be too hot.' He fiddled with the base of the oil lamp and dimmed it so that the room was plunged into near darkness. He had slipped under the sheet, his own sheet, and Rose felt safely tucked away from him.

'And as soon as you realise you're hot, you'll also realise that they're not quite loose enough to allow you to breathe easily and then you'll spend tomorrow feeling like hell because you've had a sleepless night.' He yawned widely and rolled over on to his side with his back to her, leaving her to ponder, in a very unfocused manner, his words of advice.

She waited a while, thinking that, yes, the jeans *did* feel very tight, now that he had mentioned it. It also felt ridiculous to be trying to sleep fully clothed. It was a psychological thing, of course, but once she got it into her head that she was uncomfortable, she couldn't rid herself of the notion that she wouldn't get a wink of sleep unless she took the damned trousers off.

So she did, as unobtrusively as she could. And, while she was at it, she also removed her bra and breathed a little sigh of relief. Both items she placed very carefully next to the mattress, within easy reach for when she got up to stick them back on.

Gabriel, she could tell, was already asleep. She could see it in the rhythmic rise and fall of his shoulders, and her own eyelids were beginning to droop.

The alcohol was working on her like an anaesthetic. She could almost physically feel it drugging her into slumber and then she was gone.

Peace lasted all of an hour and a half. Then came her need to go to the bathroom, something she had failed to take into consideration when she had been happily allowing the rum and sodas to relax her.

The wind was still howling. Rose was tempted to grope her way to the window and peep outside, just to see what was going on, but that would risk waking Gabriel, which was something she intended to avoid.

So she made do with going to the toilet then, with just the flickering light from the oil lamp, her wandering eyes fastened on the one thing she didn't want to see. Right there above the door was something the size of a small saucer, and it was alive. Motionless but alive. And hairy. The sound of the storm outside was nothing compared to the pounding of her heart. Could spiders *smell* fear? she wondered. Like sharks?

She washed her hands. Then, and she didn't know how she managed to achieve this, she tiptoed across to the door, one eye on the spider, the other on her flight path, yanked it open and literally leapt on to the mattress, colliding with Gabriel, who awoke with the sudden alertness of a cat.

'What the hell is going on?'

'There's a tarantula in the bathroom!' They both spoke at the same time but her shriek was definitely a few hundred decibels above his.

'*Get up!*' Rose demanded frantically. 'You have to go and kill it! Now!'

'You mean before it kills us?'

'It's not funny, Gabriel!' Rose felt close to tears. 'I have a…real fear of spiders.' She imagined it crawling out of the bathroom and scurrying across the wooden floor to her mattress and she broke out in nervous perspiration.

'Okay. You wait here.' He levered himself up, glanced around for something, finally settling for one of the glasses, and disappeared into the bathroom, taking care to close the door behind him.

In his absence, Rose huddled as tightly as she could in her sheet and tried not to think of small, furry creatures finding their way underneath it.

Where was the calm, practical secretary *now?* She groaned to herself. She could barely look at him as he exited the bathroom with a grin on his face. Not that she could actually *see* the grin, but she knew it was there from the lope of his walk.

'Where is it?' Rose asked in a small voice. 'I'm sorry. I'm not being much help so far, am I?'

Gabriel lay down and turned to face her. 'I put it through the window. It was more scared of me than I was of it.' He lightly stroked her hair away from her face and Rose didn't tense up as she normally would have. 'I know you don't like being the damsel in distress, but there's no need to apologise for being afraid of a spider. You're not the exception. Most people are afraid of spiders.'

'Except you.'

'I fear nothing.'

That drew a smile from her, but only for a second, then she sobered up and said quietly, 'But that's not why I'm here. To be a burden that needs looking after—scared of spiders, scared of thunder and lightning. I'm not functioning properly at the moment, I'm afraid.'

'Why is that, I wonder? Maybe you're homesick.' Gabriel had never been so intensely aware of a woman in his life before. If he edged one inch closer to her, he would explode.

'Maybe you're missing what's-his-name…' He realised, with some surprise, that *what's-his-name* had actually been on his mind. 'What *is* his name? Did you ever say? Oh, yes. You did. Joe. Maybe you're missing Joe. Being in love can do strange things to a woman.'

Rose, lulled into a cocoon of security, with the gale force winds gusting outside and the rain as clamorous as hailstones clattering down on a tin roof, was yanked back to reality by the mention of Joe. Joe, whom she had completely forgotten. Joe, perfectly nice and suitable Joe, who was supposed to be her passport to overcoming her feelings for the very inappropriate Gabriel Gessi.

She pulled away, suddenly horrified by her compromising position.

'Can it? Yes, I suppose it can.'

Not the answer Gabriel was hoping for. Not when he was in the process of freely admitting to himself that he wanted this woman, for reasons beyond his comprehension.

'What does that mean?' he found himself asking.

'It means that this conversation is inappropriate.'

'Nothing that's going on here at the moment is *appropriate,* or hadn't you noticed? We're halfway across the world. We're being buffeted by a hurricane outside. We're sharing a mattress on a floor. I'm all but naked and so are you.'

'I…I…'

'Yes?' Gabriel prompted silkily. 'You…what? Want to disagree with something I've said?'

'I don't think we should be having this conversation!' Rose heard the panic in her voice and wondered whether he had detected it as well.

'Why? We *could* talk about work but somehow…I don't think the circumstances are quite right for that.'

'We should go to sleep. Tomorrow will be a long day. Lots to do.'

'I *was* sleeping until you jumped on me.'

'For a reason!'

'But now I'm fully awake and so are you. So let's discuss this sudden love you think you've discovered. I'm curious how it can all happen so quickly.'

'And *I'm* curious as to why you're *curious* in the first place!' Desperation was beginning to lace itself in between the panic but the option of returning to her room was now non existent after the tarantula episode.

'Because it's out of character,' Gabriel told her. 'And anything *that* out of character can't be right.'

'You think you know me, but you don't,' Rose muttered, half truthfully because he sure as heck didn't know how she felt about him.

'You mean you've *always* hopped into bed with men you've only known for a couple of hours?'

'I haven't *hopped into bed* with anybody!' Rose objected and immediately regretted her talent for telling the truth when she saw him smile smugly.

'Now, *that's* more like my Rose.' Some men knew women and Gabriel was one of them. Women loathed being stereotyped. Rose might be sharper, cleverer, funnier and a damn sight more on the ball than the women he had always dated in the past, but she was still a woman. And a woman he wanted. Increasingly. Everything about her had been getting to him recently and lying on a mattress next to her, admittedly under some pretty weird conditions, was not conducive to his attraction abating.

Every primitive instinct in him reared into ferocious life. He had never felt anything like it before. His need to have her, right here and right now, was overwhelming. Accustomed as he was to being in control, the sensation of suddenly being swept along on a roller coaster ride of desire was strangely erotic.

'Because I'm dull?' Rose snapped.

'Anything but.'

'I haven't slept with Joe because we're still in the process of getting to know one another.' She wondered how this situation fitted in with her getting to know another man. And, never mind the situation, how her feelings of suppressed excitement at lying next to Gabriel fitted in with her plans for moving forward with her life, trying on a bit of healthy dating for size. How was she ever going to progress any relationship with a man if her body was still so stubbornly and frantically aware of her boss? How? 'I don't believe in rushing into things. Not if they're to last.'

'And you think what you and some man you've spoken to a couple of times have is *going to last?*'

'Why not?' Rose said defensively. She was finding it impossible to tear her eyes away from him and the soft, lazy drawl of his voice seemed to drown out the chaos of the weather outside. How was that possible? she wondered. And how was it *fair?*

'All relationships have to start *somewhere,*' she whispered. She turned away abruptly and lay on her back, staring upwards at the ceiling. He hadn't laid a finger on her but he might as well have, because her body was responding to his proximity with a mind of its own. Her breasts ached and the moistness between her legs was a shameful reminder of how insanely attracted she was to him. She knew that she was breathing heavily and quickly but she didn't care because it was a feat in itself to have broken the mesmerising spell of his gaze.

'No truer word was ever spoken,' Gabriel murmured.

The soft, feathery touch of his finger on her arm made her swivel to face him.

'What…are you doing?' she croaked.

'Touching you. Do you like it?'

'No.' Rose felt faint.

'Yes, you do.' Gabriel's voice was as soft as silk. 'Every relationship has to start somewhere. You're absolutely right.'

'I don't know what you're talking about, Gabriel.' Her words were punctuated by the sound of the shutters being blown back as the gale force winds ferociously tried to attack the inside of the villa. Gabriel jumped up and even for him it was a struggle to secure them back into place. When he was finished he turned to her, arms folded, and walked towards where she was now half sitting up on the mattress.

'I'm going to check on the rest of the place,' he told her, 'make sure that everything's as secure as it's possible to be.'

'I'll come.'

'No.'

'But…'

'If anything needs securing, you won't be able to help with it. I'm no chauvinist, but even I have to acknowledge that I'm probably going to be better at doing something that requires brute strength.' And besides, he thought to himself, he didn't want her putting on her secretarial hat. He didn't want her sticking on her jeans and gathering herself together. He wanted her warm and wide-eyed and lying next to him. He wanted…

He could feel his body responding to the thought of what he really wanted.

'I'll be half an hour. You stay here.'

Right, Rose thought, as soon as he had left the room. Time for a think. Time to get the brain processes into gear. Put some clothes on. Maybe even drag the mattress back into her room.

She might be scared of errant tarantulas but how much scarier was the thought of Gabriel returning, touching her, talking in that low, husky voice that made minced meat of all her good intentions?

She groaned softly and her hand strayed to where her cotton underwear was mortifyingly damp. Just talking to her—that was all he had done—had left her body throbbing and on fire. One touch there and she knew she would fall helplessly off the edge into mindless orgasm.

No!

Before she could dwell on the heat coursing through her body and on her own craving to have him quench it with his touch, she sprang to her feet and began dragging the mattress towards the door. It was pretty heavy and cumbersome. He had made it seem lightweight when he had dragged it through, but then, as he had said, he was equipped for the heavy duty stuff.

She had her back to the door and was busily trying to get some sort of grip that would turn the unwieldy object into something more manageable, when he spoke and Rose jumped in shock.

'What are you doing?'

Rose blinked in confusion. 'I thought you were going to be gone for at least half an hour? Checking that everything was nailed down?' She was still clutching one tip of the mattress and noticing that he was damp, probably caught out by the rain in one of the rooms. His black hair glistened.

'Everything's nailed down. What are you doing?'

'I'm going back to my room,' Rose mumbled. 'I think it's for the best.'

'Mind if I ask why?'

Rose dropped the mattress and it thudded against the back of her legs, making her stumble. Unless she suddenly developed the secret of body displacement, there was no way she was going to leave the room, not while Gabriel was standing in front of the door, arms folded, as immovable an object as she had ever set eyes on.

'Because the situation seems to be getting a little out of hand.' Rose aimed for her usual crisp voice but it had deserted her. In its place, was something nervous and unsteady and her eyes skittered away from his face.

'I didn't come over here…to…for…' Her words faltered and she cleared her throat. 'The weather's making us both behave out of character and…'

'The weather has nothing to do with it,' Gabriel said dismissively. 'And we're behaving perfectly in character…'

'I don't know what you mean,' Rose said faintly.

'You can scuttle back to your room, Rose. I'm not going to stand in your way, but make no mistake—we want one another. There's no use you pretending that you've got the perfect man in the background. He might be perfect but he's not perfect for *you* or else your whole body wouldn't quiver when I touch you.'

'How dare you?' Rose said weakly. 'That's simply not true…'

'No? Then you wouldn't mind if I put it to the test…'

Rose's mind shrieked a frantic, *Yes, yes I would mind!* But when she opened her mouth, nothing came out. Worse, her eyelids fluttered and, as his mouth touched hers, every bone in her body seemed to turn to water. That probably explained why she found herself leaning against him and why her hands curved upwards around his neck, drawing him down to her as she hungrily, *greedily,* returned his kiss.

Nothing had prepared her for this. That first kiss had been a taster but this was the real thing. He had told her that he wanted her and, just in case she was in any doubt, his kiss was putting paid to that.

His tongue invaded her eager mouth and his hand was on her waist, making sure that she was pressed against him so that she could feel the hardness of his arousal.

Rose whimpered and, when he drew back slightly, she moaned, wanting him back.

'Do you still want to go back to your room?' Gabriel murmured. 'Because, if you do, then tell me now, right now. And I'll take the mattress in for you. But if you stay, then…' He left his sentence unfinished but Rose knew exactly what he meant. If she stayed, then there would be no turning back. They would make love and to hell with what came afterwards, to hell with reality waiting just around the corner. He was giving her the opportunity to change her mind.

'What about…tomorrow…?' She had to ask the question and she didn't mean *tomorrow* in the literal sense. He understood immediately.

'For me, tomorrow is a bridge to cross. But not now. Too much planning for tomorrow dilutes the chance of enjoying today. But that's me. For you…decide now, Rose.'

Rose realised that she knew him too well to escape his meaning. Strip away all the waffle about bridges and enjoying todays…he was telling her to either give in to lust and enjoy the moment because there would be nothing else forthcoming, or else abandon the exercise while he was affording her the chance.

Rose met his eyes steadily and then smiled ruefully. 'But I'll always blame it on the weather,' she murmured before reaching up to touch his face against the palm of her hand.

CHAPTER EIGHT

WORLD WAR THREE could have been happening outside. In terms of the weather, World War Three probably *was* happening outside, but Rose was unaware of it. Gabriel pushed the mattresses back together and then turned to her.

'Don't take anything off. I want to undress you. It's been my fantasy for a while.'

'Has it?' Now *that,* Rose thought, was a truly sexy remark and not one she had ever thought she would hear, least of all from Gabriel, the object of her own fantasies for as long as she could remember.

'Oh, yes,' he murmured. 'You have no idea how erotic some of your buttoned-up suits can be.' He circled her waist with his hands and then, slowly, oh, so slowly, pushed up her T-shirt, savouring every minute of her gradual exposure. First her stomach, silky smooth and flat, then, he drew his breath in swiftly, her breasts, full and perfectly formed with big rosy nipples that begged to be taken into his mouth.

He thought of her, sitting in front of him in his office, legs crossed, notepad on her knee, the epitome of sensible efficiency. When he equated the image with the woman standing in front of him, half naked now as he carelessly tossed the

T-shirt on the ground, groaning as he took her breasts in his hands, he had to will himself to go slowly.

He led her towards the makeshift bed, wishing that he could make love to her in his own king-sized bed in his house. Then he thought that there were lots of other places he would like to have made love to her, not all of them feasible, so a couple of mattresses on the ground was no big deal.

And the storm outside lent a certain something to the ambience.

He got undressed when she was lying on the mattress, gazing up at him. He had never been the sort of man who gloried in his good looks but it was a hell of a turn-on to be performing a strip tease of sorts in front of her.

She was still wearing her panties, white cotton ones. He liked them. In fact, he preferred them to the raunchy, lacy numbers he had encountered in the past, the sort of knickers that left very little, if anything, to the imagination. For the first time ever, he wondered why women seemed to think that obvious won over simple when it came to underwear.

He lowered himself gently on to her. He would take this very slowly. He would savour every leisurely minute of it. And he would start with her mouth, her full, inviting mouth.

Under him, her breasts were soft. He would get there later. The anticipation was excruciating.

Having him lie on her, feeling him hard against her thighs… Rose knew, without a doubt, that she was doing the right thing. At least for the moment. The years, she could now see, had tipped her infatuation into something much, much deeper, and while for him this would only be a physical act, for her it was everything. She moaned softly as his mouth found her neck and he trailed feathery kisses down to her shoulders. When he reached her breasts she squirmed and then sighed blissfully as he began suckling on one aroused nipple, drawing it into his mouth, tasting it the way someone would taste an exquisite morsel of food.

The storm inside her was raging. Even with the savage noise of rain and wind, she could hear herself groaning as she writhed under his exploring mouth.

He was in no hurry. He seemed prepared to linger over her breasts for ever. Rose had always been self-conscious about her body. Her face was average, which was something she could handle, but her breasts were too big. She had been an early developer and had never quite recovered from the shame of being the first in her class to get a chest, and a sizeable one at that. That she had been slim at the time had only made matters worse. So she had put on weight. What couldn't be hidden could at least be camouflaged. Her weight had, in turn, made her self-conscious in front of men and she had never really relaxed or enjoyed sex with the partners she had had, all two of them.

She was making up for lost time. She didn't feel an ounce of shame or modesty as Gabriel continued his attentions to her breasts and when he raised his head and told her that she had the most beautiful breasts he had ever seen, she felt heady with pleasure.

'Fantastic nipples,' he murmured, rising up to kiss her and at the same time pressing himself against her sensitised, swollen clitoris so that she shuddered in swift, immediate response. 'I could lick them for ever. Did you like me doing that?'

Rose nodded and he nuzzled into her ear. 'Then why don't you tell me…?'

'I did. Like it. You know I did.'

'Do I?'

'You should and in case you're in any doubt… I loved you

licking my nipples, teasing them, playing with them with your tongue…'

'Good.'

Rose felt him smile against her neck.

'Now I'll just go and do a bit more exploring before I get you to talk dirty to me again…'

He did. He massaged her breasts, enjoying the weight of them in his hands. Women tended to be too skinny. Rose had lost weight, yes, but she still maintained her curves. There were no ribs showing and she was magnificently well endowed. He hadn't been lying when he had told her that he could spend for ever playing with her breasts. He could.

He nipped the tip of one nipple between his teeth, drawing a pleasingly vocal response from her, and then he felt her gasp as he edged his way lower, circling her belly button with his tongue.

He placed both his hands firmly on her hips and then he was there, breathing in the sweet, musky scent of her womanhood through the cotton briefs.

Rose grasped his hair and tugged him to look at her.

'You can't…'

'Have you never…?'

'I…No…'

'I promise you, I'll do nothing you won't enjoy…' Gabriel focused his mind. He was so close to the edge that he had to physically pause for a few seconds just to get a grip. Never before had he felt so out of control in bed. He gazed up briefly at her. Her back was arched, her head thrown back and her breasts were heaving as though she had run a marathon. He knew exactly how she felt!

She was as close to orgasm. He knew that all he need do was thrust into her and they would both be there. But he wasn't going to do that. Not yet.

He tugged the crotch of the briefs to one side and breathed softly on the fine, downy hair and Rose groaned. When he flicked his tongue along the moistened groove, she wriggled against his hands and then thrust up, offering herself to his eager, questing mouth.

Gabriel tugged down the underwear and it joined the T-shirt somewhere on the ground.

Now they were both naked, flesh against flesh. He parted her legs, hitched them over his shoulders and, amidst the noise of wind and rain, he took her to a place she had never been before.

The sensation of his invading tongue unleashed a wild, unrestrained ecstasy in her. Rose gasped and groaned and she would have come right there against his mouth if he hadn't reared up, sensing the fragility of the moment, and entered her.

Fulfilment was not a long time coming. For either of them. Afterwards, when Rose would normally have felt the need to get back into her clothes, she lay curled into him and sighed. 'Is it my imagination or is the storm beginning to abate?'

'Is that, my darling, all you have to say?'

Did he just call her *my darling?* Was that how he talked to *all* his women after they had finished making love?

'What would you like me to say?' she teased, curling her arms around his neck and sliding against him. Even in the aftermath of their love-making, she could still feel him stir in arousal, and that gave her a delicious, heady sense of power. That she could do that to him!

'You could tell me that the earth moved…'

'No…I don't think it would be morally responsible for me to inflate your ego even more than it already is…'

Gabriel laughed under his breath and brushed her lips with his. 'So tell me now that you're still interested in what's-his-name.'

Rose stilled. 'Is that why…you…because you wanted to prove that I found you more attractive?'

'What sort of man do you think I am?' Gabriel asked. 'I wouldn't be above lecturing to you on your choice of man but I would never sleep with you to prove a point. What I don't want is for you to wake up in the morning and tell me that we have to pretend that none of this happened so that you can pretend to be interested in someone you obviously don't care much about.'

'I do like Joe!' She was, however, finding it difficult to even remember what he looked like. The blond hair and blue eyes which had impressed her because of their boyish charm had been completely obliterated by a man with devilishly dark good looks and a sexy charm that could turn any woman's head.

'But you're not attracted to him. Forget about how *nice* it is to take things slowly. Fast and furious…' he gave her a slow, crooked smile that made her toes curl '…is the mark of physical attraction…'

Rose would dearly have liked to disagree but how could she? 'Fast and furious isn't a good thing all of the time,' she said wistfully. It only worked when it was part of a developing relationship, when the fast and the furious eventually matured into joy and contentment and all the silly little things that Gabriel wanted nothing to do with.

'Helluva lot of fun, though.' Gabriel stroked her thigh and then slipped his hands between her legs so that he could cup her womanhood in a gesture that was almost territorial. And, much as she hated admitting it, very pleasurable.

'And the only reason I want you to admit what you feel for me is because I selfishly want us to carry on enjoying this…'

For how long?

'You're my boss.'

'And so can tell you what to do...hmm...?'

Rose couldn't help herself. She felt her lips twitch. 'Only when it's to do with work,' she said gravely.

'So if I tell you that we're going to make love again...?'

'I might agree or I might not...' But already his fingers were gently exploring her, turning her brain to mush. She closed her eyes and reached down, taking his erection in her hand and sensuously massaging it, then she pressed it against her so that they could be yet more intimate.

'What about if *I* tell *you* that we're going to make love again...?' Rose murmured wickedly. 'Would you be prepared for the shoe to go on the other foot?'

'Absolutely. I'm a feminist. More than prepared to take orders from a woman...'

Later, after a long and lazy bout of love-making, during which they touched and caressed each other everywhere, exploring each other's bodies with the fascination of kids opening presents at Christmas, they fell asleep.

When Rose next stirred and opened her eyes, it was to find that Gabriel was no longer in bed with her and sunlight was doing its best to stream through the wooden shutters that had blown open the night before in the high winds.

Then memories of the night before flooded her mind and she lay back for a few seconds savouring them.

Cold reality, just a heartbeat away, had her dashing to the bathroom so that she could get changed before Gabriel returned from wherever he had gone. They may have made wild, abandoned love but the extraordinary circumstances had disappeared and she didn't want him to return, perhaps regretting his actions of the night before, to find her lying in bed dreamily waiting for him to return.

She realised that she was ravenous, though where they

were going to get food she had no idea. Just as she had no idea what damage had been done to the exterior of the villa, or to the island, for that matter.

She dressed quickly in a small silk skirt, several variations of which she had purchased during her time in Australia. She had brought them with her because they could be rolled into a small ball and unrolled back to their pristine state—and a blue T-shirt. She would have worn slippers but, not knowing what sort of destruction she would find outside, stuck on her flip flops as an afterthought.

The body of the place seemed intact, as she hurriedly left the bedroom and made her way to the front door. Somehow debris had found its way in, but there appeared to be no structural damage. When she ventured out, the scene was slightly different.

Rose stood and gaped. Raging storms were not part of the English weather pattern. She had never witnessed firsthand what destruction their wrath could unleash so it was a shock to look around now and see the uprooted trees, the branches transported and scattered across the lawns, the detritus of building work that had managed to escape its confines and be blown to all four corners. It seemed incredible that the sun was now shining and the sea was blue and calm in the distance. From her vantage point, she couldn't see the beach but she could imagine that it was as littered as the gardens higher up here were.

Then, glancing to her left, she spotted Gabriel, deep in conversation with two local men who were gesticulating and laughing. He wasn't looking in her direction and Rose took a few seconds to appreciate his immense physical appeal. He was wearing a pair of low-slung khaki shorts and an off-white T-shirt with some indecipherable logo on the back. He looked casual, relaxed but, at the same time, totally in command. The two dark men were both shorter than him and were nodding now and pointing. Even from here, Rose could read the deference in their body language.

She took a deep breath and walked over to where they seemed to be inspecting the distant horizon, not forgetting that her role on the island was one of a practical nature, even if last night had blurred it wildly beyond recognition.

She also couldn't allow herself to forget that sex, for Gabriel, was not an indication of anything meaningful, at least not according to *her* definition of meaningful. He might not even want to remember what had occurred between them the night before and, even if he did, he certainly would not expect her attitude towards him to have changed substantially.

Either way, Rose was going to be braced for all eventualities.

Most of all, she was going to be adult about everything. She had slept with her boss and, yes, it had been blistering, but that didn't mean that she would allow it to scramble her brains.

She got closer and hid her growing anxiety under an easy smile.

As soon as Gabriel smiled back, she knew that at least he wasn't going to look at her with disgust at her behaviour the night before and, when he pulled her towards him and slung his arm over her shoulder, Rose tried hard not to read anything into it. This wasn't about love and commitment, it was about a man whose needs had been satisfied and who anticipated further satisfaction of those needs.

She remembered just how blissfully satisfied her own needs had been met and relaxed into his casual embrace. After a while, it seemed natural to be pressed against him and she actually began paying some attention to what was being said.

It seemed that however frightful the destruction appeared to her, the island had actually only received the tail-end of the hurricane. The brunt of it had swung away from the small island, reserving its devastation for American shores. Hence no real loss of buildings and the roads, or rather the one main road and its few tributaries, were intact. Electricity would be back up and running by mid-morning, they were assured, and the clean up programme would only take a couple of days.

It was treated as more of an irritation than anything else. When she worried aloud how the gardens would be cleared of the debris, she was told that it would be taken care of. Most of the workforce would be back by the following morning and they would see to it that everything was sorted.

Wilson, the foreman, was neverendingly optimistic about the timescale involved in the clearing up and even more optimistic about completion of the project. While the boss man was over, he said, they could go through what was left to do, although if he had a look around he would see that there was very little. They could take a boat over to the mainland, choose some of the fixtures and fittings. By Christmas, he told them, everything would be ready. They could come and have a little holiday there, enjoy the sunshine.

Rose thought that by Christmas the chances of them still being together bordered on the unimaginable, although Gabriel, ever diplomatic, was making all the right noises.

By the time they had concluded their conversation with Wilson, Rose was beginning to feel hot. And very hungry. It was nearly eleven. They had not actually got to sleep until the early hours of the morning and she had slept the sleep of the drugged. Heaven only knew what time Gabriel had got up!

'I'm sorry I got up so late,' was the first thing she told him as they headed back towards the villa. 'You should have woken me up.' Just in case he thought that she might want to start taking liberties now that they had slept together.

'You look very sexy,' Gabriel told her, spinning her to face him and pulling her close. 'Did you bring that skirt to turn me on?'

'Of course not!' But she barely had time to protest when his mouth crushed hers and her body reacted automatically. She thought, in a daze of sudden, fierce desire, that it was as if she had now been programmed to respond to him. He kissed her and she kissed him back, hungrily, greedily. His hand grazed her breast, like it was doing now, and her nipples became acutely sensitive, so sensitive that she had to stop herself from pushing his hand under her T-shirt so that he could touch her right here and now, in the middle of the garden and in sight of whoever happened to be around.

'You're wearing a bra,' he murmured into her ear. 'Very bad. In this hot weather, the constriction to the blood circulation could be downright dangerous.'

Rose laughed huskily. 'Would you recommend that I take it off?'

'Without further ado. Right now, in fact.'

Rose went red and looked around her. Daring and sexy was fine in the safety of a dark room at night, but daring and sexy in the middle of the day, in full view of spectators, was a different matter.

'There's no one around,' Gabriel drawled, placing both hands on her bottom and grinding her against him. 'In fact, you could wear your birthday suit here safe in the knowledge that you would be free from prying eyes.'

'What about Wilson and the other chap who was with him?'

'Gone. And because we're on a hill top, we have a commanding view of anyone coming up, not that anyone's likely to. They'll all be too busy cleaning up after the storm. They'll have put their binoculars away for the moment.' He slid his hands up, under her T-shirt, and efficiently unclasped her bra. When he saw her shocked expression, he grinned wickedly. 'Not something else you haven't tried, Rose?'

'There isn't much opportunity to strip off in my back garden,' she told him, 'not unless you want an audience.'

'So you've never made love in a public place?'

'No!'

'Close your eyes.'

'What?'

'Close them and go with the flow…'

She did, helplessly allowing him to pull her T-shirt over her head, followed by the circulation-constricting bra. The warm sun felt wonderful against her bare skin, as did Gabriel's sudden intake of breath as he looked at her abundant breasts.

There were a million things he should be doing. For starters, he needed to go into the town, find the local bar and a telephone point so that he could connect to the outside world and start doing some work. Life in London hadn't ground to a halt because there had been a spot of bad weather on an island halfway across the Atlantic.

He also needed to start thinking about doing some basic clearing up. The workmen would take care of the outside, but he would have to ascertain what kind of damage had been done, if any, to the interior of the villa, see what would be covered by insurance and start working on it.

On the other hand…

He could, as he had advised her to do, go with the flow…

What harm was there in playing truant for a day or two? When such irresistible delicacies were on offer?

'Of course, if you're going to enjoy the sunshine, you're going to have to apply some sun cream.' His eyes blazed across her bare breasts, sending a shudder of electric awareness zinging through her. 'Why don't we have a look around the grounds, just make sure that nothing too immediate needs to be seen to, and then we can take some lunch down to the beach? See what damage has been done there. Hmm?' The irresistible delicacies were too powerful a temptation and Gabriel flicked his thumbs over the pert nipples. Rose felt her breath catch.

'Good idea,' she croaked.

'And I'll take my shirt off as well, to keep you company. Now we'll *both* need to apply the sun cream...'

Rose thought that the trip was developing into some kind of wonderful, surreal experience. Having sun cream smoothed over her bare breasts by Gabriel was beyond even her wildest imaginings, and she had had a few of those over the years. She didn't have an idea where the experience would take her but, for the first time in her life, she was living in the moment and for the moment and relishing every second of it.

They strolled around the grounds, which had been damaged by the high winds, but not substantially so. Gabriel pointed out what would need to be done and filled her in on his plans for the place, pointing out what was intended to go where, asking her what she would choose for this place or that place, seemingly interested in everything she had to say.

Her own private preferences spilled over into her professional advice. How could she remain the consummate secretary when she had slept with her boss and was now walking side by side with him in nothing more than a slip of a skirt? How could she be clipped and businesslike when every so often, as though he couldn't help himself, he would turn to her and kiss her, then touch her breasts, caress them, tease her pouting nipples into peaks? Impossible.

And the scene was almost domestic when they prepared a

light lunch together to take down to the beach. They chatted as though they had known each other for years, as indeed they had, Rose reflected. Four years of picking up all the bits and pieces that comprised someone's personality. They had never shared an intimate moment in all those years, but she still felt as though she knew him intimately and she was surprised how much he knew *her* even though she had never allowed him entry into her private life.

The beach was much as they had both expected. On the walk down, Gabriel pointed his plans for converting the rocky ledge halfway down into a sunbathing patio.

'With the perfect view of calm blue sea,' he said.

'Provided the calm blue sea decides to behave itself.' She had become used to her breasts being bared to the sunshine. It felt wonderfully free. Ahead of her, Gabriel was holding a makeshift box in which they had packed some corned beef sandwiches, some water and a packet of biscuits. It was the best they could rummage up at short notice, not that he seemed to mind. For someone who could afford caviar and champagne on a starched linen cloth with a butler to pour, Gabriel seemed surprisingly happy with the scant offerings from the cupboard.

Rose thought that no picnic could have been better. Even the clutter of branches and coconuts on the beach, not to mention the seaweed and coral that had been dredged up from the storm, was enough to ruin the perfection of the experience.

They had managed to unearth a huge blanket of sorts from a cupboard that contained various assorted items of linen, presumably used by the workmen. To Rose, this was as close to paradise as she could possibly get.

'Now,' Gabriel said, settling down next to her on the blanket, 'I think there's still a spot of sun lotion to be applied considering you'll have to take off that very impractical skirt you're wearing.'

He whipped the sun lotion out of the box and squirted a generous amount on to the palms of his hands. Rose gave herself over to the smell of the salty air, the warmth of the sun and the expertise of Gabriel's hands as he stroked the cream onto her breasts, paying a disproportionate amount of attention to her nipples, which were standing stiff and erect. She felt like a luxuriating cat. Whenever she stirred, he told her to lie back and relax. He needed her, he told her huskily, to remain perfectly still if he was to do a thorough job.

'And close your eyes,' he commanded. His need to possess her, mentally and physically, was overpowering. He worked his way down her stomach, massaging the cream into her skin. She was silky-soft and warm from the sun.

But this time, before he could get her to that mindless point of no return, Rose scrambled up and pushed *him* back on to the blanket.

'*I'm* going to make love to *you* this time,' she told him. 'You'll do everything I tell you to do…and the first thing is to keep absolutely still…so that I can rub this lotion over *every inch of you…*'

Rose thought that she could easily get used to making love in a public place, or at least in a deserted cove on an island in the middle of the blue ocean. With this man. The man she loved and always would love to the ends of the earth.

She didn't want to think beyond the feel of the blanket under her, the sound of the sea, gentle and docile now as it lapped against the sand, the sensation of the salty breeze on their bodies.

If Rose could have captured that moment in a bottle and hung on to it for ever, she would have because she knew that, once it was lost, it was lost for all time. They would never recapture it again.

And neither could she exist in a bubble, living from one moment to the next.

'…much as I'd like to…' she finished explaining to him. They had just finished having the most amazing sex and a long swim in water that was so transparently blue and calm that it was mind boggling to think of it churning against the rocks the night before. The sun was rapidly drying them. Staring up at the cloudless azure sky, it was hard to believe that she was having this conversation.

Gabriel propped himself up on one elbow and stared down at her, tilting her face so that she couldn't avoid looking at him.

'Who said anything about living in a bubble?' he asked.

'What do you call this…?'

'I call it…my perfect secretary…' He trailed his finger between her breasts, then circled first one nipple, then the other, finally rotating the sensitised nub of each between his fingers. His eyes lazily feasted on her body, the flat planes of her stomach, already turning a pale shade of gold, the V of soft downy hair that shielded her ripe womanhood. The taste of her still lingered in his mouth.

Rose turned on to her side to look at him seriously. 'But it's not reality,' she persisted quietly. 'Reality is London. Reality is me working for you, coming into the office in a suit, sitting at a desk… Reality isn't the two of us on a beach. This is stolen time.'

'It's only stolen if we leave it here,' Gabriel said, bending to place a kiss on the corner of her mouth. It beat the hell out of him how he could have failed to notice just how perfect her lips were. Full and well defined. Like her. 'When we're back in London things can carry on just as they were before…in the office. And just as they are now with you in my bed.'

But she wanted to spend the rest of her life following it through.

The kiss at the side of her mouth deepened into something more urgent, something that sent her body into immediate meltdown. He pulled her close and she rubbed herself against him, head flung back, nostrils flared in pure sensuous pleasure at the abrasive feel of his hard erection against her. When he rammed his thigh between her legs and began pushing against her, she let her thoughts fly from her head.

And that, for Gabriel, was the end of the conversation. It had literally gone from his mind. Rose knew that with unerring instinct and, for a short while, she was prepared to enjoy what was spectacularly on offer. They made love with an intensity and driving passion that was almost uncontrollable. And they overstayed their original four day plan! Rose was amused because, for Gabriel, it was unheard of. One of the bigger islands was a boat trip and short flight away and they made a day of it, buying clothes and various other luxuries not easily found on the small island.

They would stay for a week, Gabriel told her. Things were being accomplished with the villa and, besides, he needed the break. But the week turned into two. They filled the time with trips to other islands, with a bit of work, with lots of love-making. Together they even chose tiles and accessories, which felt treacherously good. At night, wakeful when Gabriel was asleep and still hot with the imprint of his touch on her, Rose lay awake and pondered her options.

Sooner or later, Gabriel would rouse from his unfamiliar slumber and the call to arms would sound its trumpet. He might like the idea of continuing with their loose affair back in London, but Rose had seen too many examples of what happened to the women he slept with once they had outlived their sell-by date. There was no doubt that, sooner or later, and probably sooner, she would end up sending the goodbye flowers to herself.

And Gabriel had no intention of committing to anything other than a fling. He never had and he never would, not until he found the right woman and it certainly wasn't her.

Rose wasn't going to wait until she became an embarrassment. Nor was she going to try and pin him down with questions of permanence. So when, after two weeks, he began making noises about regrettably returning to work, she did the only thing she could think of doing.

She arranged a phone call to herself. It was a little tricky. It involved a call to her neighbour, instructing her to call and to leave an urgent message. Rose would take it from there. Her neighbour was bemused but blessedly tactful and the following lunchtime, hurrying from the public telephone in the town and wearing an anxious expression, Rose told Gabriel that she would have to leave immediately. An emergency. She had run through the various *emergency* options in her head and had settled on one that couldn't be fixed with money.

'A death in the family,' she told him, packing as she spoke so that she wouldn't be able to make eye contact. 'An aunt—' she crossed her fingers '—very sudden. I must go. Mum… Well, they were close, put it like that…'

The clean break she had anticipated when she had returned from Australia was the only option now. If she didn't take it, she knew that at some point she risked her longing and love for him to be transmitted, like osmosis, out of her and into him and her mind shut down when she tried to contemplate the humiliation of that eventuality.

She would see him back in London, she lied, flinging things into her case, knowing that she would get rid of everything, every last memory. Three days—she laughed, half turning to him—not long!

There was a bittersweet poignancy when he held her from behind, when his hand found those places that could send her soul soaring, when later they made love, enjoying each other for what seemed like an eternity.

She wanted to commit every second of it to memory because it would have to last.

CHAPTER NINE

GABRIEL looked at the photographs of the villa that had been scanned and emailed to him. It was virtually complete. Two and a half months ago it had withstood the fury of the weather and it was as if that in itself had been a catalyst for change. Equipment and materials that had been a source of problems, suddenly became available. The workforce had resumed with renewed effort. Everything had dovetailed neatly into place.

He logged off, sending the twenty-two scenic shots back into cyberspace, and pushed himself away from the desk, swivelling his chair around so that he was staring broodingly out of the window at an ever-darkening day.

The sun, the island, the passion, that night of rain and wind and untamed sex, followed by two weeks of the most liberating love-making he had ever experienced, seemed like a dream. *She* seemed like a dream. And not one Gabriel particularly liked springing into his head when he least expected it. Like now.

Three days after she had left, destination one deceased relative, so called, Gabriel had returned to London to find an empty office and a note.

Don't think this is going to work after all. Please don't contact me. I have arranged for a replacement to start work as soon as you return. Rose.

He could recall word for word what she had written because he had kept the note. He wanted it close to him at all times as a reminder of why any sort of emotional involvement with a woman was a mistake and, yes, he *had* become emotionally involved. Not much, of course, but enough. Too much.

He had followed his natural pattern of replacing her with someone else and had been to the right places with the right six-foot leggy blonde clutching his arm and gazing up at him in awestruck adoration but the formula for forgetfulness had failed to work. He had been distracted and unable to find the energy to court her. She, in turn, had been hurt, mortified and ultimately enraged by his apparent slur to her pulling power.

Gabriel had immediately abandoned himself to work. It would have been successful had it not been for moments like…this, when he found himself grimly subjected to the merciless power of memory.

He had no idea why he couldn't rid himself of the inconvenient image of her popping up in his head like a burr, determined to cause maximum irritation. He assumed it was because, for the first time in his life, he had been wrong-footed by a woman. In every single instance he had always been the one who gave the rueful speech about it being time to move on. Now he had been given a taste of his own medicine and he didn't care for it.

Not, of course, that he had any intention of seeking her out and prolonging the debate. That would have been unthinkable.

Gabriel stood up, stretched and loped over to the window. He shoved his hands in his pockets and stared down at the fading day. Curiosity, a visitor he did his utmost to repel, gnawed tenaciously at the back of his mind. *What was she up to? Had she started that course of hers? Was she seeing anyone?* He assumed she would have taken up again with Mr What's-his-name she had left behind. Thinking about that made his teeth clench in anger. *After she had slept with him, proved to them both that Mr What's-his-name was one hundred per cent lacking in the sexual compatibility department, she would go back to the guy just because he represented God knew what...security, he supposed!*

Gabriel glowered through the window at nothing in particular. So far up, everyone and everything looked pleasantly small. He had had nearly three months to mull over her disappearing act and had come to the conclusion that underneath the sexy, responsive woman beat a heart that longed for security. Of course, he should have guessed that she would have eventually been terrified of having an affair with him, terrified of the limitless freedom of expression he offered her. He had allowed the fiery, sexual, hungry side of her to be expressed and she had decided that it was all a little bit too much.

Serve her right if she ended up living a life of drudgery and monotony with a man she clearly didn't love and never would!

Gabriel sat back down at his desk and glared at the computer screen, which obligingly offered him the relaxing vision of company accounts. He lightly tapped one of the keys and the screen shifted to a draft report that needed checking.

It was just as well that she'd vanished if security was the thing she longed for! Because she would know only too well that he was the last man in the world to offer that gem of a prize to any woman. When the time came he would settle down, but that time was still a long way away! The last thing he needed was a messy situation involving someone who worked for him!

He couldn't help but speculate, with satisfaction, that she was probably bitterly regretting her hasty impulse to leave. When she sobered up, it pleased him to think that she would realise just what a financial package she had tossed down the drain. How many companies were prepared to offer an employee a part-time week at an escalated salary, with no guarantee that said employee wouldn't walk straight out of the door the minute they qualified in their studies? Frankly, none, and especially not considering she would be a recent employee at whatever company she had deserted him to join.

No, he was pretty sure that she would be suffering.

Fortified at the thought of that, Gabriel retrieved the photos of the villa and contemplated them in a less aggrieved frame of mind, flicking through them with satisfaction because the place looked stunning even in its as yet unfinished state. Amazing what painting and decorating could achieve! The landscaping, including the golf course, was yet to be completed but that would be the last thing, and the pools, three smaller ones and one large infinity overlooking the sea, were all but up and running.

He wondered whether he would aggressively advertise it as a luxurious, fairly private resort available to a select handful of people who were willing to basically rent an island or whether he would keep this treasure to himself, lend it out to friends, enjoy it with his family whenever he could find the time. His mother was always angling for a family reunion. She could have her reunions in style there.

He was just beginning to pleasantly contemplate the myriad uses to which the villa could be put when he heard his secretary knock tentatively on his door and he bit back the immediate surge of annoyance.

Karen Davis was proving to be an excellent replacement

secretary if efficiency was the only prerequisite. Unfortunately, on most other counts, she didn't press the right buttons for him. She was too young at twenty, too timid and too reluctant to take the initiative. He told himself that he really had to give her time to grow accustomed to his ways but, whenever he thought like that, he began thinking of Rose and then his mind, freed of its leash, would gallop all over the place.

'What?' he snapped, modifying his voice to a more polite, 'Yes?' when Karen poked her head around his door.

She was thin. Some might call it fashionably thin, but to his eyes, she appeared emaciated. Her hair was very long and she was very pale and had a tendency to look away whenever he spoke to her. She *was,* however, extremely good when it came to the basic mechanisms of her job. Gabriel reminded himself of that and of the succession of no hopers he had employed when Rose had gone to Australia. He tried to soften his expression.

'There's someone here to see you, sir…'

Gabriel had tried hard to make her call him by his first name but she persisted in sticking to *sir* and he had given up. 'Who? There's nothing in my diary.'

'No, well, sir…'

'Tell him to book an appointment through you. I won't be working late tonight.'

Karen hesitated and glanced over her shoulder.

Rose, standing by the door, knowing that Gabriel wouldn't be able to actually make her out, sent her a sympathetic glance back. Poor kid. This was probably her first real job, fresh out of secretarial college, all primed on her computer skills but totally green when it came to handling a man like Gabriel. For a few seconds, Rose forgot that she, herself, felt sick to the stomach with nerves. She gently lifted one finger to her mouth, instructing the girl not to pursue the matter and noticed the flash of relief in her eyes.

Karen nodded at Gabriel, who had already lost interest in the identity of his mystery caller, and quietly shut the door.

'You go home,' Rose said gently. 'And I'll go in.'

'But…' Karen looked back at the closed door and chewed nervously on her lip, 'he'll *kill* me if you just walk into his office. Part of my job is to…you know…vet the people who want to see him…'

'Don't worry about it. I'll make sure you survive the ordeal.' Rose smiled, although her mouth hurt from the effort. 'Don't forget I used to work for him. You're not allowing a complete stranger into his hallowed presence…' Rose had met Karen briefly, on the very day she had returned to clear out her desk. Two days before Gabriel returned from the island. She knew that the young girl had been curious about the suddenness of her employment, but she had been easily convinced by the generosity of the pay package. So hers was a familiar face and if Karen suspected that she might not be an entirely welcome visitor—or else why would she have arrived unannounced for a surprise visit?—she was still happy to follow the path of least resistance. Which involved her making a quiet and speedy departure from the office.

With the outside door firmly shut, Rose drew in a deep shaky breath.

She had spent the past four days trying to predict how she would feel standing right here, inside this office. She could have come earlier in the day, but she knew how the office worked, knew that if she timed it well she would arrive when most of the staff were leaving, which would be the better option.

She had anticipated nerves, but nothing could compare to the wild, sick fluttering in her stomach now.

She smoothed her perspiring palms on her skirt and forced herself to walk towards his door. To knock or not to knock? Rose knocked and got exactly what she expected, which was a, *'Yes! What is it now?'* that paid even less lip service to courtesy than when Karen had knocked previously.

She pushed open the connecting door.

Gabriel didn't bother to look up. He was frowning heavily at his computer screen and, for a few seconds, Rose took the opportunity to just look at him.

His masculine beauty, as it always had, jumped out at her, making the breath catch in her throat, although he looked more gaunt than when she had last seen him on that fateful night before she'd walked out of his life. For good. Or so she had planned at the time.

'Gabriel!' Her voice seemed over loud in the confines of the room but it had the desired effect. Gabriel's head shot up and his expression was one of utter shock, very quickly replaced by one of unreadable stillness.

They stared at one another. To Rose, it felt like hours. Her legs felt weaker and weaker but no way was she going to make her way to the chair, that chair facing him that she used to sit on every time she entered his office to take notes. He was the first to break the silence.

'What are you doing here?' Gabriel pushed himself away from his desk so that he could cross his legs and survey the woman standing in front of him, as nervous as a kitten. The fact that he was still raw from thinking about her only a few minutes ago left a bitter taste in his mouth.

Suddenly Rose found that the speech she had rehearsed wouldn't emerge from her dry, stricken throat.

'Sit down. Although I have to tell you…' he glanced at his watch, then back at her face '…I don't have much time to chew the fat with you. I'm out on a date and I don't think the lady in question would appreciate being kept waiting because of some ex-fling.' There was no date in point of fact. He had cancelled the redhead a few days ago, preferring the option of a bit of solitude and the company of his faithful laptop computer but he didn't flinch at lying. He also knew that dismissing her as little more than an ex-fling would cut and, sure enough, he saw her wince, although, to her credit, she didn't take her eyes off his face.

'So. What do you want?'

'I…I…'

'…you were in the area and thought that you'd just pop in and see how I was doing?' Gabriel raised his eyebrows in patent disbelief. 'Now, why do I find that hard to believe?'

'I know you were probably surprised when you got back to London…and found…found that I had left…' This wasn't exactly how she had planned on broaching the conversation, but just looking at him had thrown her off balance.

'Now, what would give you that idea?' Gabriel asked, with blistering sarcasm. 'Is it because, the night before you left, we had made lingering, passionate love? I was obviously deluded into imagining that you might have wanted to prolong our affair.'

'Things change.'

'When did you decide that clearing off was a good idea?' Gabriel found that he was compelled to hear the answers to questions he hadn't even known existed in his head but obviously did. 'Was it when you made it back to the UK?' He digested the barely discernible flicker of hesitation on her face and pounced with deadly accuracy. 'You'd made your mind up *before,* hadn't you…?' Gabriel intoned slowly. She neither denied it nor did she confirm it and her silence was answer in itself. He had been *used.* Gabriel felt as though he had been hit in the gut with a sledgehammer.

'You don't understand, Gabriel…' Rose could feel herself descending into a quagmire of ugly accusations.

'Oh, I understand all right. Shall I tell you how I see things…?'

'No!'

Rose tried to control her shaking hands but she was mesmerised by his cruel, handsome face. She would hear him out. She didn't have much choice anyway because Gabriel, when the mood took him, was an unstoppable force.

'You became my lover because you were frustrated by the boyfriend you left behind here… Don't ask me why—maybe you found that he couldn't satisfy you.'

Rose gaped at him incredulously. She would have burst out laughing if he hadn't been so absorbed in own ridiculous theory.

'And, as fate would have it, we ended up in bed. Although…maybe fate played less of a part than I think. After all, it was *you* who came running into my bed at the first sound of thunder and it was *you* who fled out of the bathroom from a spider, just coincidentally happening to land on top of me…'

'If you recall, I was also the one who told you that I didn't want anything…to happen between us!'

'An impossibility and you knew it!' Gabriel dismissed. 'You must have known that we would have ended up making love. Tell me, did you give your boyfriend the benefit of what you learnt from me?'

Rose clenched her fists tightly. If she had been within hitting distance, she would have struck him across his sexy, sneering face. *How dared he jump to his horrendous conclusions and reduce her in the process?* And why bother to tell him that Joe was no more? The man who'd lasted one date!

It was a joke but she had known, beyond the shadow of a doubt, when she'd returned, that there could be no one for her but Gabriel. At least not for a while. It just wouldn't have been fair to have any man suffer the humiliation of comparison.

'How *could* you think that of me, Gabriel? How could you think that I would be...*calculating* enough to jump into bed with one man just so that I *could practise?*'

'Then when did you make the decision to leave and *why?*' Gabriel loathed himself for his weakness in wanting to know and he gave her a look of cold contempt that she could show up and extract the shameful admission from him.

'I did you a favour, Gabriel.' She looked at him steadily, even though inside she felt as though her nerves were being twisted into knots. 'I knew that you would tire of me sooner or later. I spared you the embarrassment of knowing that you wanted to get rid of me and I spared myself the pain of...'

'The pain of *what?*'

'Never mind. It doesn't matter. It has nothing to do with why I'm here. None of it has.'

In her head she had played around with all the various possible outcomes of her visit. None of them were very comforting.

When he didn't say anything, she frowned and asked unsteadily, 'Don't you want to know why I'm here?'

'I already do.'

Rose's eyes widened. 'You don't! How could you?'

'It's easy.' Gabriel gave an elegant shrug. 'When you cut through all the nonsense, the only thing that speaks volumes is money.'

'But...'

He raised one imperious hand. 'How are you doing on your course?'

'I haven't actually…started it, as a matter of fact. But what does that have to do with anything?'

Gabriel couldn't contain the grim stab of disappointment. Had he really thought her to be any different from the rest of the human race?

'How much?'

'How much what?' Rose asked, dazed.

'How much money are you after to fund your course?' He stood up and strolled over to the window so that he could perch against the ledge and give her the full benefit of his contemptuous stare. 'I wondered how long it would take before you realised just what a good financial deal you gave up here. I guess I could be heartless and tell you to clear off, but hell, what's a bit of money in recognition of your…effort?'

'Forget it, Gabriel.' Rose stood up on trembling legs and turned blindly for the door.

It had been a huge mistake coming here, but she had talked it over with her sister, had seen it as the right and decent thing to do. Now, she could only ask herself what aspect of right and decent Gabriel Gessi would understand when his whole world was ruled by the concept of money.

'Sit back down!' he commanded, but she was already heading for the door.

She didn't get far. In fact, she hadn't even made it to the outer door when he was by her side, spinning her around so that she was forced to look at him.

The touch of his hand on her was like the heat of a branding iron and nor did he release her. He just stared down at her, his fingers digging into her skin, until she finally pulled away.

'I didn't come here to listen to your accusations!' she said in a rush. 'I didn't come here to be accused of being some kind of gold-digger or anything else, for that matter!'

'Oh, why did you come, then? To check and make sure the secretary you procured for me was doing all right? She is. You need have no worries on that front.'

'I came to tell you that I'm pregnant!'

The silence that reverberated around the room was deafening and, for the first time since she had known him, Rose was treated to the one-off sight of her boss rendered utterly speechless. The colour drained from his face and he stared at her for a few seconds, during which she would have sworn that her heart stopped beating.

But he rallied fast. Shock gave way to suspicion. 'That's impossible. We were careful.'

'We were careful most of the time, Gabriel. But we weren't careful on that first night… Do you mind if I sit back down?' If she didn't, she might *fall* down because her legs felt as unsteady as rubber. She sat on the chair and for a while he remained standing behind her, as if locked in one spot. Rose refused to twist around and face him. She couldn't imagine what was going through his head but she was pretty sure that she wouldn't like any of it. Fatherhood was a high price to pay for a couple of weeks of sex with a woman who was destined to be yet another one of his ships that passed in the night. She would never have featured on his agenda at all if she hadn't returned from Australia several pounds lighter, several shades darker and more in keeping with what he considered *attractive!*

She daredn't look at the horror that would be stamped across his beautiful face.

Eventually she heard him walk towards her, past her, towards the window, through which he stared in complete and telling silence.

Most of all, she wanted to tell him that she was sorry but it had never occurred to her, not for a minute, that she would fall pregnant because of a single slip-up. She had stupidly allowed passion to overwhelm the simple matter of taking precautions. Gabriel, mistakenly, had assumed that she was on the pill and the following day, having been assured by her that no, she wasn't protected, but that they had been absolutely safe the night before, he had taken the issue of contraception into his own hands.

She hadn't guessed that, by then, it was too late.

It had taken her sister six months of trying to conceive!

'When did you find out?' Gabriel asked coolly, turning to look at her.

'Ten days ago.' Her eyes fluttered away from his cold, shuttered expression. 'I...I didn't think about my periods until I had to go to the dentist and she asked whether I could possibly be pregnant because I needed an x-ray to be done. Then it occurred to me that I hadn't had one for ages.' She knew that her words were tripping over one another but that look in his eyes...

When she had rehearsed what she would say, the scene had never unfolded in her head like this. Yes, she had anticipated being nervous, but she had her speech all down pat. She was pregnant. She took full responsibility for what had happened. She felt it only right that he should be aware of the situation but she wasn't about to impose on him, either emotionally or financially. In her head she emerged from the messy situation as proudly independent, open and willing to negotiate whatever visiting rights he might want, but also open and willing to accept that he might want very little. After all, a child had never been part of his game plan and she should know because, in a weird way, she knew him like the back of her hand.

'What makes you think that I believe you?' Gabriel asked.

Rose looked at him, startled out of her gut-wrenching apprehension. 'What do you mean?'

'I *mean,*' he said, his tone of voice implying that what he was about to say would be logical beyond all dispute, 'I suddenly discover that you find me irresistible. You've worked for me for years and yet, five seconds after arriving on the island, I've suddenly turned into the man of your dreams. Odd, wouldn't you say?'

To refute this sweeping, inaccurate observation would have left her wide open and vulnerable, so Rose remained silent, waiting for him to develop what he meant.

'Particularly odd,' Gabriel continued, 'considering you'd just got yourself a boyfriend…' He thought of the way she had run out on him and his fiercely wounded male pride was like the sharp edge of a knife, goading him into accusations which her changing expression was making a nonsense of. He couldn't help himself. He particularly couldn't help himself when he thought about what's-his-name and the possibility that she might, actually, be seeing him again, sleeping with him. Who was to say differently?

'Now you swan in here, months after you've walked out on your job, with some story about being pregnant.' His mouth twisted into a cynical sneer. 'If you *are,* and I'm not even willing to admit to that, who's to say that you weren't already pregnant when you came with me on that trip? Who's to say that your sudden, overwhelming need to hop in the sack with me wasn't a ruse for you and your lover to con me out of money?'

Rose's shock showed in her white, disbelieving face, sufficient for Gabriel to feel a morsel of guilt at his casual shredding of her character.

She made to stand but he was in front of her before she was halfway to her feet and she fell back into the chair, wincing away from his dark, oppressive anger as he leant over her, his arms on either side of the chair like steel bars.

'Don't even think about it!' he grated. 'Don't even think that you can come in here and tell me that you're pregnant with my child and then leave!'

'And don't *you* think that you can accuse me of being a gold-digger or of *using you!* That's the most insulting thing anyone has ever told me! *How dare you think that I had some kind of ulterior motive for sleeping with you?* It says a lot about you, Gabriel Gessi, that you could have such a...*vile* opinion of another human being!'

Gabriel shot to his feet and walked away, hands shoved deep in his pockets. He raked his fingers through his hair and swung round to look at her.

'What can you expect?' he muttered. 'You've come in here with a bomb and detonated it at my desk.'

'I'm sorry.' An icy calm had settled over her. Yes, he would be in shock, but his extreme reaction was somehow easier to bear than if he had offered help or compassion or even money. She wasn't even sure why she was so surprised and wounded at his raw accusations. Gabriel was filthy rich and he had the instinctively suspicious mind of someone who *was* filthy rich. And she could concede—just—that pregnancy was the fastest way to a man's wallet. The hurtful part wasn't his cold, detached approach to what she had said, it was that he had thought it in the first place, that he had allowed his flawed intellect to take precedence over what he must surely know about her by now.

'I know you're in a state of shock,' she said tonelessly. 'I debated whether I should come and tell you or not but in the end I felt you should know. And, before you leap in with any more accusations, let me tell you straight away that I'm not after your money. This wasn't part of some elaborate plot to rip you off. I can't go back in time and take back what happened between us on that island but I didn't *connive* for it to happen.' She risked a glance at him and felt a sharp stab of compassion. 'And it's yours, Gabriel. I haven't seen Joe since I got back to England and, anyway, I never slept with him.'

She suddenly felt desperately weary. The past ten days had been a struggle. In fact, the past two and a half months had been a struggle. She had returned to London, jobless, and had immediately found herself a decent enough temp job. But it was uninspiring and left her ample time to mourn what she had abandoned. She was tormented by the thought that she should have stayed, had the affair he had offered, waited to see what happened. She had salvaged her pride, saved herself the eventual let-down, but her bed was cold and lonely at night and her mind chattered ceaselessly with argument and counter-argument.

She had also dropped her plans to go on her business course. Somehow she didn't feel herself to be in a positive enough frame of mind.

So she had drifted miserably from one day to the next until, ten days ago, when two bright blue lines on a home pregnancy testing kit had galvanised her out of her depressed torpor.

Now here she was, having done the right thing, facing down a barrage of accusations. She gritted her teeth against the desire to cry.

'Okay, let's just say I believe you…' He did. The truth was written all over her face. Nor had he really believed for a second that she would have wilfully slept with him so that she could later spring a pregnancy tale of woe on his shoulders. Nor did he know what had compelled him to lay into her with such force. But he believed her. She was carrying his baby.

Gabriel, who had never once contemplated the reality of

fatherhood except as some distant situation that might or might not arise in the fullness of time, was shocked to realise that his initial feelings were ones of pure, virile satisfaction.

He felt as though he had *triumphed.*

'Yes…?' Rose was treading warily.

'Which isn't to say,' he added, 'that I won't demand a DNA test somewhere along the line…' He wouldn't.

'I'm not lying to you, Gabriel. Would you believe me any quicker if I told you that I didn't come here today to try and get money out of you? That I came because I thought it was the right, moral thing to do?'

'You must know that there's no way I would let any son of mine go without…'

'*Son?* Hang on a minute…'

'Or daughter, of course.' He gave an elegant shrug and then began prowling the room, forcing her to turn around to keep up with his progress. 'Whatever. No child of mine will be allowed to go without.'

'Naturally it will be up to you, whatever you decide to contribute to his or her welfare.'

'Contribute?' He gave a bark of laughter and paused to look at her with incredulity. '*Contribute?* You speak as though my own flesh and blood would be on the receiving end of the occasional donation! No, my involvement will be *much* more far reaching than a cheque sent out once a month…'

For the first time since she had disappeared, Gabriel felt the angry restlessness inside him begin to ebb away as he contemplated, with calm acceptance, a future he had not banked on.

'What do you have in mind?' Rose asked, her voice even more guarded.

'Put it this way, Rose…' He sat behind his desk and looked at her. Yes, he could see now that she had put on a bit of weight. Not so much that you would notice, but enough. She looked glowing. 'No child of mine will be a bastard.'

'Meaning…?'

'Meaning that you'll have to marry me.'

Rose gazed at him, shocked by his Draconian solution. 'I don't intend to do any such thing!' she informed him adamantly. 'We're no longer in the Dark Ages, Gabriel. Children are born out of wedlock all the time. There's no longer any social stigma associated with that.'

'Irrelevant.'

'No, it's not *irrelevant!*' Marry him? Live a life knowing that he had tied himself to her because of a child? Was there a faster way for a marriage to turn sour between two people? 'I can't marry you because I'm pregnant!' Rose struggled to make him see her point of view, aware that she was battling against the traditionalist core of a dinosaur. 'It's the worst idea I've ever heard. You didn't *ask* for this situation!'

'That I won't deny…' So why, he wondered, didn't he feel worse about it?

'And I'm sorry but I won't let you bury yourself in matrimony with me because you feel obliged…'

'I don't think I mentioned that you had a choice.'

Rose thought about marriage and her expectations of it. None of them included her loving a man, having his baby, desperately waiting and hoping that one day he would return her love. Nor had she ever looked forward to the inevitability of a husband who would stray because he would eventually become bored with her, bored by the sight of her. A child was many things but superglue wasn't one of them and a marriage artificially sustained because of one would be a marriage made in hell.

'You will marry me, Rose. It can be a small affair or you can lay on all the trimmings, but marry me you will.'

CHAPTER TEN

GABRIEL, in what was becoming a familiar situation of disgruntled uncertainty, clicked off his mobile with a frown.

He was sure that there had been a man's voice in the background. Or maybe it was his imagination playing tricks on him. It had been doing that lately. Ever since he had found himself on the receiving end of Rose's determination.

No marriage.

Naturally, he had assumed, with his boundless self-assurance, that he could steamroller over her objections, and he had given it a damn good shot.

For every point she raised he had countered it with ten of his own.

To claims that he was behaving like a Victorian tyrant, he had pointed out that his intention was merely to honour his responsibilities and ensure that his progeny was born with the greatest advantages of having a mother and father, both living under the same roof, both sharing the decision making.

'You will never be able to accuse me of not doing the right thing,' he had told her with pride.

And, just in case she remained unconvinced, which she surely couldn't be, given the indisputable logic of his arguments, he had ticked off, on his fingers, every reason for marrying him.

The benefit of security for his son. Or daughter, he had hastened to add. The benefit to *her* because she would be financially secure, able to fully appreciate motherhood without feeling the need to go out to work. Additionally, he had told her, they got along and were attracted to one another. It was hardly as if they were sworn enemies being forced into an unnatural alliance!

To any further obstacles and to reassure any misplaced sense of pride, he had informed her that she could look on it as something of a sensible business arrangement.

'As you do?' she had asked blandly, and he had nodded thinking that, yes, it really *was* something that made sense. And, to top it off, it made him *feel good.* He had never thought that the prospect of marriage would make him *feel good.* Rather, he had always privately maintained that, whatever tales he had heard to the contrary, most men, himself included, would view the institution of marriage as a regrettable cessation of the sheer joy of the affair, the vigour and excitement of the chase.

But, surprisingly, he had felt nothing like that and he could only assume that the prospect of fatherhood was more powerful than he had ever imagined.

So it had come as a brutal shock when she had stuck to her guns. No marriage.

Threats to drag her up the aisle had met with stony silence and he had resorted to dangling all manner of financial carrots in front of her, at which point she had turned her back on him and thrown over her shoulder that, unless he stopped pestering her, not only would she not marry him but she would find it hard to have *anything* to do with him at all!

Pestering her! Just the memory of those two words made Gabriel's teeth snap together in baffled fury.

He was certainly left in no doubt that the last thing she was was a gold-digger! In fact, he sometimes caught himself half wishing that she was more impressed by his wealth. At least then he might have been able to pin her down!

As it was, she was now in her sixth month of pregnancy and there was still no prospect of any ring going anywhere near her finger.

Gabriel had even consulted his mother on the best way of tying her down, expecting keen support from that area—after all he came from a family of traditionalists—but he had been woefully let down. His mother had quizzed him, asked all the right questions, sympathised with his dilemma which, as he pointed out, was the irrational dilemma of a man thwarted from doing the right thing, and then confounded him by saying that he couldn't make someone do something they didn't want to do.

He had been reduced to *visiting her,* as often as he could, and he had arranged his work life to fit in accordingly.

He said nothing when she told him that there was no need and, over time, she had stopped telling him. Of course, he didn't like the fact that she was still working but, when he'd mentioned that she had laughed and told him that pregnancy wasn't an illness, that it was a perfectly natural condition and putting her feet up would only make her put on too much weight.

However, he was reassured that she had postponed the business course, which would have been sheer lunacy.

Apart from the marriage issue, which appeared to be going nowhere fast, things seemed to be progressing nicely and privately Gabriel had been working on a plan to buy them a house. He would let her choose it. Would let her fall in love with it. And then, maybe, he could entice her into doing what he realised he wanted more and more.

Now this.

Had he heard a man's voice in the background? It occurred to him that she had seemed a bit breathless down the phone.

It was nine-thirty at night! Why would she be breathless? Gabriel, on the way to the airport, tapped on the partition separating him from his driver and gave him immediate instructions to turn around.

He wasn't turning around *to check up on her,* he told himself. Naturally there was no man in the house! Why should there be? She was six months pregnant with his child! And over the months he had come to appreciate that she was not deceptive by nature. She could no more lie to him than she could flap her arms and fly to the moon.

On the other hand, it wasn't as though they were married, was it? She had maintained her freedom even if he was convinced that she had no intention of using it. Damn it, they were still making love! He had done his homework. Read the pregnancy books. Was convinced that sex in the latter stages of pregnancy was absolutely fine, provided there were no contra-indications.

For a few seconds, Gabriel's mind drifted to the eminently pleasing recollection of their passionate love-making. He wasn't ashamed of admitting that her ripe body was a massive turn-on for him. Her breasts were now more than a generous handful and her nipples had swelled and darkened and seemed to have become ultra-sensitive, judging from the way she squirmed whenever he licked their stiffened peaks.

He shifted as his body responded swiftly and inevitably to the mental pictures in his head and he told the driver, in a clipped voice, to hurry.

If she sounded breathless, he decided, then he had to check it out. Purely on health grounds. His deal halfway across the world would just have to wait. He phoned his secretary, utterly unapologetic about disturbing whatever she happened to be doing, and told her to cancel all arrangements for him for the next couple of days. Thrown in at the deep end, she had certainly smartened up her act over the months. He still had to spell certain things out for her and she would never attain the level of responsibility that Rose had, but she would know what to do in this event.

That dealt with, Gabriel stared through the window as the car tackled London on a dark, dank, wintry Thursday night.

His thoughts were all over the place. Right there and then he made the decision that he would not leave her place until he had persuaded her to move in with him. Okay, she hadn't yet agreed to marriage, despite his reasonable approach, an approach that made sense from whichever angle it was viewed, but they would live together. Not ideal, but that way he could keep an eye on her.

The journey took thirty-five torturous minutes and, as the chauffeur-driven Jaguar pulled up to the kerb outside her house, Gabriel was witness to the one thing he didn't want to see.

The male voice in the background hadn't been a figment of his over-active imagination after all. It had been all too real and Gabriel didn't need to look very hard to know the identity of the mystery guest. Who else could it be but the ex-boyfriend?

He sat in silence for a few seconds, clenching and unclenching his fist, watching the man sling on his coat even as he walked down the road away from the Jaguar, reminding himself that he had no control, ultimately, over what she chose to do with her life.

He was overcome with a feeling of failure, an emptiness that was quite unlike how he was used to feeling.

He rubbed his eyes with his thumbs, clearing his head,

trying to silence the roar in there, then he told his driver that he could head back.

'I'll make my own way home,' Gabriel said tersely, pushing open the car door. Jealousy was threatening to overcome every shred of self-control he possessed. He made it to her front door before she even had time to hit the staircase.

Rose heard the banging and immediately assumed that Joe had left something behind.

She wasn't prepared to find Gabriel standing outside her door. Not that it wasn't a wonderful surprise. It was. Because she had thought that he would be at Heathrow, waiting for his plane, although in truth her mind wasn't as sharp as it had been before she became pregnant. She smiled and waited for his responding smile but none was forthcoming. Instead he stepped wordlessly into the hall and turned around to face her.

'What are you doing here?' Rose asked, hesitating at the expression on his face. 'I thought you were on your way to Hong Kong…'

'It would seem that there was a change of plan.' His instinct was to lay into her with questions about what the hell that man was doing in her house, but he restrained himself. Over the past few months, he had discovered a reservoir of patience he had never known existed in him and he called upon it now. Arguing would be no good for her in her condition and, besides, it occurred to him, he seldom won.

A change of plan and so he'd rushed over to her house. Rose tried not to feel flattered but she was. The man who had never actively pursued any woman was pursuing her now and it took all her strength to remind herself of the reason for that. The baby. Had it not been for the baby, she would no longer have been a part of his life. He hadn't bothered to search her out when he had returned from the island and found that she had left his company, after all. And his marriage proposal. That, too, was all about the baby and she respected him for his alacrity in accepting responsibility, but he was no closer to seeing now than he had been months ago that a loveless union was worse than no union at all and he didn't love her. He was willing to take care of her because she would be the mother of his child and he was, as he had pointed out in various ways, an Italian traditionalist through and through. But not once had he mentioned love.

Rose could see all the advantages in marrying him. He would be a generous husband and a fantastic father, but she knew him well. Playing the dutiful husband to a woman he didn't love would grind him down and, over time, inevitably, his eyes would begin to wander. And, looking the way he did, it would be all too easy for temptation to meet opportunity.

There was no such thing as guaranteed fidelity within a marriage but, as far as Rose was concerned, most marriages at least started out with the expectation. For her, it would be like waiting for an axe to fall and there was no way she was going to do that.

But it was hard. When they made love, the feeling of total completeness was as uplifting as it was painful.

'What was the change of plan?' Rose asked, leading him towards the sitting room. Too much standing about tired her out these days.

Normally, he would sit next to her on the squashy sofa, but this time he settled for the chair by the fire.

'We need to regulate this situation,' Gabriel said abruptly. He had waited for her to raise the subject of the man leaving the house, but she hadn't. She obviously thought that they would have missed each other by a few minutes and he was damned if *he* was going to ask questions. He felt sick with rage and jealousy.

'Regulate…?' Rose was baffled by the statement. She yawned and was startled when he asked her, rather coldly, if she would mind staying up so that she could listen to what he had to say.

'What's the matter?' Rose asked, suddenly sitting up. 'What's wrong? Is it work?'

'Work couldn't be better,' Gabriel said icily. 'And if I appear to be in a bad mood it's because I am angry with myself for allowing this situation to go as far as it has done. It is no longer satisfactory for us to be living apart. In three months time you will give birth to our child and I don't intend to remain an occasional visitor to your house.' Nor, he thought savagely, do I intend to let other men have contact with my child!

'But, Gabriel, we've talked about this!'

'And, like a fool, I have indulged your crazy desire to maintain your freedom!'

'It's got nothing to do with *maintaining my freedom!*' Rose told him painfully. 'What exactly do you think I'm going to with this so called freedom I'm desperate to maintain? When I'm at home with a baby?'

Gabriel ignored that. He couldn't think straight. In his mind, the only thing he could see was that man leaving the house. He burned to lay into her, demand to know what the hell she was playing at, inviting strange men into her house, and he loathed his own weakness in feeling so desperate.

'Good. Then we compromise. And I really don't care if you refuse, Rose, because I will simply stay put until you agree.'

'What's brought on this change of mood?'

'A clear head,' Gabriel snapped. 'You don't want to marry me. Fine. You're right. I cannot drag you kicking and screaming up the aisle, although how your conscience allows you to jeopardise the stability of our child's future is beyond me.'

'I don't know h…'

Gabriel raised one imperious hand to silence her protest. 'But there is a limit to what I will tolerate. If you won't marry me, then you will live with me.'

'Be your mistress?'

'Call it whatever you like. The description is immaterial.' He gave one of those nonchalant shrugs of his although his eyes remained very firmly focused on her dazed face.

'I don't see the point,' Rose muttered, but she was exhausted by his drip, drip technique. He had used a sledgehammer to crack a nut but once he had clocked into the fact that she wasn't budging, Gabriel had changed his techniques and over the months had become the master of subtlety, making small but consistent measures to chip away at her resolve. Sometimes she had the unsettling suspicion that part of his persistence came from the fact that she presented a challenge he felt compelled to overcome. It was a disturbing thought.

'What was the urgency to rush over here at this hour to discuss this?' she asked, stifling a yawn. 'I'm really tired.'

'I'll bet.'

Something in Gabriel's voice made Rose stiffen. Now she knew that something was wrong. 'What does that mean?'

'What do you *think* it means?' Gabriel threw out belligerently.

'I have no idea. Are you going to tell me or are you going to try and make me guess?'

'Who was he?' Gabriel heard himself ask the question and it was as if his vocal cords were functioning without the agreement of his brain, because he certainly hadn't intended to reduce himself by asking.

'Who was *who?* What are you talking about?'

'Don't give me that *butter wouldn't melt in your mouth* act! I wasn't born yesterday, Rose!' He sprang to his feet and began pacing the room, releasing some of the high voltage energy that was threatening to make him really explode with her. He daredn't look at her bewildered expression when it must be obvious to her exactly what he was talking about. I mean, he thought savagely, how many men did she entertain when he wasn't around?

Now frankly disturbed, Rose padded across to where he was standing by the window, arms folded, his eyes aggressive slits. She placed her hand worriedly on his arm and he shrugged it off.

'I have *no idea what you're on about.*'

'There was a man leaving this house when I drove up,' Gabriel said, struggling to maintain his composure. 'Why do you think I flew over here? What do you imagine I meant when I told you that my plans had changed? I heard his voice in the background when I spoke to you earlier on the phone and, sure enough, I get here and what do I find? A man leaving this house. Cool as a cucumber! And you acting as though nothing's happened! Well, it won't do! You're going to move in with me and that's the end of it!'

'Are you *jealous,* Gabriel?' Rose couldn't squash an excited flutter of hope. If he was *jealous,* surely that meant that he felt more for her than lust, which would pass, and a sense of duty?

'Should I be? I come here, I see a strange man leaving your house late at night… Tell me, *should I be?* Furthermore, I notice you still haven't told me who the hell he is! No need. I can guess! What's-his-name off the business course! Am I right?' He looked away from her and tried not to imagine the worst. Somewhere inside, he knew that his fears were groundless but, like a leaf caught up in a storm, he was incapable of anchoring himself. 'I hadn't realised that you two were still in contact.'

'We're not.'

'No? The figure leaving the house was really just a figment of my imagination?'

'Joe's called me a couple of times…'

'Joe's called you a couple of times…'

'Well, yes.' Now she felt guilty that she hadn't mentioned the calls. Partly her lapses in memory were to blame and also the fact that she had known that Gabriel's reaction would probably not have been too understanding. She hadn't reckoned on it being as extreme as it was, however, and guilt brought a tinge of colour to her cheeks. Gabriel was on to that in a flash.

'But I don't know what you're so worried about. I mean, there's no need for you to be jealous…' Rose laughed self-consciously and, in some corner of her mind, she was aware that this time Gabriel had not denied that he was jealous. 'Look at me, Gabriel and tell me what you see!' With her smock dress and thick, forgiving cardigan, she was like a ship in full sail.

'A very sexy woman…' Gabriel affirmed through gritted teeth.

Something in Rose melted. She walked over to her handbag, which was on the chair, and rummaged inside, finally extracting a piece of white card which she handed in silence to him. Gabriel glanced at it, then read it.

'He's invited *us* to his engagement party,' Rose said. 'He phoned a few weeks ago because he's a nice guy and he wanted to find out how I was doing with the pregnancy. He mentioned that he'd met a woman and things were serious. I was pleased for him.'

Gabriel stared down at the invitation. He should have been alarmed at his huge overreaction but he wasn't because he knew why he had reacted the way he had. Why he was so desperate to marry her, why, when faced with her constant refusal, he was now desperate to have her live with him. The writing on the card looked blurry and he realised that he was no longer focusing on it but travelling down the blindingly obvious paths his mind was revealing to him.

He looked at her and cupped her amused, gently quizzical face in his hands.

'Okay. Here's the deal,' he said sombrely. 'You have to move in with me because it's driving me nuts living apart from you.'

'What are you saying?' Rose wanted to hold her breath, close her eyes and wish as hard as she could that he would say what she wanted to hear, but reality never worked that way, so she held his gaze steadily and waited.

'I'm saying…' Gabriel ran his fingers through his hair and fidgeted. Finally he led her to the sofa and tugged her down to sit next to him, close enough for him to still touch her face. 'I'm saying…that I can't think straight with you living on your own here. I've felt it for a while but I denied it. Now, I *know.*' He sighed and looked as if he might be trying to put his thoughts into some kind of coherent order. 'Seeing that man leaving here…imagining…well, I can't tell you…seems crazy but that's what you do to me. You make me crazy.' He kissed her gently on the mouth but pulled back before they could find themselves unable to break apart. He needed to talk without the distractions of her amazing body. But, as if he was still compelled to have some level of physical contact with her, he placed his hand on her stomach and she, in turn, placed her hand on his.

'I can't concentrate properly. I worry about you.' He

looked at her carefully. 'I thought I wanted to marry you for the sake of the baby,' Gabriel told her. 'But somewhere along the line things have changed… No…things had changed *before* then. Sometimes I wonder whether what I felt for you was there all along, from way back when, just something waiting to be revealed…'

'*What you felt for me?* What do you feel for me…?'

'I need you…' Gabriel felt as though he was falling off the side of a precipice. 'I'm in love with you…'

Rose looked at him and smiled, a slow, mesmerised smile that only touched the depth of her happiness. 'Will you marry me?' she asked. 'Because I'm in love with you too and you have no idea… I've been waiting so long for you to tell me that you love me too… I never dared hope…' The baby kicked and they both looked down.

'My darling,' Gabriel murmured, marvelling at how his frantic life suddenly made sense, 'I'm yours for ever…'